Sophie Hardach was born in 1979 and grew up in Germany. She studied in Edinburgh and Singapore, and on graduating worked as a correspondent for Reuters news agency in London, Milan, Tokyo and Paris, where she now lives.

www.sophiehardach.com

The
Registrar's
Manual *for*
Detecting
Forced
Marriages

Sophie Hardach

SIMON &
SCHUSTER

London · New York · Sydney · Toronto

A CBS COMPANY

First published in Great Britain by Simon & Schuster UK Ltd, 2011
A CBS COMPANY

1 3 5 7 9 10 8 6 4 2

Simon & Schuster UK Ltd
1st Floor
222 Gray's Inn Road
London
WC1X 8HB

www.simonandschuster.co.uk

Simon & Schuster Australia
Sydney

A CIP catalogue record for this book
is available from the British Library

ISBN HB 978-0-85720-118-8
ISBN TPB 978-0-85720-119-5

Typeset by M Rules
Printed in the UK by CPI Mackays, Chatham ME5 8TD

For Dan, with love.

So that wise men cannot say: The Kurds
Did not choose love as their aim.
They neither desire nor are desired,
They neither love nor are loved

– From Mem û Zîn by Ehmedê Xanî

Why didn't he give me to the master, Agha Hassan,
    Bahri's uncle,
Why did he give me to Ibrahim Temo, who looks like
    the old rat from the granary?

– Kurdish folk song, recorded by Gérard Chaliand

PART ONE

Hair by Hair, You Make a Beard
1

PART TWO

Brides, Sheikhs and Anarchists
161

PART THREE

The Difficulty of Lighting a Fuse in the Rain
277

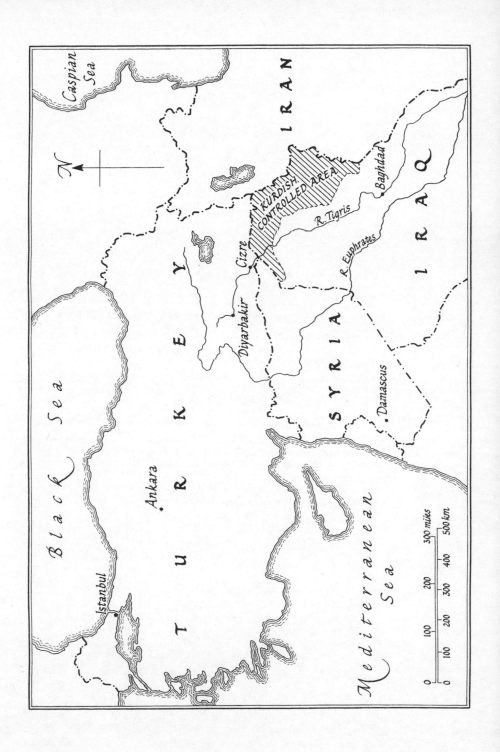

Caspian Sea

IRAN

Baghdad

KURDISH CONTROLLED AREA

R. Tigris

Cizre

R. Euphrates

IRAQ

Diyarbakir

T U R K E Y

SYRIA

Damascus

N

Black Sea

Ankara

Istanbul

Mediterranean Sea

300 miles
500 km.

200

300   400

100   200

100   200

0
0

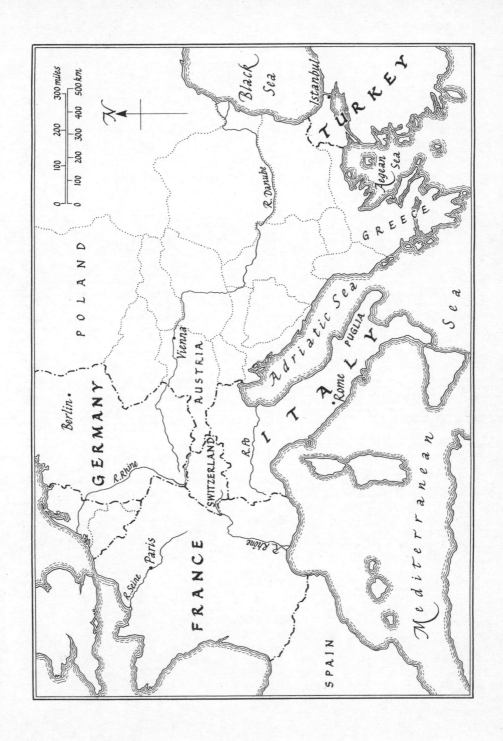

300 miles
500 km

N

POLAND

R. Danube

Black
Sea

Istanbul

TURKEY

Aegean
Sea

GREECE

Adriatic Sea

Berlin

GERMANY

Vienna

AUSTRIA

ITALY

PUGLIA

Rome

R. Rhine

SWITZERLAND

R. Po

FRANCE

R. Rhône

R. Seine

Paris

Mediterranean

Sea

SPAIN

PART ONE

Hair by Hair, You Make a Beard

1

Selim's first view of Europe was a vast, thick carpet of shit. Layered on the waves before him, bobbing on the water, there loomed an impenetrable barricade made of tons and tons of excrement pumped out by the generous stomachs of southern Italy; as if the shores of Europe, fed up with thousands of washed-up refugees, had decided to surround themselves with a man-made security cordon of slime and stench. *Better turn around now*, said the slime. *And please don't come back*, said the stench.

But Selim, his ears full of saltwater, limbs struggling to keep his body afloat, sight blurred by a wig of seaweed, did not hear the message. The heat on the creaking boat had not stopped him, the watchful coastguards had not stopped him, his own fear and seasickness had not stopped him. A stinking mass of digested pasta would not stop him now.

And so, holding his head high like a splashing dog, leading a trail of men, women and a toddler strapped to her mother's back, Selim broke through the barrier before him, parted Europe's soft defences with his bony chest and hands, and swam right through to the other side.

Closer to the beach, the green water became warmer, the

foul smell gave way to a nose-tingling mix of fresh air, surf and seaweed, and the brown suds turned into white foam that tickled his stiff neck.

Selim swam on and, when he could feel his legs brushing against the sand, collapsed then crawled on, his fingers clawing the moist grains, his elbows sinking into the ground. He dragged himself ashore, and, panting and sobbing, his left hand clutching a fistful of damp Puglian sand, curled up on his side.

He had arrived.

'Get up.' A hand grabbed his shoulder. 'GET UP. Quick quick quick.'

Selim sat up. The man had moved on to the next tired body, giving it a quick shake, rounding up the creatures that littered the beach like corpses. They rose to their feet, grouped in a wet tangle and shifted through the gentle light of dawn towards the waiting trucks.

The traffickers barked nervous orders. They ran up and down to steer their flock, hurrying the slow ones, restraining the fast ones, looking even more afraid than their charges. Selim had been told they would be rowed ashore in the middle of the night, under the cover of darkness. Instead, the men on the boat had told them to jump, and here they were, dozens of Kurdish refugees brightly illuminated by the early morning sun like so many incriminating pieces of evidence.

The group stopped. Selim looked back at the beach. Two thin figures, a man and a woman, remained there, saltwater dripping from their hair and blackened clothes, their backs bent over something on the sand. Hurry up, people, Selim thought. Let's get going. A few of the traffickers detached themselves from the group and jogged down to the couple.

The man turned around to face them, and now Selim could make out the thing lying at his feet. The traffickers motioned towards the trucks, but the man shook his head. The traffickers motioned towards the trucks again.

'Just leave it,' one of the traffickers shouted. 'Come.'

The man shook his head again. And all of a sudden, the woman, who had been perfectly still, dropped to her knees and started digging a hole in the sand with her hands. Selim, shivering in his clammy jeans and jumper, walked away from the trucks and towards the beach, the fabric chafing against his thighs. He felt a hand on his shoulder, shook it off, broke into a trot.

Someone seized his arm.

'Come, quick, here, COME!'

But Selim, used to people trying to pull him this way and that, easily twisted his slippery twig of an arm out of the trafficker's big hand and ran to the mourning couple.

He knelt down next to the woman and pushed his fingers into the cold sand. The father and the traffickers had formed a circle around them. It did not have to be a big hole. A small hole was enough.

The mother took the limp toddler into her arms, tenderly, as if she had fallen asleep and needed to be carried to bed.

A sand-coated limb slipped loose, dangled, was tucked back in. The mother lowered her child into the hole. Her lips moved silently as they raked the sand back with their hands and smoothed it over the little body.

Officially, Selim's truck was loaded with crates of tomatoes: the Taste of Sunny Puglia, ripe, red and fragrant, destined for canning factories in foggy northern Italy, where they would be packaged and stacked into trucks rumbling through Switzerland all the way to Germany, unloaded in dark warehouses, sold to pizzerias, mixed with olive oil, herbs and rotten tomatoes from rusty tins, spread onto sickly pale dough, baked in the seventh circle of hell until all the germs were killed off, served to lip-licking German owners of holiday homes in southern Italy who would frown, take a bite, smile and sigh: 'Ah! The Taste of Sunny Puglia!'

Unofficially, secretly, illegally, Selim's truck was loaded with Selim and his fellow sufferers: the Taste of Sunny Kurdistan.

They were exhausted, grey and smelt of shit. They would be unloaded, washed and dressed in dry rags somewhere in the north. Crammed into another truck. Waved past indifferent Italian border police. Better not check the trucks; not our problem anyway; *chi se ne frega*; good thing they're off to Germany. Bye!

As they rattled through Switzerland's winding roads, the man to Selim's left started to retch. A pool of vomit licked at his feet.

The mother had not spoken since they left behind the little mound of sand on the beach.

The father hid his face in his hands.

Back in the village, they were Selim's neighbours. He had a photo of the little girl, Evin. She was in the big group shot of his family and all the neighbours. It was his only photo of home, but he'd already decided to give it to Evin's parents. It was in his bag. He'd give it to them when he got his bag. Come to think of it, where was his bag?

It was dark now. The thin line of light along the top of the back doors had disappeared. The truck stopped. Selim held his breath and willed it to move again. Instead, the back doors swung open and a torch shone brutally inside. The Kurds cowered in the far corner like mice. Satisfied, the torch disappeared, the doors slammed shut, the truck roared on.

The Sunny Taste of Kurdistan spilled out of the truck, onto the concrete floors of a dark warehouse in Germany and was portioned out into manageable bites: Selim's neighbours into one vehicle, he into another.

'We'll find each other later,' Selim told the father, who briefly looked up from his hands and ruffled Selim's hair.

'You're a good boy. We'll find each other.'

The mother did not hear him. She climbed into the truck, a dead woman walking.

And then Selim was alone. He did not know any of the other men in his truck. The clothes he was wearing were not his clothes. His bag was somewhere between his village, the town of Cizre, Istanbul, an unnamed secret port, Puglia, Switzerland and Germany. He had three passports, none of them real. He did not possess any health records or a birth certificate. Since he swam through the putrid moat and entered the magic fortress, he had ceased to exist. You would have to travel all the way to the mountains of Kurdistan, to the wild and remote region where Turkey knocked against Iraq and Syria, all the way to Selim's village, and talk to his mother, his father, his neighbours, to find out the most basic details such as when he was born.

Even then, the question would prompt a lot of head-scratching and murmuring and: 'I think it was the night after *Newroz* and before Cevim's wedding . . .'

'No, it was long before that, after we bought the second goat but before we fixed the hole in the roof, no, not the new roof, the old roof.'

'No, it was the new roof.'

'No, it was the old roof.'

'The old roof didn't have a hole! I laid it with my own hands, these hands, look.'

Hands would be examined, calluses admired.

'I'm not saying it was a bad roof, but one day we noticed there was a hole in it and you climbed up there to fix it, *remember*?'

'That was the new roof, the one your brother put up when I was in prison.'

And so on.

And eventually, after many glasses of sugared tea and stories about happy days at weddings and terrible nights in Turkish prisons, a consensus would emerge on the year when Selim was born, and give or take a few days or weeks or months, that estimate would mean that when Selim swam through the sewage and crawled ashore and helped bury his neighbours' child, on that first day of his bright new life in Europe, he was about thirteen.

2

I met Selim several years after he was smuggled into Germany, a skinny Kurd disguised as a plump tomato. By then, his estimated birthday, based on the purchase of goats, the death of an aunt, the jail terms of male relatives, had been converted into a neat number that was typed on forms and slid into folders and sorted into filing cabinets by manicured hands at a German immigration office.

Selim had entered Germany with three passports: Turkish, Italian, and for some reason, Bulgarian. The Italian one in particular had been a source of worry. The trafficker had handed it out soon after the beach, holding the passports before him like a card trick, opening them one by one and reciting the name inside, since few in the group could read. Selim eagerly lifted his hand when it was finally his turn. The trafficker, looking puzzled, repeated his name to confirm it. Selim nodded. It was not until after the trafficker had left that Selim opened the soft booklet and myopically peered at the black-and-white photo. It showed a woman.

In any case, the passports were soon discarded. And then the guesswork began. A dentist prised open Selim's mouth and a radiologist X-rayed his hands.

'Thirteen sounds about right.'

'Thirteen? Bones like a ten-year-old. That child wants feeding.' This from a matronly nurse, whose broad hips and quivering double chin made Selim feel strangely homesick.

'Not everyone has big bones. Thirteen's about right.'

A more detailed verdict was dictated to the receptionist and sent on to Selim's case worker. Dentist, radiologist and nurse (who felt vaguely offended but could not quite say why) washed their hands and went their separate ways.

Among the many numbers that came to dominate Selim's life, from his case number to his lawyer's phone number, his date of birth occupied a special place.

He did not immediately realise its significance. He was illiterate and alone. In offices steeped in coffee and disinfectant, he was asked strange questions in a strange language; and then, strange questions in a familiar language by a Kurdish interpreter.

At some point in the process, a series of numbers appeared on his forms, and he could not exactly say where it had come from or who had first mentioned it.

'It's your date of birth,' the interpreter told Selim in Kurdish, flicking his chin towards the grey form before them. 'The day you were born.'

'How do they know when I was born? I don't know when I was born.'

'You don't know when you were born? Man, those *villages*,' said the interpreter, who had been born in Cizre in south-eastern Turkey, which was surely very different from having been born in a *village* outside Cizre in south-eastern Turkey.

10

'I wasn't there, was I? Or rather, I *was* there, but not in a record-keeping role.'

'You sure you're thirteen? Smart-arse. Wonder if I should tell the potato over there that you sound more like an eighteen-year-old.'

Their eyes swivelled towards a placid German bureaucrat who was watching them from behind his desk.

Selim smiled at the bureaucrat. The interpreter smiled at the bureaucrat. The bureaucrat did not smile back. He had three hundred asylum-seeking minors to deal with, and he wished the one in front of him would get on with it.

'He's getting impatient,' the interpreter hissed. 'See the way he's worrying his pinkie with his thumb? If you don't sign the papers now he'll throw us out, and you see if you can get another appointment before they kick you back to Kurdistan.'

'I just want to know who said this is my date of birth. How can they know if even my parents don't know?' Selim sighed.

'They know everything,' the interpreter said with conviction and gave Selim a pen.

Selim signed as best he could. It was only a number, after all. At the time, it did not seem any more important than the question of where he would sleep, and what he would eat.

But by the time I met him, this short row of digits was so central to his life that it might as well have flashed from every form and every folder in bright, bright red.

Come to think of it, Selim's artificial date of birth, and the fact that it was only a few weeks away from my own, more

11

reliably recorded date of birth, was the only reason why we met, and why our lives became very tightly intertwined.

But more of that later.

For now, Selim was the latest arrival in the German borough of Neustadt, a jumble of medieval cottages, timbered houses and modern council flats that also happened to be my hometown. *Willkommen!*

His memories of that time were hazy, blurred by a heavy tiredness. He recalled a series of camps and disused barracks. Days passed by. Weeks.

'So what was it like when you first got here?' I asked him.

He took a long deep drag from his cigarette and said thoughtfully: '*Hmm. Es war Scheisse.*'

He remembered sitting in a Volkswagen van, hurtling along narrow country lanes, past bright yellow fields and neat farmhouses, squashed between the windowpane and another Kurd, on his way to yet another camp, and he remembered thinking, Why don't they just attach a handle to my back? That would make it easier. And he giggled and considered telling the joke to the Kurd next to him, but, as he turned to face the older man and his serious, set face, a face that looked like a mountainscape, all sunburnt ridges and ravines, as he looked at this battered old fighter next to him, Selim swallowed his joke and turned back to the windowpane.

They entered a forest of conifers. Selim pressed his forehead against the vibrating glass, and through the trees caught a glimpse of a clearing in the forest, where broken washing machines and a fridge were piled up like offerings. This time he really did need to tell the other Kurd because this was too strange to be ignored; but when he turned, oh, the van had already whizzed past and trees obscured the vision.

They drove up to a metal gate that hummed open to reveal a cluster of rusty containers. Before them was a bleak military compound with high walls, its entrance strewn with scattered junk and rolls of barbed wire ready to be fitted around the fence.

'We can't get out here,' Selim whispered to his neighbour. 'It's a prison.'

'Don't worry,' the older Kurd said. '*We çêtir be*. This is where we're going to live.'

Linoleum floors and a sour dampness. In a cramped communal kitchen, Selim glimpsed a battered Kurdish teapot before the social worker hurried him on. He was shown his bunk bed. He sniffed at the mattress. It smelt of dirty hair.

'I need to find my relatives,' Selim told the older man, who was inspecting the bunk next to his, testing the springs with his hand.

'They'll find you.' The Kurd unzipped his bag, took out a tattered red, yellow and green flag and, with a serious nod, gave it to Selim. 'It might take a while. They'll need to prove that they're your family. Because, you see . . . well, sometimes people come in to pick up children, and then it turns out they're not their family at all.'

Selim pinned the flag above his bunk. He had been given a bottle of apple-scented shampoo and a pile of second-hand clothes, and he stored them carefully in his metal locker, leaving the shampoo bottle open in the hope the apple scent would waft out and settle on the musty socks and T-shirts.

13

A black man kneeling on the top bunk turned around, looked down at Selim, flashed a big white grin.

'Johnson.' He pointed at a poster he was tacking up above the bed, a picture of a blue-eyed man with long blond hair and girly hands that encircled a flaming heart. 'Jesus.'

'Selim,' Selim responded and pointed at himself, then at the poster. '*Isa.*' They nodded to each other, then Johnson in the top bunk went back to pinning up Jesus.

At night, Selim could not sleep. He had not slept since he helped his neighbours bury their daughter in the sand. Sometimes, just before dawn, his tiredness knocked him out and left him unconscious until the alarm clock shook him back to something closely resembling life. That did not count as sleep, did it?

He imagined the gentle snoring of sleeping babies around him, the giggles of his little sister Aynur, the bleating shuffles of the sheep.

Instead, above him, below him, there were hundreds of men and boys who lived, ate, slept in this gigantic waiting room on the edge of town.

There were nameless Liberians who were really Nigerians, and stateless Palestinians who were really Egyptians. Every now and then, the men were summoned into dark corridors and dusty offices where they were asked lots of questions and no one believed the answers.

'So you say you are Palestinian, from the Gaza Strip.'

'Yes.'

'Right. So if you're from the Gaza Strip, how come you can't accurately name a single village or landmark or neighbourhood or even a road in that area?'

'Forgot.'

On day two, Johnson stopped talking. Selim greeted him in the morning, and he merely smiled back in silence.

Selim pointed at Jesus and said '*Isa*' in a small attempt to make conversation.

Johnson stayed silent.

The Liberians were Nigerians, the Palestinians were Egyptians, the Kurds were just Kurds. But since Kurdistan did not, as such, exist; since it was an imaginary land, stretching over scraggy mountains and deep valleys in Turkey, Iraq, Iran and Syria; since they were as landless as the Palestinians and as nameless as the Liberians, the Kurds didn't really exist either, and so, officially, they were Turks.

Selim could describe every single tree, every single village around Cizre, even the villages that remained only as blackened stumps along a potholed road. He could draw the shepherds' paths that criss-crossed the mountains with the certainty of someone who had followed them at night, blindly. But in his case, none of this mattered very much.

Back at the immigration office, he watched his interpreter talk to his new caseworker, who was as blond and blue-eyed as the man on Johnson's poster. The caseworker nodded, nodded, nodded and then curtly shook his head.

'So he says you've just turned thirteen and you're claiming to be a political refugee, and according to your story you started your political activities when you were . . .' The interpreter paused. 'Eight.'

'Yes.'

'He says that's obviously not possible. Either you're a child or you're a political activist.'

15

'Eh, you know what it's like back home,' Selim suggested. '*Here, bêje wî.* Go on, tell him.'

'Listen, I haven't been back in ages, and I'm not going to get involved. I mean, I'm here as your interpreter, right, but this job gets paid by the hour and frankly there's only so much I can do. *Afû.* It's not like I'm an expert.'

The interpreter was Kurdish, but he looked completely different from the men in Selim's village. His skin was smooth. His grey suit fitted well. When he laughed, he laughed like a young man in a TV advert, and all his teeth were straight and white. He told Selim he was born in Cizre, went to school and college in Istanbul, and was now studying at a German university.

What a nice life, Selim thought. Nice teeth.

He sighed.

'So what now?'

'Just tell him exactly what happened. It's your case, just give him the facts.'

Selim did. He looked at the inscrutable German behind the desk and told him the whole story. At the end of his statement, the German's expression had softened, maybe out of sympathy, or maybe pity because he knew Selim's case was hopeless.

3

I thought of Selim one morning long after I had left Germany, when I received an unsettling visitor in my office, and an unsettling book in the post.

Back home, I was quite rebellious, a teenager with green hair, pierced eyebrows and radical ideas. By the time I finished my degree at Panthéon-Sorbonne and started looking for a job in Paris, my hair was brown and my views more pragmatic. Having heard that the Paris town hall was looking to recruit staff with a 'migrant background', as they put it, I re-wrote my CV with an emphasis on cultural outreach (a stint as head of the Franco-German friendship society came in handy) and turned up for the interview wearing a black polyester jacket and a navy skirt. That was my idea of 'professional'. That day, my interviewer from human resources, a kindly Senegal-born man with round glasses, nodded patiently through my rehearsed answers, and just as the conversation drew to a natural close, he smiled at me and asked: 'Would you like to see the wedding hall?'

He took me up the main staircase, a flight of red-carpeted marble steps that split into two and swerved up, up to the wedding hall: an oval, wood-panelled room with views over the city, one wall entirely covered by a nineteenth-century oil painting of a wedding party, all straw hats and bustles. On the opposite wall was a picture of cattle traders haggling over cows, the animals bowing their heads in harnessed submission. In the centre of the room, under a high ceiling painted with an image of a bare-chested man wielding a knife over a bull, stood a kind of secular wooden altar.

I assumed man and bull were part of an allegory or myth – about Zeus, maybe – and, forgetting for an instant that this was an interview and I was supposed to show myself at my most knowledgeable, I asked my companion about their significance.

'It's the old abattoir down by the meat market,' he said cheerfully.

'Oh.' I glanced back at the painting, noticing now that the knife-wielder was wearing a butcher's apron. 'I thought it was an allegory.'

'It's symbolic, like all the paintings in this hall.'

'I see. So what does it symbolise?'

'An abattoir.'

Despite the slaughterhouse fresco, the room was one of the most impressive I had ever seen, and I knew there and then that this was where I wanted to work.

'It must be wonderful to take weddings for a living,' I said. 'All that happiness.'

My interviewer shrugged.

'Some like it, some don't. Either way, it's the Deputy Mayor who conducts the ceremony, and Monsieur Dubois, the registrar, just helps. He's about to retire, so you will fill his shoes.'

I tried to picture myself standing next to the Deputy Mayor.

'I wonder if my accent will be a problem. It's quite strong. And German.'

He smiled at me.

'Nothing they can do about that. If they don't like us, they can go to Las Vegas.'

I smiled back.

He called the following week to offer me the job in earnest tones, like an old abbot taking in a novice, and right at the end he said he had an important piece of advice for me. I actually took out my pen, thinking he would share some town hall secrets.

'The thing is,' he said, 'you need to improve your posture, or you will get problems with your lower back. You will be sitting a lot. I noticed that you sit straight for a bit, then you sag and hunch, then you suddenly remember your posture and straighten up again like a rod. Then you sag again.'

'Er, thanks,' I said, putting away my pen. 'I was often told to sit up straight as a child. But maybe not often enough.'

Weddings remained my favourite type of ceremony. There was the romance, the suspense, and just the tiniest risk that one of the two protagonists would have a change of heart.

After a wedding, I usually went back to my keyboard-tapping routine, but occasionally my thoughts lingered on the couple that had just walked down the marble steps, imagining how their life was going to play out.

I was in that kind of mood this morning, grinding some coffee beans for the second cup of the day, when the door was flung open. In came a man, followed by Sandra, our secretary. He muscled into the room the way most men here do, a blast of testosterone, and I instinctively drew back when he leaned across my desk to shake my hand. He sat down, reached between his thighs to grab the front of the seat and dragged it closer to my desk.

'I'm here for the papers,' he said, stating his name. He shared Selim's surname; not unusual in a part of the world where the villages were small and the families large.

Sandra gave a helpless shrug and withdrew. I reluctantly abandoned the coffee grinder and sat down, pushing the lever on my swivel chair to raise the seat a little.

'Well, congratulations!' I smiled at him. 'You're the lucky groom?'

'His cousin.'

'Oh. I see.' I shifted some books so that they were in front of me, like a barrier. 'I'm really sorry, but you know, you can't actually do that for them. They'll have to complete the papers themselves. Don't worry, it won't take all that long.'

'Yeah, so, I'll pick them up and give them to my cousin, they fill them in, return them.' He drummed his fingers on the armrest of his chair.

'It's one of those new rules . . .' I raised my hands as if to say it can't be helped.

'My cousin's busy.'

He was sizing me up like a boxer now. I rubbed my eyebrow, a tic I had tried and failed to shake off. It went back to those rebellious days. The green hair dye grew out quickly enough, but the telltale holes remained for years after the rings had been removed. Sometimes my fingers would still find their way to my face, twisting phantom rings.

'I'm afraid it's just the way it is. The prospective—'

'You the one who's doing the weddings now? There was a guy here who did all the weddings and he knew exactly what he was doing. So, if you ask him how it works with the papers, he'll tell you. We pick them up blank, return them filled in. Everybody's happy.'

We were not off to a good start: I could see it as soon as I uttered the words *new rules*.

He straightened up and pushed out his chest, eyeing me defiantly. New rules for whom, he seemed to be saying. Those *new rules* are what you people make up to aggravate people like me.

He shared Selim's surname, but looked nothing like him. They didn't even seem to be made from the same raw material. My visitor could have been hewn out of a rock by an angry giant, from the block that formed his head and neck through his triangular torso to his bulging thighs, all barely restrained by a white ribbed T-shirt and jeans. Selim, on the other hand, most resembled a folding chair, just waiting to be doubled up and put away.

My visitor sighed, as if being forced to explain something painfully simple and obvious.

'You know they're already married, right? We already did the religious wedding *là-bas*, before Ramadan.'

'But this is the town hall!' I said, suddenly feeling rather indignant. 'It's an important ceremony, it's the only wedding that counts here. I've looked at the papers, and as I understand it, the groom came over from Turkey, from Cizre, right, and the bride is a French citizen. So by law, I need to make sure they understand what this is all about.'

'You know Cizre?'

'I know the name. There are lots of Kurdish families in this neighbourhood.'

He laughed, surprised.

'How do you know we're Kurdish?'

'I'm a registrar. And I live here, too.' I immediately regretted that second sentence, then told myself not to be so paranoid.

'Right. OK. You win. I'll bring my cousin over tomorrow and we'll fill the papers in together, OK, me and you and him.' He shifted his weight to one side, extracted a mobile phone from his back pocket and started texting.

I waited for him to finish his message and put the phone away, which he eventually did with a grin.

'Look,' I tried once more, 'you've probably been told that this is the way it's usually done, that you can just fetch the papers and get the couple to sign them. But things have changed.'

He clenched his fist around his mobile, and for a moment I thought he was going to hurl it across the room. His face, which had briefly relaxed into an expression not unlike friendliness, snapped shut. He glared at me.

'I'm sorry,' I repeated. 'But the girl will have to come.'

4

Our *mairie* was perched atop a hill, overlooking what used to be a village but was now one of the poorer areas of Paris. A park with a duck pond stretched out in front, divided by a stream that ran all the way to a set of staggered tower blocks; a lot of our weddings ended with a raucous picnic on the grass. A few streets down, by the canal, illegal immigrants had pitched tents in a playground, suspending blue-plastic sheeting between the slide and the swings. The town hall itself looked as if it was hijacked from a much wealthier place, all turrets and pillars, and an imposing carved portal crowned by a fluttering French flag. The rooms inside were far less glamorous – archives, cubicles, corridors – except, of course, for the ceremonial wedding hall.

Ceremonies were important to me. In that, I agreed with the French. Maybe I even learned it from them. I used to loathe their pomp and protocol, but now I found it reassuring, soothing almost.

About a year ago, we celebrated a Republican baptism, a ceremony invented in 1790, during the Revolution. Behind the walls of the *mairie*, I had feared a blue, white and red orgy of Frenchness, the kind that made outsiders like me feel uncomfortable at times. Instead, when the white-swaddled baby howled its outrage at the vaulted ceiling, drowning out my boss's eulogy to solidarity and mutual acceptance, I found myself strangely moved.

'*Citoyenne, Citoyen*, do you want to place your child under the protection of the Republican institutions?' asked my boss, the Deputy Mayor, looking festive with a blue, white and red sash draped across his pot belly.

The ceremony reminded me of the political rallies I organised as a teenager: the jargon, the conviction. And yet I was touched by my boss's seriousness, by this rotund man addressing the baby's parents as if they were fellow revolutionaries storming the Bastille.

Not everyone felt that way. The man who had just stormed out of my office, for example, couldn't have cared less about our ceremonies.

Once he had left, I finished grinding the beans and made myself an espresso. Then I turned to the booklet I had found in the post amongst the usual letters and pamphlets. I took a swig of coffee, letting it slosh around in my mouth in an attempt to ward off that yearning for the first cigarette of the day, and looked at the cover. It showed a hand forcing a wedding ring made of barbed wire onto the finger of another hand.

FORCED MARRIAGES ARE ILLEGAL IN FRANCE, it said in big bold letters.

Of course I knew forced marriages were illegal in France. Everyone knew that. It's why parents here lured their daughters away on family holidays that involved a trip to the ancestral village and a visit to the matchmaker. Then they came back to France for the civil ceremony, and at that point there wasn't much we could do about it.

The other day, Sandra showed me a magazine article about terrified brides who had fled their families; there was a quote from the Justice Minister saying a campaign was needed to put teachers, social workers and registrars on higher alert.

'They want us to be *des superflics*,' Sandra said with contempt: supercops. 'As if we could tell whether a marriage was real. Sometimes I can't even tell whether my own is.'

I agreed with her. Since I took this job, I'd started making regular donations to a shelter for battered wives, and that was as far as my involvement went.

So I was about to shift the booklet to the to-be-dealt-with pile, the one that was never dealt with, when I saw the title: *The Registrar's Manual for Detecting Forced Marriages*.

I thought of Selim, and the time he came back from that journey to his Kurdish village, his first visit since he had left. We were both in our early twenties then, twenty-three, to be precise. I was already living in Paris, and I'd flown back to my hometown to see my family and sort out some problematic paperwork with my friend.

We sat on cushions on the floor, and he served me Kurdish white cheese and sweet tea and told me about the trip. There had been a wedding in the village. He showed me the pictures of the celebrations: old men in sagging suits, boys drowning in their fathers' oversized jackets. They were leaning on their rifles and frowning through black moustaches or grey beards, except for Selim, whose shadow of upper-lip fluff in the photos suggested a last-minute attempt to grow a moustache.

Selim placed the photos on the low table. He tapped on the pictures of the old men and boys and labelled them: cousin, uncle, uncle, cousin, uncle.

'See, the suit and the big moustache, that's Kurdish.'

I noticed something odd about the photos, something vaguely disconcerting. It took me a while to figure out what it was: there were hardly any young men in the pictures.

'Where are the men?' I asked. 'I mean, the ones in the middle, between the grandfathers and the boys.'

'Prison,' Selim replied with a smile. 'Or in the mountains. Or gone, like me.' His lips trembled a little. They often did.

He sat hunched over the table, propping up his right hand, his smoking hand, with his elbow, nervously flicking the ash off a cigarette. He smoked roll-ups when we first met, then later proper cigarettes from a pack that he would offer around; it was a point of pride, I think, pulling out that little cardboard box rather than a packet of tobacco.

Always nervous, always smoking. Sometimes I thought that, if he let go of his fag, he would simply crumple to the ground. That was all that was holding him up, a Marlboro Light.

With his high cheekbones, sleepy eyes and slightly trembling lips he looked at once very old and very young, and very afraid. His round glasses and long nose gave him the squirrel-like appearance of a young academic, and the chain-smoking and nervousness compounded that effect: he could have passed for one of those underground masterminds, the brains behind the battle. So what if he couldn't read or write. An illiterate intellectual: the world was full of them.

'And the women?' I asked.

26

'In the house,' he said and slid his finger from the photo to the napkin. 'But not all of them. Some are in the mountains, fighting. Some of our women are very strong.'

I went on perusing the photos. A wedding celebration made up of teenagers, children and the aged.

'So which of the boys is your little brother? The one who was born after you left?'

Selim pointed at a boy in a suit jacket that almost came down to his knees, standing wedged between two gnarled and crooked men and staring defiantly into the lens.

'It was the first time I met him. My own little brother. He said I sounded like Satan. They're all very religious there, they sit on rugs like this' – he squatted down – 'and everything is *Allah, Allah*, and I don't talk like that. My little brother, he told me killing an American gives you a free ticket to heaven, *automatisch*.'

'Hey, I thought the Kurds were supposed to love the Americans! You know, the Kurds in northern Iraq and all that.'

'Yes. But not my little brother.' Selim nervously rubbed his cheek. 'He's very interested in chemistry. He likes it more than all other subjects. When I was there, he was always busy with little experiments, he had some bottles and things.'

And then, like every time there was a new piece of vaguely disturbing news from Selim's village, we looked at each other and laughed.

'But I think, maybe he simply likes chemistry, maybe he's playing. Anyway I don't know so much about chemistry, so I didn't ask,' he added cautiously.

When Selim laughed, he cupped his mouth with the hand that held the cigarette, his long, jittery fingers sprinkling bits of ash over the tabletop. The plucky boy who had led a group of refugees ashore had turned into an observer, watching life from the sidelines, from the corner of a room, from the protective shadow of a doorway; like a man on the run.

And yet, when he arrived in Germany in 1992, at the beginning of that lukewarm decade between the fall of the Berlin Wall and the attacks on the World Trade Center, he was as quick and astute as any boy guerrilla east of Istanbul.

I picked up the photo of Selim's little brother in his oversized jacket.

'Little Al-Qaeda, hmm?' I said, shaking my head.

'Yes.' He sighed. 'Little Al-Qaeda, yes.'

I let the memories settle back into the crevices of my brain and opened the manual.

Serious signs that you may be dealing with a forced marriage include the following, I read. *When a middleman fills in the required documents ahead of the wedding. When the future bride is not visible, does not appear at the town hall at any point before the wedding day. When there is a big age difference between the man and the woman.*

I got up from my swivel chair and went to the office next door, where Sandra did her best to impose order on my files and folders. Most of the room was still taken up by the archives of my predecessor, Monsieur Dubois, who ruled over this corner of the town hall for decades. He had retired by the time I arrived, but his methodical spirit continued to pervade the older filing cabinets. I sometimes imagined him sitting there, forever labelling his brown-cardboard folders with a black pen and a stencil, until his skin began to resemble the soft, yellowing paper that held our most ancient records. (During my first week at the town hall, I spotted a note scrawled on the margins of one of his papers, his tidy handwriting distorted by haste or rage: *Putain!* I laughed out loud.)

Despite the unruliness of my own papers, it did not take me long to find what I was looking for: only a few sheets for now. The man was twenty-eight, roughly the same age as his cousin looked, a couple of years younger than me. The woman was eighteen. Not necessarily a big age difference, some might say.

This morning's aggressive errand boy could, of course, be called a middleman. But maybe the bride herself preferred to organise things that way; maybe she was shy, maybe she was illiterate, maybe she simply liked bossing her future husband's cousin around.

And even if I had the couple here, right here before me, how could I begin to guess their true feelings? How often did we look at a couple and think, What can possibly keep these two together, surely this won't last, surely they must be on the verge of a break-up? For all we knew they went on for years, decades, outlasting the ones we judged to be perfectly matched.

Even on the big day, you can look for signs at the wedding ceremony, right there, at the town hall!! the booklet continued, the double exclamation marks adding an incongruous note of jollity like a smiley face in an e-mail.

In which case should you be suspicious? If, for example, the bride is behaving abnormally. If there are tears.

Most brides cried at their wedding. Old brides, young

brides, thin brides, fat brides. I liked to think of it as tears of happiness, but sometimes I wondered.

After all, everyone got nervous at the bit with the signature. The forty-something bride with her noisy trail of children, entering the third round; the thirty-something with the relieved look in her eyes; the twenty-something who truly believed this would last for ever.

They all hesitated that fraction of a second after they picked up the pen, before they placed the nib on the paper. I was sure no one else noticed it. They probably didn't even notice it themselves. But I, I noticed it always.

I'd look at them, and think, But are you sure? Are you really sure?

Moments later, they would put down the pen, exhale and laugh, and turn to beam at the groom, glowing with joy and relief; and that single heartbeat of doubt (and, why not say it like it is, fear) would never be remembered again.

The men, of course, exuded nothing but panic.

As Selim would say: for a man, a wedding day is never a good day.

None of these signs should be taken as evidence individually, my inquisitive little manual said. *But together, they may be enough to arouse suspicion.*

There was a subtle menace in those words. Suspicion: well, everyone knew that feeling. My young visitor earlier this morning had probably suspected me of harbouring unfair prejudices against his family. I had, at one point, suspected Selim of not being entirely truthful with me, even of manipulating me. And yes, maybe I had my suspicions about the young Kurdish bride-to-be.

The law allows suspicious officials to hold pre-wedding interviews with the couple, either together or separately, to try and determine whether they both consent to be married.

That passage gave me a bit of a tingle. But it was the last sentence of the introduction, written in the tone of an earnest older registrar lecturing an inexperienced newcomer like me, that made me get up and go back to my filing cabinet: *If you have good reason to suspect that the marriage is not consensual, you should stop the ceremony.*

5

While Selim watched TV and sipped sugary tea, repeated his story before a series of immigration officials and tried to contact his relatives scattered across Germany, my home-town slowly froze up around him. Late summer turned into autumn and autumn turned into winter. Puddles became slippery bone-breakers, icicles hung from the roofs, and the pale men and women who passed Selim on his way to the immigration office blew out little puffs of steam like empty speech bubbles.

The older refugees stayed in bed and listened to Kurdish songs and reggae tunes that drifted out of the dorms and into the deserted corridors. The more recent arrivals were still full of energy. The Liberian-Nigerians explored the nightclubs on the edge of town, looking for girlfriends among the middle-aged German women who shook their broad hips on the dance floor every Saturday night. The Kurds piled into the TV room and talked about politics.

Initially, Selim had been excited to find they could watch broadcasts and videos that were banned at home: blurred footage of guerrilla fighters running down a steep moun-tainside, overlaid with an aggressively strummed *saz*.

Pictures of Kurdish demonstrations in Germany, Holland. Protesters shouting *Biji, Biji Kurdistan.*

To Selim's right sat the older Kurd, dressed in jeans and a woollen jumper with a black-and-white geometrical pattern, a *keffiya* wrapped around his neck in thick coils that came up to his ears. With his face half concealed by the scarf, he berated the newsreader, praised the boys in the mountains, half shouted, half sang along with the martial music.

'See this,' the older Kurd said, gesturing towards the fuzzy images on the screen. 'This is the future. Technology!'

In kebab takeaways, university corridors, dry-cleaning shops all over Europe, men in shabby woollen jumpers or sharp black suits were collecting funds for a project that would set the Kurdish diaspora on fire, that would make hardened old men weep tears of joy in the streets: a proper Kurdish TV channel broadcast from London, with news, woman's hour, announcements from the workers' party and a children's cartoon about a furry animal in Kurdish folk dress.

For now, the broadcasts were somewhat limited, but the older Kurd did not seem to mind.

To Selim's left sat an uncle a few times removed who had just arrived at the shelter with his wife Hanife and his son, Şivan, a shy boy who rarely ventured into the common room.

The uncle, a squat, brooding man with a moustache like an untrimmed hedge, would sit in silence for hours, then erupt in a blast of passion at the most unexpected moments; for example, when the broadcast showed a group of guerrilla fighters boiling water for tea.

33

BIJI KURDISTAN! the uncle shouted, then settled back into the sofa.

Selim sighed and went into the kitchen to make another pot of tea, stretching out every step of the process. The day before, he had turned over a wooden stool, tied a kitchen towel to its four legs and filled it with curdled milk, which was ripening into cheese. That had filled a good chunk of time.

Now he pushed aside the crusty bowls and plates on the worktop. The solidified cold fat covering the bottom of a frying pan had been traversed by tiny paws. He shuddered and inspected the saucepans until he found one that looked, on the whole, usable. He carefully steamed the green, red and black tea leaves. Moistened them. Moistened them again. Suspended them over another pot to collect the bitter extract. He poured the tea extract into the top half of the Kurdish teapot, water into the bottom. But however slow his motions were, in the end the tea was ready, and there was nothing more to be done. He looked at the sieve, the teapot, the stove. They were all getting along by themselves now, doing their tea-thing. Did not need his assistance.

He poured a little tea extract into three glasses, carefully topped them up with water, added sugar, stirred. Paused. Took a fourth glass from a cupboard with broken doors, filled it with tea, picked up the hot glass by the rim, placed it on a saucer and carried it into his dorm.

Johnson was lying on the top bunk, as expected, just his blue-eyed Jesus and a scratched Bob Marley tape for company.

'Johnson?' Selim said, tugging at Johnson's blanket.

Johnson was still refusing to speak, though sometimes Selim, out of the corner of his eye, saw him silently exercise his lips. It was an old trick, playing dumb so that the immigration officials couldn't find out where you were from. Once Selim had figured that out, he felt nothing but pity for his friend. Because in his short life he had already learned one thing: if someone wanted to make you talk, he would.

He placed the glass on the windowsill, fetched the other glasses from the kitchen and carried them into the TV room, where the fake Liberians and Palestinians were trying to take over the remote control.

The older Kurd was shouting at his challengers in Kurdish, cursing the day their mothers had been born. Selim's uncle was shoving a smuggled videotape into the hungry mouth of the recorder. A Liberian wrested the remote control from the older Kurd and zapped to a music channel.

Dance
Dance
Everybody in the house!
Dance

Selim's uncle pressed play and the music channel was replaced by blurred guerrilla footage.

Biji
Biji Kurdistan

Back to the music channel.

Everybody – khhhrrrrr . . .

'You broke the TV!'

 'No, you broke it!'

 'No, you . . .'

The older Kurd and Selim's uncle grumpily withdrew into the kitchen. A handful of Liberians plopped down on the sofa, clapping their hands and stretching out their long arms on the backrest. Selim enjoyed their easy banter, even though he did not understand a word. The TV sprang back to life and blasted out thumping beats, and some of the men got up to dance.

 'Ya, Selim, look!'

A Palestinian boy, the only other refugee of Selim's age, had entered the TV room. He sat down on one of the orange plastic chairs and showed Selim a novel way to drink tea: wedge a sugar cube between your teeth, then filter the tea through the sugar.

 '*Kıtlama*,' Selim said, intrigued. He had heard that the old men in Van drank their tea that way, but it had never occurred to him to try it himself. It was one of those practices that belonged exclusively to the elderly, like sitting under a tree and playing backgammon.

Selim unwrapped a twin packet of sugar cubes and positioned one of them between his front teeth. He pushed out his lower lip, rested the rim on it, and slowly tilted the glass while sucking the liquid through the sugar.

Just then, the older Kurd came back from the kitchen, looked at the two boys with disintegrating sugar cubes between their teeth and shook his head.

'We should talk about your appointment tomorrow, go over what you're going to tell them.'

Selim nodded and tried to answer, but the sugar cube crumbled between his teeth, half of it falling on the floor, the rest dribbling out of his mouth in a tea-soaked mess. The Palestinian boy, who had just taken a big gulp from his glass, burst into giggles, spraying sticky tea all over the linoleum floor.

'Eh, and if you drink your tea like that, your teeth will fall out,' the older Kurd sighed.

Yes, but it tasted nice.

6

At night, enveloped in the sour-sweet mist that rose up from hundreds of feet and armpits and mingled with the ghosts of generations of German soldiers, Selim lay on his mattress, listening to his snoring room-mates, the sound of air being sucked in through snot.

He heard Johnson warble and sigh in a strange tongue, vocalising all the thoughts and fears that had been locked in his throat during the day.

How could they sleep? He feared that, if he fell asleep, he would dream of drowning, of being buried alive, of being caught. But every morning, waking from his few hours of unconsciousness, he felt he had in fact dreamt nothing at all.

Not many hours from now, it would be time to get up for the first prayer of the day.

He lay there and listened for creaking doors, alien footsteps, his whole body an antenna trying to detect enemy intruders, to hear above the snoring uncle and ticking alarm clock. What if the German police were to crash into their room, take him away, put him on a plane back to Turkey? They were not supposed to take away children, but the day before they had taken away the Palestinian boy. As it turned out, he had not been from Palestine at all.

Selim's mind swerved across Europe, back to Italy, to Greece, to Turkey, and then south and east to the mountains, giving in to the pull of memories. He was running along winding paths and through dark alleys, squat beige buildings and tangled electric wires to his left and right. There was a funeral procession. The older boys were carrying the coffin, the younger children waving a flag that kept wrapping itself around the pole. The mothers and fathers stayed at home; if they were arrested, who would look after the children?

Selim and his cousins had snapped branches off trees. An uncle helped Selim tape a photograph of a man to his branch. Selim was shaking the branch, following the crowd. He turned around and saw his sister Aynur, clasping her own big branch with pudgy hands. He angrily gestured to her to make her go away, give him her banner, go home. She was too small for this.

Then there was a bang and everyone started running.

He turned over, pressing his throbbing chest against the mattress, forcing himself to think of something else.

His first time in Istanbul: he had never seen so many people, so many cars and buses, so many ragged refugees looking for ways to leave. Kurds, Iranians, Pakistanis, Afghans sleeping in doorways, basements, tent cities, crumbling houses in the city centre, tower blocks on the outskirts. They drifted in and out of dimly lit bars that offered no entertainment, restaurants where no food was served. Selim's traffickers passed him on to men whose only business was to put people in touch with other people, establish connections, make sure you found your man.

The first choice was a truck ride across the border to Greece and from there, snaking through Europe, to *Almanya*. A German passport was the most expensive, the most desirable, especially for the Kurds, with their thousands of relatives in Germany. Britain, that was also good. But Britain was a lot harder to reach.

Selim's family had sorted it all out for him, paying for the luxury route, the first choice. It would take about three months, with a variety of trucks and passports and long walks through cold darkness, but he had heard from many people, who were now settled in Frankfurt or Bremen, that it was the safest way. Unfortunately, by the time he met his man in Istanbul, that route had been closed. Tighter controls. On to the second choice, then, the truck to Bulgaria, and from there on foot to Albania; from there, quick little boats across to Italy, taking less than a couple of hours. That was fine; Selim was used to walking, and so he agreed to the change of plan.

On his third day in Istanbul, where he slept in the back room of a bar, he was told that the Bulgarian route was closed too. However, there was a new option. No problem, very safe, not so many controls, tomorrow night you leave, no problem: the ship.

'But . . . I can't swim,' Selim told the trafficker.

'No problem, that's why we take the ship.'

Selim had heard the rumours about ships sinking somewhere between Turkey and Italy. Men, women, children, all drowned, going down in a vast rusty metal coffin.

'OK,' he said.

The journey took six days and six nights. By the end of it, Selim learned that he could, in fact, swim.

Better not think of that. His thoughts returned to the snoring and warbling and clock-ticking around him, to the cave-like bunk. If he fell asleep now, he would definitely dream of the ship. He hugged his pillow and forced the thoughts away. Tried to think of something else.

In the village, during those long winters when all the little houses were covered in snow, and the roads and mountains were covered in snow, when there was nowhere to go and nothing to do but bake bread, his mother would entertain them with stories. Those were the years when his father was in jail, when his mother kept the family together, sold the house to pay for a lawyer, moved them into a smaller house, comforted them with her tales. Selim buried his face in his pillow and imagined she was there, big, soft and warm, keeping the winter cold out and her voice down so as not to wake the others.

Brother and Sister went into the mountains to collect milk thistles, she would say softly. *They climbed up the steep mountain, plucking thistles on the left, thistles on the right, until the bag was full.*

Sister carried the bag on her back. Brother said, let's sit down and rest and drink some water and see how many thistles we have collected. Sister said yes, let's see.

But when they opened the bag, it was empty. Sister, you've eaten all the thistles! Brother said. No I haven't! Sister said. Yes you have! Brother said. (And here the voice of Selim's mother faded away and the shrill little voice of his naughty sister

Aynur took over.) 'No I haven't! Yes you have!' *No I haven't, and if you don't believe me, take a knife and cut open my stomach and you'll see there are no thistles inside.*

Brother took his knife and cut open Sister's stomach. No thistles inside. He walked back down the path and spotted a neat trail of thistles. They had dropped through a hole in the bag. Sister, you were right! You didn't eat the thistles! Brother shook Sister, but she did not respond.

Oh Sister! Oh Sister!

He wept and broke into a mourning song. He dug a grave for her by the stream, and since then . . .

Why had he let that particular story worm its way into his brain? Now sleep would be impossible.

Tick. Tock. Tick. Tock. Tick.

Every tick a jab. On all fours, Selim crawled over to the neighbouring bunk. Reached for the alarm clock. Took the batteries out. Waited there for a bit, exhausted, resting his cheek on the bristly rug between the beds. Listened. Breathed in the dust and dirt collected in the rough fibre of the rug, tried to convert the smell into the warm sheepy odour of the stable. Tried to imagine the bristly rug was straw. Tried to remember how the story ended.

Tick. Tock.

Argh! Where did it come from?

The building, he thought. It's the heart of this building with all its waiting rooms full of waiting chairs and waiting corridors full of waiting people.

My own heart goes thud-thud-thud, Selim thought. The heart of this building goes tick-tick-tick.

7

The address and number of the Ligue pour la Défense des Droits de la Femme were listed at the back of *The Registrar's Manual for Detecting Forced Marriages*, along with the phone numbers of helplines and women's shelters. The name had led me to expect quite a large and professional organisation, but when I went there during my lunch break I found a rundown alleyway near the canal, a gate that gave way to a junk-filled courtyard, and at the bottom of the courtyard a scratched metal door. I heard angry voices from behind the door and stopped to listen.

'I don't know where you got that number,' a women cried, 'because I've now seen it in five pamphlets with five different sources – no, you listen now—'

'It all goes back to that bogus survey they did in '99, doesn't it? Doesn't it?' another woman interrupted her, her voice deep and raspy. 'Just tell me if it's based on that survey, yes or no, because if it is we might as well throw out the whole study.'

'You questioning my methodology?' a third woman cut in. 'Frankly, it sounds like you're questioning my methodology. And just to remind you, I did my PhD in methodology.'

There was a brief pause, and then the first woman said in an almost timid voice, as if aware that she was saying something unforgivable: '*Et oui*, Derya. I question your methodology.'

The other two fell silent.

Then the woman with the deep voice added, less timidly: 'And I have a PhD in methodology, too.'

The door swung open and a woman with short black hair stormed out into the courtyard. She snatched a cigarette from her breast pocket and lit it, inhaling grimly as if to punish the tobacco. I pretended to be reading one of the posters by the door, something about a Turkish film festival, then fiddled with my mobile phone. After a while, two other women came out, ignored the smoker and stomped through the gateway into the street.

I turned around to face the woman, who was glaring after the other two with tight-lipped scorn.

'Excuse me, I'm looking for the Ligue,' I said.

'Well that's me,' she snapped. 'I'm the head.'

'Sorry, I didn't mean to interrupt your break.'

'I'm just having a smoke,' she said defensively, waving her cigarette and glaring at me. 'I'm in there all day, right, and I don't see why a five-minute smoke should do any harm.'

'No, no,' I said hastily. 'Of course not. By all means enjoy your break and I'll come back a bit later.'

'Ha! I wish I could take a proper break!' She gave me a sour smile. 'God knows, I need one. I'm just going to finish this and then it's back to work, but you know, I really don't see why I shouldn't allow myself five minutes of pleasure.'

'You should, definitely.' I tried to look encouraging. 'In fact, you should take a proper lunch break, it's your right.'

'Exactly, as you say, it's my right.' She softened a little and took two slow drags before stretching out her hand. 'Derya Çelik. How can I help?'

'I'm from the town hall, I found your organisation on our contact list,' I began, but she didn't seem to be listening.

Instead, she looked at the mobile phone in my hand and said: 'You should use a filter for that, or it'll fry your brain. You can buy one at the phone shop next door.'

'Sure . . . I probably should have made an appointment—'

'Let's go inside, and we can talk properly.' She finished her cigarette, bent over to stub it out on the concrete and dropped the end into a sealable plastic bag from her pocket.

I followed her into a dimly lit room that was bursting at the seams with stacked folders, books and rolled-up posters. She sat down, pushing aside an open folder and a tub of half-eaten tomato salad.

'So,' she said, wiping her fingers on a crumpled tissue. 'Someone from the *mairie*. We were just about to send you lot another letter about our funding. Or lack of it, rather.'

I laughed nervously.

'It's more of a private visit. Or maybe not exactly private. I get a lot of couples from the communities you work with, Turkish and North African and all that, so I thought it would be good to get in touch.'

'Oh right, I thought you had come to ask about our girls' empowerment campaign. We sent you a pamphlet a couple of weeks ago,' she said.

'So that was you?'

I looked at her folder and noticed that some papers were fastened together with hairpins. A thick book on family law was stained with brown rings from a coffee mug; the mug itself was balanced on a stack of crumb-strewn plates. Strangely, the mess only made her appear all the more authoritative as she sat there with her neat, spiky hair and steel-rimmed glasses, reigning over the general disorder.

'The manual on forced marriages, that was from your organisation?' I pressed.

She shot me a puzzled look. 'No, it wasn't a manual, just a pamphlet. What manual are you talking about?'

I tried to think of a way to describe the manual, but the whole idea of registrars poking into private matters suddenly seemed bizarre and amateurish. I felt embarrassed about the town hall's bumbling efforts.

'The town hall has produced a book on forced marriages,' I finally said. 'You must have heard, we're all supposed to be more alert now, and I just wanted to ask for your advice. It's pretty new to me, this idea that we're supposed to meddle.'

'Well, my job is all about meddling,' Derya said. 'I don't know if you read our pamphlet, but we get a dozen calls a week from girls asking us for help. This one's due to be shipped to Turkey next week.' She tapped the open folder. 'They've already printed the invitations for the wedding. Only there won't be a wedding.'

'Hmm. I guess it's different for us at the town hall.'

I thought of Sandra, of my retired predecessor, Monsieur Dubois, with his love of methodical file-keeping. They would be shocked to hear that I was snooping around like this, spying into people's private matters, singling out a certain community when we were surely all gloriously French, united by the Republic, regardless of where we had been born. Maybe they were right.

'What exactly do you want to know?' Derya picked up her mobile phone and attached filter and put it in her canvas satchel. 'I'm having another crazy day, not that I'm saying you should leave, we definitely need to improve relations with the town hall. But if this is going to take a while we might as well talk by the canal. It's so hot in here.'

'Sure . . .'

'You know, I work night-shifts and weekends all the time, so I don't see why I shouldn't take a walk along the canal every now and then. It's like the cigarettes, why shouldn't I?'

I smiled and nodded to show my complete agreement.

'The girl is going to run away tonight, we're putting her up in an emergency shelter,' Derya said as we left the office. 'Not that it's ideal, plonking her into a dorm full of junkies. Some decide they'd rather be locked up in a room with their cousin on the wedding night than spend another day in the shelter.'

It was cooler by the canal. We walked past crowded pavement cafés and cars with their windows down, rap music from the *banlieue* blasting out over the cobblestones and broken bottles. The hip young interns from the advertising companies and tech start-ups around us had left their offices and were sitting on the bank, legs dangling over the water, paper wrappers and cans of Coke by their side.

'What about talking to the families?' I asked. 'Say, for instance, if I had a suspicion, or if the bride asked me to help, hypothetically speaking, could I ask you to mediate or something?'

47

She paused. We had reached the lock and were watching the bridge beside it slowly rotate sideways, inviting an empty, *chanson*-playing cruise boat to pass.

'Sometimes that isn't such a good idea.' She gazed at the boat, and for the first time in our conversation, she looked calm, almost a little deflated. 'We did have a case once where the social worker thought it would work. Basically, the girl wanted the family to be reconciled, and the social worker wanted the family to be reconciled. As it turned out, the family didn't want to be reconciled. The only family member who turned up at the mediation centre was the girl's brother, the youngest son, just turned eighteen. He came into the room, ran to his sister and stabbed her. By the time help arrived, it was too late. It's usually the youngest son, and he'll say it was all his idea and he'll take the blame, because he'll spend the shortest time in prison.'

The boat disappeared down the canal, and she turned to face me.

'But you must know all this, right, given that you work in this neighbourhood. And the press are all over these kinds of stories now, though they usually get it wrong. It's not like all Muslim girls are victims. I'm a Muslim, and I'm certainly not a victim. I just refuse to be a victim, you know?'

'Well, that's exactly the problem, isn't it, figuring out who's who.'

'Can I tell you what I think?' She didn't wait for my reply. 'Frankly, you're not going to answer that question, ever. It's not just that the girl is scared, it's that . . . well . . .'

The bridge pivoted back into position, latching onto the dock with a satisfying clank of stone meeting metal.

'Stay there, I'll be right back, I'm just going to . . .' And without finishing that sentence or the previous one, she slipped across the street and into one of the shops.

I sat down by the bridge. A couple of metres to my left, two dishevelled boys were sleeping on a mattress. Their friends sat near by, chatting, bathing their feet in the canal. A splash; something had fallen into the water; someone, in fact. He ploughed his way towards us through the milky green liquid, churning up a trail of foam, and when he reached the bank propped himself up on his elbows, shook a spray of sparkling drops out of his black hair and showed his big white teeth, laughing. Hands reached down to pull him up, slapped him on the back, and then the next boy dropped into the canal and swam across.

They were Afghans, I think; I had read about them in the paper. They had set up camp along the canal, Afghan teenagers planning to make their way to Britain. These boys, the ones who were laughing and playing and jumping into the water, would at some point disappear and re-emerge up north, trying to sneak a ride across the Channel. But the makeshift camp would stay, to be refilled with bright young things treading the Jalalabad–London path.

It was just before two o'clock and apparently time for midday prayer. One teenager was kneeling on an unfolded cardboard box laid out on the cobbled promenade, the stones shiny, glazed by the urine of dogs and drunkards. His head was pointing east, toes west, his forehead touching the cardboard. Lunchtime couples skirted around the praying boy, trying to keep a respectful distance without falling into the canal. Out of the fifty or so Afghan teenagers by the canal, he was the only one praying. Or maybe the others prayed in their head now, like Selim.

These days, all over Paris, there were these little clusters of hope and despair; humans fashioning settlements out of nothing. Mattresses, bundles of African cloth, pots full of bubbling stew: little villages amid the urban grit and exhaust fumes.

And yet, for now, they were simply teenagers taking a summertime dip. Because even if you're a homeless Afghan sleeping under a bridge, even if you're a landless Kurd on the run, I guess it's not possible to be unhappy all the time.

Derya came back, carrying a newspaper.

'Look at this.' She rustled through to the local news pages and pointed to a two-paragraph piece. It was something about a knife fight in the neighbourhood. 'See, I'm from a Turkish family, I grew up in this neighbourhood, I know the entire story behind it, the families, the girl herself, in fact. It's like this with everything that goes on here, everyone knows everything, marriages, fall-outs, whatever, we're big gossips. I'm not saying that your campaign is useless, but . . .' She waved her hands towards the canal, the Afghan boys, the passers-by. 'Where do you start?'

'Right, so there's no point in me getting involved because I'm an outsider, but if I stand back and ignore it you'll accuse me of turning a blind eye.'

'I'm not accusing you of anything. I'm just saying it might be better to leave it to people with a bit more experience. And to support us a bit more. Last month, we sent the town hall half a dozen invites to our fund-raiser, and not one of you came.'

I offered some lie about having been on holiday. She raised one eyebrow, clearly not buying it.

We walked back and soon reached the junction where she would turn left to her pamphlets and combative colleagues and I would turn right to my filing cabinets.

We shook hands in a rather formal way and she looked at me quizzically. 'Do you mind if I ask why you're this interested?'

If only I'd gone to that bloody fund-raiser, I thought, then this would be so much easier. I could have bought some goodwill, reached some general agreement on offloading tricky cases onto their organisation. Anyway, too late now.

'I guess there's a certain personal link,' I said cautiously. 'I'm dealing with a couple right now where the girl is Kurdish, and I once had a Kurdish friend who was involved in a, well, a strange kind of wedding. And then there's something about the couple . . . I'm sure it's totally fine, but the bride seems to be staying away, or she's being kept away, and she's very young.' I caught myself rubbing one eyebrow and clasped my hands to stop.

'She's Kurdish?' Derya said with sudden interest. 'You do need to be careful. With some of those families, it's no joke. We really have to make the girl completely disappear, because the father will track her down. It doesn't matter if she's a teenager. They have networks, so if it's not the father it's the uncle, the brother. He doesn't care if it takes years, decades. If he sees her again, even if it's years later, even if she's forty, he will kill her.'

'Sure, I understand,' I said, thinking to myself, That's the one thing I find a bit annoying about these social activists, they always exaggerate.

8

Back in the early 1990s, when Selim was doing time in the refugee shelter, we never heard about Kurdish forced marriages. We never heard about Kurdish honour killings. Back then, Kurdish men weren't perpetrators. They were victims.

I remember one night when I was halfway through my homework and decided, lazily, that I couldn't be bothered with the rest. I trundled into the living room, where my brother was watching the *Tagesschau*. A crowd of Kurds were blocking the motorway. They had formed a circle, leaving a kind of clearing or arena in the middle. The camera zoomed in on a man pouring something over himself out of a squarish metal container. He struck a match, and turned into a man-shaped column of fire. He ran into the centre of the circle, waving his hands and trailing flames, drawing a frenzied, violent spiral. Within seconds he had collapsed onto the ground.

The camera cut to a traffic jam. A man was bursting out of his car, his features distorted with anger.

'I'm not having this!' he shouted into the camera. 'Me, here, stuck!'

The Kurds had barricaded the Cologne ring road, the

newsreader said. It was *Newroz*, the Kurdish New Year: 1994. Three Kurdish men immolated themselves that day.

'The terror has reached a new dimension!' our usually stoical Chancellor barked.

At my school, someone had put up a poster, secretly, at night. It showed nine Kurdish men who had sought political asylum in Germany, claiming Turkish militias had blacklisted them as members of the PKK. The claims were rejected and the men deported back to Turkey. The picture showed the nine men in a row. They were up on a hill, their silhouettes black against the sunset: nine men dangling from nine gallows.

Now, of course, the newspapers were full of stories about what really happened. European politicians were all very surprised and outraged. The Turkish government itself had deployed official investigators to swarm among the remains of the villages up in the mountains around Cizre. To peek into acid tubs in abandoned factories, lower themselves down deep wells and ravines, dig up fields, while being watched by a crowd of dead-eyed widows.

But I am getting ahead of myself. In the early 1990s hardly anyone was interested in the fate of the Kurds in general, or Selim in particular.

Every few weeks, Selim took the bus from the barracks to the cobblestoned alleys and timbered houses of the medieval town centre. There, he walked down a narrow passage, a mere crack between two warped old black-and-white houses, turned left into a green doorway, and climbed the wonky wooden stairs that led to the flat of his ponytailed lawyer, Dr Habicht.

Dr Habicht's dark little rooms smelt of exotic spices and damp. There was what Selim assumed to be his bedroom, separated from the main living area by a red batik curtain fashioned out of a shawl. In the kitchen, slivers of apple quietly desiccated in the oven while a cracked old teapot dispensed endless cups of verbena tea.

When he sat on Dr Habicht's toilet, Selim was confronted by a big poster with a wheel on it; between the spokes of the wheel grew different plants with descriptions he could not read. On the front of the door was a poster of men with moustaches holding up a PKK banner.

Dr Habicht had a proper office somewhere that he shared with other lawyers, but he preferred to receive informal clients, or, as he called them, solidarity clients, in his living room. A cluttered desk and a small filing cabinet gave one corner of the room a slightly more officious air. It was in that corner that Selim and Dr Habicht would sit down, drink their cups of herbal tea, nibble dried apple slices, talk in a mixture of Kurdish, Turkish and German and pore over Selim's paperwork.

'I'm not feeling too well today,' Dr Habicht sighed, adjusting the chequered scarf around his neck.

'Cough?' Selim had already learned the names of the most frequent visitors to Dr Habicht's home.

The lawyer shook his head.

'Cold?'

He shook his head again. Selim studied his lawyer's sunken cheeks and bloodshot eyes. He wasn't looking too bad today. The ends of his ponytail stuck out in different directions, like the ends of an overused paintbrush. Selim had the slight suspicion that Dr Habicht chewed on them when he was by himself.

'A general feeling of being unwell. Ah, Selim, if you knew what kind of unpleasant stuff lurks inside this!' Dr Habicht rapped his knuckles on the whitewashed wall. 'I've asked a toxins expert to come over and investigate, but part of me prefers not to know. I should keep the windows open for my lungs, but then my health can't take the draught.' He stroked his right ear. 'And my tinnitus. Please remember to keep your voice down today.'

He excavated a folder from underneath one of the piles on his desk. Selim recognised the pink label. He had brought his own folder, too, and now man and boy opened the folders on their knees and sighed in acknowledgement of the complex situation before them.

'So, here we have your latest application,' Dr Habicht said. 'God, this noise!'

He put aside the folder, went to the window and, running his fingertip along the frame, checked that it was firmly shut. But like the rest of the house, the wooden frame had shrunk and swollen through centuries of wet winters and dry summers, and nothing quite fitted the way Dr Habicht would have liked it to. To plug the gaps, he used little squares of cloth that he cut from old vests and kept in a floppy pile by the window. He was now stuffing one of the greyish rags down the side of the frame with the help of a fork.

He sat down again. Selim looked at him expectantly. Dr Habicht shook his head.

'I'm not going to beat around the bush. Rejected, unfortunately. Sorry. *Bibûre*. But you know, they won't deport you while you're – God, this noise!' He grabbed the fork, but one look at Selim made him put it down again.

Selim peered at Dr Habicht through heavy-lidded eyes, leaned forward and put his long, thin fingers to his mouth as if about to take a drag from a cigarette.

'Can I smoke?' he asked with his trembling smile, knowing the answer but feeling he really needed a cigarette, now, right now.

The lawyer gasped.

'Please, Selim, at your age! And my lungs . . . you could go downstairs, but maybe try to shake out your clothes, you know, to air them a little before you come back up again.' He shook his limp jacket to show what he meant.

Selim smiled and nodded.

'I wait.' He picked at his lips with his fingers.

Dr Habicht asked him to sign a few forms. He told him about the next meeting of the legal aid group. He told him not to lose hope, the situation was difficult, but not entirely without hope. They would appeal again, and again, and again.

'And even if we lose, even in the very, very worst case, even then, there are options. Some Kurdish men, well, boys, well, you know. Some go underground, go into hiding. There are options . . . oh, oh, here comes another bad one.' Dr Habicht gave way to a wheezing cough.

Selim left the flat clutching the bag with his documents, willing himself to believe that, somewhere in this folder, or in Dr Habicht's folder, or in one of those intimidating folders at the immigration office, there was a piece of paper that would turn out to be his ticket to a proper, legal, signed and stamped life. He emerged from the narrow passage, tucked the bag between waist and elbow, took a cigarette out of the breast pocket of his denim jacket – he had rolled it earlier, in wise foresight – lit it and inhaled deeply.

He was lucky to have Dr Habicht, he thought.

In some ways, it was fortunate that Selim could hardly read. He did not notice that on his letterhead Dr Habicht had misspelt the name of his own street.

Dr Habicht, the elegant letterhead read. *Mauergassse 13*.

It should have been *Mauergasse*.

When I had the dubious pleasure of meeting Dr Habicht a few years later, it was still *Mauergassse*. I never found out whether he stuck to the wrong spelling because he had ordered the letterhead in bulk and was too broke to pay for a reprint; whether he did not care about spelling because it was not immediately relevant to his health; whether he did not notice details like a misspelt official letterhead; or whether he simply did not know how to spell *Mauergasse*.

None of the possible explanations increased my trust in Dr Habicht's abilities as a lawyer.

But, as I said, it was probably a good thing that Selim was unaware of the letterhead; because in any case Dr Habicht was almost free of charge, and that was the only fee Selim could afford.

9

A few days passed after that strange visitor wrestled his way into my office, and I did not hear from him or the couple he claimed to represent. Then, one day, I took a lunchtime stroll around the park. When I arrived back at the town hall, another visitor was lying in wait for me. She looked as if she had just emerged from a street market and accidentally dragged along a tangle of tie-dye foulards and dangling jewellery, like someone coming out of the undergrowth with half the forest in their hair.

I tried to slip past her, but she ambushed me with a toothy smile and outstretched hand.

'I am *so* glad I caught you – I just felt I *had* to come and see you about Azad. Would you have time for a chat?'

There are few things more frightening than a toothy woman with foulards asking for a chat, and, as I quickly made clear to her, I had not the faintest idea who she was talking about.

'Gosh, right, sorry – first things first, I'm Azad's social worker, but do call me Carole. I just want to try and roll this whole mess right back to the basics' – and here she actually performed a winding motion with her hands – 'it's such a mess. He says you've already called the family asking to meet the girl.'

Oh, I thought, the little bully has shopped me to the ethics police. I took a step back.

'I'm afraid I can't receive visitors without an appointment, but if you phone my secretary, she can help you arrange one. Though to be clear, I don't discuss individual cases, Madame . . .'

'*On peut se tutoyer*,' she suggested chummily.

'Well, if you phone my secretary—'

'I have already called your secretary. She offered me a date in two months' time.'

Bless her, I thought gratefully. Pay rise.

'I'm sorry, but we are all rather busy here.'

I moved towards the entrance. And here Carole turned from soft to steely and, with unexpected decisiveness, grabbed my arm.

'I'm not going to let this one go. You have to understand, someone like Azad can feel a lot of anger if he senses that he is being emasculated.'

'Emasculated! Where did you get that from?'

'Just think about his role in the community, his responsibility for the wedding. This kind of interference from the authorities can be perceived as very threatening.'

'Well, I'm sure you're only doing your job, and I'm doing mine. We've got new rules, and it's my job to meet the bride and make sure she knows her rights. We can't skip it just because Azad feels castrated.'

'Could you tell me a bit more about these new rules? I haven't heard of them.'

'As I said, they are new.'

'Were they especially invented to humiliate migrant families?'

Look here, I thought. Who would have thought the woolly thing could be so sharp. She was sticking up her nose now, pushing it towards me like a suspicious terrier. Standing on the steps, we were trapped in the early afternoon heat; behind us were the stone-chilled halls of the *mairie*, before us the park, tempting me back with its leafy coolness. How nice it would be to take another wander and sit down on a bench and reflect. I crossed my arms.

'I assume they were "invented", as you put it, to make sure unusually young brides are aware of the legal implications of marriage.'

'Eighteen is unusually young?'

'I can send you a copy of the new guidelines, but, sorry, I was just about to . . .'

I was annoyed with myself; why was I lying? I didn't have a copy of the rules, for a very simple reason: there were none. Not in the legal sense. There was a flimsy, well-meaning little manual I had received in the post, and should probably have ignored. Show her that and watch her sue me for discrimination.

'Look,' I said. 'I think it's fair to say we all want the best for this couple, and I fully appreciate your, er, expertise. So how about this, we arrange a meeting with the family and you help me explain that the business with the bride is now pretty much part of the procedure.' I grappled for a phrase that would win her over, and finally settled on: 'It's all about cultural dialogue, isn't it?'

'This isn't dialogue, it's a disgrace. No other bride in this neighbourhood has been asked to do this kind of interview. You have no idea, you have no idea what you're doing.'

She stood too close to me, her eyes wide with outrage suffered by proxy, her skin exuding a potent mix of patchouli and perspiration. She had, I assumed, stomped all the way uphill to the *mairie* in the heat.

'I wish you'd spoken to me first,' she continued. 'I could have given you the whole back story, the years of work it's taken me, well, us, to get Azad to where he is now.'

'To east Paris?'

She shot me an irritated glance.

'To his place in life, his place in the community. We're talking real rites of passage here. Dealing with the paperwork for his cousin's wedding, that's a milestone for Azad. I was talking about him just the other day, in a workshop, as a brilliant example of how it can all work out, how he's completely kept himself out of trouble since I took him on. And now, half the community is gossiping about this wedding being held up, and who will be blamed? Azad!'

Oh Carole, I thought, I know your kind. You have been dreaming about this job ever since you read *Tristes Tropiques* at the *lycée*, followed by *Intifada of the Heart*. You probably take belly-dancing classes. You have learned to make Kurdish tea in a tin pot, you listen to Moroccan music, you buy your kohl eyeliner in a Salafi shop, you love Middle Eastern and Turkish and North African culture because it's so *sensual* and so very different from your petit bourgeois suburban background; you think veils are empowering because they free women from the dictates of Western fashion, you get excited

61

by your own anger on behalf of all the world's oppressed, you love the rush of passion when there's a cause to defend, you think Azad's main problem is *lack of confidence*, yes, Carole, you really believe that Azad is actually quite *shy* and *helpless* and *misunderstood*, and in my life I have known far too many people like you, and don't take it personally, but I am sick of them, and already I am sick of you; because people like you have created nothing, nothing but trouble for me.

No, I did not share my thoughts with her.

Instead, I used that old passive-aggressive trick: I smiled with great warmth.

'Do you know her?' I asked.

'Who?'

'The bride. Do you know her? Have you ever met her?'

'Well, not personally.'

I wondered what other ways of meeting people there were, but let it go.

'So just to be clear, do you know whether she's actually against this interview?'

Ah, but she had known Azad and his family for years and—

'Yes, but the girl, Carole. The girl. She's never shown up at Azad's place? She's never met you, or talked to you, even though you seem to be so heavily involved in this whole process, and so, hmm, close to Azad?'

At this point, it turned out that Carole had indeed never met the girl. She did not find this unusual, as the bride was meant to be modest and reserved before the wedding. In any case, the traditional wedding had already been performed in Turkey. My role was simply to add an official French seal to the whole procedure, and surely that wasn't asking too much, especially considering that, as a town hall official, I was meant to be respectful of . . .

Wishing I had closable ear-flaps like a dog, I tried to think of a way to get rid of her. We had entered the drab waiting area behind the portal of the town hall and were moving towards a group of polymix-covered sofas in various shades of greyish beige. The taupe synthetic carpet clashed violently with my guest's henna-red hair.

She was still talking at me. However, sobered by the familiar taupeness of my surroundings, I reminded myself that I was not on a crusade. I felt sheepish for having been so emotional earlier on. Here, the very furniture exuded stern rationality: the plastic name-tags, the earnest, typed reminders on the noticeboard, the felt-covered partitions on their black metal legs.

I was not out to castrate Azad, after all, or stage a rescue mission for a girl I knew nothing about, or stamp my version of what I thought of as a free relationship on a family I had never met. I simply felt an impulse to sit up and be watchful. I did not want to be the one who was fooled, who, out of negligence or ignorance, failed to help when help was required. I did not want to be an unwitting accomplice. And to gain even a most basic understanding of what was going on here, I needed allies. I had hoped for assistance from sensible, no-nonsense Derya; as it turned out, I would also need flaky Carole.

So I asked her to come into my office.

When she sat down in the chair where angry young Azad had parked his buttocks, and positioned herself as if she was about to give me another lecture on the importance of respecting migrant traditions, I put my hand on her arm and whispered: 'But, Carole, what if the girl doesn't want to be married? What if they are forcing her?'

She shook her head, exasperated.

'I just don't get why you're so absolutely determined to wreck this wedding. I mean, what do you know about the Kurds?'

'I have my reasons,' I said, and at that point I almost told her everything. I felt such an urge to convince her, to make her see and understand what I believed I was seeing and understanding. I almost told her everything about Selim; the whole sorry tale. But instead, I simply repeated: 'Believe me, I have my reasons.'

10

Almost a year after Selim arrived, right in the middle of the school year, when he was about fourteen, someone, some-where, decided that it would be a good time to introduce him to the joys of formal education.

Since his arrival, he had learned a few words in German: *Schlepper*, people-traffickers. *Asyl*, asylum. And one that took him a while to learn: *Asylbewerberheim*. Shelter for asylum seekers.

Armed with those words and a rolled-up prayer mat, Selim ran down the linoleum-covered stairs of the *Ah-zeel-beverber-hime*, all the way down to the steel gate, where a woman with practical short blonde hair bundled him onto a bus, then dropped him off in front of a long grey building with reinforced windows and graffiti-smeared doors. A secretary took him to a classroom at the top of another set of linoleum-covered stairs.

There, Selim, his three words and his prayer mat slipped into an unassuming seat in the back row, hoping to go unnoticed. The chair to his right was empty. The next one was occupied by a broad-shouldered boy in a black T-shirt.

The boy leaned over and jerked his chin in a questioning way.

'*Adın ne*?' the boy said.

'Selim. *Seninki*?'

'Hakan.' They gave each other a brief nod.

The others were too busy with their own activities to pay much attention. Selim looked left, right, left again, amazed to see himself surrounded by so many teenagers after months of living like a smaller than average adult, drinking tea and waiting and drinking tea again. Here the girls chatted or painted their nails and wiggled their fingers to let the varnish dry. The boys teased the girls and circulated obscene drawings and aimed the occasional spitball at each other. One boy tried to set fire to the swishing ponytail of the girl in front of him.

There was one adult in the classroom, a tall, thin string of a man who had taken cover behind a wooden desk and was writing words on the blackboard that Selim could not read. The teacher.

Every now and then the teacher edged away from the blackboard and towards the class. Guiding him were two principles he had learned in a three-week course retraining jobless academics as teachers of difficult pupils: Ignore destructive and attention-seeking behaviour. Reward and praise positive behaviour.

Ignore the nail-painting, the spitball-firing, the smouldering ponytail. Reward and praise . . . well . . . this required a certain creativity.

'Well done, Dynasty, you brought your pen . . . and Hakan, your notebook, excellent . . . ah it's Dwayn's notebook . . . anyway, well done, Hakan, well done, Dwayn . . . and here we have Selim . . . welcome, welcome . . .'

Ignore the spitballs.

Selim leaned back in his chair and looked out of the window. Occasionally, he caught a Turkish word or phrase bandied around between the Turkish-German boys, whose fathers had arrived in Germany as guest workers decades ago. Across from the Turkish-Germans sat a small cluster of Kurdish boys, sons of asylum seekers.

Just as Selim began to enjoy observing the circus around him, easing into his first day at school, the teacher, encouraged by a temporary absence of spitballs, took a deep breath and decided to ask the class a question.

Not a difficult question.

Certainly not a controversial question.

Just a friendly, testing-the-waters, trying-to-establish-contact kind of question.

'So,' the teacher repeated. 'Why do you think Michael returned the apples to the shop at the end of the story?'

No one replied, as usual. The teacher bravely turned to one of the baseball caps in the back row.

'Dwayn Olshevsky? Any idea why Michael returned the apples?'

''Cause he's gay.'

The class briefly stopped chatting, manicuring, antagonising and let out a brief collective chortle.

The teacher crossed his arms and twisted his mouth into a pained smirk.

'The story does not specify his sexuality, but you may of course have spotted a sub-text that I missed. Selim, any idea why Michael returned the apples?'

Selim hadn't understood a word of the story, hadn't

understood a word of the question. From his seat in the back row, he was gazing out of the window at the trees in the yard. The snow covered the naked branches in thick white layers like whipped cream, making them look strangely edible. It was nice and warm in the classroom. He yawned.

'Right. Hakan, any idea why Michael returned the apples?'

The class hunkered down and held its breath.

'Hakan? OK, OK, no problem, sorry, next one, Dynasty – Dynasty?' There was a note of panic in the teacher's voice. Establishing contact with Hakan had not been a good idea.

Dynasty Schmidt, her blonde hair pulled back into a tight bun, silver hoops swinging from her ears, dipped the little brush back into its bottle of Stardust Sexy Sprinkle. She wore a pink hooded jumper that matched her permanently blushing cheeks.

'Dynasty? Care to share your thoughts?'

''Cause he's feeling guilty, I guess.'

The teacher pursed his lips in surprise.

'Yes, Dynasty, that's correct. He's feeling guilty. Michael is feeling guilty, and that's why he returned the apples. That's a very sensitive observation, well done. And why do you think he's feeling guilty?'

''Cause he saw the shop owner's son washing cars in the posh neighbourhood, didn't he.'

'That's correct. Dynasty, if you were to spend less time painting your nails and more time taking notes, you could do really well in this class.'

'Your story is pretty lame, frankly. It's, like, for three-year-old spazzos.' Dynasty carefully applied a coat of Stardust

Sexy Sprinkle to her thumbnail. 'You think we're thick or what?'

'Oooh, look at Dynasty,' someone shouted from the back row.

The teacher retreated, trying to fade into the blackboard.

'Well, if you'd prefer to read a different short story, Dynasty, I'm open to suggestions. Pushkin, Kafka, whatever you like.' The teacher sighed. He opened a drawer and took out a pile of dog-eared notebooks. 'In fact, your written composition was very good. Well, it was good. Well, it was—'

'Just leave it right there,' Dynasty said. 'Before we get to "it was shit".'

'No, no, what I meant to say – Cengiz, on the other hand.' The teacher held up an opened notebook with a single line scrawled across the page. 'Cengiz, when I ask you to write a composition on what you did over the weekend, you are expected to hand in more than a one-line response.'

The class reacted with an appreciative chuckle.

'Especially if the response is *I fucked your sister*.'

The chuckle erupted into laughter, but the teacher's final words swiftly silenced them.

'So I think I should have a word with your father.'

With the exception of Selim, who was still completely unaware of what was being said, the entire back row glowered at the teacher in silent menace. The word *sister* was a mere provocation. The word *father*, however, was a declaration of war.

The back row planted their feet firmly on the ground, leaned back, spread their massive thighs a bit wider, crossed their arms, raised their chins. The teacher slowly, very slowly began handing out the homework, starting with the desks in front, where the relatively docile students sat. His progress seemed to stall somewhere between rows three and four; he rifled through the papers, buying time while he tried to work out what he would do when he reached the back row.

Salvation came from an unlikely corner.

'You calling me gay?' It was Dwayn Olshevsky, who had taken his time to examine the teacher's response to his initial comment, had mulled over it, analysed it, and now suddenly jumped to his feet with such violence that his chair toppled over and crashed into Selim.

'Dwayn?'

'You try calling me gay and I'll—'

'Dwayn, would you please sit down, please . . .'

'You try calling me gay—'

The bell sounded, ending their brief exchange. Dwayn spat in the general direction of the blackboard, grabbed his bag and pushed through the door with the rest of the class.

Selim stayed in his chair at the back of the room, his eyes open but his mind seeing the stone houses of his village. He tried to remember what the smell was like in winter, when the fields were hard and bare.

11

At break time just after noon, prayer mat rolled up and tucked under his arm, Selim walked out of the classroom, out of the building and into the snow-covered schoolyard. On the far side was a concrete shed that housed the toilets. Selim noted with relief that it was empty. He found it hard to concentrate as he washed himself at the scummy sink, worried that someone would burst in. He went back out and cleared a patch of snow, shivering at the touch. Rolled out the patterned brown rug with his fingers, frozen red. Silently recited his intention to pray, raised his hands, declared God to be great, then let himself glide into the gentle rhythm of prayer: '*Bismillahi r-rahman ar-raheem* . . . In the name of God, the most gracious, the most merciful . . .'

When he got back on his feet and rolled up his damp rug, he noticed the girl from his class leaning against the brick wall opposite, watching him from underneath her pink hood. Selim gave her an uncertain nod and walked back into the building, the limp rug wedged under his arm like a frown.

The next day, during break time, Selim prayed again. New snow had fallen and the old snow had turned to ice. His joints were stiff and frozen. His knees hurt. He could hear their rusty-hinge creak as he knelt down and stood up, knelt down and stood up.

'*Bismillahi r-rahman ar-raheem . . .*'

A crowd of boys and girls gathered under the basketball hoop across from his icy patch. They were staring at him and whispering to each other. He finished his prayers, walked towards the main building, and they stepped back to let him pass. One of the boys, spottier and lankier than the others, called out something that sounded vaguely hostile. A tall girl in a headscarf gave the boy a push. Selim smiled at the girl, and, just in case, smiled at the boy who had shouted at him.

Overnight, the temperature stabilised, and the next morning it rose just enough to melt the top layer of snow and turn it into dirty slush. Selim tried to clear the wet ground with his bare hands. He covered it with a plastic bin liner before rolling out his mat.

'*Bismillahi r-rahman ar-raheem . . .*'

He got up from his knees. The blonde girl was standing there, wearing the same pink jumper. What's there to stare at, Selim grumbled. His hands were numb. He tried to grip the soggy rug, grip his nylon bag with the school books he could not read. The bell sounded and he quickened his pace, slipped on the slushy brown snow, hit the ground hard, sending his books and rug and bag flying. He scrambled to his feet, brushed the soft, wet leaves off his trousers and elbows and tried to dry the books and rug with his sleeves.

He looked up. The schoolyard was deserted, the girl gone.

Selim's right hip still hurt when he came back the following day. The winter air tasted of burnt wood and smoked sausages. He breathed it in, savoured it with a vague sense of guilt and blew it out again.

Where slush and mud had soaked his mat the previous day, a mirror of solid ice now stretched out, hard and glassy. Selim suspected it was the same water assuming many different guises to torture him, as slush, as ice, as snow that melted into his shoes and socks, as crystals that trickled down his neck.

He laid out his mat, tested the surface, sighed. A thin layer of softness over icy rigidity.

And then he knelt down and he prayed.

Two days later, Selim left the *Asylbewerberheim* without his prayer mat.

He had stashed it away without really thinking about it, as one would fling a pair of shoes or a jacket into a corner. But the next day, he did not take it along to school. Or the day after.

In fact, he never unrolled it again.

It was not a conscious decision. Like most things in his life, it happened, and he let it. Day after day, he put on his shoes, his jacket, but left behind the mat. And, at some point over the next few years, it simply disappeared. He did not know when or how. It took him a while to notice it was gone. He had kept it in a corner of his room at the *Asylbewerberheim*, and when he moved out he bundled it together with his other belongings. It moved with him from place to place, part of a lengthening trail of bits and bobs that he dragged through the years: clothes, boxes, a broken tape recorder, a CD player. One day, he realised the tape recorder was gone. How? When? Who knows. Got lost. And while he was at it, rooting through his stuff, he looked for the prayer mat: in all the boxes, under his bed, in this corner, that corner. Nope. Gone. Lost.

He scratched his head.

Couldn't remember when he last saw the thing.

Maybe it had gone to find someone who would make better use of it.

And that was that. You would think abandoning prayer would be a momentous decision for a good Kurdish boy, wouldn't you? You'd think it would involve much anguish and internal debate. And maybe it did, but when I asked Selim why he had rolled up his prayer mat on that bone-chilling winter day and stowed it away for good, he shrugged.

'It was so cold,' he said, adding after a little pause: 'I do believe in Allah. But . . .' He shrugged again, contemplating. 'When I arrived here, my first days at school, I rolled out my prayer mat in the snow, like that, and prayed in the snow. Can you believe it?'

I couldn't. The Selim I knew blended easily into his social circle of pot-smoking hippies, rude boys, hobby conspirators, party animals, political geeks. The usual small-town adolescent mix. Even when I met his uncles and cousins, prayer was never mentioned. Those were the 1990s, you see: religion didn't seem like a big deal.

Having abandoned his prayers, Selim would spend the noon break in the classroom. He would sit in his seat in the back row, his eyes closed, his mind roaming the valleys and mountains of Kurdistan. As a small boy, he had helped feed the family's sheep, the ones who were too old or too young to be taken to the mountains. He remembered the smell of hay, and the velvety softness of the lamb's muzzle in his palm. Also, the musky taste of mutton stew.

A lingering vapour of nail varnish bit his nostrils.

'You asleep?'

It was the spotty boy, peering out from underneath a grey hood.

Selim smiled at him and shrugged.

'*Afû, tênêgîştim.*'

The boy pointed at his chest.

'*Ich bin Flo.*'

Selim pointed at his own chest.

'*Ich bin Selim.*' He looked around. Everyone else had left.

The boy gestured to a desk in front of them and gave it a thumbs-up.

'Desks in the middle, good. Good choice.' He pointed both his thumbs towards the ceiling, smiling, wide-eyed and emphatic, like a manic hitchhiker. 'Desks in the middle, no trouble. Desks in front are also OK, but no need to be quite so eager. Desks in the middle, safe.'

Then he pointed at Selim's chair and the other chairs in the now empty back row.

'Back row, bad. Baaaad. Asking for trouble.' He pointed his thumbs downwards, shaking his head, then put both his hands to his neck as if to strangle himself. 'Your mates in the back row, lethal. Better stay away. Wouldn't advise you to sit there.'

Selim nodded. He should have thought of that himself; the back row was always trouble, everywhere, in Kurdistan as in Turkey as in Germany. An unwise choice for a skinny, bespectacled young Kurd.

He picked up his shabby nylon bag and accompanied the boy to a well-placed desk that was not too near the front and not too near the back. Just right. Just the right place to pass a few years without attracting too much attention.

When the bell sounded, everyone raced down the stairs three at a time: holidays!

Selim and Flo trotted out of the building, towards the gym with its vast grey concrete walls. They walked past the broken bike stand and the shed that reeked of vomit because someone had emptied a bottle of acid all over the desks. Walked past the crumbling stone wall that hid the old botanical gardens. To Flo and Selim, the gap midway along the wall was an invitation, almost an order in fact, to spy on the half-naked university students sunbathing on the lawn.

'There's a topless one over by the gazebo, look,' Flo said, trying to draw Selim's attention to a reclining, flesh-coloured figure in the distance. 'Topless!' he repeated, rubbing at his chest.

But Selim already knew that trick.

'No topless,' he said. 'Man.'

Their bus shelter was heaving with intertwined arms and legs, ponytails, baggy trousers, trainers, cigarettes and hoop earrings: girls and boys from Selim's school with their latest conquests.

'Right, everyone, listen to this! Hey!'

Selim looked up to where the voice had come from.

Dwayn Olshevsky had climbed on top of the glass shelter and was waving a notebook.

'Got Dynasty's diary . . . wait for the filthy bits!'

Dynasty, who had been busy snogging one of the baggy-trousered boys, detached herself and looked up.

'It's my fucking maths book, you idiot.' She stuck her face back into the hood in front of her.

'Yeah, so it says here every night I dream about Dwayn Olshevsky . . .'

No one paid him any attention. He hurled the book in front of an approaching bus and hopped off the shelter, landing next to Selim. Snarled, considering whether to pick a fight, then walked over to his mates.

Selim noticed a group of university students who were also waiting for the bus. They appeared to have given up on the area around the bus shelter, preferring the safety of the stone pillars at the university gate. None of the male students wore baggy jeans, none of the girls wore hoop earrings. Selim studied their faces. They're scared of us! he thought, puzzled. They don't even want to board the same bus.

And indeed, when Selim and Flo and their classmates thronged into the next bus, the crowd of academic hopefuls in gypsy skirts and corduroy trousers stayed behind, patiently waiting for the scum to depart.

Flo's father sold bikes for a living; his mother stayed at home, looking after Flo as well as two foster children. Taking the lift up to their flat on the ninth floor of a grey tower block, Selim was terrified, but as soon as he arrived he was hugged, handed a glass of juice and planted in a chair at the table with the affectionate authority he knew from his own mother and aunts.

One of the foster children, a fat-cheeked toddler, stared at

Selim in wonder while he pushed a pea up his nose. Selim instinctively reached out and tickled the toddler under his chin, making him giggle and snort so the pea popped out. Flo's mother came hurrying over, throwing Selim an appreciative glance, and Selim, looking at the children around him, was flooded by a feeling of ease and familiarity. Children, he thought, are always children.

Still smiling, he turned to his plate, piled with pasta in a sauce of cream, peas, bits of meat and tinned pineapple chunks.

'Mmmmm,' Flo hummed, grinning at Selim. He rubbed his belly, then dug in, loading his spoon with cream-slathered pasta.

Selim wondered what the meat was, then decided it would be rude to ask, especially since he did not know how. He plunged his own spoon into the mound on his plate and shoved the spoonful into his mouth. The food tasted creamy, sweet and salty.

Flo's mother asked Selim a question. He smiled at her vaguely. They gestured for a while, until he understood.

'*Asylbewerberheim*,' Selim said, rather fluent all of a sudden because he was finally talking about his one area of expertise. 'Wait for asylum and residence permit.'

He parted his lips, wanting to explain that he had hoped to move in with his uncle, aunt and Şivan, but their asylum claim was still pending and so all of them had to remain at the shelter for now. He couldn't think of the right words, and instead put another spoonful of pasta into his open mouth.

'And how many people are in that . . . place?' Flo's mother asked, wiggling her fingers. 'How many?'

'Ah.' Selim waved his hands through the air, signing masses and masses of invisible people. 'Many, many, many.' He smiled again and held up his right index finger. 'One bathroom.'

Several months and many forms and visits to the immigration office later, Selim moved in with Flo's family, sleeping on a sofa-bed in their living room. After school, he and Flo spent most of their time at the bike shop amongst rusty chains and mutilated frames. Selim did not learn to read or write very well over the next few years, and the teachers did not seem to mind much either way. He did, however, learn quite a lot about bikes.

12

When I left my office, the sun was still out. I decided to walk home along the canal. The Afghans had moved on, leaving behind only one boy who lay across the mattress, guarding it with his body. I took the long route, crossing the canal and weaving through a maze of narrow back streets, walking and walking to straighten out my muddled thoughts, almost forgetting that I had to get ready for my friend Anna's birthday party later that night. By the time I got home, the sun had set and my street was crowded with people gathering in celebration.

I was pushed along past trestle tables overflowing with snacks and treats. Men were ladling out couscous and stew for the homeless; children were stuffing their mouths with syrupy, glossy, orange *zlabiya* spirals and honey-soaked pastries. *Of course*, I thought: Ramadan. At the town hall, the fasting month brought about a lull in activity, followed by a slew of post-Ramadan weddings.

Our neighbourhood probably housed more mosques than any other in Paris, and the pavements thronged with Moroccans, Senegalese, Algerians breaking the daytime fast. There must have been some Kurds, too. Cheered by the happy crowd and mounds of fried food, I decided to buy a *zlabiya* coil. The man behind the trestle table waved away my cash with a smile, and as I bit into the tooth-achingly sweet crust and savoured the taste of honey and orange blossom I thought I could hear Selim's voice, so full of yearning.

'You know, at home, we have the sugar festival, after Ramadan and when the pilgrims come back from the hajj,' Selim told me, using the German word, *Zuckerfest*. 'And it's always been my dream, just once more, to see the *Zuckerfest*.'

That's how it was with Selim. He had a tendency to cross my mind at the most unexpected times. Tripped up by a song, a name, an accent or simply a sweet, crunchy taste, I would suddenly feel a sharp sadness or, at other times, a kind of defiant hope.

'Three days of celebration, toys for the children, and everyone is kind,' he said dreamily one morning when we were sitting in his flat in Germany, drinking sweet tea. 'And during the *Zuckerfest*, the children are allowed to do anything. Can you imagine? They are even allowed to smoke.'

I looked at him, incredulous.

'Yes, really,' he insisted. 'When I was small, I sometimes smoked secretly, you know. We collected old cigarettes and made new ones. So I looked forward to the *Zuckerfest*, because then I would be allowed to smoke, even my parents couldn't say anything. But then, always, something bad happened. Someone got killed, people were sad and once again, no festival. And then I would think, Damn, now I have to wait again for such a long time.'

*

I wiped my hands on the *zlabiya* wrapper and entered my door code with a sticky index finger. The staircase was filled with the ricey steam of the Thai restaurant on the ground floor. The smell was delicious, although I often wondered about the link between the warm humidity, the traces of condensation on the staircase wall, and the peeling grey wallpaper. The scent of rice followed me into my dark studio flat on the first floor, and I opened the windows and leaned out, watching the flow of revellers navigate their way between teetering stacks of cardboard boxes and vats of olives in brine.

My street was one of those bourgeois-bohemian favourites; you know the type: a burqa shop at one end, a sex shop at the other. In between lay a row of crumbling nineteenth-century houses where generations of immigrants had warmed their feet before moving further west.

I used to come here as a student, buying kebabs from a stall that puffed out clouds of rancid oil and charred meat, hanging out at a nearby bar where I worked part-time as a waitress. I hadn't been back to that bar in years; it held too many memories of drunken heartbreak. Still, the boozy nights spent there were among the reasons why this was the part of Paris where I felt most at home. When I moved here, my friend Anna was working on a travel feature that described the neighbourhood as *run-down*. In more recent articles, she had switched to calling it *up-and-coming*. Sweatshops were turning into art galleries, halal butchers into banks. The kebab place in my street was holding on, but others had been gutted and converted into restaurants that served cauliflower cappuccino under exposed steel pipes.

I closed the window, and after a quick shower changed into a blue shift dress. Just before leaving, as an afterthought, I dabbed on some lip gloss. Then I made my way through the crowds to Anna's chosen spot: a dark, bottle-lined wine bar next to a basement mosque.

Anna and her friends took up most of the bar, the backs of their chairs occasionally clinking against bottles of Pinot Noir and Chablis, sending the owner into a barely masked tizzy as he discreetly moved the most expensive wines to higher shelves.

My arrival caused much moving about of chairs and plates, and I smiled apologetically at the owner. After a round of congratulations, an exchange of gifts and gratitude and a bubbly aperitif, Anna gave me a hug, fuelled by genuine affection as well as several flutes of champagne.

'So, what's new at the town hall?' She adjusted her brown ponytail, loosened by too many rounds of enthusiastic embraces. 'Let me find my flower.'

'The usual, plus it's the wedding season,' I said to her husband, Philippe, while Anna dived under the table and emerged with a plastic hibiscus, as red as her flushed cheeks.

'She does weddings,' she told those who didn't already know, clipping the flower to the side of her head.

'Weddings!' one of the girls exclaimed. 'That must be so special.'

'Well, it . . .'

Everyone was looking at me, expecting a funny anecdote, and usually I had one ready for precisely this kind of situation, some sweet story I could whip out like a TV chef: *Here's one I prepared earlier*. But my mind was too crowded that night, and so I had to disappoint them with a mere: 'Yes. It's special.'

With that, the conversation moved on to Philippe's archaeology project, and from there to everyone's holidays past and planned, briefly swerved to politics, brushed the economic crisis and settled on wine, red versus white.

Feeling rather exhausted, I sipped my wine and observed the group around me, half of them chatting in French, the other in English.

There were certain people in this world who spoke like glass. I don't know how else to describe it. Their English was transparent, clean and flavourless. It was strange in its flawlessness, too perfect for a native and yet, too casual and comfy for a foreigner. Anna spoke like that, as did most of her friends. They grew up in a sort of geographical limbo, attending international schools and tagging along with their peripatetic parents, and so their language was like one of those fashion collections that mix a dozen ethnic costumes. They used *dorky* in one sentence and *dodgy* in the next, like designers combining Eskimo boots with Inca hats.

I usually enjoyed their company. They tended not to ask questions about personal history: they were bored enough with repeating their own. And usually they didn't have much of a political opinion, a result maybe of their itinerant upbringing. This suited me well; having overindulged in politics as a teenager, I was now like a bloated boa that was happy to sit out the next decades and digest it all.

As I said, Anna was a typical member of the modern nomadic tribe. She would say things like, 'Let's blow this popsicle stand,' then talk about eating *sarnies*. Hong Kong British by birth, American by education with a Swiss savings scheme and an east Asian love of the durian fruit, she moved to Paris to cure Philippe's homesickness and work as a journalist.

We met while I was still at uni – she interviewed my ex-boyfriend about his bar as part of her food-and-wine feature for an expat magazine – and when the boyfriend disappeared from my life Anna stayed on. She was already living with Philippe at the time and he was keen to marry her, but she had her doubts.

'Mixed marriages are hard,' she would tell me again and again. 'It's fun at first, but once the children are there . . . it's about values, you know. I may not look Asian, but I *am* Asian.'

'Hey, you've got so much in common – Philippe doesn't look Asian, either!' I would reply.

Or I would tell her that French values were OK, weren't they, and anyway she would be free to instil whatever values she wanted in their children, given that Philippe was always away digging out lost cities.

Then, one night, we were sitting in her flat, Philippe was abroad looking for Atlantis, it was 5 a.m. and we were drinking his Glenlivet even though neither of us liked whisky – what a waste, I know – and as she poured the last drops into our glasses she said regretfully: 'He's perfect. But he's not Chinese.'

'No,' I said, downing my drink without waiting for her. Philippe Levy is not Chinese.'

They married about a year later.

And there they were now, sharing a crème brûlée. Anna, always very affectionate when drunk, passed her spoon to Philippe and pulled me towards her.

'You're so quiet,' she complained. 'Talk to me. It's my birthday.'

'I'm sorry. Work is a bit annoying.'

'How come?'

'It's . . .'

But I wasn't in the mood to explain and anyway, she wasn't in the mood to listen. She smiled mischievously, moving on to her favourite subject.

'You never told me how your date went the other night.'

'I didn't go.'

Unfortunately, Philippe heard this.

'You didn't go? But I hand-picked him!'

Anna waved him away.

'Philippe, this is private.'

'I'm useless, I know,' I said, lowering my voice. 'And this work thing, it's one of those marriages where you aren't too sure if the bride is doing it of her own free will, but you don't really want to interfere.'

'Maybe try talking to her,' Anna counselled vaguely. 'But what about Philippe's mate? I thought you liked him. You two got on so well at the party, he was really keen.'

'That's the thing, I sent her a request for a meeting but she hasn't replied. I mean, if someone summoned me like that maybe I wouldn't go, either.'

'You can't stay single for ever,' Philippe added wisely, having rejoined us despite Anna's ban.

'It's like being pregnant, you know. This Kurdish couple turns up and all of a sudden I see Kurds everywhere.' I had downed quite a few glasses of wine. 'It's like, everywhere you look, it's Kurdish. Did you know, even Mount Ararat is actually Kurdish.'

'Mount Ararat? Not if you ask the Armenians.' This from the bloke next to me, who was somehow managing to smile at me while simultaneously addressing the group.

'Well, whatever, the mountain where Noah's Ark landed.'

'That's not Mount Ararat anyway, it's kind of a mis-translation. The Ark probably landed much further south, in Turkey, towards Iraq, near a place called Cizre. If it ever existed at all. What the Bible actually says is the *mountains* of Ararat, which refers to that whole area.' He paused, rubbing his biceps. He had rolled up the sleeves of his grubby green T-shirt, a style I had last seen at an anti-nuclear camp. 'Interesting place, though. That's actually where I'm off to next week, though the security situation is a bit dicey.'

'See what I mean!' I said triumphantly.

'David is the raider of the lost Ark,' Philippe slurred. 'Eternal quest for the dragon-shaped knockers.' He gave his friend a brotherly slap on the back.

'Dragon-shaped door knockers,' David said by way of explanation. 'On the door of the mosque in Cizre. Philippe seems to find that hilarious.'

'Not at all,' Philippe said. 'I think dragon-shaped door knockers are fascinating. Wish I could see them. Wish David had hired me for this project, in fact.' He waved his wine-sloshing glass in David's general direction, as if to indicate there was no ill-will, whatever little dispute there had been over the hiring decision.

How strange, I thought to my tipsy self. I spent all those years talking to Selim, and he never once mentioned any of this. I used to think of Cizre as a random spot on the map, whose only significance was that I had to memorise its name.

And yet, Noah's Ark. A mosque. Dragon-shaped door knockers. Fascinating.

'Fascinating,' I blurted out, but had evidently missed a vital turn in the conversation. They had moved on to a kind of late-night, booze-soaked confessional.

'What's the most criminal thing you've done in your life?'

'I used to switch on my parents' washing machine when they were out and climb inside,' Anna giggled. 'It was one of those old, slow, top-loading ones back in Hong Kong, I'd pour in a bottle of detergent and go round and round and round in the foam.'

'That's not criminal,' Philippe said. 'That's silly.'

'Well, I stole a car once,' a petite blonde said, rather surprisingly.

'I once stole a bike.'

'I stole cash from the till once, well, actually, twice, yeah OK, loads of times.'

'God, how boring, can't we have a bit of variety?'

'Insider trading.'

'Fiddled my expenses.'

'Pimping.'

'Pimping?'

'Pimping my dog, actually. What happened is I had this pedigree Dobermann, right, such a cool dog, a kind of uber-dog really, and one of the neighbours down the road had a Dobermann that was OK, not really a prize one but OK, and . . .'

'Right, no need for details,' the blonde intervened. 'So, how about you?'

'I'm a town hall official,' I said. 'A bureaucrat. What do you expect?'

David put down his glass and rested one arm on the back of my chair, leaning towards me.

'That's exactly why. A bureaucrat. A bureaucrat. An anonymous official hidden in the deep, deep bowels of the administrative underworld, a woman versed in the dark arts of council-tax fraud and rogue dog-walking. What better job to mask a criminal past?'

I looked at him, surprised. That's exactly what I used to think. What better job to mask a criminal past? And as the others continued boasting about their brushes with illegality, I let my mind linger on the thought.

People with an assumed identity always seemed to work as doctors. War criminals, terrorists, torturers: the newspaper stories of their discovery were all the same, a faded headshot of the murderer as a young man, next to a picture of a bewildered octogenarian in his surgery in Buenos Aires.

A strange choice for a fugitive, medicine, motivated maybe by an unconscious desire to be hunted down and exposed. One of the most sociable professions, after all; one of your patients might well end up denouncing you.

You could of course argue that there was a certain advantage in making yourself useful to the community. It helped to build a network of allies, to make sure you were the first to know what was going on in the neighbourhood. But there were other jobs that offered such benefits. Town hall official, for example.

There was a time in my life when I was quite eager to reinvent myself. I would, in fact, have liked to take on a new name and identity. The name remained the same, for a variety of reasons, but the new identity had, to some extent, worked out. Nothing dramatic – my official CV matched my life, except for one detail. And because it was not a dramatic shift I was after, but only a small adjustment, I did not need to go very far. I merely moved across the border. Once I had secured French citizenship, which was not all that hard for a German, my new host did not ask too many questions. That was France for you. It lifted its blanket and you quickly slipped underneath and then, at least officially, you were covered by that warm, thick layer of Frenchness.

'Sex,' someone said.

'Excuse me?'

'I was saying, you seem so tense these days.' I hoped Anna's confidential whisper was as discreet as she intended it to be. 'Come on, loosen up, have a bit of fun, get yourself a nice man, you can't spend your whole life thinking about work and your ex. Trust me, I'm the same.'

'Oh, is that what you said, ex?'

'Yes, ex. But before that, I said sex.' She giggled. 'What about David? He's easy.'

I looked around, embarrassed. To my relief, the chair next to me was empty.

'He's not my type. And that Indiana Jones attitude gets on my nerves.'

'But everyone gets on your nerves! You know what, you're working too hard. And not drinking enough water. Take a holiday and fly to Iraq with David, he'd love it, and, more importantly, you'd love it.'

'What's wrong with thinking about work and Lucien?

Keeps me busy.' I smiled to show I did appreciate her help, in a way. 'It's too hot in Iraq.'

David came back and noisily reoccupied his chair. He was fingering an intricate stone pendant that hung from his neck on a leather string. Probably stolen from someone's tomb.

'We were just talking about school,' he announced. 'What's the worst thing you ever did at school? And I was saying, I bet you were such a good girl.'

'Yes,' I said. 'Exactly.'

13

My school was just around the corner from Selim's. In our town, everything was just around the corner. The medieval centre consisted of a mound studded with timbered houses and a dozen churches, the jagged ruins of a castle rising above it all. To the east, an industrial park flanked the high-rises where most of Selim's classmates lived. To the west, the wealthier families spread out in houses that mutated over the decades, sprouting garages, extra bedrooms, conservatories. The rubbish dump and my neighbourhood were to the north; the town's schools, right at the foot of the hill.

In fact, Selim's school was so close that we used their gym, since our school didn't have one. We would traipse down the road, across the gently arching old stone bridge, past the university building and into the gym. Other than that, there was no interaction between the pupils from my school and those from Selim's.

Let me rephrase that. There was some interaction. Once a girl from Selim's school punched a girl from my class on the nose; I can't remember the reason. I do remember that the girl from my class had a spectacular nosebleed (which she was prone to anyway). After that, we were not allowed to spend the break at Selim's school. We had to go straight to the gym in one big group, and come straight back in the same big group.

My school was very different from his. No one there was called Dynasty or Hakan or Dwayn. My classmates had names like Anna, Benjamin, Sebastian. No one at my school would have dared hand in a one-line composition, let alone one suggesting sexual relations with the teacher's sister.

There were some similarities, though. At my school, the Kurdish question was a hot topic, almost as hot as nuclear power and endangered whales: we discussed it in and out of class, wrote essays about it, drew posters and went to demonstrations and watched videos that highlighted the plight of the Kurds.

At Selim's school, the Kurdish question was also rather hotly discussed.

One day, as Selim was leaving school with Flo, eating an ice cream from the nearby shop, a group of mainly older boys blocked his way. At the centre of the human road block stood Cengiz, the Turkish boy from the back row of Selim's class.

'*Selim, komm her, lan.*'

Selim smiled and shrugged, motioning to Flo to go away.

'*Gel lan buraya!*' Cengiz called out, louder this time.

Selim walked towards the boys, still holding his ice-cream, wondering whether it would be wiser to discard it. Too late. The boy wrested it out of Selim's hand and crushed it on his face. The cone fell off and pink blobs slid down his cheeks.

Teenagers were streaming out of the gates, some stopping and watching, others looking away and hurrying off. Flo lingered, uncertain what to do, then disappeared.

'Nice friends you have. So, what you're going to do now is you're going to run around in a circle until I say you can stop and then you're going to sing, "Cengiz is great, Cengiz is the boss, and I'm a Kurdish wanker." Right, run.'

Selim did nothing. Cengiz gave him a shove. Selim began to walk in a circle.

'Run!'

Selim broke into a trot.

'Sing!' Selim repeated the Turkish words.

'In German, you idiot! So these potatoes here can understand you.'

'I don't know how to say it in German,' Selim shouted.

Cengiz tore away from his friends, raced towards Selim and landed a punch on the side of his head, knocking him over and sending his glasses flying into the crowd. He kicked Selim in the side, wham, in the stomach, smack, in the kidneys. Selim's thin body curled around Cengiz's trainers, and he felt something inside him crack. Yet he took the blows as he had taken most things in his life, silently, in the expectation that this, too, would pass.

He shielded his head and waited for the next kick, but his attacker had suddenly left off. Selim looked up. Someone yanked Cengiz back and shoved him forward so he collapsed on the road, not far from Selim, who was still sobbing with pain, his cheek on the rough, warm pavement. Even without his glasses, he could make out the solid shape of Cengiz, lying there not far from him and being stomped on by white, black, yellow trainers.

Someone helped Selim to his feet. Someone else handed him his glasses. The frames were bent and a lens had dropped out. Selim straightened the wire as best as he could, put the lens back in and watched the brawl.

There was his cousin, Şivan, the once shy boy who had grown as bulky as his shovel-handed father and then some more, and had learned to use his body efficiently with the help of the local kick-boxing club. He was kicking Cengiz as if that was how he would spend the rest of his life, thrashing the soul out of the body on the ground.

Flo loomed behind Şivan like a shadow. He sidled up to Selim, and the two, feeling rather cowardly but concluding that their skinny presence would not contribute much to the scene, took refuge in the crowd.

Others joined in the fight: Turks, Kurds, and, for good measure, Eritreans, Germans and Russians.

'What the fuck is going on?' someone shouted in German.

'The Turks are having a fight, watch out for the knives.'

'It's something about honour.'

'Let's go. Let them sort it out among themselves.'

It was unfortunate that Selim's teacher had been off that very week. He was in hospital, having his infected tonsils removed. The nurse told him that, tonsil-free, he would be less likely to catch the colds that plague teachers.

Therefore, when he entered the classroom on Monday morning, he had not heard about the big street battle between the Kurds and the Turks just outside the school.

He had not heard about Cengiz's concussion and Şivan's torn ear.

He was humming a happy tune. He had had a week to think about his job, his pupils, what he was doing with his life. He had thought about the bored back row and the frustrated girl who had complained that the stories they were reading were boring and stupid. She was right. None of them deserved stories that were patronising and silly. They deserved stories that were relevant to their lives, their problems. He was brimming over with excellent ideas.

Which is why, in his leather briefcase, he carried a stack of photocopied A4 sheets, the pages of a brief story about a football-loving Kurdish boy who, against all odds, makes friends with a football-loving Turkish boy.

To be fair, the class did not immediately explode.

For one, the back row was busy making paper planes and penis sculptures out of the pages and therefore ignored the words. Then Dwayn Olshevsky loudly objected to being given a story about gays. Then Dynasty Schmidt told Dwayn Olshevsky to shut up. That it's a story about kids and stop being such a pervert.

The trouble started when Murat, intrigued by Dwayn's comment, unfolded his paper plane, read the first line of the story and stood up to share his opinion.

'The Kurds don't have any land and that's where trouble starts and why they're all dreck,' he announced calmly. 'At least we came here as *Gastarbeiter* but they're asylum fakes and scroungers and there's no way I'm going to read a story about a PKK brat.'

He sat down again. The teacher, still not realising the full significance of the situation, nodded thoughtfully.

'Thank you, Murat,' he said gently. 'Now, I think this would be a good time to talk about *respect*. We all want to *respect* each other in this class, don't we? So we should try to stay calm and leave the insults for later. Or, er, just leave them out altogether . . .'

'. . . And fuck all Kurds. FUCK ALL KURDS.' That was Cengiz, sitting in the back row with a bandage around his head and ribs, which did not stop him from shouting out with red-faced rage.

Between the four sunshine-yellow walls of the classroom, a buzz of murmured insults and whispered curses and hissed threats began, accompanied by the annoyed sighs of the ninety-five per cent of the class who really did not want this to develop into yet another fight.

Over the buzz, a handful of boys with black jar-top haircuts and broad shoulders in tight T-shirts spat words at each other.

Go back to Mongolia . . . Fucking Turks . . . And what's your problem . . . Why can't you let us learn Kurdish after school . . . It's none of your business, is it?

The teacher made one last attempt to intervene. There was, after all, scope for a compromise.

'Now, if you would like to discuss the possibility of Kurdish-language lessons for students at this school . . .'

That briefly united the disintegrating class. They all stared at the teacher, Turks, Kurds, Eritreans, Russians, Russian-Germans, Germans, all stunned by so much stupidity.

'In *Turkey*,' Dynasty, who considered herself neutral, said slowly, deliberately. 'They are talking about Kurdish lessons *in Turkey*. The Kurds are not allowed to learn Kurdish in Turkey, even though the Turks are allowed to learn Turkish *in Germany*.'

'Yeah but it's Turkey, Turkey pays for our lessons and

mosques here, with my taxes and good money!' Cengiz yelled.

'Cengiz, you don't pay any taxes,' Dynasty pointed out.

'Whatever. Ask your PKK pimps and junkies to send over cash to pay for your Kurdish lessons if you're so fucking keen.'

Still, the teacher thought, at least they are talking. I'm not entirely sure what they are talking about, but for the first time in this class people are actually talking to each other.

Hakan, who usually preferred to remain silent and dangerous, had climbed onto his desk.

'Show me on the map, come on, show me on the map! Here's the map! Now show me where your Kurdistan is, you shepherd! Where is it, huh?' He was standing next to a glossy map of the world, his clenched fist angrily hammering Australia.

'You cannot find Kurdistan on any map, you can find it in my heart, and do you know what you get when you cross a Turkish woman with a spider, an EIGHT-LEGGED CLEANER!' Kurdish Aziz shouted.

'Not a single, not a single stone from us, hear me?'

'YOU ARE SLAVES! YOU ARE OUR SLAVES!' That was Hakan, still pounding Australia.

Dwayn Olshevsky also wanted to contribute but did not know how to.

He started a half-hearted: 'Shut up everyone . . .' but was shouted down by Aziz who had climbed onto a desk across the room from Hakan.

Aziz grabbed the window frame to either side of him and arched himself like a bow, ready to unleash a kick.

'Yep, not a single stone but we get all your women—'

And that was it.

When the police arrived, the teacher had barricaded himself in the next classroom together with most of the class.

Unsurprisingly, whoever had torn up the map and smashed the chairs had left the scene.

Interviews with the pupils led to nothing, because no one had seen or heard anything. However, the entire back row of Selim's class was expelled, and from then on his mornings were a little quieter.

14

'People have different ways of dealing with anger,' my teacher declared. 'One man goes down to the basement and hammers his punch bag, another shaves his dog.'

I lowered my head and continued to read my book under the desk. It was clearly a fake: chapter one explained how to get high on dried banana peel, and everyone knew that was a myth.

I looked up. Julian was standing in front of the blackboard with a piece of chalk in his hand, looking lost.

The teacher, wearing a tight jumper that throttled his neck, eyed Julian's dreadlocks with a mixture of pity and disdain, then theatrically wrung his hands.

'Oh Lord, let it rain brains from heaven!'

Chapter two of my book was about bombs. I suspected the recipes for explosives were no more reliable than the ones for drugs. Friends had told me the book had in fact been written by the CIA in a ploy to make anarchists blow themselves up. I nodded. That made sense.

'What do we have here?' A hand reached over my shoulder and grabbed the book. '*The Anarchist Cookbook*.' The teacher handed it back to me, shaking his head. 'If I catch you again, you'll be on my list.'

I grunted submissively.

He scratched his chin.

'You know, in the Middle Ages they would have burnt you as a witch.'

'Maybe,' I said.

'And if I catch you carving political slogans on the desks, which may I remind you are public property and should therefore, in line with your convictions, be treated with respect, then woe betide you.'

I grunted again, and he turned back to Julian, who was tentatively chalking some numbers and symbols on the board.

A few streets away, two of Selim's classmates had tied the teacher to his chair and were opening his bag, looking for cash.

And yet at my school we were seen as rebellious just because we read books under our desks.

The sound of the bell freed us, and I rushed downstairs to the car park for a smoke.

The school's pale-yellow façade with its curled gables looked down on us disapprovingly. It had been looking down on hundreds of unruly pupils for more than a century, first as the Koenigliches Gymnasium, then briefly as the Heinrich-Heine-Schule, after the Jewish poet; then as the Adolf-Hitler-Schule; then simply as the Gymnasium.

After the war, years were spent discussing what to do about the name; the school needed a proper name, Gymnasium was not a proper name, but which to choose? There were those who felt that going back to Heinrich-Heine-Schule would bring back unpleasant memories of the 1993 name change. Later on, the older teachers did not particularly want to be reminded of that change, which they had embraced eagerly, feverishly, along with the new regime, happily expelling dozens of pupils, who, yes . . . what exactly had become of them? They preferred not to think about that, and so Heinrich-Heine-Schule was out of the question.

'How about . . . Friedrich-Ebert-Schule? That's a solid name, Social Democrat and a mayor to boot,' one greying, nervously blinking teacher would say to another.

'But he's not Heine.'

'No, he's not Heine.'

'I guess,' the other greying teacher would say thoughtfully, tugging his moustache, 'we could go back to the old name and call it Heinrich-Heine-Schule.'

'You know, my friend, secretly I always wanted the school to keep its name. I always liked Heine.'

'Oh yes, so did I. It was such a sad day when they renamed · it . . . we had no choice, did we, but inwardly I was full of rage.'

'Inwardly, yes.'

The two men studied the dusty red tiles in the corridor, each trying to ignore the images that floated through their minds – of two young men with razor-sharp side-partings, one nervously blinking, the other stroking his first hint of a moustache, cheering the workmen who polished a huge sign saying *Adolf-Hitler-Schule*, raising their right arms in the Nazi salute.

'But I feel that naming it after Heine again would be a step back in history, so to speak.'

'Yes, I feel the same. But if we don't name it after Heine, people will think we have something against him.'

'I never had anything against Heine.'

'Nor did I. One of the greats.'

'One of the greats.'

And they smiled to distract themselves from the next wave of memories that rolled towards them, of two young men pulling book after book from the shelves in the library and throwing them onto the big bonfire in the schoolyard.

Then one of them gently patted the other's bony shoulder and they walked towards the classrooms: two friendly if somewhat stiff, grey-haired men who had taught generations of German schoolchildren.

And so my school went without a name for decades until, in a ceremony packed with heartfelt hypocrisy and passionately boring speeches, it was officially renamed Heinrich-Heine-Schule. It was 1989, more than forty years after the end of the war.

A few months later, the Berlin Wall came down, and if we had been East German we would have faced yet another rebranding. But we were in West Germany, so it was all fine and my school was allowed to keep its name.

Hidden behind the third H of HEINRICH-HEINE-SCHULE, Martin, my older brother, was squirting speed up his nose with an old hayfever spray, undetected by the teachers.

'Don't forget to wipe your nose before you go back into class,' I murmured.

Martin laughed and twisted his neck to read the title of the book sticking out of my canvas bag: The Anarchist Cookbook.

'Oh man, I can't believe you're reading that. I read it, like, when I was five. Everyone knows it's full of shit.'

'I'm just reading it for a laugh.'

'You're reading it 'cause you want to make bombs.' He pulled the book out of my bag and waved it about. 'Look at my little sister, intense!'

'Give it back!' I yelled, then tried to switch to indifference. 'Whatever. If you're that keen on it, why don't you keep it. Idiot.' I turned around and walked off.

'Think I should tell Mum you're trying to learn how to make bombs?'

My ears were burning and it felt like half the school was watching.

'Is that Granny's nightie you're wearing?'

Still walking, I lifted my hand and stuck up my middle finger. It *was* in fact one of my granny's nylon nighties, which she had handed down to me. I had dyed it black and teamed it with laddered, tartan-patterned tights. It was an excellent look. My brother didn't have a clue.

I wandered over to Julian, who was sharing a cigarette with Andy. Andy was new; he had been forced to repeat the year, which meant he was the only one who had a driving licence. He passed me the cigarette.

'Can we talk about the amp?' I suggested, taking a drag.

'Here? Sure?' Julian glanced over his right shoulder and rubbed his head, either out of nervousness or because his dreadlocks were itching. The secret to twisting straight hair into dreadlocks, he had told me, was to wash your scalp with nettle soap a few times, then stop washing it altogether.

I had known Julian since primary school. He had always had the same straight brown mop until the day Andy showed up in our class with hair hanging down to his hips in thick black ropes. The next day, Julian started talking about nettle soap.

'Well I don't think the school is bugged. It's less likely to be bugged than our bedrooms,' I said.

'Yeah, as if our bedrooms are bugged,' Andy sniggered. (He had moved on from the long dreadlocks, claiming that a shaved head was better for the summer. I wondered how long it would take Julian to get out his razor.)

'You didn't read the legal aid leaflet, did you?' I reproached him.

'Lost it.' He grinned.

'Well here's another one.' I opened my bag and rummaged through leaflets, notebooks, Rizlas. 'Never know when they might come in handy.'

Instead of reading the leaflet, Andy stuffed it into his pocket and studied my dress. I blushed. He stretched out his hand and fingered one of the nylon straps.

'Is that a nightie you're wearing?'

'So, the amplifier.' I backed away and caught Andy smirking at Julian. 'We still need wire cutters and surgical gloves,' I said too loudly.

Julian shook his head.

'Fingerprints show through surgical gloves.'

'Where did you get that?'

'*Anarchist Cookbook.*'

'Damn, I just read the first two chapters and they're full of shit.'

'All the good stuff's in chapter three.'

Meanwhile, at Selim's school, a janitor entered the empty classroom, saw the bound and gagged teacher and released him. The perpetrators were thrown out of school. They switched the classroom for the arcade and the car park in front of the supermarket, where they met with the boys from the back row who had been expelled a few months earlier. Some would start an apprenticeship, others, a long relationship with the benefits office.

For Selim, the future looked a bit different. Thanks to Dr Habicht and the frowning gang from the immigration office, he now understood the significance of the series of numbers that followed the words DATE OF BIRTH on his personal forms.

He was still unsure how that number had come to be, who had been the first to mention it, who had been the one to approve it, to validate it, when even his own mother would blush and scratch her head and shrug if asked when her son was born.

But that was it, his official launch date, stamped, signed, saved on hard disks and in databases, and lately, it had started blinking in red, numbering his days on this earth in general and in Germany specifically.

Because, in a couple of years, like most of the people in his class, he would be celebrating his eighteenth birthday. And on his eighteenth birthday, he would officially be old enough to drive, vote, marry, buy a house, rent porn and – and this was the reason why the date had begun to flash like the warning light on a detonator – be deported. On his eighteenth birthday, the German government intended to put him on a plane back to Kurdistan.

15

Julian, Andy and I stood on the bridge between the two schools and stared at a piece of paper covered with lines, dots, arrows.

'Everyone, memorise the drawing,' I ordered.

'Memorise?' Andy yawned. 'Let's just take it with us.'

'No way! If they stop us and search the car and find this—'

'Then we're fucked.' He shrugged. 'They won't search us if Julian remembers to cover up his dreads and look respectable.'

'I'd rather memorise it,' Julian said defensively, twiddling a dreadlock. 'By the way, not sure looking like a skinhead is any more *respectable*, quite frankly. If that's why you shaved off your hair.'

'It's because of the summer, mate. Like, you know, the smell?' Andy sniffed. 'Nettle soap.'

I sighed and pointed at the map. We put our heads together and studied it. I had copied the tracks and access routes from a pamphlet using different coloured crayons, for clarity.

'Right. Let's go.' I tore the drawing into pieces and scattered them over the river.

A few hours later, Andy parked his mum's car near a bright-yellow rape field. We got out, plucked some blades of grass and chewed them with studied innocence, a green-haired girl and two grubby boys, taking a stroll in the country. Julian took off his sweatshirt and slung it over his shoulder, whistling. The rail tracks were not fenced off; we had chosen a good spot. A quick look around, a few steps uphill, and we were standing by a metal box sprouting cables and wires.

Julian unzipped his backpack and took out the wire cutters. Every move counted now. I scanned the horizon for trains and walkers. Yellow rape fields, the red rooftops of a village in the distance, cows. It was a quiet and peaceful place, an unlikely spot for sabotage. Then again, maybe not that unlikely; trains and railways have always been favourite targets of anarchists. There is a famous true story of three young nineteenth-century German anarchists who tried to blow up a train full of aristocrats. The youngest, eighteen years old, was told to go and buy string for the fuse, but when he got to the shop it had run out of thick, expensive string. So he bought cheap, thin string and didn't tell the others. After the three had carefully planted the explosives, laid the fuse, hidden behind a bush and finally, as the train appeared on the horizon, lit the fuse, it . . . fizzled out.

They lit it again . . . and it fizzled out. The string didn't light properly. The three started to argue about how and who and why and let's try again – and then they looked up and watched the train carrying the aristocrats pass out of site.

At the next annual anarchists' conference (very big, very secret, in some dripping underground vault near Berlin), the red-faced three had to stand up and report their botched mission. They justified themselves as best they could: they really had intended to blow up the train, they had enough explosives, it was all because the shop had run out of thick string.

Unfortunately for them, of the two hundred anarchists attending, two were secret police. All three failed plotters, including the eighteen-year-old, were arrested and executed.

Our mission was less brutal. We didn't want to blow up anyone, for a start. In the jargon of the scene, we disagreed with violence against human beings, though we agreed with violence against objects. In particular, we agreed with using violence to stop the transport of Castor casks. They contained spent nuclear fuel, freshly reprocessed in La Hague, France. Germany sent its used fuel to the French recycling plant, where it was separated into plutonium, uranium and high-level nuclear waste. The toxic waste was sealed in glass and sent back to Germany, to be buried in the ground and quietly radiate away into the next millennium.

Not that the trains on this specific track in rural Germany carried nuclear waste. Our mission was just meant to make a general point. The general point being that German railways should not allow their network to be used for the transport of Castor casks. The even more general point being that Germany should stop using nuclear power.

We had a few minutes, I reckoned.

Julian was still holding the wire cutters and thoughtfully biting his lower lip.

'Is there a problem?' Andy sounded as nervous as I felt.

'Shit.' Julian lowered the wire cutters. 'I don't know where to start.'

'Let's look at the drawing,' I suggested.

'You ripped it up,' Julian reminded me.

'Well, good thing I did, what if someone had searched the car?'

Julian glared at me.

Andy, even more annoyed, glared at Julian.

'Mate, at least do me a favour and cover up your hair again. You're scaring the wildlife. That cow over there looks like it's about to moo.'

'Chill,' was all Julian came up with, prompting irritated snorts from me and Andy.

I surveyed the scene. Buzzing bees and birdsong. Smell of hay. Fields, cows, village, all fine. No sound of tractors or dog-walkers. No sign of any approaching trains.

'Let's call Carl and ask,' Andy finally said.

'OK, ask him which one I should cut, but don't mention the tracks. His phone is tapped.'

'Carl?' Andy pressed his ear against the brick-like phone. 'It's Andy. We're looking at the amplifier. Yes, for the electric guitar. And we're just wondering, which is the right button? Yellow or red?'

Pause.

'Nope. No green button. There's a yellow button, yeah, with a cable attached to it.'

Andy sounded worried now. His eyebrows almost met and he looked like a spy, one of those men in trench coats with upturned collars who talk in muffled tones into phones.

'No, yellow. There isn't anything green on the amplifier.'

He put the phone away.

'It's supposed to be green but there's no green button so

he says it must be the yellow cable. Let's just cut the fucking cable and run.'

Andy took the wire cutters from Julian and cut the cable. It was that simple.

Julian looked a bit pissed off. The wire cutting was meant to be done by him. Andy was communications. I was safety and security. Julian was mechanics. Now Andy was communications *and* mechanics and Julian was, well, a failure.

Julian stuffed the wire cutters back into his bag, we skidded down the slope, swished through the field with the cows, not too fast, not too hurried, and bundled into the car.

We turned up the volume on the radio, and when – a little later – they announced that there were problems with the trains, Andy stopped the car by the road and we cheered. Then we lit a joint.

16

We never found out whether it was in fact our tampering with the signal box that caused the problems with the trains. According to the website, cutting a certain cable automatically switched the signal to red. That had been our plan. Who knows if it had worked. In any case, the right people believed it had.

With hindsight, our pathetic little act of sabotage was probably where it all started. Like many teenagers, I had long been into politics. Not party politics, which I wrote off as corrupt and boring, but the politics of values: justice, equality, freedom. Words we printed on our banners and paraded down the streets.

However, I had the suspicion that our protests were pretty useless. I imagined grey-suited businessmen and politicians observing us from afar, nodding at each other with satisfaction: *Glad they're marching, keeps them busy and away from any real trouble.*

And I remember that, when I sat in that little car with Julian and Andy, careering along the road away from the signal box, I felt a sense of awakening. A sense of: so this is what it's like. We don't have to follow the approved route.

We don't have to sit in classrooms, and lecture halls, and parliaments, and offices and throw words at each other. We can, with a bit of courage, step outside all that and surprise the powers that be. I remember the feeling very clearly, and like any awakening it was exhilarating as well as frightening.

As it turned out, Carl and his group had taken notice of our action. And, as a reward for our apparent success, they let us in on their plan.

'We're planning something for Carl's birthday, something really big,' his girlfriend, Meredith, told us one evening when we were all sitting outside the cooperative Red Star pub by the river, her voice strangely squeaky with excitement. 'A really, *really* big party. You know, like, *big*. And we were wondering whether you'd like to help.'

She was barefoot and wearing a jade toe-ring, her blonde dreadlocks gathered back to reveal matching jade studs in her ear lobes. Her feet sank into the muddy riverbank as she sat down next to me, brown sludge engulfing the jade stone, but she did not seem to mind.

Julian looked a bit puzzled. We hardly knew Carl and had never really spoken to him, let alone partied with him.

'Well, if you want us to set up the stage or something . . . I can bring my guitar . . .'

'It's in June,' Meredith interrupted him, staring into his eyes as if she wanted to hypnotise him. 'We're planning a *big bash*.'

Julian broke off a twig from the weeping willow overhanging the river. He snapped it into little pieces which he flicked, one by one, across the dark water.

'Sure,' he said, watching the last piece of twig make a

dozen rippling circles. 'Sounds fun. Party. Happy to help. Hey, that thing where you chuck something into the water and it jumps, does that only work with stones?'

Meredith turned to me, impatient and somewhat irritated now. Her toes, complete with jade stone, had disappeared under the sludge.

'Carl's birthday. Are you with us?' And in a desperate last attempt to make the penny drop, she added: 'You know, you're looking *radiant*.'

Finally, it occurred to me that this was not about a birthday party at all. June was when the next Castor trains would be rolling from France to Germany.

'Of course we're with you,' I said, wondering what the appropriate facial expression was: conspiratorial? Enthusiastic? Inscrutable? I opted for inscrutable, in keeping with the undercover tone of the conversation. 'We're with you,' I repeated, looking straight at her.

'Brilliant.' With a squelching, sucking sound, she pulled her feet out of the mud and wiped them on a patch of grass.

And so Carl's group let us join their action. Well, a small, specific part of it. It was carefully segmented, and each unit only knew their own task, so that potential spies would not be able to endanger the mission.

The only one who knew all the elements of the plan was Carl.

Carl wasn't our leader. We were grass-roots activists and did not believe in leaders. He was just the one everyone listened to. He wore leather trousers he hadn't taken off since his first anti-nuclear camp in 1982, had long black hair and allegedly hid Kurdish refugees in his flat. Most importantly, he kept telling us that there was no leader and whatever happened would be purely a consequence of our own decisions. Impressed, we agreed.

In truth, like all anarchist movements, this one was intensely hierarchical. So when, one Saturday morning after our encounter with Meredith, Carl met the three of us on a rickety wooden bridge, hidden by abundant foliage, and invited us to another meeting in a different location at a different time, when we would be given more details, we felt slightly confused but very excited.

We met in what was considered a safe flat in the old town centre. The owner, a lawyer, was away at a retreat. His kitchen was all chipped mugs, verbena-tea bags and necklaces of dried fruit dangling from the ceiling. Bits of greying cloth dangled from the window frame. In his bathroom was a poster of a wheel with cannabis leaves and opium poppies between the spokes. Julian said the retreat was one of those where you learn to drum on your own body and heal yourself with your innermost vibrations, though where he got that from I don't know.

We sat down on threadbare cushions and arranged ourselves with Carl at the centre: iron filings tracing field lines around a magnet.

'In some ways, you're actually the most important people in the plan,' he intoned, scrutinising our eager faces as he massaged his feet.

I was sixteen and had not yet learned that when someone uses those words, *In some ways, you're actually the most important people in the plan*, alarm bells should go off all the way from your ears to your toes. And because I did not know this at the time, I hung on Carl's every word.

What he told us was this: under the cover of darkness, a few hours before the nuclear-waste-carrying train was expected to roll by, they would chain themselves to the tracks. He did not give us any details of who else was involved, how many they were, how they would prevent the police from simply unchaining them. All we knew at that point was that they would use a novel method, a magic technique that would be immune to saws and wire cutters.

'What you are going to do is, you are going to stop the train before it reaches the people on the tracks,' Carl said.

We nodded. Even Andy held back whatever snarky comments were going through his mind. Sure. Anything you say. We'll stop the train. Sounds like a good idea.

'You'll stop the train. Now, you may wonder how. We'll discuss different ways, but the most efficient would be with your bodies.'

We nodded. Sure, we'll stop the train with our bodies.

'It'll be going really really slowly so it shouldn't be that hard,' Meredith interjected.

Andy rolled his eyes. Meredith had far less authority than Carl. In fact, we had started to find her a bit ditzy.

Carl was sitting on his cushion, cross-legged, eyes closed now. Still massaging his feet. Even though I liked and admired and in fact secretly wanted to be Carl – not just be *like* him, you understand, but *be* him – I often wished he would not finger his feet in meetings. His black hair was streaked with grey and framed his weather-beaten face, giving him the appearance of a sage, or a member of an ageing rock band.

'We believe the most efficient thing would be for you to walk onto the tracks and unfold a banner, or something that's visible in the dark – because it will be dark – so it can be seen by the approaching train.' He paused. 'Make sure you don't get run over.'

Meredith, blonde and fresh-faced, sat by Carl's feet. I half expected her to help massage them, but instead she focused on reinforcing his instructions.

'But also, make sure you step right in front of the train because otherwise it might not stop.'

'And if it doesn't the people chained to the tracks will get run over, and that would be really really bad,' she added.

We glared at her.

She blushed, grabbed Carl's right foot and started kneading it.

'I mean, of course it wouldn't be worse than if you got run over. That's not what I meant at all.'

'No, of course not,' I said.

She was, after all, Carl's girlfriend. I remembered the woman he had been with previously: a toned, stern biology student who had led the last Castor protests. She had been caught planning an act of sabotage involving explosives, and was now in prison.

I wondered if Carl ever went to visit her.

'Anyone else finding it smells a bit, like, mouldy in here? Let's have some fresh air . . .'

Before Meredith could stop him, Julian had leapt up and unbolted the window, which swung open violently like a drowning man coming up for air. The little rags dropped to the floor or floated to the centre of the room, carried by the exuberant breeze rushing in for the first time in decades.

Julian gaped at the scattered bits of cloth, at Meredith's furious eyes, at the dust and dirt from the windowsill that was settling on our faces like monochrome hundreds and thousands. He bent down and started ineffectually wiping the floor with a hankie, mostly to avoid our stares.

Carl's eyes were still closed when he spoke, as if he were channelling a message from the spirit world.

'You will walk onto the tracks. You will unroll or unfold whatever clearly visible item you deem most appropriate for your action. The train will slow, the train will stop. You will get arrested.' He opened his eyes. They were greyish-green and looked rather tired. 'And when you get arrested, you will state clearly that further down the line there are people chained to the tracks, and the train must not proceed.'

'Sure. Sounds like a plan.'

I wished Andy would say something, too. But he wasn't paying any attention. His eyes were on Julian, who was still dabbing the floor. He gave an amused snort. I tried to ignore them and gave Meredith and Carl a reassuring nod: don't worry, we may look like a big mistake but we are in fact very competent.

'Honestly, sometimes I wish I could just press fast forward on Carl. The way he goes on and on.' Julian blew his nose with the dust-stained hankie. 'It's like, mate, we heard you the first time.'

We were walking back from the lawyer's flat in the timbered house. Julian knew a short cut down some winding steps to the river. Andy knew a better short cut. After a bit of toing and froing, we took Andy's route through an overgrown cemetery.

'Well, it's a complex project.' I stepped over a broken headstone and paused, determined to defend Carl. More importantly, I didn't want to endanger our Important Role in the Big Plan. 'And it's all about consensus, right? He can't just bark orders at us.'

'But that's exactly what he's doing!' Julian cried out. '*Walk onto the tracks.*' He imitated Carl's droning baritone. '*I can stop trains with my mind, but I suggest you use your bodies.*'

Andy slapped Julian's back in agreement.

'Nettle soap, that was actually pretty funny. Sometimes I wonder what Carl's done that makes him Jesus fucking Christ.'

'What's with you two all of a sudden?' I wanted to sound cross but it came out uncertain, doubtful.

Not that they were listening; they were too busy cackling at each other's jokes. I felt like I was on a walk with my brother and his mates.

'What about the refugees?' I said eventually, when they had calmed down a bit.

'What about them?'

'Well, he actually puts up Kurdish refugees in his flat, after they've gone underground, so they won't be deported. I mean, how many people do that? Everyone's always, like, oh, if I had lived under the Nazis I would have hidden all my Jewish neighbours and I would have been such a saint, but right now how many people actually go and offer food and shelter or really any kind of basic help to people who face deportation? Like, who does that? We don't, right?'

119

'Hey, we were just having a bit of a laugh.' Andy put his arm around my shoulders and pulled me towards him. Julian looked away.

We walked on, plotting our assault on the tracks. But a small part of me thought, Here we are, discussing sheets and torches and maps like a bunch of naughty children, and maybe this is what this is all about. A bit of mischief. Very wholesome after all, lots of fresh air, bracing walks and flasks of organic tea. The police play their part, with their night-vision goggles and wagging fingers, and we play ours. Makes everyone feel heroic. And meanwhile, aren't there much more important things going on in the world?

17

Selim peered out of a doorway in the cobblestoned town centre, his left hand holding the sticky paw of a wriggling boy, his right grabbing the collar of a little girl.

'Auntie!' the little girl shouted, straining to join the protest march before them. She pointed at a stout woman in a blue dress. 'Look! It's Auntie Hanife!'

Next to Selim, his uncle was juggling a toddler and a baby, keeping his shovel-hands busy and his volatile temper subdued.

They watched the women stream by. A camouflaged girl with a machine gun glowered from a poster high above the black-haired, brown-haired, headscarved crowd, ringed by a garland of red, yellow and green flags. Others were carrying portraits of moustached men or PKK banners.

The guerrilla girl on the poster, her features blurred by the grainy print, reminded Selim of his sister Aynur. He had spoken to his mother on the phone a few days ago; one of those precious, brittle conversations in which her soft voice was drowned due to the vagaries of international calls. A bad line, a cracked phone, a dark hole-in-the-wall phone shop, an impatient Colombian rattling the plastic door of the booth. His father's health was declining. One of his uncles had been taken away by Turkish police. His parents were worried about Aynur, but his mother would not say why.

It must be something political, Selim thought; if it had been boy trouble, his mother would have talked freely about it on the phone. In any case, Aynur was still too young for that. Or was she? Years had passed since he had left; two, three, four years, enough for a little girl to turn into a teenager with boy trouble. Maybe even enough for a little girl to turn into a warrior.

His little brother, the one who was born just after Selim left, was well, his mother said. To think that he had a little brother!

Large old women lumbered along the tarmac like steamrollers. Their voices were surprisingly shrill. '*Serok Apo*!' they chanted, and '*Jin-Jiyan-Azadî*!'

Selim had his eyes on a sulky, pouting teenager. Arms folded, she moodily shuffled along with the older women, a lone protester against being in this protest.

She was wearing a baggy black Nirvana T-shirt, her black hair hanging down in a grungy curtain, and as she lifted one hand to an irritating strand of hair the fabric of the T-shirt was pulled back and he could make out the shape of her breasts. He stood there, transfixed. And at that moment, Selim wanted nothing more than to thrust his charges into his uncle's arms and follow the girl to wherever she would take him. He stared at her, hoping she would look at him, but she kept her eyes on the ground, and Selim gazed after her feeling his lungs ache with longing.

The little boy tugged at Selim's hand as if it were an emergency brake.

'I think I've wet my trousers.'

Selim sighed. He squatted down, opened a nylon bag with a change of clothes and helped the boy out of his trousers.

By the time Selim had stuffed the soiled clothes into a plastic bag, wiped his hands with disinfectant and straightened up, the women were trying to crash through the police cordon. A potato whizzed past his ear. He ducked into the doorway.

The police responded with tear gas. Clumps of earth flew back at them, in an escalating exchange. Selim heard yells and screams from the front line.

Women rushed towards him, pressed their children onto him and ran back into the crowd. Some scooped up earth and seized plants from flowerbeds, but the supply of throwable objects in the street was limited.

Locks clicked, window shutters were slammed, blinds drawn inside the black-and-white timbered houses that flanked the street.

'Can't you demonstrate somewhere else?' someone shouted from one of the windows before it banged shut.

Through a loudspeaker, police announced the end of the protest. The women, however, had time. They sat down. Thermos flasks were unscrewed, tea poured into plastic cups.

A solitary figure stood up and, stork-like, stepped over the sitting matriarchs. A man – how on earth had he ended up in a women-only protest? He seemed to ask himself exactly that question as he awkwardly manoeuvred himself out of the crowd.

There was something familiar about him, his uncertain steps, his gawkiness . . .

Selim squinted.

It was his lawyer, Dr Habicht. Selim thought of waving to him, but felt strangely embarrassed by this misplaced, pony-tailed figure and instead drew further back into the doorway.

It was only after Dr Habicht had vanished into one of the alleyways that Selim was gripped by sudden guilt.

'What if they arrest me?' he mumbled in the vague direction of his uncle. 'My case is with the immigration office. What if the police arrest me and charge me with protesting or, you know, that other stuff? My lawyer isn't very good.'

'You'll probably get sent straight back to Cizre,' his uncle replied drily.

'Just like that? Shit. Şivan was right to stay away, huh?'

Selim's uncle frowned at the suggestion that his son was bunking off.

'Şivan was extremely keen on coming, but he had to study. Actually, in your case, this march can only help your claim. Shows you're politically active. Though really it depends what mood the judge is in.'

The toddler started crying, and Selim felt like howling along in frustration. Şivan was probably out with his mates, having fun, getting up to no good in the safe knowledge that his parents were at the demo. In fact, everyone was at the demo. Every single authority figure was safely out of the way, and Şivan was completely and utterly free. The injustice of it all!

Well, there was a tiny bit of consolation. Poor Şivan, Selim thought with a hint of glee, you may not know it yet, but the

other day I overheard Auntie Hanife on the phone and . . .
you're down to marry Aynur. He grinned, remembered
something and frowned.

'Uncle . . .'

'What?'

'The girl on that poster. Don't you think she looks a bit like
Aynur?'

His uncle squinted, then shook his bullish head.

'It's a bad print, and I've only seen your sister once, at my
cousin's wedding. I remember it very well because the roof
caved in, and everyone screamed. Except for your sister.' His
uncle paused for dramatic effect. 'She laughed.'

'She must have been tiny at the time. Probably didn't
understand what was going on.'

'Maybe.'

'You're not saying Aynur made the roof cave in?'

'She was always such a mischievous child.'

'You just said you've only seen her once!'

'Stories get around, my friend. They get around.'

'I'm just thinking, that girl could be Aynur. You're right,
it's a grainy print and there are lots of girls with thick black
eyebrows like that . . . but you know Aynur has that kind . . .
the ones that meet up.' Selim passed a hand over his forehead. 'I don't know why it got into my head.'

His uncle squeezed his shoulder in a gesture that was
meant to be comforting but made Selim wince with pain.

'Don't worry. That's some old photo they dug out from
somewhere and enlarged. It's an old photo, and the girl in it
is probably dead by now.'

Selim shook a cigarette out of a packet of Marlboro Lights,

put it between his lips with some difficulty. His hands were shaking and it was windy. He cupped one hand around the cigarette, flicked the rusty little wheel of the lighter with the other, lit the cigarette and inhaled deeply. Leaned against the wall behind him and watched the smoke from his mouth disperse in the wind.

At nightfall, the women conceded that this time they would not march through the town centre. They packed up their banners and their children and went home.

Selim, relieved of his charges, caught a glimpse of the long-haired girl and sidled up to her, listening to her chat to an older woman. Her hands were smeared with mud, her hair was tousled, and under the street lights she looked strangely wild and elated; no trace of the previous sulky boredom.

'Yeah, everyone knows that, yeah,' the girl said to the woman beside her, speaking through one side of her mouth and chewing gum with the other. 'Politicals are in the common cell in front, criminals in the back, and torture is in the basement.'

Selim knew that, too. Turkish makeshift prisons. The basement. He sidled up to the girl, hoping to stay in her general sphere of wild elation.

The girl, as if noticing an irritating fly buzzing by her shoulder, briefly turned her face towards him, then shut him out behind a wall of hair.

18

Despite Carl's attempts to divide the plan into spy-proof chunks, some news from other cells trickled through. Ours was a small town, after all, and even anarchists like to gossip. A friend of a friend who worked as a welder let it slip that he was forging metal tubes, special hooks and handcuffs in one of the hidden vaults in the medieval part of town, which was normally used for band practice.

Out of vanity or carelessness, the bassist in Andy's band mentioned that he was on the communications team: they had prepared a script to be read out to the police, learned it by heart, then eaten it.

And rumour had it that Carl, Meredith and four other people were having secret meetings in the forest to practise non-violent resistance and urinating into nappies.

Andy, Julian and I drove up to northern Germany the day before the Castor train was due to arrive. We pitched our tent in a field where thousands of protesters had settled in anticipation of the big demo. Spiky-haired punks and bearded teachers gathered around flickering bonfires, huddling in sleeping bags on damp piles of straw, spearing potatoes with sticks and holding them over fires. One of the beards picked up a guitar and began to sing 'Blowin' in the Wind', ignoring the sighs and eye-rolling from the punks.

I waited until the fires and singing had died down. Then I crept out of my clammy sleeping bag. I kicked aside a charred potato and softly, softly slid towards the forest at the edge of the field, avoiding the tent pegs and guy ropes. My clothes and hair reeked of smoke. I stopped next to a man-high banner that showed a grinning red sun holding up a clenched fist, and waited for Julian and Andy to catch up. They emerged from between the dark triangles and domes of the tents, Julian carrying a floppy bundle. We silently entered the forest.

Police were patrolling the woods, but we banked on the fact that the area was vast and three people, even if shrouded in a smoke-scented cloud, would be able to slip through. We tried to tread lightly. Every crunchy step through the undergrowth startled me, and I wished I could stop the twigs from snapping underfoot. Andy had taken the lead, as he felt the most confident about the map we had memorised.

We circled a clearing with a distinctive conical rock that protruded from the moss. Following the other two, who were faster than me, I dived back into the undergrowth, zigzagged between the trees, mossy rainwater seeping through my leather boots, wet hair sticking to my forehead.

We came out of the forest and circled the same clearing with its conical rock and moss.

'Andy . . .' I whispered.

'Ssshhh!'

We left the forest and another field stretched out before us, flat and wide and chilly. On the far side were the raised tracks.

We stopped, nodded to each other and then, hare-like, sprinted towards the tracks. At the foot of the slope we paused again to unroll Julian's bundle, a sheet that declared in bold letters: *STOP! PEOPLE ON THE TRACKS!*

That, we felt, made it quite clear.

'And now?'

'Up the slope, onto the tracks, right?'

'Right.'

We marched onto the tracks and stood on the wooden planks and pebbles and waited there in the dark, blocking the way with our white banner tacked to two broomsticks, hoping we could be seen in the black night, and I wondered what would happen if they didn't see us, if the train, however slow it was, would just roll on and over us, and I raised my broomstick a bit higher, and then there was the angry crackle of a megaphone and a deep voice ordered us to get off the tracks, NOW.

A group of border guards scrambled up the slope and trapped us in a circle of light, their faces dark behind their torches.

'Hello. So, what do we have here?'

'We're blocking the tracks. There are people chained to the tracks further down,' I recited dutifully, lowering the banner.

'We're exercising our democratic right to resistance,' Julian ad-libbed, feeling he should contribute something to the script. 'If you don't respect our lives, we don't respect your laws.'

'And we're protesting for your lives, too,' said Andy, addressing the tired family men in padded uniforms around us.

'Uh-huh. Cheers.'

They handcuffed us, led us down the slope, packed us into a police van and drove us to a nearby gym.

There, between the bare concrete walls, we surrendered our names and ID cards and waited for the others to turn up. A policeman had already confiscated the sheet.

We were asked a few questions by policewomen who offered us tea, but because we had all learned our legal aid pamphlets by heart we kept our mouths shut. Keeping your mouth shut couldn't be held against you, we had been taught. But partial statements could. Saying, for example: 'Yes I went to the demo but I'd rather not comment on the incident with the smashed window' could well be used against you.

'We're not saying anything without a lawyer,' we repeated until they got bored with us and went back to their radio and card games.

We had, however, accepted their tea and were sipping it, quietly pleased with ourselves.

I leaned against Julian and nodded off, waking up when the doors were flung open and a dozen dishevelled twenty-somethings in oddly bulging dungarees, hooded woollen jumpers and overalls piled into the room, laughing and shrieking and hugging each other. When they saw us, they swept us up in their happy celebration.

It had all worked out: they had chained themselves to the tracks and held up the train for several hours. They had stuck their arms into metal tubes, buried under the tracks weeks before, three activists on one side, three on the other. When police and border guards, called in as reinforcement, tried to cut them loose, Carl told them that he and the others had locked the chains around little metal hooks inside the tubes and were unable to free themselves; in reality, they used karabiners that they could open easily with a flick of the thumb in case things got ugly.

The set-up was considered so police-proof that the six had put on nappies, preparing for a long hold-out.

Meredith kissed me on the cheek as if we were old comrades reunited after years in some Vietcong hideout. The others gathered around us in a knotted mess of dreadlocks and jumpers from Guatemala. Most of them were people I didn't know. That was the whole point.

'Great media pics,' Meredith shouted, one arm around Carl's waist, the other around Andy's. 'TV was there, everyone basically.'

Carl studied the cup of tea I was holding with both hands; my third. Suddenly, all of them were gawking at our cups of tea.

'Tea?' asked a short, squat chap next to Carl, frowning.

Well, yes, tea. It had been a long night. What was wrong with tea now?

'Careful, eh. It's all part of their technique,' Meredith said knowledgeably.

'Have they asked you any questions?' the short comrade probed.

We shrugged.

'We haven't said anything, just took their tea,' came Julian's defiant reply.

'I could do with a cup of tea myself,' Carl said, at his most gentle and fatherly. He winked at me. 'But let's wait until we get back to the camp. Not a good idea to get too matey with the boys in uniform.'

That relaxed our uptight, supposed allies and they giddily fell back into congratulating each other.

Julian, Andy and I stood there blowing the steam off our treacherous cups of tea, trying to act as if we couldn't care less about its provenance.

I remembered a winter's evening a few months before, during a non-violence seminar on a farm in the snow-covered countryside. I had stepped outside with my glass of red wine, watching the snowflakes fall into the dark-red liquid, and turned around to find that Carl had followed me. He just stood there silently holding his glass, and we both looked at the frozen white earth and sky and the white snowflakes that melted into our red wine; neither of us spoke, and after a while we went back inside, and since then I had felt a warm, tender, unspoken connection with him that even his gross foot-squeezing could not break.

I nonchalantly wandered over to a corner of the room, put down my cup of tea, pushed my hands into my pockets and rejoined the group.

19

Half the sky was black. I pulled up my scarf, which kept sliding down my nose, and adjusted the hood that covered my hair. And I thought, If those boys set a few more tyres on fire the entire sky will be black, and I wouldn't be surprised if all the birds stop singing. This is like fucking Armageddon.

In my hand I held a rock. I was standing on a plastic barrel, scanning the flat fields of northern Germany that stretched out before me, all the way to a high fence guarding a large grey block. Its thick walls hid steel containers packed with scorching-hot nuclear waste.

I hopped off the barrel and walked towards the main demonstration. Bearded Christians and mothers in dungarees were holding a vigil on a muddy plot between farmhouses, a school and some scattered modern ruins: an abandoned service station, a half-built shopping centre. The Christians and mothers crowded around a huge bale of straw. And there, right on top, sat Carl, legs crossed, reciting some boring poem about mankind. The rest of us, the masked and hooded minority, used the peaceful gathering as a safe haven, grabbing a bite to eat in the kitchen tent before venturing out for the next clash with the police.

'Let the sun shine . . . into your hearts . . .' the Christians sang when Carl had finished, waving flags with doves and peace signs.

I turned away from them, embarrassed by their singing, embarrassed by the rock in my hand.

'Drum, my heart, for lii-iiife . . . sing, my mouth, for peee-eeace . . .'

I stuffed the rock under my waistband and pulled down my scarf. Julian came out of the kitchen tent carrying a bowl of tepid water. He had cut off his dreadlocks, pierced his left nostril and linked it to his ear lobe with a rusty chain. He smelled of vegetable scraps and dirt. We leaned against Carl's bale of straw and Julian passed me his spoon. Sad orange bits floated in the murky liquid.

'The chefs got arrested at the border,' Julian said. 'It was the kitchen knives. Potential weapons. He does the cooking for now.'

He pointed at a spindly-legged teenager with dirty blond hair who was skulking around the kitchen tent like a crow on a rubbish dump, stacking up cracked bowls and handle-less cups.

'Let the sun shine . . . into your hearts . . .'

'Can someone switch off the Christians?' Julian grumbled.

A woman in dungarees came by to collect his soup bowl. She suspiciously glowered at our hoods and scarves.

'. . . Sing, my mouth, for peee-eeace . . .'

We covered our faces and walked back to the road, where hundreds of masked, black-clad figures were busy at work, piling up wooden crates, dragging tyres, pushing shopping carts filled with beer cans and mysteriously bulging bags.

One of them slung a rope around a lamp post and beckoned a dozen others to come and help. I quickly lost Julian in the commotion. They were like bees, like ants, and their industry was infectious. I took the rock from my waistband and started moving towards the lamp post, then thought I might help carry some tyres, then wandered back to the boxy, brick school building where a black-clad mass had gathered.

A fellow hooded figure sidled up to me.

'Let's go and find more, like, stones and stuff.'

I didn't recognise the voice.

'What? Sorry, you are?'

His response was muffled by the scarf around his face. His watery grey eyes did not look familiar.

'Where's your affinity group?' I asked.

'My what?'

'Your affinity group.' I edged away and tried subtly to cross my arms over the rock in my hand, wishing I had left it tucked away. 'You know, your people. Your mates.'

It was chilly despite the bonfires and burning tyres, the northern wind sweeping across the vast open space. I hoped the grass and crops would be damp enough to prevent the fires from spreading.

'Oh, my mates. They stayed at home. They're not really into politics.' The eyes smiled apologetically. 'They're probably at the pub, getting wasted.'

Shit. I needed to get rid of that rock, quickly.

'No, I mean – listen, you know how this works, right?'

'How what works?'

'Protesting. You need an affinity group, like, basically, people you know and trust, people you practise with.' I looked at him. Black sweatshirt, black Doc Martens, Palestinian scarf hiding half his face: my mirror image.

'Practise what?' His voice was muffled by the scarf, as was mine.

We must look pathetic, I thought, two black-clad protesters chatting in front of a burning vegetable crate.

'Protesting!' I repeated. Either he was dense or a spy. 'You need an affinity group to practise protesting. Listen, I really think this isn't the time—'

'Can't be that hard, protesting. Walk down the road with a banner, right? We're protesting right now after all, and frankly we seem to be doing pretty well.' He gestured towards the row of water cannons that had appeared on the horizon.

'I'm talking about proper protesting. Road blocks and all that. You need to practise. Otherwise they'll knock you over with the first squirt from one of those water cannons.' I really needed to stop this. What if he was recording my voice? Though the scarf should help.

'Right. You know what, maybe you could be my affinity group.' He stretched out both arms.

'It doesn't work like that.' I almost laughed. It was so typical that this should happen to me; anyone else would have managed to cut off the conversation after the first sentence. 'You could be a spy.'

The water cannons drew closer, and I used the resulting turmoil to lose the boy and look for Julian, my only remaining affinity group. Andy had decided he was sick of this. He'd gone home with some girl he met. I tried not to think of that.

The cluster around the school grew astonishingly quickly. Some were gripping metal poles, traffic signs they had ripped out of the road. Who were these people? They were so efficient. What had happened to the amateurish stone-throwers? I felt that this lot were quite different, more numerous, more professional, more serious, and I was suddenly uneasy in their presence. The passage to the main road was now blocked by a barricade of smashed-up wooden fences.

I tried to smile reassuringly at one of the peaceful hippies, a girl my age in a ruffled frock, forgetting that I was masked and gripping a rock. The girl gave a shriek and fled into the crowd.

Carl started a song: 'We are water, soft water, water breaking the hard, hard stone . . .'

The little ones are out of control, I had heard him tell ditzy Meredith earlier in the day.

Yes, we are, I thought. We are out of control.

There was a loud crash. One of the boys with the traffic signs had smashed a shopping-centre window. And with that, the loitering crowd raced into action. With iron bars and poles, they smashed more windows, the door, the frame.

Within minutes, the big and solid building had had its teeth knocked out.

A hooded figure sprayed *FUCK CAPITALISM* across the concrete wall, another poured something from a metal container over the wall and windows. Flames shot up.

I ran back into the peaceful crowd, looking for Julian.

A chubby boy in combat trousers materialised next to me, manoeuvring a dented shopping cart. He thrust his arm into one of the canvas sacks in the cart and pulled out a fire cracker.

'Er,' I said. 'You sure that's a good idea? We're right in the middle of the crowd here . . .'

The boy silently lit the fuse. I ducked and pulled my hood down to my eyebrows, motioning to the hippies to move on, move on, move on. They parted before me, scurrying away like cockroaches; I kept forgetting about my outfit.

On the other side of the fence, riot police formed a menacing front. The boy hurled the firecracker at them: a green flash arcing higher and higher through the smoke-tinted sky. Before it even hit the ground, a shower of tiny pellets erupted into white smoke around us and sent us running: 'Tear gas!'

The pellet must have hit me right on the chest. A blunt ache, and then my face felt as if it was on fire, my eyes pumping out tears to wash out the burning pain, my lungs choking, my throat contracting, and I felt rage rise up inside me, uncontrollable rage, and when my eyes had cleared I ripped the rock from my waistband, swung back my body and hurled the rock at the wall of plastic shields and black helmets.

'The school!' someone yelled, and we moved as one, propelled forwards by an irresistible force.

Another column of smoke billowed up into the sky.

Carl's monotone voice whined through the loudspeaker: 'We will march peacefully . . . I call on all of you to join us and come together in non-violence, my friends . . .'

Then the chorus set in: 'Let the sun shine . . . into your heart . . .'

Stun grenades punctuated the songs.

'. . . Drum, my heart, for lii-iiife . . .'

Masked boys stormed out of our crowd and attacked the approaching riot police.

I stood there and looked at the blazing school. It's a Sunday, I told myself. It's empty. It must be empty.

The flames reached the playground. Within seconds, the wooden swings and slide and a little wooden castle were on fire. A grinning paper clown winked at me from one of the windows on the ground floor before he curled up, blackened and disappeared in the blaze.

'Run!'

I wheeled around, my feet moving, my gas-filled lungs pumping against the pain. I raced past the hippies, the village. Just get out of the open field, I thought, there is a forest. I ripped through thorny branches and crackling foliage and could hear the boys behind me and – dogs? Panic speeded me up. I had never in my life felt so afraid, and yet so exhilarated and free. My mouth stretched into an open grimace, I wheezed and laughed and ran, until I heard only the blood pulsing through my temples: no dogs, no police, no hooded boys, and I collapsed in a mound of dry leaves, my chest aching, my head exploding with excitement and exhaustion. And then I felt a wonderful sensation of peace.

20

'There are children dying of leukaemia,' I said, putting my elbows on the table. 'It's well known. The nuclear lobby is paying for all sorts of cover-ups but everybody knows. I know, even you know.'

I hadn't even taken off my torn black jumper and trousers, ripped by the thorny shrubs, nor my mud-encrusted boots, and was already heading into another argument with Stefan, my stepfather.

'Yes, yes, cover-ups,' he said, stroking his shaved head. 'Thank God for fossil fuels. Let's replace nuclear with coal. Cough, cough.'

Stefan was one of the first men in Neustadt – and the very first man in our neighbourhood – to shave his balding head, rather than mask the bald patches with a comb-over. He must have spotted the style on one of his business trips to Frankfurt, or even London, and it was brave, really, trying it out on our rather conservative streets. Looking back I don't really understand why I didn't get on with him; he wasn't a bad person, he was nice to my mother, he liked running in the forest and hiking in the Alps. He was more interested in Martin and me than our biological father had ever been.

Objectively speaking, his only flaw was that he kept saying the world should be run by engineers, because he himself was one.

My mother discreetly shifted my dirty backpack from the sofa to the tiled floor.

'I'm just glad she's back,' she said, then turned to me. 'Why don't you take a shower and then we'll have dinner.'

I rubbed my eyes, still itchy from the tear gas, got up and went to my room. When I came out of the shower, Stefan had disappeared. There was bread, cheese and jellied pig's head on the table, and I dragged my chair close and tried to remember if I was a vegan or a vegetarian, then stuffed a slice of jellied pig's head into my mouth.

'Let's wait for Stefan,' Mum said.

'Hmm yeah,' I mumbled and took another slice of pig.

'Sorry.' I got up and went into the kitchen. 'I'm just so hungry.'

I was feeling nauseous, and had thought it was just my empty stomach demanding food, but after eating I felt even worse. Everything seemed oddly disjointed and dislocated, as if someone was cutting out chunks of time and pasting them all over my brain. It hurt.

The pork and cartilage sat uneasily in my stomach. I placed a hand on the door of the fridge to steady myself. The gushing tap was very loud, the kitchen striplight very bright.

Mum appeared in the doorway.

'I think I might have concussion,' I said. 'Maybe I got hit by something when it all got chaotic and . . . I feel kind of nauseous.'

She put a hand on my forehead and told me to lie on the sofa.

Martin came into the living room humming 'Risen from the Ruins', the GDR anthem, and carrying a tray with a glass of water on it.

'Very funny,' I said, feeling a bit defenceless with my legs sticking out over the armrest and my head propped up by a brown velveteen cushion. 'I'm an anarchist, not a socialist. Actually, I'm not even an anarchist any more. I'm just a free spirit.'

'That was for Mum. She's moving east,' he said, handing me the glass of water and an aspirin. 'And this is for you.'

'Mum is moving?' I spluttered, trying to drink without splashing water on the cushion. 'But she's our mother!'

'Keep your voice down, we're not even supposed to know this. Stefan was going to arrange a proper round of consultations with us, but I overheard her on the phone. OK, OK, I was listening in on the other phone.' He paused and rolled his eyes. 'Don't look at me like that. You'd have done the same. Anyway, all the funding for archaeologists is in the east now, and she's been offered a job there. It sounds like a kind of low-cost digging job, frankly, but I guess it's better than nothing.'

'And Stefan?' I whispered.

'He's going to look after us,' Martin said gravely.

I pressed my head into the cushion and groaned.

My brother laughed.

'Hey, joking. They're moving out there together as soon as I finish school. So, officially, they're only going to do it if we agree, but basically, you'd better ask Julian's parents to get the spare room ready.'

'I can't believe this,' I said. 'Mum's defecting. And you'll be doing your military service. And I'll be all on my own.' I felt rather sorry for myself. 'You do know they're kind of serious about their no-drugs policy in the Army, right? Let me know if you want to desert.'

'Hey, you'll have so much fun at Julian's,' Martin said with unusual tenderness, lightly boxing my shoulder in what was meant to be a gesture of affection. 'And if you get bored, you can always come and watch me at target practice. And I'll be paying you embarrassing visits in full camouflage. In fact, we'll probably run into each other at the next demo. I'll be the stoned guy with the riot shield.'

21

From anarchist to civil servant: there had been stranger conversions. Certain aspects of my gently plodding job even reminded me of the anti-nuclear movement. The committee meetings, panel meetings, community meetings, not to mention the jargon and grammatical creativity. Take this sentence from my (by now well-thumbed though not well-liked) *Registrar's Manual for Detecting Forced Marriages: Mais 'attention' il ne faut pas confondre: 'mariage blanc' et 'mariage forcé'!!!*

But 'be careful' you mustn't confuse: 'paper marriage' and 'forced marriage'.

Where do I start? The rogue quotation marks, the drunken punctuation, the infantile structure? This is, after all, a booklet published by the Republic, written in a language that the French in their self-effacing way like to refer to as *la langue de Molière*.

Incidentally, my Larousse translates *mariage blanc* as *unconsummated marriage*. That, I feel, somewhat misses the point. A quick Internet search brings up a more nuanced definition: *'Mariage blanc' is a marriage of convenience, entered into in order to protect one of the partners from persecution or harm.*

So, I hear you say, never mind the linguistic niceties, what about the girl? Well, the manual had stirred up many doubts and questions, but it failed to provide much in the way of answers. It was my duty, I was told, to alert the Mayor if I sensed the marriage was not consensual. The Mayor would then alert the public prosecutor, and if the prosecutor had nothing better to do he might even look into the issue. That was the theory. In practice, our Mayor spent half the week in Strasbourg in his second job as a Member of the European Parliament, and the other half trying to win back the French President's favour. The Mayor had once been a star minister in the Cabinet, had fallen from grace, and was now far too busy with courtly manoeuvrings to be interested in the fate of a Kurdish eighteen-year-old and her clan.

As for my own tentative investigation: well, this kind of snooping around was no more part of my job description than it would have been part of a carpenter's or a librarian's. I had sent the bride and groom requests for separate interviews at the town hall, but so far only the groom had responded. We fixed a date, and that set off a whole new train of thought. What on earth would I ask him? I tried to distract myself with my other weddings, but the Kurdish girl remained on my mind.

About a week after Azad's visit, I sealed off a particularly pleasing union. A young Jewish couple and their families poured out of the wedding hall, the bride looking glamorous in a knee-length ruffled dress and jauntily perched pillbox hat, the groom gazing at her throughout the ceremony, enraptured. I stayed behind, cheered up by their boisterous happiness, and told myself that this was what I

145

was supposed to be doing, linking couples and families, not breaking them apart.

When the party had disappeared down the stairs, I closed the door and hoisted myself up onto the carved wooden table that served as a kind of Republican altar, enjoying the vague mischief of sitting on the yellow cloth. I usually stood with my back to the oil painting behind the stand, assisting the Deputy Mayor, and it was nice to be a spectator for a change.

The painting, one of those light-filled Impressionist works, showed a bride and groom standing before the Mayor, their families gathered around them. The signature in the corner said *H. Gervex 1881*, but the scene was set here, right here in this hall, and that was what I liked most about it: that continuity, that solidness. The portrayed Mayor in his tricolour sash was reading from a book, just as our Deputy Mayor had read from a book to the Jewish couple an hour before. The windows with their wooden frames and red curtains, ruched back by theatrical yellow sashes, had stayed exactly the same. The wooden table in the picture, adorned with a carved wreath of laurel – that was the very wooden table I was sitting on. I could almost feel the Mayor in the painting turn to me with indignation and scold me for occupying his ceremonial prop.

The wedding party in the picture was of course very different, the bride in a satin dress with a bustle, looking pale and blonde under her tulle veil; the groom, with his natty brown moustache, holding a top hat in his white-gloved hand. To the bride's left sat a young woman in pink, maybe her sister, gripping a summery straw hat. There was the mother of the bride in a rust-red bonnet, deep in thought, maybe remembering her own wedding. The father of the bride sat in the foreground, a big brown coat slung over his arm, as if ready to get up and walk out, like a passenger on an overheated bus. Around them stood bearded men in black suits and women in shimmering dresses, so vividly painted you could almost hear the fabric rustle, could almost hear the low murmur of a dashing officer with an impressive moustache whispering something into the ear of a blushing girl.

And then there was the balding, bearded man assisting the Mayor, holding a quill, grinning at the bride: that would be one of my predecessors.

We did once have a couple who wanted their wedding to replicate the scene in the painting. It had been the bride's idea, I think. Her mother had stitched together an elaborate satin dress, complete with bustle and tulle veil. The groom played along enthusiastically: he had even grown a walrus moustache and greeted me with a stiff little bow before kissing my hand.

The father of the bride, one of those slightly overenthusiastic amateur photographers, told everyone to stand like this and hold their hats like that as he held his point-and-shoot at arm's length.

I could see the Deputy Mayor growing impatient and muttering that they should get on with it: 'This is a ceremony of the Republic and not Disneyland!'

Finally the father of the bride lowered his camera, satisfied, and as the others left the hall he showed me the photo, held it against the painting and said: 'It's exactly the same, isn't it?'

And I nodded and said yes, it's exactly the same.

'*Oh! Pardon!*'

I slipped off the table, but it was too late. Sandra stood in the doorway, staring at me with a mixture of shock and delight. I stammered something about feeling queasy, but even as I did so I could see her mentally shaping this moment into an anecdote that would quickly make the rounds of the town hall.

'I was just wondering whether you'd like some cake,' she said, her eyes on the crumpled cloth. 'The Chinese family from yesterday brought some over.'

I followed her to the kitchenette, docile in my embarrassment. Sandra had been a secretary at the town hall for ever, probably since the brides wore bustles, and it occurred to me that she might be the person to ask for advice on my Kurdish dilemma. Asking for advice was in itself a bit of a novelty. As the nimble fingers of the state, we were supposed to know exactly how to carry out our instructions; and suddenly sticking out and questioning one of those instructions, suddenly asking *how and why should I do this*, was like your own thumb showing signs of confusion rather than bending willingly around the handle of a mug.

Munching a slice of chocolate cake, I listened to Sandra complain about being overworked and underpaid, and was once again half impressed, half disturbed by her unrivalled fund of town hall gossip.

'Have you noticed how he always smells of beer in the afternoon?'

'I haven't, no.'

'He smells of beer!'

'He probably has a *pression* with his lunch,' I ventured.

'No!' Sandra's double chin wobbled as she vigorously shook her head. 'I found out why.'

'Well . . .'

'It's because he meets a young friend during his lunch break and takes her to a hotel. Obviously he knows the soapy smell is a dead giveaway, so afterwards he buys a can of beer and dabs the beer all over his body. Then he sits here and works and then he goes home to his wife.'

I sighed.

'How do you know this? Did he tell you?'

She responded with an almost flirty giggle.

'Of course not! I heard it from the hotel owner, who's a friend, and the owner of the shop next door, who's also a friend.'

'You're not short of friends.'

'That's what you need to keep up with things.'

Not for the first time, I wondered how many of Sandra's spies were trained on me.

'The shop owner also told me about my husband. You mustn't think I'm a big gossip, it's just important to know what's going on, otherwise you're the last to know and then you look pretty daft, right?'

'What, your husband uses the hotel too?'

'Nah, he's far too fat for that kind of thing. Not that I mind him being fat, it's nice in bed, he's so big and soft. But you know, I hear him panting up the stairs, and I see people snigger at us, and our own children go, "No other daddy has such a big belly. And if he doesn't lose weight he's going to die."'

'We're all going to die,' I said, feeling sensible but also treacherous. As always, Sandra's reports made me feel slightly dirty, and yet as they went on they were weirdly addictive.

'But he's going to die before me, that's what I'm saying. So the doctor puts him on a diet. Before long, I talk to the shop-keeper. The shopkeeper says no offence but I know your husband's on a diet and guess where I saw him the other day.' She leaned closer to me, as if whispering a filthy secret. 'McDo! Scoffing burgers with his friend Pierre, who's also fat.'

We pondered this outrage in appropriately solemn silence.

'Sandra,' I began after a while, 'I was wondering whether you've heard anything about this girl, the one with the annoying cousin, or rather, he's the groom's cousin. Do you know the family?'

She shook her head.

'I don't really know much about the families from the Maghreb, they go to a different shop.'

'I think she's Kurdish, actually.'

'Well, I don't know them. Never heard of them.' Which basically meant they did not exist.

Such were the contradictions in our cosy fellowship at the town hall: curiosity about a colleague's lunchtime affair was thought of as normal, natural even, but a family's motivation for nudging their young daughter towards marriage was not to be questioned.

Sandra unwrapped a chocolate bar, broke off a piece and offered it to me.

'I've noticed you're quite upset by the whole thing.

150

Thierry said it must be trouble at home but I said no, she's upset by this business with the girl. We were never asked to be this careful before, though it's not as if it didn't happen when Monsieur Dubois was around. He'd never admit it, you'd just see him frown into his cardboard folders and get on with it, but between you and me, it broke his heart.'

'Who would have thought registrars were such a sensitive bunch, eh?'

'Not easy.' She gave a sympathetic nod, pressing her jaw into her smiling chins. 'You should talk to him. Between you and me, you know, he started here when he was very young, and he was even more, well, not insecure exactly, but . . . anxious, that's it. He was even more anxious than you are.'

'Well, I wouldn't describe myself as anxious exactly.'

'No, you're just insecure.' She laughed with chin-trembling mirth.

'It seems a bit over the top to barge into his retirement like that.'

She laughed again.

'If you want to make a retired man happy, ask him about his career.'

My predecessor had fled our eventful little neighbourhood and retired to a house in a hilly, wooded part of Normandy, about two hours from Paris. His voice sounded stiffly paternal over the phone, strict but not unfriendly. Given that I had never met him, I was taken aback when he invited me out to the country; such matters, he said, were not suitable for discussing over the phone. His tone left me no option but to agree, thank him and ask for directions.

'You don't sound all that surprised that I called,' I ended with.

'Oh no,' he replied with a chuckle, 'I knew you would. Let's hope my poor little thoughts will be of use to you.'

It was a Saturday morning. Thousands of Parisians in their Peugeots were crawling out of the city, and I wished I had left earlier. But the traffic thinned as I approached the enclave of old blood and privilege where Monsieur Dubois lived, with most weekenders heading to cheaper spots or the seaside. I slowed and pulled past the ivy-covered stone walls of a chateau flanked by two round towers. I looked at my directions, and thought, But surely he can't . . . he's only a retired town hall official. But who knows? And so I parked and stepped out of the car.

The towers stared reproachfully at my scratched old Polo. I walked up to the wrought-iron gate and gently pushed it. It was locked. A gardener emerged from the bushes by the left tower, sulkily dragging his rake through the courtyard.

'Monsieur Dubois lives here?'

Annoyed, the gardener raised his rake and pointed it up at the hill.

'*Merci, Monsieur.*'

The tarmac turned to crunching gravel and the gravel turned to silent dirt, taking me deeper into the forest, climbing uphill again and swerving into a vast clearing. Up on the hill sat a boxy bungalow with wraparound windows, of the type once built as someone's dream home.

Monsieur Dubois sat on the terrace behind the house, surrounded by bushes of white rhododendrons. He was a thin little man, and he now turned around and stood up from his wrought-iron chair with difficulty, peering at me through bottletop glasses. The young woman who had shown me to the terrace disappeared back into the house and I could hear the clatter of cups and saucers.

'You will have coffee? Tea? Some cake perhaps?' he asked once we'd sat down. 'Or a glass of wine, maybe? It's a long way from Paris.'

'That would be . . .'

'Nathalie,' he called out towards the house. 'Hold the coffee, hold the tea, fetch us a good bottle from the cellar, will you?'

In his hand he held a crumpled white handkerchief that he used to pat his face and mouth. Nathalie brought a bowl of nuts and one of crackers and an unlabelled bottle which Dubois uncorked and poured with authority. Like the unimaginative bureaucrats we were, we toasted the *mairie*.

'She won't let me do a thing,' he sighed, gesturing to the discreetly withdrawing Nathalie. 'Not even the garden.' He popped a handful of nuts into his mouth. 'Well then, are you enjoying yourself at the town hall?'

I cast around for a suitable reply, not wanting to sound too enthusiastic in case he still missed his old job, and eventually said: 'It's fun. I do love the wedding hall.'

'Oh, that Gervex is wonderful. Though it would have been much more amusing if instead of that prim and proper bride, it was Rolla.'

He'd lost me there, possibly intentionally. I made one of those neutral humming noises that could indicate agreement, dissent or indifference.

'Nathalie,' he called out. 'Have you seen that book on Gervex?'

She brought us the book so quickly that I wondered if he had planned this in advance; there was even a yellow file card stuck between the right pages. The painting showed a half-dressed young man gazing at a naked woman sprawled across a nest of sheets and pillows. She was bathed in the glare of the morning-after sun, lying next to a cast-off top hat and crumpled corset: it could have been a sequel to the wedding portrait at the town hall.

'I used to amuse myself by imagining that this was the bride after the wedding night,' Dubois said, as if he had guessed my thoughts. 'But it's actually a prostitute. *Rolla considère d'un œil mélancolique/ La belle Marion dormant dans son grand lit*. Rolla is the most debauched man in Paris, and he uses all his money to pay for the services of the beautiful Marion, a very expensive lady. You may know the poem.'

I didn't.

'My eyesight is not too good, but do take a closer look. It's a wonderful painting. If you lengthen the diagonal of his arm, it cuts right across Marion's pubis.'

'Oh,' I said. 'How interesting.'

I closed the book and tried to nudge the conversation back to the town hall.

'I like the wedding portrait. It's very cute.'

He snorted with derision. Then he slowly sipped his wine and gave an approving nod before continuing. It seemed as if he had long prepared all of this – the wine, the saucy joke about Gervex, his subsequent remarks – expecting someone to seek his advice one day. And it occurred to me that all retired people probably did this, mentally drawing up an ever-lengthening lecture to a prospective disciple, handing on all their stored wisdom and experience, real or imagined, to a successor; but presumably, in most cases, that long-awaited young listener never comes.

'So, you did not come here to talk about Rolla, you came here for advice. But where do I start! You would need to stay here for weeks, hah, how about that? Here's the first one, I see it right before me, picture this: I am alone in a room full of Berbers. A room full of Berbers!' He slapped the table for emphasis. 'I wasn't as young as you, if I may be frank, town hall officials seem to get younger every year. When I started, you still had to work your way up. Not a bad thing, in my opinion, if you don't mind my saying so.'

His fingers inched along the embroidery on the tablecloth until they found the silver bowl with the nuts; clearly even the bottlecap glasses were not doing much for his eyesight.

'Sixty men on one side of the room, a girl in a white dress on the other. Let me see if I can recall her name . . . little . . . oh, you know, one of those Berber names. And I, young and, well, if you don't mind my saying so, rather dashing in those days, I sat in the middle. Now, believe it or not, I don't even remember the groom.' He laughed. 'I don't even remember the groom! Just the frightened child and all those Berbers in one room with me. And I looked at her and thought, Oh dear, what are they doing with this poor little thing.'

'So what did you do?'

'I married them, of course.'

He gave a chuckle that was more helpless than amused. His right hand brushed against his glass, but all his gestures were so light, so exploratory in their nature, that the glass hardly shook.

'What about your suspicions, then?'

'That was a long time ago. In those days, no one married because they wanted to. I tell you' – he lowered his voice confidingly – 'my wife and I married in, shall we say, a bit of a rush. My eldest son was born six months after the wedding.'

He placed his fingertips on the tablecloth and sensed his way to the bowl of crackers. He gently lifted the dish and offered me some. They had a home-made texture to them, of burnt spices and unsieved flour, and the domestic pleasantness of the scene only made me more unsettled by this friendly half-blind wine drinker.

'But you said she looked scared, the first bride, I mean.'

'Yes, she and so many girls after her. That was only the first, you see. I had two or three every year, weddings where you could almost see the gun being pressed into the small of her back, metaphorically speaking, of course. Not just the Berbers. I had a Portuguese girl in front of me once, I tell you, I thought she would break in two with fear!'

'Well, I have my problems with that. In the case I'm dealing with now, I haven't even seen the bride but I definitely feel I should do something, that I should really make sure it's all above board.'

He shook his head.

'Just before I retired, yes, there was more talk of something needing to be done, it's our responsibility and all that. But frankly, what's the use? Marriage, you see, is all about the family. Problems will be solved within the family, or not at all. It's not for us to poke and probe like some kind of blackmailing charlady.'

'Surely if you think she's terrified, if it's obvious she doesn't want to get married, then surely—'

'Tell me then, what do we want? I told you about the first girl, room full of Berbers. Now let me tell you, that shy child came back to me ten years later, fifteen years later, a plump, proud mother of six! Came to make arrangements for her niece's wedding.'

I could not bring myself to agree with him. In fact, hearing him speak like that made things seem much clearer, obvious even. I thought, Marriage must be consensual, and that is all there is to it. This was not a question of subtleties, sensitivities, cultural differences. The law was clear; and I was puzzled that I could ever have seen any ambiguity where there was, after all, only right or wrong.

I explained this to him with a certain defiance, and, as evidence of the changing times, added: 'You may have heard about this new manual we've been given, this new booklet that really makes it all quite clear.'

At this he broke into surprised laughter. He scrunched up his weak eyes and threw back his head.

'Are you referring to the booklet on forced marriages?'

'Yes, the manual for registrars.'

'The one that was published by the *mairie*, with the wedding ring made of barbed wire on the cover?' He mimed slipping a ring on his finger.

'That's the one.'

He leaned back, savouring the pause, my confusion.

'Well, my dear,' he said slowly. 'Apparently you know many things that a simple old man like me cannot begin to understand, and I sense that you may even find me a bit behind the times, out of touch . . . No, no, don't protest, I take great delight in the company of young women but I also know that they rarely take old men like me seriously, and that is, if you allow me to say so, a shame. For sometimes you may find that old men have a thing or two to, shall we say, not teach you, I would not dare suggest that there is anything you need to be taught, but maybe, well, maybe there is room for a little advice, a little guidance. And in the case of that clever manual, the one laying out the rules which you so clearly admire, well, my dear, don't fall off your little chair and onto your little bottom, but it may surprise you to hear that . . . I wrote it.'

I nearly did fall off of my chair.

In great length and detail, he told me the whole story. Just before retiring, as his last project, he was asked to compile a guide for young officials facing the situation he had so frequently experienced. He took to the task with the unquestioning loyalty and thoroughness of a lifelong bureaucrat. He consulted lawyers and anthropologists, social workers and town hall officials, clerics and feminists, even a few battered wives. Due to his deteriorating eyesight, he had to dictate the work to a junior civil servant who typed it all up (hence the wayward style, which I decided not to mention to my host).

The resulting draft was hailed as an unprecedented tool for concerned registrars, a small revolution in the realm of officialdom that excited mayors and minions alike.

And my host spoke of the manual with the pride of a foot soldier who had accomplished a mission of great complexity if little meaning.

Editing, revising, updating, fact-checking, designing and printing it took a couple of years, and eventually the finished copies were popped into the post and delivered to thousands of officials, including me.

A triumph.

Personally, of course, he believed the manual was utterly pointless.

Yet he smiled generously, humouring me.

And I felt rather sheepish.

'Well, I never. And to be honest, despite everything you've just said, I'm still glad I read it. I still think it made me see things in a different way, a clearer way.'

He leisurely fingered his wine glass.

'Clearer. Yes.' He was unflappable now, relaxed in his freshly asserted authority. 'The fact is, my dear friend, however certain and knowledgeable you feel now, the day you get married you will realise that it's never clear. You will think, But what am I doing! Do I really want this man? No, I need more time! And then you will find that custom and ceremony oblige you to go through with it, and in fact you will be quite glad about that, because it means you don't have to decide it all yourself. Later, you will think, But did I really know what I was getting myself into? You will think, But did I actually know the person I married? You will ask yourself these questions, and find that, like most brides, you entered the harsh and stony field of marriage thinking it would be a . . . what's the word I'm grappling for . . . what's it . . . a . . . a . . .' He took a rattling breath. 'A flowerbed. Thinking it would be a flowerbed.'

'What makes you think I haven't got married yet?'

That startled him. He put down his glass and discreetly coughed into his tissue.

'Oh, I'm sorry. You're married?' And I thought I caught his half-blind eyes glancing at my bare, ringless hands.

'Not married,' I said. 'Divorced.'

PART TWO

Brides, Sheikhs and Anarchists

22

I was young to be divorced, but by modern standards my marriage wasn't even that short: seven years. Most brides started out thinking they would be married until they dropped dead, or until their husbands dropped dead. Then, surprise! They found that their marriage was much shorter than expected.

My case was the opposite. I married thinking it would be a brief, efficient and functional union. Instead, it lasted seven years.

Like the girl I had tried to summon to my office, I was a teenage bride.

When I talked to my friends about their younger siblings, or their students, or their neighbours' children, the assumption was that teenagers were somehow sillier than the rest of humanity. More shallow, more self-obsessed, more ignorant and yet more judgemental than adults. People and objects were either loved or hated, and actions were self-evidently right or disgustingly wrong. From the grown-up perspective, the teenage world was painted in primary colours, in exuberant yellow, angry red and depressed blue; while being an adult meant seeing the more nuanced shades, like appreciating wine instead of alcopops.

There was maybe some truth in that, but I liked to think that adolescence was also the one time in our lives when our actions matched our principles. Teenagers could hold tight to ideals and convictions, and act on them, and feel the pain of an unjust world the way few others could. As children we didn't yet understand what was happening in the world; as adults, we no longer cared. As teenagers, we still thought we could change the weather.

And so, when I was seventeen, I offered to marry a man I had never met. In that sense, without having the slightest link with Kurdistan, and despite being European through and through, I was the perfect Kurdish bride.

I was sitting in the sun with Julian. Andy had taken to keeping his distance. He had won some success as a techno DJ and was no longer interested in politics, but Julian and I were closer friends than ever. I moved in with his family after Stefan and my mother left, and although I missed my mother (and, to my great surprise, even Stefan), I felt quite at home in Julian's little village just outside town. We cycled to school together at dawn and spent most weekends getting drunk by the river with our friends, enduring the bongo-drumming around us. I thought of it as character-building.

That morning, we were both nursing a terrible hangover, the consequence of several bottles of Kadarka at an open-air concert in the botanical gardens. We had once again descended into a lament about the state of the world, the plight of the Kurds, to be precise.

And Julian said: 'You know Selim? Flo's friend? Guy from the BlueBlue bike shop?'

'Hmm. Don't think I've met him, but guess I've heard of him,' I said. In my hometown, everybody had heard of everybody else.

'He lost his appeal. Against being deported on his eighteenth birthday. Appealed, lost. Shit, huh?'

'Yeah,' I said. 'That's really shit.'

'Totally shit.'

'Yeah. '

'Turkish police went to his village with a list. Apparently, Selim's name was on the list.'

'How come?'

'Got caught when he was thirteen, like, putting up posters for the PKK or something.'

'But if he was only thirteen . . .'

'Well, listen to this. So he puts up those posters, gets caught, beaten up, then they set him free. Next day, his mum scrapes together all the money she can get from his uncles and cousins and shit, pays some *Schlepper*, gets him onto the next truck to Europe. All the roads are blocked, right, so they take him to some secret port, put him on a boat, throw him into the sea somewhere near Italy. I mean, he almost drowned. He hasn't seen his family since. If he goes back he'll be killed.'

We sat in silence.

'And he's definitely going back? That's crazy. Really shit.' (I was not the most eloquent teenager).

'He can't launch another appeal. That was the last one. End of the line. Finito. He could marry a local, but we all asked around and none of the women from the legal aid group want to help.'

'The what?'

'The legal aid group. It's like this help-thingy for asylum seekers that Carl runs. Network, sort of. But they just sit around and talk and feel fucking great about themselves. We asked some of the women if any of them would marry Selim so he could stay. I mean, they're old, in their twenties, right. But they all said they were against marriage, for ideological reasons.' He paused, picked up a stick and drew a star in the dusty gravel. ''Cause it's, like, patriarchy.'

'Carl hides people.'

'Carl needs some space, apparently. Meredith is preggers, right, and apparently she also needs space. They all need space so there's no space for his pet Kurds any more.'

'I would maybe consider it.' I didn't know that I would, until the words left my mouth.

Julian looked at me, astonished.

Ultimately, it boiled down to a very simple equation. For me, getting married was a charade, just another act in a farcical bourgeois system. A signature, a piece of paper, a bit of print. A grown woman dressed up as a virgin. A grown man dressed up as a penguin. Wearing a top hat, for Christ's sake.

I didn't believe in marriage as an institution. I didn't believe that the state had any role to play in a relationship between two people. I didn't believe in princessy wedding gowns, and I certainly didn't believe in top hats. And so, all it meant to me was two names on a piece of paper. A signature: that was nothing compared to a human life, now, was it?

Julian nodded respectfully.

'You would?'

'I'd need to meet this bloke, obviously. But as an option, yeah, I'd consider it.'

A few days later, I met up with Selim.

23

He looked frightened as he slipped in through the wooden door, and terribly embarrassed. We greeted each other with shy smiles and handshakes. Minutes after coming in, he asked if he could smoke; and his apologetic tone, his soft, sleepy eyes, his gentleness in everything he did immediately made me feel protective of him.

Someone from the legal aid group had helped fix the meeting, passing each of us the keys to a garden shed in an abandoned allotment. Selim turned up alone. In hindsight, that was a rarity: a private meeting, with no one lecturing or cajoling us. If I had known how precious such occasions would be, I would have made much better use of that time, asked more questions, listened more carefully.

The shed had been converted into a kind of miniature cottage, a doll's house really, with a rose-patterned sofa, a wicker chair and a table with a plastic kettle and a few mugs. I poured us some orange juice, we sat down and he told me his story.

'Julian mentioned something about posters for the PKK,' I interrupted him, trying to show I knew what this was all about.

He gave me a blank look.

'In Kurdistan?' I tried again. 'He said you put up posters and got caught by the Turks or something, and then your family sent you here.'

He shook his head.

'If they catch you with PKK posters, they execute you right away. I didn't have anything to do with the PKK. But yes, my uncles arranged for the *Schlepper* to take me to Germany. My father was in prison. The Turkish special units came to our house and beat me, the first time I was maybe eight. You know those boots, from the Army? They kicked me in the head with those. The skin came off. You can see the scars when I shave off my hair.'

The wicker chair creaked as Selim fingered his scalp.

I did not ask him any more questions.

Really, he told me very little about himself, and what he said was somewhat jumbled, contradictory in parts. Despite all this, I trusted him, and I wanted him to trust me.

The simple fact was, I had never before met a victim of that particular kind of violence. My grandparents had talked about the war the way most German grandparents do: my grandmothers had stories about swapping antique chairs for rashers of bacon; my one surviving grandfather about stealing a lump of butter as a prisoner of war.

If the violence my grandparents had suffered was very rarely talked about, the violence they had possibly perpetrated was even less of a topic. There were some neighbours in my village who had not spoken to each other for fifty years – rumour had it that one side denounced the other to the Gestapo over fraternising with the POWs. Who knew.

169

When the Americans arrived, the village priest placed their hands on the Bible and swore that there was not a single Nazi in the village, and that was that.

Selim laid bare enough of his personal suffering to convince me of his cause, but most of our conversation was not really about that. Maybe he did not want to be seen as begging for help. Instead, he mostly talked about his friends, his family back in Kurdistan, his political hopes.

'I didn't spend so much time in school, but you know, no one in Kurdistan does,' he said. 'If we ever get our own country, none of the ministers will be able to read the laws.'

We giggled.

His documents said he was almost eighteen. He was an *almost* away from being deported. He was, I discovered, uncertain as to when exactly he was born.

'How can they know how old you are when even you don't know how old you are?' I asked.

He shrugged.

'They know everything.'

24

'You're planning to do *what*?'

Unlike Selim, I knew my exact date of birth. I was two months away from my eighteenth birthday, and according to German law, I could not get married without my mother's consent.

I fumbled around in my pocket for more coins and jammed them into the payphone. Calls to eastern Germany were expensive, but I should probably have taken more time to present the facts. I tried again.

There was a brief silence, which is unusual for my mother.

'But he sounds like one of those . . . I don't want to be horrible, but he sounds a bit like, you know, those men who marry women for their passports.'

'Mum, that's exactly the point! This is a political act. I'm marrying him so he can stay. It's not a love marriage, it's political, you see,' I said helplessly, feeling the conversation slip out of my hands.

Remember when you were five years old and you tried to explain to your mother why the bedroom light had to stay on? That was the tone of the conversation. That was the level of mutual comprehension.

'The Kurds,' I said, watching the display and regretfully sacrificing another coin. 'This is about human rights, and solidarity. It's horrible. Don't you understand? If he goes back, he might die. If he goes back, he'll be arrested, and he might be killed.'

'The day I see my only daughter get married,' she said with unusual decisiveness, 'I want it to be the most beautiful day of her life. I want her to marry a lovely man who will take care of her, and I want it to be a lovely, happy, beautiful day.'

'But you watch the news, right? I was hoping you'd support my decision. I was sure you would.' I remembered my conversation with Selim. 'It's like with the POWs. Some sat back and did nothing, and others did their best to help, right?'

'Darling . . .' She sounded less certain now. 'The POWs, that was more than fifty years ago. And the Turks are not POWs, are they? They came here of their own free will.'

'I know,' I said helplessly. 'That was just an example. And he's Kurdish, not Turkish.'

'Well . . . I need to discuss it with Stefan.'

'It's OK, Mum, forget it,' I said. 'Sorry I brought it up.'

'Bad news. We can't get married now. They won't let me.'

And Selim, who went through life expecting at any time to be smacked in the face by another piece of bad news, just lowered his eyelids another millimetre. He was good at taking blows.

'But if you're still up for it,' I added, 'I'm still up for it. If you can hold on until I'm eighteen, until my birthday in a couple of months, that's the only way.'

'I'll try,' he said with a resigned air. 'Thank you, really. I'll ask my lawyer. You should meet him too, so he can give you some advice. The legal aid group will pay the fee, I think. Or I can pay the fee.'

'Oh he's with the legal aids? What's his name?'

'Habicht. You know him?'

I shook my head.

We met the lawyer the following day. I was surprised to recognise the crooked, damp room where only a few months before Carl, Meredith and the others had told us about the Great Plan. Dr Habicht sat hunched behind his paper-laden desk, peering out from behind thick glasses. He looked unwell in the way of someone who carefully grooms his misery, sadly blowing the steam off a mug of herbal tea. His ashen blond hair fled his temples towards a measly little ponytail, and he had knotted a purple scarf around his scrawny neck even though it was spring. In any case it might as well have been winter, as no light penetrated the cramped alleyway in which stood the wonky timber house.

'It's quite straightforward,' I said. 'I'll be eighteen in a couple of months' time and I'd be willing to do it then.'

He pulled out a crumpled hankie and discreetly coughed into it.

'Excuse me. I seem to have caught . . . you see, it's in the air.' He gestured towards the window. 'And every time something's in the air, I catch it. But yes, I think we should be able to arrange something.'

He pushed some forms towards me.

'You both need to fill in the paperwork, and there's certainly scope for an emergency appeal – no, please don't, sorry, but that pen . . . take this one, here's a better one, take this one. Just your name and so on for now. Harrumph.' The hankie came out again.

'It seems kind of damp in here, that's probably not doing much for your lungs,' I remarked, and for the first time since I entered the flat, he looked genuinely interested.

'You think so? That's an accurate observation. You see, it's in the walls . . .' He stood up and thoughtfully knocked his yellow knuckles against the stained plaster and gnarled beams.

I completed the forms.

'There's one really important thing,' I said.

'Mmm?' He was still examining the wall.

'Dr Habicht, there's one very important thing.'

'Should get someone in, rip out the whole bloody beam-and-plaster stuff, rip it all out!' His nostrils widened with a sudden passion. 'Out, out, *alles raus*. Fuck the heritage people, why should I be a slave to history? Rip it all out, seal it off with Saniplast, let them sue me and I'll sue right back, no animal would live like this! Get double glazing in while I'm at it. You were saying? Yes, that should be fine.'

'There's one really important thing. My mum must never find out about this.'

'Well don't tell her, for a start. If you don't tell her and no one else tells her, that should be fine.'

'What I'm saying is, it's really crucial. Just to be sure we're all talking about the same thing, OK? My mum really mustn't find out.'

'I'll check, but there's no reason why she should.'

He went back to his desk and made a little note on the

back of an envelope. Then he sighed, turned to his computer, with two bony fingers hammered out a few lines relating to Selim's emergency appeal, printed it out and passed me a copy. And with that we were dismissed.

'You should probably keep all the stuff about your appeal,' I said as I handed Selim the copy on our way out. By chance, I glanced at the letterhead. *Mauergassse* it said. With three s's. I felt uneasy, as if it was some strange warning sign.

'Look, Selim . . .'

'Mmm?'

'Oh, nothing.'

25

I woke up just as it got light. Through the car window I saw the porn cinemas, grimy pubs and banking towers of Frankfurt, that centre of high finance and low provincialism. Selim's cousin Şivan had picked us up at dawn, hoping to beat the long queue at the Turkish Consulate. He was steering the car with his left hand, his right hand playing with a green-and-yellow cardboard aroma tree that dangled from the rear-view mirror. The smell of fake pine and vanilla wafted towards me.

'Almost there,' Şivan said, looking at me in the mirror.

It was the first time he'd spoken to me. He had been helpful, borrowing a friend's car, getting up early to take us to Frankfurt, even swapping his tracksuit bottoms and tight T-shirt for jeans and a blue shirt.

We drove past tired prostitutes in Puffa jackets and perky bankers with their ties slung over their shoulders. Selim was silent. I could see him nervously scratching the back of his neck. He had told me that he hated going to the Turkish Consulate, but there was no way around it. His passport was Turkish, after all, and we needed a certificate showing he was not already married in Turkey.

Şivan dropped us off in front of the Consulate and drove on to find a parking space. I grinned at Selim in what I hoped was a vaguely optimistic way. He sighed.

Inside, the corridors were crammed with matronly women in headscarves and men in woollen jumpers. The women sat on metal chairs, solid and proprietary as if the corridor were their living room. The men leaned against the wall or stood next to the women, feet apart, hands in pockets, looking thoroughly in control until a door opened somewhere and they spun round, suddenly all hopeful and alert, and then the door closed again and they realised it wasn't their turn and settled back into waiting.

We found a single free seat and took turns sitting down. I was the only green-haired woman in the corridor, and I could feel everyone looking at me out of the corner of their eyes. To distract myself, I asked Selim to show me his passport. After everything he'd told me about his pride in all things Kurdish, it was odd to see his picture in the booklet with Turkey's golden crescent and star on the cover. I looked at his picture and personal details, stopping at the date of birth.

'Hey,' I said, pointing at the open page. 'I'm so sorry, I totally forgot!'

'What?'

'Happy birthday!' I was about to hug him, then glanced at the women around us and squeezed his arm instead, handing him his open passport. 'It was yesterday, look.'

He shut it and slipped it back into his pocket, not even glancing at it.

'Oh, don't worry, it doesn't matter now,' he said as if to

reassure me. 'I've got an emergency permit so I can stay for the wedding and then I will get a longer permit. You know, the one we talked about, the permit for three years.'

I shook my head, yawning a little because I was so tired from getting up early.

'No, I don't mean that, I mean it's your birthday . . . I just thought you'd have a party or something. Eighteen, that's pretty big.'

'Hmm.' Selim yawned too. 'But it's not really my birthday. It's only a date, made up, you know? And it's not a nice date. For such a long time, it only made me worry.'

Şivan joined us, his shaved head and single earring looking oddly out of place between the flowery headscarves and woollen jumpers. He leaned against the wall and started fiddling with a photo calendar of the Swiss Alps until a passing official told him to stop it.

A man emerged from behind a chipped wooden door, barked something at Selim, then disappeared again.

'What was that about?' I asked.

Selim shrugged.

'It's always a bit difficult here.'

'Why, because it's so crowded?'

The woman next to us was now eyeing me with open curiosity.

Selim looked embarrassed.

'No . . . they just always treat us badly, you know, as Kurds.'

The woman frowned, but I could not tell whether she had understood him.

And then it was our turn. The Turkish bureaucrat behind the desk grunted a barrage of questions in Turkish, asked

Selim to write his name here, here and here. And I simply sat there. The official ignored me, naturally, as one would ignore a chair or a table.

I was taken aback when he suddenly turned to me and drily asked in flawless German: 'So you want to marry him?'

Surprised, I nodded.

He studied me with sudden interest: another dumb girl taken in by a shrewd Kurd.

And with an expression not unlike sympathy he insisted: 'He asked you to marry him and you said yes?'

Again, I nodded. I knew what he was thinking: *The Kurd has duped her, has romanced her and promised her love, and the provincial little tart fell for it and doesn't realise all he wants is her passport.*

He mumbled an aside to a young clerk at the back of the room. I felt Selim stiffen, but he pretended not to have heard the remark, the insult.

And I felt a rush of anger, an urge to shout at the official, *No, you're the stupid one, you're the one who doesn't get it, I know exactly what I'm getting into.*

Talking back was so easy. Protesting was so easy. Shutting your mouth, that was very hard, even though you'd think it would be the natural position of a mouth at rest. If the official had doubted my sincerity, my good intentions, that I could have taken. Appearing insincere and sinister before a bureaucrat, that would not have affected me. I would even have quite enjoyed it. But being studied with that kind of pity laced with disdain, or disdain laced with pity, being marked as stupid and malleable, *that* hurt my pride in a way I had never before considered possible. In fact, I had never

179

before considered the importance of pride, or honour, had never realised they meant so much to me.

'You are young,' the bureaucrat said, impatient now. 'You may want to think about it. Make sure you really want to do this. Do you really want to do this? It's an important decision.' His impatience erased the hint of kindness he had shown a second before, and he now regarded me with tired contempt.

'Yes,' I said. 'I want to marry him.'

26

French town halls tended to resemble miniature chateaux, all charming turrets and conical roofs. The German town hall where Selim and I were married looked more like a fortress, built for sturdiness rather than beauty. At its inauguration in 1513, hundreds of merchants, peasants, fishwives and general medieval riff-raff pushed into the square to gape at what was considered then an unrivalled work of thick-walled durability. The local baron, notorious for his hot-headed outbursts, fuelled the crowd with free beer provided by a nearby convent. When he tired of their sweaty revelry he sent in his troops to clear the square. A few dozen beggars and children were killed in the resulting crush, and the town hall would henceforth be known as Blood House.

I turned up on my bike, pedalling furiously up the steep cobbled slope to Blood House. Feeling that I should make an effort, but at the same time not wanting to overdress as I had to go back to school after the wedding, I had picked a dark-blue skirt, a black top and my only pair of tights without any holes or ladders. I locked my bike to a lamp post. Selim came towards me, looking very relieved. Flanked by Flo's family, Julian and the legal aid lot, we entered Blood House.

The registrar was a friend of Dr Habicht's and knew everything, which meant we could skip the amateur acting; I did not need to shed fake tears of joy or display any particular exuberance. We didn't even bother booking the ceremonial wedding hall, using the registrar's office instead. Still, I remember feeling extremely nervous and strangely ashamed.

Looking back now, I believe that right up until the signature Selim thought I was going to pull out.

He signed with difficulty. I picked up the pen and hesitated. And then, in a flash, with sudden, lucid, powerful clarity, I realised the last thing I wanted to do was to write my name on the document before me. This was a ludicrous mission. We had no idea what we were doing, I did not trust the people advising us, and once I signed this I would be tied to someone I hardly knew. For better or worse, and quite possibly for worse, this one signature would change my life, and change it irreversibly. I would never be able to unsign this piece of paper. Even if the marriage itself was eventually dissolved, it would not erase my act of marrying Selim, no more than felling a tree would mean ungrowing it.

And as I felt the strange, sharp pain of those thoughts, I signed my name next to Selim's.

We stood up and walked out of the registrar's office.

The people from the legal aid group filmed us with a video camera so that we'd have a proper wedding video if the officials came to check on us.

'And it's really really important to make this really credible, right,' Meredith said, chucking a handful of rice at me.

They gathered around us, women with henna-red hair

and men with greasy ponytails. Carl had sent his excuses. I had not spoken to him since the riot.

Julian was my witness. Flo was Selim's witness. Flo's parents looked surprised when they saw me. I think they had expected someone older. The legals threw rice at us and we put on big grins and they filmed everything. Then we went to a café for breakfast, but I had to rush off to school. In any case, I did not feel like celebrating.

'You're off? Surely not! If this were a Kurdish wedding, we would be celebrating for three days!' Flo's father said. He was sitting next to me and nudged me in a jovial way. 'At least eat something – what can I get you?'

But this wasn't a normal Kurdish wedding, and I did not feel like eating. I'd had enough. I slipped away, unlocked my bike, swung myself onto the saddle and pedalled to school, just in time for my lesson.

About a century after the Blood House was inaugurated, builders extending the vaults discovered a cavity where the jealous baron had walled up his mistress. Her remains were buried in a mass grave outside the cemetery, along with the local witches.

27

So that was that. We got married in 1997. It was supposed to last for three years. In the end, it lasted for seven.

The seven years quite neatly straddled a date that changed so much for so many of us; certainly for the Kurds living in Germany: 2001, the year when a group of men, several of whom had lived and studied in Germany, hijacked planes and flew two of them into the World Trade Center. Those years saw a lot of trouble. For now, my point is this: considering that it lasted seven years, it is surprising that I know so little about the Kurds.

In the early days of our marriage, I was still eager to ask, eager to learn.

'*Jin, jiyan, azadî*,' Selim recited. 'It means woman, life, freedom. They shout it at the demonstrations, you may have heard?'

A couple of weeks had passed since our wedding, and we were having our first date as a married couple, sitting on low wooden stools in the kitchen. Well, it wasn't exactly a date. Selim had called me a few times after the ceremony, but I had been in shock and unable to meet up, spooked by visions of police interrogations and fraud convictions. Finally, I agreed to see him.

'*Jin, jiyan, azadî*,' I repeated. 'I should learn Kurdish, huh? Though I'm having trouble just remembering the name of your nearest town.'

'Cizre,' he said quickly.

'Only joking, of course I remember it. Cizre. With a soft C, like Jizre. See how I remember.'

'Yes, very good,' he said and smiled. 'If you want to learn, I can teach you. *Evar bash*, that's goodnight. *Roj bash*, good morning.'

'*Roj bash*,' I repeated. 'Let's leave it at that for now.'

He had suggested that we cook something together, and I had agreed, too embarrassed to tell him I hardly knew how to scramble an egg.

Now we were sitting in the kitchen. To buy time, I asked him about his favourite Kurdish food.

'Lentil soup,' he cried before I'd even finished the question. He was in high spirits in those early honeymoon days.

'Well, let's make that then,' I said, relieved. 'I've never had it, but you could show me how to make it.'

He shook his head.

'I don't know how to make it either. What's your favourite?'

'Hmm, don't know. Pizza, maybe.'

He brightened up.

'We could make bread! Have you ever had Kurdish bread?'

I hadn't.

He fetched a pen and notepad, very excited now, and drew a kind of beehive with a round hole near the top.

'That's the oven,' he explained, jabbing the pen at the beehive. 'You make a fire at the bottom, then you take the dough

185

and slap it on the walls inside. When it's cooked, you take it out.'

'Doesn't the bread fall into the fire?' I asked.

'Not when my mother makes it,' he said. 'It's the most delicious bread I've ever tasted. If you get a loaf while it's still warm, you're the luckiest person in the world. Then you bite the crust, and the inside is all warm and fluffy. We can have it with a yogurt drink. And cheese. And tomatoes and cucumber.'

'Well, we can't,' I said. 'We don't have a Kurdish oven.'

He looked crestfallen, as if this minor detail had escaped him, and I wished I had kept my mouth shut. He frowned and studied his drawing, eventually sketching in a pile of firewood with his pen as if that would change anything. I stood up and walked around the kitchen, inspecting the gas oven, the toaster. Selim followed me, notepad in hand.

'I guess we could just bake it in this oven. The walls are quite smooth,' I said doubtfully.

Selim nodded with enthusiasm.

I closed the oven door.

'Do you know what goes into the dough?'

'Just flour and water, I think,' he said. 'And yogurt. And a little oil, maybe. Maybe even salt. Then the dough has to rise, I think, before you shape it into loaves. There are lots of different kinds, some are huge and very thin, others are ring-shaped, others . . .' His voice trailed off. 'But this one is the best.'

I was about to ask whether he had actually ever made bread, but stopped myself.

'Sounds good,' I said.

I watched Selim pour a mound of flour onto a wooden

board, add water, yogurt and oil and knead it all into a ball. He was dextrous, working the dough with his long, thin fingers, as if he had done this many times before; only the surprised look on his face, he astonished at his own skill, revealed that this was in fact a first.

I fiddled with the oven, cranking up the heat, sticking little bits of dough to the inside walls. They dried into solid white balls. I raised the temperature another notch.

Selim portioned out dough balls that we squashed and stretched into flat loaves. We slapped them on the oven walls. Miraculously, they stuck, which was heartening.

'It should be really quick,' he said, surveying the neat row of loaves, hanging there like gravity-defying cowpats. He straightened up, then took another peek, excited by his experiment.

I was less confident in the result.

'What do you mean by quick – seconds? Hours?'

'Hmm.' He opened the oven door and poked a pale loaf. 'Seconds, maybe, in the real oven. I mean, they should be done about now.'

I wandered over to the fridge, a loudly humming model with rust stains. It contained a wilted bunch of radishes, three cans of beer, a bag of tomatoes and a tub of yogurt. Flo's family were away on holiday, leaving Flo and Selim to look after themselves.

'Would you like a beer?' I cracked open a can for myself. 'Is that what you'd have with it at home? Beer?'

'No . . . no alcohol usually, just the yogurt drink. *Ayran*. We'll make that later.' He looked a bit exhausted. 'OK, I will have a beer. But the bread will be ready. It takes seconds.'

'Maybe in Kurdistan. This bread will take hours.'

We went out onto the tiled balcony, sat down on plastic chairs and toasted with our beer cans. I shook traces of flour from my baggy purple T-shirt. When I had finished my first beer, Selim lit a cigarette and used the empty can as an ashtray. We split the third can.

The front door slammed shut; it was Flo, who poked his head out, gave us a quick little wave and disappeared again. I heard the door open and shut several times, heard people talking in the living room, but Selim did not seem interested in checking who was hanging out in the flat. I thought about asking him who these visitors were, but did not want to seem rude.

Eventually, the kitchen door opened and Şivan came out, looking a bit surly as usual.

He shook Selim's hand in the twisty, abrupt way that boys in Neustadt considered cool, then smiled at me with surprising affection. They exchanged a few words in Kurdish.

'My sister will join us in a bit,' Selim said to me, translating.

'You have a sister? Here?'

'She's his older sister. Lives in Bonn,' Şivan said, took a packet of Marlboro Lights from his back pocket and handed it round.

He tried to perch on the armrest of one of the plastic chairs, still assessing whether it was worth joining us and sitting down properly. The chair tipped and he shifted his weight to his feet in an awkward rocking motion, letting the chair topple over with a dull clatter.

Selim got up and they rearranged the chairs together, with

Şivan somehow pretending that this had been his plan all along.

'She came here a couple of years ago, with the *Schlepper*,' Selim said over his shoulder. 'She has four children. My younger sister is still . . . she's over there.'

'Well, it must be great to have at least one sister here.'

'She's your family now, too!' Selim cried in a happy outburst. 'We all are. We should have a big family reunion, I could come to your house for . . . what's it called . . . Christmas!'

'Well, my mum doesn't even know about all this,' I said quickly, waving my cigarette towards him, Şivan, the geraniums. 'It's a secret, right?'

'Yes, yes, of course,' he said. 'But you will like my sister.'

Selim had an older sister: that was the first of many tiny pieces of information that gradually changed my view of him. Originally, I had seen him as a bit of a lost cub, abandoned and alone; then, slowly, it emerged that there were in fact people around him, there were uncles, cousins, friends, a sister, nephews and nieces even; and yet, this big, loud, interfering crowd was ultimately unable to help him, and in the end, when it really mattered, he came full circle and was alone again.

'I don't see her often. Travel to Bonn is expensive, and I can't move there,' he explained.

We were all sitting now, like guests at a polite tea party.

'Well, now that we're married you can,' I said, feeling rather pleased.

He shook his head.

'I don't have a permanent residency permit, just one that I have to renew every three years. I have to stay here in

Neustadt, to prove that you and I are really married, that we are together. If I move to Bonn without you, the immigration people will say our marriage is fake.'

'OK, but one day you will.'

'Yes. One day.'

Şivan had grown bored with the conversation and was plucking the leaves off a tired geranium. With the other hand, he flicked his cigarette over the railing.

'Hey!' I grabbed his arm.

'What?'

'You can't do that! What if it hits someone down in the street?'

Şivan looked intrigued and leaned over the railing.

'No one there,' he drawled with an air of disappointment.

I sniffed. And sniffed again. There was the definite smell of something burning.

'That's your bloody cigarette. It probably hit someone's laundry.'

We stretched over the geraniums, trying to spot any signs of a smouldering clothes-line. Nothing.

'It's down there, definitely, you can smell it too, right?'

Selim, who had been observing us from the comfort of his plastic chair, suddenly jumped up and raced into the kitchen.

The bread!

The flat loaves had turned a shiny black, and smoke filled the kitchen. We banged shut the door to the living room and ineffectually flapped our hands at the smoke. The door swung open seconds later and a woman came into the kitchen, exclaiming something in Kurdish. In a series of swift, efficient gestures, she turned off the oven, opened the

190

kitchen window, grabbed a towel and used it to fan the room, expelling the smoke as if it were an unruly child.

'My sister,' Selim declared with admiration.

She hugged him and beamed at me, then went back to fanning the kitchen, shooing us into the living room, and there we sat, waiting for her to master the situation. She was one of those energetic women with a low centre of gravity, as confident as Selim was jittery. Şivan, who for once looked rather intimidated, left the flat shortly after she arrived.

Plastic tubs heavy with stews and pickles made their way from her bulging bags into the kitchen. She spoke no German and Selim was not a great interpreter, and so we simply smiled at each other across bowls of minty yogurt soup, plates of stewed red peppers, aubergines, tomatoes and lamb, and finally a mound of deliciously honey-sticky baklava, piled high on a metal platter. I don't think she even knew I was Selim's wife.

'She is asking if you don't like baklava. Maybe they're too sweet for you?' Selim said at one point.

'No, I love them, they're amazing,' I protested, popping a third pistachio-and-pastry concoction into my mouth. I tried to smile in a particularly approving way as I chewed it and almost did a thumbs-up; I must have looked insane.

Selim said something to her, and she laughed and reached across to squeeze my hand.

I felt like a dancing monkey, then thought, oh well, I might as well perform some more dancing-monkey tricks, and so I grinned and said: *Evar bash*!

She stared at me, then giggled.

'*Evar bash*!'

191

28

Unlikely as it sounds, it was David, Philippe's archaeologist friend with his dragon-shaped door knockers in Cizre, who prompted me to discover more about the Kurds, beyond *evar bash* and flat bread. Because really that was all I had gleaned from my years of marriage; that and the strange story of Aynur, Selim's wildly wayward little sister. At some point, it sort of petered out, my curiosity, maybe because I felt frightened, stuck knee-deep in Selim's life, sinking further and further into this morass of politics and traditions I did not understand.

I saw David again a while after Anna's birthday party. It was Saturday morning and the phone rang: Anna announced she would pick me up to go shopping.

'But I don't like shopping.'

'I've noticed.'

'What's that supposed to mean? I've just had a really disturbing dream about dead people filling up the train station.'

'Can't wait to hear all about it. Let's get you some clothes.'

Like most younger siblings, I instinctively tended to choose friends who continued my brother's gentle patronising, who made my decisions for me. The one advantage was that, frankly, other people's decisions were often less

192

disastrous than my own. And so I was not entirely surprised when Anna led me into a courtyard café in the Marais after our unsuccessful attempt at joint shopping (she had two bags dangling from each arm; I, none) to see David, who just happened to be sitting at a corner table, wearing a greyish striped T-shirt and beige combat trousers.

Anna ignored my annoyed sigh and pulled me over to his table. To be fair, he looked surprised to see us.

'I've actually got to go and meet Philippe, but why don't you two go ahead and have lunch,' Anna said quickly.

'I'd really love to but I've got something on as well,' I said, then backed away from my own bluntness. 'Actually, lunch would be great.'

Anna let herself be persuaded into staying. It turned out to be quite fun, with David talking about Syriac-Christian monasteries and Anna talking about covering the latest dairy farmers' protests. He was much less attention-seeking in a small group, listened carefully when I told him about my mother's adventures in archaeology, and I in turn found myself asking him more questions than I had intended. He spoke about practising his Aramaic with the last three monks at an ancient monastery on the Turkish–Syrian border, about crossing into northern Iraq with the help of some Kurdish builders.

'What I want to do on my next trip is travel from Turkey to Kurdish Iraq, and then all the way down to Baggers,' he said, then shot Anna a guilty glance. 'Sorry. Baghdad.'

'*Baggers*!' she snorted. 'I hate the way Brits abbreviate everything. Honkers and Shanghers, that's the worst. Shanghers! It's like, dude, it has a name and it's *Shanghai*.'

She wandered off to look at the cakes by the counter.

David moved his chair a bit closer.

'So how's your Kurdish bride?' he asked, looking genuinely interested.

I smiled.

'I shouldn't have brought it up at that party. So unprofessional, right? Sometimes I still feel I'm getting used to being a civil servant, the responsibility and privacy issues and all that.'

'I don't think anyone else at the table heard you. I'm just curious because I've got my own Kurdish connection.'

'Have you?' I put down my glass, taken aback. What an unlikely potential ally.

'Well, the research.'

'Oh. Of course.'

'Though I won't be heading back there any time soon after all. We've lost our funding.' He waved off my expressions of sympathy. 'It happens. Now it's back to paperwork and writing applications for grants.'

'Hmm. Paperwork.' I gave an understanding sigh.

And then I told him about the manual. After all, there was nothing confidential about the booklet; it had been handed out to thousands of officials and charity workers.

'I guess it's meant to protect us from making a wrong judgement,' I said. 'Though my problem is, I don't want to pass any judgement, wrong or right. I'm not that kind of person.'

'It sounds bizarre.' He looked at my bag. 'You don't happen to have it on you? I'd love to see it.'

I hesitated, then opened my bag and handed him the

194

booklet with its barbed-wire wedding ring on the front. He crossed one leg over the other, resting his ankle on the other knee, and propped up the booklet with his thigh. As he flicked through the pages, he looked like a backpacker relaxing on the terrace of some guesthouse, planning the next route.

'I love where it says at the top of the page, *If you have a suspicion, you must stop the ceremony*, and at the bottom, *You must avoid any acts of cultural prejudice that could harm or embarrass innocent couples; be sure to act with extreme sensitivity at all times.*'

'Exactly!' I cried. 'Exactly. That sums it all up. It's mad. What am I supposed to do?'

'Well, if you need some background, cultural context, anything that would help you with your case, just let me know. I've got lots of friends from that area, from southern Turkey and northern Iraq, you know, most of them are Kurdish.'

'Thanks,' I murmured, wondering whether he was about to offer some kind of private cultural tutorial, and whether that would be a bad thing. 'In fact, you know what, that would be great.' I tucked the booklet back between my folders.

He brightened up and pulled out a big lined notebook from his own leather bag just as Anna came back with a *tarte aux pommes*, which she had taken suspiciously long to order. Then he furiously scribbled down a long list of titles and authors, tore out the page and passed it to me with a smile.

'Right, this might give you a better idea. You'll find them in the Kurdish library.' He paused, bent over the table and scrawled an address across the top of the paper.

'Thanks,' I repeated, inwardly cringing because I had mis-interpreted his helpfulness.

He nodded with satisfaction, put the cap on his pen, carefully shut the notebook, packed it all into his bag, leaned back with a smile and ordered a coffee.

Not one to give up easily, Anna urged us both to come over for dinner the following week. She insisted on walking to the Métro with me, even though her stop was in the opposite direction.

'He's definitely interested, but you've got to do your bit as well,' she pleaded when we reached the entrance of the Métro. 'Don't let me down here, OK? And what's with that appointment, or did you just make that up?'

'One of those boring work things,' I replied vaguely.

Between a Chinese restaurant and a cheap clothes shop, I located the big brown door where I pressed the buzzer for the Institute of Oriental Studies. I took the lift up to a reception area where a young woman sat up expectantly behind her computer. The walls were lined with photos of women with blue stars and moons and *ghazals* tattooed on their faces.

'I'm looking for books on Kurdish marriage,' I explained. 'And Kurdish women in general, their role in society, for a research project.'

'The library is on the next floor,' she replied, pointing back towards the lift. 'But the librarian is on holiday, so we've got a volunteer helping out.'

The volunteer sat in a wooden cubicle with a little work-top. From the reading room, I could only see the henna-red top of her head, bowed over a book, and the wires leading

196

out of her ears and into her thickly knitted scarf. I knocked several times on the wall of the cubicle, and finally she looked up. It was Azad's social worker, Carole.

She didn't exactly brighten up at seeing me. Instead, she leaned back and folded her arms. I motioned to her to take out her earphones.

'It's switched off. Well, I'm glad you're finally responding to my calls,' she said with studied coldness, leaving on the earphones.

'It's been pretty manic at the town hall, but I'm glad I caught you here, I've been looking for you,' I ad-libbed. 'I thought you could help me find some books.'

I had prepared a complicated story about fictional research projects but that was now of little use.

However, Carole seemed to approve of my interest.

'I wish more public servants would do that, expand their horizons.' She stretched her arms above her head, and I half worried, half hoped the scarf and wires might become tangled in her ornate earrings. 'Though you can't read up on everything unless you've got years. I did almost an entire degree in Kurdology and I'm still nowhere near . . . and if this is about Azad—'

'No, no, it's more general, you know, part of, er, learning about the communities in the neighbourhood.'

'OK, but you'll still have to pick an area, I mean, we've got Turkey, Syria, Iran, Iraq . . . which part of Kurdistan do you want?'

'Cizre,' I said, automatically naming the only Kurdish town I knew, and whose name I had memorised so carefully a long time ago.

She gave a quick nod of recognition.

'You might as well start with the legend then,' she commanded, evidently pleased with the role reversal: I the pleading visitor, she the one in charge. 'Since you deal with couples. And it might un-distort your view of Kurdish relationships and romance. It's not all coercion, you know.'

'Yes, yes,' I hastily agreed, though I had winced at *un-distort*. Well, Carole was Carole.

As far as Kurdish towns went, Cizre was actually fairly well known. Archaeologists liked the mosque; tourists liked the tombs of Mem and Zin, a sort of Kurdish Romeo and Juliet. Their story formed the basis of the most famous Kurdish epic, *Mem û Zin*, by a seventeenth-century poet called Ehmedê Xanî.

According to the legend, one New Year's Day the Emir's younger sisters, Zin and Siti, dressed up as men to explore the streets of Cizre and check out potential suitors. They bumped into Mem, a young scribe, and his friend Tajin, who in turn were disguised as girls. Zin and Mem fell in love, a starlit encounter in a secret garden ensued, and their friends devised an elaborate scheme to allow the two to marry. But the traitor Bakr conspired against them. Mem was thrown into jail and wasted away; after his death, Zin lay across his tomb, where she died of heartbreak.

It was there, in that little reading room not far from the Gare du Nord, to the faint sound of Carole playing bellydancing music on her iPod, that I gradually coloured in some of the blanks on my mental map of Kurdistan.

198

29

In the shadow of Mount Ararat, where a trickle of water formed the source of the all-conquering Euphrates and Tigris Rivers, there lived a cluster of tribes whose arcane dialect, harsh customs and surprisingly joyful folklore had intrigued generations of writers and travellers.

For there is a Kurdish nation, although there has never been a Kurdish state, writes Jacques Tournesol, a Frenchman, in the foreword to *The Kurds*, a seminal tome on Kurdish culture published in 1932. *Seminal* not so much because of its insight or intellectual force, but because there were no competitors at the time. Théophile Leveque, a rival French anthropologist, obsessed with beating Tournesol to the presses, was working feverishly on the only other ethnography of the Kurds; but poor Leveque contracted syphilis during a stay in Constantinople in 1929, just before the city's name was changed to Istanbul, and had to abandon the manuscript and relocate to a sanatorium in Switzerland, where, bitter, lonely and noseless, he watched Tournesol's publishing success from afar as the disease gnawed away at his features.

Leveque was bewitched by the spiritual life of the Kurds, by the way their ancient Yezidi religion merged with newer

Islamic beliefs, muddying the literal Quranic instructions and infusing them with an earthier, more sensual, more mystical view of God and his creatures. Persian-influenced poems and songs, peacock angels, holy fires and bloody codes of honour: that was how Leveque saw Kurdish culture. But because of Leveque's syphilis-infested dalliance in Constantinople, no one was to discover his take on Kurdistan, and readers had to make do with Tournesol.

Tournesol did not dwell on Persian dialects and peacock angels. He was a man of science, with a fondness for psychoanalysis. As a student, he once travelled all the way to Vienna in the hope of meeting Freud. He spent an hour waiting outside Freud's rooms before a secretary told him the great man was not in town. A persistent type, Tournesol pretended to leave while actually hiding in an adjacent room. And sure enough, ten minutes later, his eye on the keyhole, he spied someone bearded scurrying down the corridor. Hurt, Tournesol left Vienna that same night. Despite the slight, he could not bring himself to renounce psychoanalysis.

Never mind; now Tournesol himself was almost famous, only one ethnography away from academic glory. In his draughty little flat in Paris, he adjusted his fez (a souvenir brought back from his journeys through the Orient), threw another log onto the fire, and with a sigh picked up his pen. Ten pages before lunch, that was his target.

They pass the winter in the valley. Months of waiting, it seems, months of baking bread, sipping tea and telling folk tales; but really, underneath the hibernating calm, one can detect the most frantic and nervous activity: cloaks and bags are mended,

200

lambs and babies are kept warm and fed with milk, so that the young ones grow quickly, become strong and healthy, and, when the spring comes, are prepared for the strenuous exodus into the mountains.

When the snow melted and the first green shoots emerged, the Kurdish tribe began to stir.

At dawn, the people packed their belongings.

Women strapped pots, pipes, plates and babies onto their backs. The heavier bags, tents, rugs, sacks of grain were loaded onto bony mares that had been shivering in cold stables all winter. After the long, dark months in the valley, the mares staggered under the new weight and awkwardly found their balance on worn legs and frayed hooves. At the end of the summer, they would make a sinewy stew.

Here and there a sick sheep was tied on top of the baggage like a misshapen hump, bleating pitifully.

The men rubbed their thick moustaches and patted the knives and pistols on their hips. Someone shouted an order and a handful of boys rushed to fetch the last bags.

Among the roughly woven cloths, the older women's smoke-cured faces, the men's threadbare waistcoats, the animals' dull and dusty fur, there was a splash of bright colour: the Agha's elaborately painted trunk. In it were his best clothes, his tea set, his precious rugs, his ornate daggers.

'And,' the little boys, drawn to the trunk like magpies, whispered, 'dried fruit, halva, magic and lots of dangerous stuff. And if you open the trunk you'll die.'

'No you won't, it's just a trunk.'

'Yes, you'll die.'

201

'No you won't.'

'Why don't you open it then?'

'Hush, the Agha!'

The Agha strode towards his trunk, placed his hand firmly on the lid to check it was well fastened, was satisfied, nodded to his men, and with much shuffling, rattling, clinking, rustling, bleating and clattering, the people set off into the mountains.

Tournesol, excited by the chaos around him, busily observing and taking notes, suddenly realised he had forgotten his hairnet and made a red-faced dash back into one of the deserted huts to retrieve it.

The first day was always the messiest.

Like a new flock, the group was finding its rhythm. One of the younger women stumbled and the baby almost slipped off her back. A fat-tailed sheep fell into a ravine, was caught by a protruding root, was hoisted back up by a gang of young men.

Tournesol, panting, found it hard to keep up.

That night, the Kurds erected their black tents on the mountainside, feasted on cheese, and marked the first day of summer.

From afar, Tournesol wrote shakily, *their one-night settlement looks like a military camp.*

In the morning, before dawn, the tents were already rolled up and the tribe was on the move again. The handwriting in Tournesol's notebook, so neat and tidy in his first entries in Constantinople, flattened into a collection of hasty, exhausted scrawls that would later, back in Paris, frustrate him with their illegibility.

The second day passed more smoothly and in the early

afternoon they reached the sheltered ravine where they would pitch their tents. Here, it might have been worth taking a closer look at the women of the tribe. Tournesol, for one, did; though his adventures in the jealous Orient had taught him to go about it with caution. He shrewdly pretended to have a headache, was brought to an elderly woman who looked at him with suspicion, then smiled and mashed up some herbs in a mortar. While she was at work with her pestle, he observed the commotion around her.

The women had untied the broad belts that held their babies and were inspecting the blisters on their callused feet: not yet callused enough.

In the preceding weeks, travelling through Kurdish villages on the plains, Tournesol had already gathered enough material to write confidently in Chapter One: *The Kurds are among the most liberal Muslims with regard to the treatment of women. The women load and unload the animals; they feed the lambs and milk the sheep; they collect firewood and milk thistles; they cook and bake, retrieving hot loaves from ovens with their bare hands, all the while carrying their babies on their backs.*

Tournesol got up, stretched, leafed through his notes. Anything he'd forgotten? Ah, yes, they also made cheese. He swiftly added that to the list.

But, he continued, *they are also skilled horse riders and do not fear even the toughest climbs.*

Here he pushed away his manuscript, closed his eyes and thought of the girl. He had to stop thinking about the girl, otherwise he would never finish the book. And finish this book he must: his publisher had taken to sauntering in

203

unannounced, the meagre advance was disappearing fast, and somewhere out there another Leveque was surely penning a rival ethnography. Meanwhile, that *connard* Posniawski's book about the sexual lives of savages was selling like silk corsets at an Arabian bazaar.

Tournesol sighed. He should have chosen a less conservative research subject for his major oeuvre: the body of work that would make him known to future generations of anthropologists, and, more importantly, to the book-buying public. It was the 1930s, after all. The salons of Paris wanted scandal and exoticism, shocking tales from the harem, eunuchs cavorting with concubines; and all Tournesol could write about was Kurdish shepherding.

The girl. She was fifteen, sixteen maybe. It was dawn, that morning of the exodus, when the tribe was packing for the mountains. Tournesol emerged from the hut, shaking fleas from his hairnet. He looked up and saw a girl swing herself onto a dusty horse, the only horse that was not yet laden with bags and rugs, and as the women called over and told her to help, she cantered up the mountainside, laughing.

In his dimly lit study, Tournesol opened his eyes, sighed and thoughtfully tugged at his greying hair. Oh, he admitted it, she was thirteen at the most, but they did grow up fast. Her hair was wrapped in a scarf, but her face, like that of the other women, was uncovered. In the milky light of dawn, her laughter – her face . . . Oh stop it, Tournesol, he told himself and picked up his pen.

They grow very strong through their work, though they quickly lose their feminine charms, except for the Agha's wives, who lead a more leisurely life and conserve their beauty.

He spent the rest of that week trying to catch another glimpse of the girl. He was cautious, talking to the men while discreetly eyeing the women filling water-sacks and loading mares. He was surprised when one day one of the women put down her pail and told him she had been listening to his comments and frankly, she had never heard such nonsense.

The women do not veil their faces; they mix with men and always have a word to say in communal debate, he had scribbled in his notebook that night. *There are numerous reports of men being received and talked to by wives when their husbands are away, unlike Turkish or Persian women. Before marriage, there is an important period of courtship.*

The next day, halfway up the hillside, the girl reined in the horse and turned around to face him. She caught him standing there and staring at her, and for all he knew his mouth hung open. She laughed, kicked the horse and galloped on.

They marry very young. Everyone marries; there are no spinsters or confirmed bachelors. Marriage is central. This is one of the reasons why prostitution is unknown among the Kurds. If they talk about it, they have to use Turkish words.

Several weeks passed before Tournesol dared to raise the subject. He was out with some of the younger shepherds. A boisterous and confident bunch: he amused them with his inept climbing and awkward downhill stumble-sliding. Their boyish giggles encouraged him to broach this delicate topic.

At first, they had no idea what he was talking about.

'Women who . . . are paid?'

'Well, yes. You understand, loose women, you know the

205

sort. You pay and they, well, they give you a good time, don't they?'

The youngsters looked about uncomfortably, sharply inhaling through their teeth. The eldest, a broad-backed hulk who could sling a sheep over each shoulder, glowered in a way that made Tournesol think hard and fast about what exactly he had said that they found so upsetting.

Fortunately, it came to him quickly.

'Not here, of course! Sorry! *Bibûre*! I'm not talking about the women here!' he cried, madly waving his hands in denial.

This only seemed to upset them more.

'Which women are you talking about then?' the hulk grunted. 'There are no other women here. There are only our women.'

'Oh, women, you know, in general. In other places! Elsewhere! You must have heard of women like that – not here – far away—'

'In Constantinople.' The boy who spoke up looked barely twelve.

Tournesol nodded at him gratefully, as to a life-saving witness. *See, here, I am not a dirty old man offering to buy your womenfolk; I am a traveller faithfully reporting the bare facts from the world out here.* He nodded again encouragingly.

The boy looked down at the yellow grass.

'My uncle told me about them once. Went to Constantinople. Saw them. Whores.'

The others relaxed into a less menacing posture. Ah, yes. Whores. They had heard about them. Someone cracked a dirty joke that Tournesol did not quite understand, even

206

though he prided himself on his Kurdish. He laughed along anyway.

When they rejoined the rest of the tribe, the boys were back in their mood of boisterous camaraderie. But after that, Tournesol resumed his more cautious attitude. He did not dare ask after the girl on horseback. The way she laughed at him . . .

Only on his very last day with the tribe did he summon up the courage to wonder openly where some of the women had gone. Had they set off on a separate expedition?

'I noticed that some of them . . . disappeared,' he said to the hulk.

The hulk smiled.

'My sister, you mean? I saw you staring at her. I didn't know you or I would have warned you. When you were away, that week when you went hunting with my cousin, remember the big wedding that you missed?'

'Well, I can't say I remember it, to be accurate, since I was away, as you say. But yes, I do remember coming back and being told there had been, as you say . . .'

'My sister. The Agha made her his wife. One of his wives.'

'Ah.'

The hulk patted his back.

Tournesol felt a sharp disappointment; how surprising that the loss of something he had never possessed should be so painful.

He consoled himself in Constantinople, where he visited his favourite brothel and chose a fourteen-year-old whore who looked not entirely unlike the Kurdish girl.

Ah, the Orient!

*

207

Back to the manuscript. The Agha and his many wives. That was an exception, most men had only one wife. Married life in Kurdistan: Tournesol had been wise to stay away from all that. Here, in grey and rainy Paris, it all seemed quite adventurous and passionate; but not, after all, something one would want to become entangled in.

Monogamy is the rule. Female adulterers are likely to be murdered by their brothers or another close relative.

Still, it was nice to imagine her under that tent, her young skin protected from the glare of the sun, her head resting on embroidered silk cushions, her soft hands caressing not some bristly beast but . . . well, caressing the randy old Agha, probably.

And then Tournesol walked over to his red-velvet chaise longue, lay down and sank into what had recently become his favourite activity: daydreaming. This was what was slowing him down, and what was behind his current financial troubles and the never-ending arguments with his nagging wife (enough to drive a man back to Kurdistan).

He closed his eyes and saw the mountains of Kurdistan, saw himself, with bushy eyebrows and a thick moustache, leap on a horse and gallop up a hillside, leap from the horse and bellow a few orders to his men. He was an Agha now, he had shed that chafing, uncomfortable role he loathed, that of the cash-strapped explorer, the awkward outsider; in his daydreams, he was chieftain and treated and respected as such; and he strode into his tent, clapped his hands and was greeted by the laughing girl (Selim's great-grandmother, perhaps).

Some of Tournesol's daydreams infiltrated his book,

208

which was supposed to be a reliable record of Kurdish life and lore, and more than seven decades later, as I leafed through the worn pages of *The Kurds*, I couldn't help wondering if Tournesol in fact ever went to Kurdistan, if he dreamed up all these tales of mountain shepherds and tented brides in a lush, comfortable inn in a Constantinople back street.

30

On my second afternoon in the Institute, the full-time librarian was back at her post. When I had looked up the library, I had imagined discreetly slipping into a reading room lined with books, shelves and greying researchers, joining their studious silence, and after a few sessions vanishing as quietly as I had arrived. But the place wasn't overrun by visitors. I was the only one, as I had been the first time. I started chatting to the librarian, a chirpy woman who happened to be a translator as well as an expert in Xanî's *Mem û Zîn*.

'That's great!' I exclaimed. 'I've been trying to figure out some of the passages . . . this bit where he goes on about real versus symbolic love, I don't quite get what he means. In fact, I don't get it at all.'

'It's a Sufi concept,' she replied enthusiastically. 'For him, human love is basically a symbol for real, all-encompassing, divine love. A reflection of divine love, if you like.'

'I see,' I said. 'It's very Shakespearean, isn't it? The cross-dressing and all that.'

She nodded.

'Actually, that's another Sufi thing . . . for Xanî, the point is that true lovers recognise each other even if they are in disguise. In fact, Zîn tells her old nurse all about Mem after she meets him dressed in women's clothes, and the nurse tells her that it's not possible, that she can't have fallen in love with a woman. But Zîn is sure of her love because, well, their souls recognised each other.'

She walked over to the bookshelves that lined the walls, reached up and pulled out a bent paperback, opening it with the familiar ease of an old friend and translating spontaneously: 'Our hearts were bathed in light . . . we burned without understanding what had happened to us.'

'Who would have thought,' I said. 'Shakespeare's Kurdish soulmate.'

The librarian laughed.

'So what is this research of yours?'

'I'm researching for a . . . a script,' I improvised, having mislaid my initial, more convincing excuses. 'For a film.'

'Oh how interesting. What's it about?'

'It's . . . there are some Kurdish characters, but it's mostly about France. About a French girl who marries a Kurdish refugee as a political act, to help him stay in France, and then it all goes wrong.' Not very original, I agree, but I had learned from experience that the safest lies were those that stayed closest to the truth.

'Hmm,' she said thoughtfully. 'A mariage blanc, eh? I assume you're going to play with that a little, after reading so much Xanî. They could fall in love.' She pointed to the Kurdish copy of Mem û Zîn.

I blushed.

'No, I don't think they would do that. No, I don't think it's like that at all.'

211

31

Selim stood bent over a mountain bike, a spanner in one hand, a dirty rag in the other, his floppy hair falling into his eyes. He heard the jingle of the wind chimes over the door, put down his tools, straightened up and turned around, brushing his hair back with his arm. A blonde girl in a pink hooded sweatshirt and jeans walked in.

'Hey, Selim!' she exclaimed. 'Fancy seeing you here. It's been a while.'

'Diana,' Selim said. 'Very nice to see you.' He wiped his greasy hands on his trousers.

'Dynasty, actually,' she said. 'Can't believe you forgot my name, and you were in my class for, like, years! At least you've learned to speak.'

'I'm sorry,' Selim said. 'And yes, I can speak now.'

'You know, I don't think I ever heard your voice before. Can't believe we spent years in the same class. That was a shit school, eh?' She laughed a big, happy laugh. 'And our class was well out of control.'

'Yes,' Selim said. 'It was always very loud.' He picked up the spanner again to have something to fidget with.

Dynasty looked around at the bikes.

212

'So you've got, like, an actual job?'

'Flo's father owns the shop.'

'What, as in, Flo's rich? Then why did he go to our school?'

Selim considered this for a bit. She had a point. Either way, it was better not to go into it.

'Not sure,' he murmured, worried that he had said something wrong, something that would embarrass Flo or his family. He tried to think of a way to change the conversation. 'You want to buy a bike?' he asked with a bright smile.

'Nah, I don't cycle, do I. I'm looking for one for my little brother. He wants one for his birthday. Been saving up for it but it looks like I'm still a long way off.' She fingered the price tag on one of the children's bikes.

She was quite plump in a bouncy, cheerful way, but her hands were surprisingly slender. Selim remembered that she had always worn some kind of glittery nail varnish at school, and her nails had been long and curved like claws. Now her nails looked very neat and rosy and polished.

'I think I saw you the other day, in Frankfurt. I was there on a shopping trip. Should have said hi but you were kind of busy,' she said, still studying the price tags. 'One of those big demos. Thought it would be a bit stupid to walk up to you guys and go, yo, Selim.'

Selim smiled as he imagined Dynasty walking up to him, police in riot gear on one side, German neo-Nazis on the other, the Kurdish protesters in the middle, all men this time, and Dynasty walking right up to him, ignoring his grim-faced comrades and temperamental uncle, leaning over the big white, red and black PKK banner he was holding, and

213

then, why not, maybe she would even have given him a kiss on the cheek.

All things considered, the demo had not gone as badly as it could have done. They had originally planned to cycle to the Swiss–German border to protest against Europe's asylum policy, after weeks of debate on the best location: *Hey, why not the French–German border, the Polish–German border, the Dutch–German . . .*

'This one is a border between the EU and the outside world, so it's as good a symbol as any,' Selim's uncle eventually thundered, slamming his fist on the table. 'And if we can't even decide on a place, we might as well scrap the whole idea.'

Switzerland it was, then. They set off from Neustadt on their rickety bikes, a group of a dozen chain-smoking Kurds and their friends that swelled to a hundred as others joined them along the way. A convoy of cars followed them, transporting banners and megaphones for the actual demo.

A couple of hours into the tour, Selim's uncle, purple-faced and out of breath, hailed one of the cars, stuffed his bike in the back and plopped into the passenger seat as the others pedalled by, puffing and wheezing.

They gave up just before Frankfurt.

'Frankfurt, in many ways, is just as symbolic as the Swiss–German border,' Selim's uncle declared outside a service station, and the others nodded and massaged their backsides.

A boy of about thirteen or fourteen sidled up to Selim. Selim registered the startled look on his face, his old-fashioned haircut, the way his T-shirt was tucked into his tapered jeans: a recent arrival. The boy's eyes kept flitting to the far

214

side of the service station where a few bored policemen were leaning against their vans, waiting for the Kurds to get on with it.

'They're just here to escort the demo,' Selim reassured the frightened boy.

How good it felt to be an old hand, to dispense advice to newcomers. He recalled something his uncle had told him years before: *If it's because of your case, don't worry. Sometimes it can be helpful to show you're politically active, it can back up your story.*

'So . . . you're not worried at all?' the boy asked timidly.

'Oh, my case is different. Come.' Selim straightened his bike and pushed it towards the road, following the others. He almost added, *My case is different, I have a German wife, there's no way anyone can kick me out now*, but caution stopped him and he simply repeated: 'My case is different. Every case is different.'

The newcomer, somewhat confused but trusting, accepted this.

They left their bikes and cars at the train station and marched towards the centre of Frankfurt, walking past sex shops and porn cinemas, chanting slogans about an independent Kurdistan. In Kurdish. *We need a change in strategy*, Selim thought, his fists gripping the white hem of the *FREE KURDISTAN* banner, his knees brushing against the sheet as he walked. *We should be chanting in German. We should be organising rallies in German, huge rallies. We should be doing something big, much bigger than this.*

For now, he hoped at least the spelling on the banner was correct.

They left the seedy streets around the station and proceeded past the rustic pubs, and pink-topped flowerpots of old Frankfurt. At the square where the rally ended, near the shopping mile where Dynasty was trying on baggy jumpers and faded jeans, they bumped into a horde of neo-Nazis: pissed hooligans in bomber jackets, their heads smooth and hard as if they had shaved them for the occasion.

Selim dispelled the unpleasant recollection. He gestured towards the bikes.

'We have some cheaper ones, second-hand,' he offered. 'If you want, you can come here with your parents and I can show you some bikes for your brother. We have some broken ones.' No, that sounded wrong. The words did not quite line up the right way. 'I mean, you could buy a broken one, cheap, and I could help you repair it.'

He was not quite sure if Dynasty had heard him. She was looking at a poster showing a laughing blonde woman on a red bike with a laughing blond toddler strapped into a little yellow seat behind her. Next to them was a laughing blond man on a green bike.

'Though I'm wondering if he could actually ride a bike. Like, he's really small. He says he wants a bike but I think what he needs is a tricycle. Or I'd have to learn to ride a bike and drag him around in one of those little carts.'

'We have little carts. We don't have tricycles. But I can ask, maybe we can find some. You know, I have a little sister. Aynur. But she's in Kurdistan.' He paused. 'And I have a little brother, too.'

He was born after I left, Selim thought. Maybe one day I can buy him a bike.

216

Then he realised Dynasty was beaming at him as if he had offered her a new car.

'Oh cheers, wicked, yeah. I'd definitely be up for that. Bring my boyfriend along, he's good at buying cars and shit.'

Selim smiled a little less brightly than before.

'Yes, why not.'

32

'Welcome to your new job at the Superdiscount Centre,' my new boss said, beaming. 'Part-time, but fully appreciated!' He passed me a white overall, a red-striped apron, and a form to fill out.

Then he weasled away to the shelves with the special offers, adjusting a price tag here, buffing a metal rail with a cloth he kept tucked under the belt of his coat there.

I read the form. *Name, date of birth, available hours . . . marital status.* I stuffed it into my bag. So soon! Two months after my marriage, my first test. There was only one answer, of course. I was married, and would need to say so on all forms, visas, applications, contracts.

Meredith had mentioned it in passing before the wedding.

'And make sure you always tick the right box, because if you don't tick the box and they notice that you didn't tick the box then it could land Selim in deep, deep trouble!'

Such a simple thing, yet I found it impossible. Which box should I tick? Well, the married one of course.

I couldn't bring myself to do it.

When I turned up for work the next day, the box was still

218

blank. I tied my apron over my overall and wandered over to the fruit section.

Frau Brock, the head of fruit and vegetables, handed me three squashy fruit I'd never seen before: purple-black and heart-shaped.

She gestured towards the tag.

'Cherimoya. It's our fruit of the month.'

I turned them around in my hands and sniffed them. I wasn't convinced: a rotten-banana smell with a sour overtone.

'Let's demote it to fruit of the day,' I suggested. 'Do you peel them or slice them or what?'

Frau Brock raised her palms in a gesture of helplessness.

We managed to dig out a leaflet on exotic fruit that had come with the crate. It recommended scooping out the soft white flesh and spooning it into little plastic cups for sampling.

Unsurprisingly, my plastic cups of white slime did not tempt the customers of the Superdiscount Centre, and by the end of the day the crate was still full.

'You'll have to mark them down,' I said apologetically, an hour before closing time.

Frau Brock seemed unconcerned.

'I don't mind. The headscarves won't buy them anyway.'

The headscarves were Frau Brock's front-line enemies. Every night, half an hour before closing time, a group of three or four women in black, brown and blue headscarves, accompanied by a tall bearded man, would materialise at the vegetable section, patiently waiting for Frau Brock to mark down the prices with a metal gun that stuck the new tag on

219

top of the old one. They did not appear to speak German, though I have to confess I never tried to talk to them. I usually cringed into a far corner of the deep-freeze section, embarrassed by Frau Brock's efforts to thwart their innocent siege.

This night was no different. At about half past seven, there they were. Frau Brock, gun in hand, pretended not to notice them.

Slowly, she moved towards the aubergines. Slowly, the women followed her. The man remained on the sidelines.

Gun still unused, Frau Brock drifted away from the aubergines towards the red peppers, with her appendage of headscarved women.

'I just wish they wouldn't follow me around. I hate it,' she hissed at me. 'They never stop following me around!'

'Why don't you just mark down the prices and be done with it?' I said.

But she wouldn't. She would hold out.

'Why don't they pay the normal price like everyone else?'

'Well, at least you're selling aubergines by the crate.'

'Like vultures. *Wie die Geier.*'

Frau Brock let the price gun hang loosely by her side, as if she had no intention of using it. Even our spurned cherimoyas were still at the original price. She began to wipe down the chopping board, the scales, the gun itself. The women were not fooled.

At seven forty-five, with a kind of violent spasm, Frau Brock leapt to the crate of aubergines, yanked up her gun and angrily slapped on the new price tag. As she was pulling away the gun, one of the women lifted up the crate and

220

passed it to the man. Furious, Frau Brock whipped over to the peppers. There: 50 per cent off. There: a whole crate of tomatoes for 3 Deutschmarks. And there, and there, and there. She shot down the old prices and slapped on the new ones, and one by one the crates were snapped up and passed to the man who loaded them into a trolley, and by seven fifty, the trolley was full and the group had disappeared to the checkout and Frau Brock leaned against the empty rack, defeated.

The crate of cherimoyas was still there.

I cleared up my little stand, folded up the cardboard table and stashed it away in a cupboard at the back. The others were already untying their aprons, complaining about having to stand by the deep freeze.

'At least you're not trapped in Frau Brock's little war zone,' I pointed out.

'Did you know, her husband is black,' one of the girls said. 'From Africa.'

'Right.'

'Nigerian.'

'Oh.'

'I mean, he basically married her for the passport, right.'

'Who knows.' I chucked my apron into the laundry basket and unbuttoned my overall.

'Yeah, but it's obvious. I mean, she's nuts anyway.'

My boss came panting down the aisle.

'Hang on, let me give you that form,' I called over to him.

I dug the form out of my bag, ticked the box that said *married* and passed it to him.

'You're married?' He shot me a curious glance.

221

The others stopped chatting, expecting a good story.

'Yes.'

'But you're only eighteen!' He held the form close to his face and frowned, then held it at arm's length, like a wine list. 'Only eighteen,' he confirmed, nodding to the others.

'Yes.'

'But why?'

'Well . . .' I took a deep breath, buying time, trying to come up with something convincing. 'We were together for a few years, as a couple, and then we decided to get married.'

Why not, I thought. In a different life. Got together at fourteen, first boyfriend, very happy, turned eighteen, married him, bought a cat. Mum elated, chucking rice at us. Maybe, in a different life. Why not?

'But, Frau . . . from his point of view . . . or anyway, why would you buy the car when you only want the wheel? Or to put it another way, why buy the cow when you can drink the milk?'

The others sniggered.

I crumpled my overall into a ball and tossed it after the apron.

'It's love, isn't it?' I said, grabbed my bag and made for the exit.

Frau Brock was on the far side of the fruit section, resentfully stacking the empty crates and cleaning the metal racks. She lifted a plastic bucket and rested it on her hip like a toddler.

'Lucky you, out already! I've got to hurry, my husband's waiting outside!' she shouted, pushing one arm elbow-deep into the bucket. 'Actually, if you see him, could you tell him I'll be there in ten.'

222

'Sure. What does he look like?'

'He's black. Tall black guy, with a shaved head like a snooker ball.' She put down the bucket and squeezed the sponge with her reddened hand. Soap suds and water dribbled down her wrist. 'He's Nigerian. We've been through quite something together. Quite something.'

I'd had enough of the supermarket and my nosy colleagues and just wanted to leave, but she interpreted my irritation as disbelief.

'No, really.' She lowered her voice as if she were confiding something mildly shameful as well as exciting. 'He was actually in prison for a bit, not his fault though. He went a bit mental, called me the Antichrist, but that was the loneliness talking.'

She moved to the next rack, dipped the sponge in the bucket and vigorously washed the metal.

'And now he picks me up from work because of my ex . . . he usually hangs around the car park and shouts at me, so I need my husband there.'

Frau Brock had pushed up the sleeves of her overall. She smelled strongly of onions. Her stringy blonde hair was pulled back, revealing her bullish face, and yet all the ugly features together formed something not entirely unattractive. Something earthy.

'So when Johnson, that's my man, when he came out of prison, I married him.'

'Even though he called you the Antichrist?'

'I'm not really religious in that way. And he's funny. Once he put on my high heels and lipstick and danced around the bedroom.'

223

I pointed at the price gun.

'Frau Brock, you know, they're going to come back every night. The women in the headscarves.'

'I know. That's what I hate about it.'

'I read this book the other day. It's called, *I'm OK, You're OK*. It's quite interesting. I can lend it to you if you like.'

'But they're not OK.'

'Frau Brock, that's not what it's about. I mean, it's about everyone sort of accepting each other. I can bring in the book if you like.'

'It sounds a bit dull.'

I gave up. Plus, she was right. It was quite a dull book.

She wiped her hands on her apron and picked up the price gun.

'It's the way they loiter around, as if all this—' She gestured with the gun, taking in the deep-freeze section, the discount corner, the tills. 'As if it's, like, theirs. And you know, today they take over the Superdiscount Centre, tomorrow the whole country, and then we'll all be wearing headscarves.'

'I don't know,' I shrugged. 'Maybe they just want to buy cheap aubergines.'

33

A few months into my marriage with Selim, our first problem emerged. In hindsight, it was a small, manageable problem, a tiny one in fact compared with what was to come. But it was the first time that a problem had kept me awake at night. Previously, as a typical sleep-loving teenager, insomnia had been something I only read about in books.

In a different situation, I would have asked my brother Martin for help. He would have told me not to be so neurotic, and then proposed some practical solution. Like on the day our parents got divorced: we were living in a tower block at the time, and, while our parents were out finalising their separation, we went up and down in the lift between the basement with the washing machines and the very top floor, ignoring the pitying glances from the neighbours, until our mother came home.

Anyway, Martin had successfully completed his military service, which astonished us all, and, much to Stefan's delight and my surprise, secured an Army scholarship to study engineering, so he was the last person I wanted to involve in this. And he wasn't living in our town any more, which meant he couldn't have helped us even if he wanted to: our problem was that we needed to find a safe flat where we'd have an address without actually having to live together.

I knew that I would leave town as soon as I finished school. Selim, however, would stay, and our marriage would only remain valid if we had a common address. This should not be difficult, we thought. After all, this town was full of political activists who lived in flat-shares and would surely be willing to help us out.

The prospective flatmates would need to know the basic facts of our marriage and be reliable; when asked, they would need to say that yes, we were living there, yes, together, yes, as a married couple.

'There might be a problem,' Dr Habicht said. 'The immigration office doesn't recognise a flat-share as a suitable residence for a married couple.'

'That's outrageous!' I immediately flared up like a blister in the sun, as was my style at the time. 'How dare they tell us how to conduct our marriage – how dare they define what a proper marriage and a proper flat look like, when it's our life and our marriage and we can lead it whichever . . .'

So enraged was I that for a moment I felt I really was married to Selim, heart, soul and body, that our marriage was deep and meaningful and just as valid, surely, '. . . Just as valid as any of their fucking hypocritical tax-avoiding middle-aged German marriages, surely . . .'

Dr Habicht coughed.

'Those are the rules. It has to be a private apartment or house, inhabited only by the couple, and of course their children, if children are present. An enclosed, private space. A flat-share does not qualify as an enclosed, private space.'

However, neither of us could afford such a space. We reached a compromise with the immigration officials: we would be allowed to use a flat-share as an interim solution, while continuing the search for a suitable private place.

Selim was earning enough at the bike shop to afford a small room, and in any case was keen to move out and give Flo's family some space. Flo might even follow. I would continue to stay at Julian's, while officially sharing Selim's room.

We were surprised, then, to find that none of the people we had identified as politically reliable were willing to share a flat with Selim.

The reasons were never quite clear.

The socialist biology students muttered regretfully that they had just, literally, given the room to someone else.

The organic-food-eating electricians said they liked Selim but . . . one of the key elements of their communal lifestyle was really *communication*, and of course they were more than willing to teach Selim proper German and help him integrate, but they were worried that . . . well, really, for them the key issue here was *communication*.

Then we tried a crummy former squat. The flat was horrible but we thought our chances were pretty good as the occupants loved anything vaguely illegal. However, it turned out that half of them were living on benefits. Selim lived on his bike-shop money as well as some benefits, but he was planning to get off benefits and move into proper mainstream employment. All this he tried to explain to his potential future flatmates, sitting on a flattened beanbag in their living room.

'Why don't you just go on the dole, man?' This from a

227

pallid youth lolling on a corduroy sofa that reeked of cannabis. Behind him, a black-and-red Che Guevara stared into the distance with visionary zeal.

'Because then I'm not part of the workforce, and then it is actually more difficult to turn my job at the bike shop into proper work. I don't know how to explain it well, it's difficult.'

'Right, then just get off the dole.' The youth languidly rolled another joint.

'But every time I ask the woman to stop my benefits, she says how do you make money then? Tell me the truth, you're dealing drugs? Because that's what the Kurds do.'

'Shit, that's what they tell you? Fucking racists. Fuck them,' a girl with spiky orange hair grumbled.

'We-ell,' the pallid youth said, lighting the joint. 'Fact is, either you're on or you're off, but we don't want a war with the benefits office. Don't take this the wrong way but we've had a pretty peaceful relationship with them so far and, you know, don't rock the boat, man.'

He stroked his shaved head and offered the joint to Selim.

'No hard feelings, OK? Life is shit.'

'Thanks,' Selim said, taking the joint.

34

'She'd be willing to let you stay with her and pretend, you know, help with the whole official address thing,' Flo said.

They were walking past Dr Habicht's flat in the wonky timber house and down another cobbled alleyway.

Every time I get turned down, Selim thought, someone new turns up. The day before, he had been rejected by a bunch of feminists after mentioning, in a moment of carelessness, that one of his aunts wore a headscarf.

'It's only because the sun is so hot there,' he had added in a hurry. 'And it's white with some lace, and you can almost see through it.'

Too late.

He told himself it was all for the best; their spare bedroom had been tiny, anyway. He hummed a happy little tune and asked Flo what this new woman's name was.

'Pushpa.'

'Uscha?'

'Pushpa. But do me a favour and don't ask about her name, I don't really get it either. Listen, can you stop humming?'

Selim hummed a little more loudly.

'Yeah, very funny. Anyway, she's part of the whole legal aid shit so I guess that's why she's sort of keen to do this.'

They stopped by a little red gate, and Flo read out the name on the hand-painted terracotta sign: *Angela Baumann (Pushpa)*

A thin, short woman opened the door of the cottage, shaking her wiry curls with delight when she saw them. Her tight orange strappy top matched her ambitious tan. Her breasts, Selim noticed, were unusually pert and pointy. He had to stop paying so much attention to women's breasts, he told himself. They probably noticed.

'Come in! Come in! Oh, you . . .' She greedily ushered Selim into the cottage, but Flo slipped away before she could grab him, muttering something about the bike shop.

A monstrous piece of furniture awaited Selim in the living room: part sprawling divan, part sofa, part nest. Hidden under layers of pink, red, purple throws and blankets. Piled high with cushions. Like a living, fleshy thing, ready to engulf him.

Selim cautiously opted for the only other seat, a wooden chair whose main function was to prop open the door. When he moved it to sit down, the door closed; he jumped up, opened the door again, moved the chair so it held back the door, and sat down again.

Pushpa came in, her breasts perkily sticking out over a tray on which were mugs, a teapot, a plate of biscuits.

'Your friend said he'll pick you up later, he seems rather shy.' She put down the tray and flung herself into the cushions on the pulsating divan. 'Make yourself feel right at home. I thought we could relax a bit and . . . get to know each other a little. Tell me about yourself, everything!'

230

She appeared to chew each sentence with her athletic jaw and lips, intently producing those carefully articulated words.

'And Selim, I hear you are in fact Yezidi?'

'No,' Selim said, surprised. 'Not at all.'

Her mouth worked itself into a knowing smile.

'Ah, but you Yezidis are so secretive about your faith.'

She dug herself out of the cushions and poured him more tea. A faint trace of incense lingered in the velvet curtains and plump red cushions, which reminded Selim of the smell of Dr Habicht's flat.

'Come here.' Pushpa patted a cushion. 'Make yourself comfortable, make yourself at home, relax. You're so tense.'

Selim, cowering in the corner by the door, hunched over his mug of tea, grinned nervously.

'Thank you. It's OK.'

'I'll put on some Yezidi music.'

Strange to hear the twang of the *saz* in this curiously padded room, with its cushions and rows of books lining the wall and strips of red gauze dangling from the ceiling. Selim leaned against the hard door and felt his chest soften.

Pushpa had her back to Selim and was swaying her narrow hips, awkwardly tapping out the rhythm of the song with her fingers as she scanned the books. Her bottom, too, was rather pert. It was probably as wrong to stare at a woman's arse as it was to stare at her breasts, but at least it was less noticeable.

She pulled a heavy book from the shelf, slid her finger into the pages where the bookmark was and sank back into the cushions, somehow gathering up the startled Selim from his

231

creaking chair and sweeping him along with her in the process.

She smelled of soap and patchouli in a way that was vaguely pleasant.

'Gorgeous, gorgeous book. Isn't it magnificent? A gift. Look at the colours, pure jewels. Extremely sensual.'

Selim nodded. She had placed the book on his lap.

Her fingers stroked the glossy page, tracing the image of a peacock proudly fanning out his wheel of feathers.

'Of course you know this.'

'It's a bird?' Selim ventured.

'The peacock angel, Tawusi Melek. You mean you're really not Yezidi?' she said, a note of disappointment in her voice. She pursed her muscly lips.

'I know a lot of Yezidi Kurds. Some Muslims say they pray to the devil.' When he saw the expression on her face, he hastily added: 'I don't believe that at all.'

He drank some tea. It was the cinnamon and cardamom mix he often drank at Flo's place.

Nice. She was studying the illustration now, gazing at the sapphire blue peacock and his red and green tail feathers with an air of wistfulness. When he sat up straight, looking down at the book, he had a perfect view of the top of her breasts. No bra.

The next page showed another preening peacock; this one was white.

'They don't pray to the devil,' she murmured, suddenly looking slightly sad. 'They pray to the sun. It's a very beautiful and fascinating religion, in many ways. Very strict of course. I once had a Yezidi lover, you see.'

232

She closed her eyes and tilted back her head, running her fingers through her hair.

'He was unbelievably passionate. Did you know they don't eat lettuce? Fascinating culture. But of course his family had no idea. They would have mauled me.'

Selim sat up, feeling here, at least, he could contribute.

'Please, it's not because of you.' He smiled knowledgeably. 'Yezidi only marry other Yezidi. I know some crazy Muslim girls who chase after Yezidi men. It's the same problem.'

Pushpa shot him an annoyed look.

'Well, with the Muslims I'm not surprised really. You people hunted them down for centuries. It's why they don't eat lettuce.'

'I'm sorry.'

'No, I'm sorry. I don't know . . . we shouldn't let this derail our conversation. Please tell me if you feel I'm being insensitive, but I wonder if there's not some Yezidi streak in you. You seem so . . . different.'

'But we were all Yezidi, a long time ago, before Islam. Your friend didn't tell you?'

'Oh, I see.'

She took the book from his lap, carefully closed it and put in on the table. Then she took the mug from his hands and poured him more tea. She stretched out and turned over onto her stomach.

'One of the wonderful, wonderful things I learned is Yezidi foot massage. It's a very sensual religion, you know, full of sensual rituals – sorry if that's a little too direct for your taste. Even I was a bit surprised at first, but then . . .'

Selim had never heard of Yezidi foot massage. Given the

extreme conservatism of the Yezidi, he very much doubted such rituals existed anywhere outside the mind of Pushpa's former lover. Still, he thought, not a bad trick.

'Yezidi are the true Kurds, in many ways,' he ventured, clinging to his mug of tea. 'All Kurds were Yezidi in the old days, but now many are Muslim . . . but before, many were Yezidi . . . we are all, in a way, Yezidi . . . no thank you, I have a foot problem.'

'I promise this will cure your foot problem.'

'It's a very bad foot problem. It means . . . no one can touch my feet.'

'Relax, Selim, you'll see, it's nice. Relax.'

'Eek!'

'Selim!'

'I'm . . . heeeeeeeee! It tickles!'

The doorbell rang, and then rang again, more persistently. Selim dug a shoe out of the biscuits and retrieved his T-shirt from underneath the cushions, dressing hastily on his way to the door.

Flo and Şivan stood in the doorway: identical Puffa jacket twins with baseball caps and button-up tracksuit bottoms.

'You coming or what?'

'I'm . . . can you . . .' Selim nervously smoothed his hair.

'What?' Şivan looked over his shoulder and Selim worried that any minute he would enter the house, the living room, sit down on the sofa. If his cousin heard about Pushpa's bogus Yezidi tales, Selim was finished.

Selim hobbled back into the living room, grabbed the second shoe, blushed, patted, squeezed, kissed, rushed back out.

234

'Heya!' Pushpa had followed him into the hallway, barefoot, one strap falling off her shoulder, and was waving at the other two, unaware of or unbothered by their grins.

'Hi.'

'Hi.'

Selim steered them towards the street, calling over his shoulder: 'Pushpa, sorry, we have to go, yes, I'll call you, yes, I will.'

He hurriedly led them down the steep stone steps, trying not to look at his cousin.

'Who,' his cousin spluttered as they emerged onto the street, 'was that?'

Selim ignored him and turned to Flo.

'Did you tell her I'm Yezidi?'

'I thought it would help with the room. She's well into Yezidi guys.'

'I noticed.'

'She's got a cheap room. I should warn you, she's a bit possessive, I heard, and a bit mad.'

'Great help, Flo. Really, a great help.'

He thought of Rojan, a girl he had met at a concert. A bubbly girl. Her family lived in the town, she had a proper permit, she had gone to a proper German school, she was planning to study biology. She was confidently, charmingly, naturally trilingual. Kurdish, German, Turkish. Plus a smattering of Arabic. In her spare time, she sometimes volunteered as an interpreter for a Kurdish charity.

He was a little scared of her but, miraculously, she had given him her number.

Every day, he told himself he would call.

235

It didn't help that she was a head taller than him, and as beautiful as the sun.

He shook Pushpa's patchouli scent out of his sleeve and sighed, thinking of the past hour or so. Pushpa was a nice woman in many ways. Many, many ways. Some of the unexpected excitement of the afternoon was still with him and refused to be dispelled. He felt restless, knowing that he would have to spend the next few hours in the company of these two. He should have made up some excuse. He should have told them to get lost. He should have. But that would have made it look as if he was really into Pushpa.

Şivan grabbed his arm and stopped him, looking at him intently.

'Eh, if you're looking for a girl, I can help you. Give you some advice. Introduce you to girls. No problem, man, just ask, right? Just ask me. If you've got problems because they've got to stay virgins, there are tricks, you know, there are ways. No need to . . . get desperate.'

Selim slapped him on the back and told him to shut up.

35

A million men marched in Washington, DC. The camera zoomed in on one of them, a bearded weeping giant who dropped to his knees and raised his face up to the sky and wrung his hands, begging for forgiveness.

'That's pretty impressive,' I said.

Frau Brock sat in a squeaking armchair, cutting a length of salami into thick slices and putting them in her mouth. She rolled her eyes.

'Impressive, my arse,' she mumbled through stuffed cheeks, waving the salami at the chest-beating man on the screen. 'I know his type. Tomorrow they go back home and thrash their wives.'

She speared a slice of salami on her knife and passed it over to me.

'Johnson's OK though. The Nigerians are all OK. And at least they're fun.'

She wiped her hands on her apron and got ready to head back to work, then seemed to remember something.

'No offence, eh? Guess your husband is German.'

'Actually,' I said, 'he's Kurdish. Muslim, in fact.'

'God!' She gave a little shriek. 'Well, guess that explains

why you're always so nice about the headscarves. Only joking. Anyway, make sure he treats you right.'

'Yeah. Thanks.'

She pulled a piece of cloth from her ample cleavage and dabbed at her glowing face.

'I feel like I'm melting,' she groaned. 'Aren't you going to be done with school soon?'

I nodded.

'And then? Plans?'

'I'm probably going to move away.' I already knew I was going to move abroad, but something stopped me from sharing my precise plans with her. 'With my husband, of course.'

She gave an approving grunt.

'Just make sure your husband doesn't change his mind at the last minute. Men are strange like that.'

'Sure.'

Selim did not move in with Pushpa after all, but she helped him rent a flat owned by some friend of hers. Officially, we lived there together. Unofficially, I stayed on at Julian's place. I wasn't sure how Selim paid the rent or why Pushpa's friend was supporting our cause; I was busy working at the Superdiscount Centre, saving up for university and making plans for life after school, and so I never asked.

Once the housing issue was solved, the next problem emerged: child support.

'Child support?'

'Benefit. The money that the state pays to your mother,' Selim said.

We were sitting in the underground vault in the old town

238

that was used for band practice, the porous limestone walls partly covered with empty egg cartons. Dr Habicht had made his excuses.

The benefit should have ceased once I got married. However, since I had not told my mother about my marriage, she was probably still drawing child benefit. And she would continue to do so until the state informed her of my changed status; or until someone knocked on her door and charged her with benefit fraud.

'Dr Habicht says he is very sorry,' Selim said, looking at the egg cartons. 'He forgot to think of this before the marriage.'

'He . . . he forgot?' I stood up, walked over to Selim and sat down right in front of him, leaning against the cartons. 'Did you know about this?'

Selim lifted his hands, his palms a shield against my implicit accusation.

'No, no, I swear. I didn't even know the German state paid money for children.'

Somewhat sceptical, I glanced at Julian. His short, bristly hair was flat-topped and, for some reason, bleached, which made his head look like a sun-scorched football pitch.

He shrugged.

'I guess you'll have to tell her, and then she should ask the benefits office to stop the payments.'

'Yes,' Selim agreed, nodding with relief. 'That's a good solution.'

I stared at them in disbelief.

'That's not a solution at all. I mean, telling my mum, that's not an option, right? I told you that right from the start. That was my only condition.'

239

Selim frowned.

'Yes, I remember, that was a condition. Dr Habicht should have made sure that was OK.' He raised his palms again, expressing helplessness but also, I realised, a kind of resigned acceptance of the changed facts. 'I'm sorry. I hope your mother won't be too angry. I can come and explain, if you want. Maybe your brother can help explain, too.'

'No! No, definitely not.' I felt an urge to lock them both in the band-practice room there and then. 'My brother doesn't even know! He's on an Army scholarship. There's no way I'm going to drag him into this.'

I cast around for some way to gain control of the situation, to make them both realise how important this was to me, but all I could come up with was repeating what I had told them a couple of months earlier.

'I really meant it when I said I couldn't tell my mum about this,' I said, feeling a bit desperate. 'She'll go mental. She'll think I was tricked into this. She'll probably tell Stefan, and he'll report Selim to the police or something. And she'll think it's all her fault for moving to eastern Germany.'

I caught Julian and Selim glancing at each other. It confused me: Julian and I were supposed to do that, the smirking, the quick locking of eyes to confirm to each other that we were right and the others wrong.

'Selim, you always go on about family and all that,' I said, pathetically trying to address him alone rather than the wall of two. 'So, I may not show it in the same way, but that's how I feel about my mother and Martin, right? I don't want them to find out that I'm running a . . . well, a scam.'

'To be honest, it might be a good idea to tell them at some

point anyway,' Julian said. 'Even after the divorce, that whole financial side is always going to be there. Like, if Selim loses his job or something, you'll obviously have to support him, pay maintenance and stuff.' He let his palm glide back and forth over his bristly bleached hair. 'That only occurred to me the other day, actually. Maintenance.'

'Maybe we should just focus on the child-support issue for now,' I said weakly.

'I'm sorry,' Selim said. 'I thought Dr Habicht . . .'

'For fuck's sake, can we forget about Habicht for a second?' I cried. 'I thought *you* knew what you were doing.'

Selim pressed his lips together.

'OK, folks, the only remaining option is we take a gamble,' Julian said, frustratingly unfazed by my outburst. 'Dr Habicht said in theory the child-support people and the marriage people aren't in touch, and there's no reason why they should suddenly link up.'

'Dr Habicht said that?' I said. 'Lovely.'

'He said he would come here,' Selim offered. 'He wanted to explain it to you properly. But then he had another meeting.'

'Sure.'

'Look,' Julian said, suddenly nervous, 'we just need to stay calm about this. Let's not blow this out of proportion.'

'Oh, don't worry, I'll do it. I mean, I won't do anything, I'll keep quiet. I only hope it won't spill out. Just promise me that I never have to see Dr Habicht ever again.' I tried to think of a way to make them understand why this was bothering me so much. 'I mean, if something this simple wasn't considered before, then God knows what else is out there.'

241

It was around that time that I started obsessively twisting the rings in my eyebrows. I did it unconsciously at first, only noticing there was a problem when the holes became red and infected. I treated them with antiseptic, thinking the inflammation was a result of my general grubbiness, but it only got worse. My left eyebrow became sore and swollen. I made a deliberate effort not to touch it, with great difficulty controlling the impulse, the urge to fiddle with those metal rings. Julian gave me a string of Tibetan worry beads, which helped a little, but not much. In the end, with a twinge of regret, I took the rings out.

36

My insomnia worsened during our first year of marriage. I was nervous, irritable, paranoid. Nothing stayed secret for very long in a small, bored community. Julian fell in love with a girl who played the tuba in our school orchestra. One weekend, when she stayed over, she 'accidentally' went through my desk drawer, supposedly because she was looking for sticky tape. There, between my diary and archaeology-themed postcards from my mother, she found my marriage certificate.

'What did she need tape for anyway?' I cried.

'To wrap a present for me, apparently,' Julian said. The worst thing was that he didn't even look angry: he looked *flattered*.

'There's a great big roll of tape on my desk!' I ran into my room, which of course was not really my room at all, but Julian's family's spare room, and came back holding the roll of tape high over my head. 'Look, it was sitting there, *on* my desk. It couldn't have been more visible if it had been walking around saying I'm a roll of tape, I'm a roll of tape.'

'She told me she didn't see it,' Julian said. 'And she apologised. Don't be cross.'

He fled into the kitchen and I followed him, ready to continue, but his mother was there, sitting at the table.

'What are you two arguing about?' she asked without looking up from her crossword puzzle.

'Nothing,' we replied in unison.

She gave me a quick glance, the briefest reassuring smile; she probably thought it was a case of jealousy.

Naturally, Julian said his girlfriend was sound and could be trusted with the truth. I felt the exact opposite, but reckoned it was still best to come clean to her about my fraudulent marriage, then hammer home the fact that this was a life-or-death situation.

'If the immigration office finds out about this, Selim will be deported. I'll go to jail, Julian will go to jail, our lives will be fucked, and Selim's life will be over,' I said. 'And they'll probably find his body in the Tigris.'

She gulped.

Her relationship with Julian did not last long. However, contrary to my expectations, she turned out to be discreet. At least I never had any trouble from that corner.

Once I had left Germany, I began to feel altogether less jittery. My eyebrow tic became less marked and I threw away the worry beads. Selim stayed behind; at least one of us had to live at our registered address and deal with potential visits from immigration officials. Julian moved to Berlin to study Klezmer music. I plunged into my new life in Paris, first waitressing at a café, then enrolling at university to study sociology.

Among my laid-back new friends in Paris, I began to talk

244

more freely. I wasn't a naturally duplicitous person, I wasn't good at telling lies, and it felt liberating to shed some of the secrecy. It was a relief, in fact, to be able to mention the marriage the way others might mention a mild cocaine habit: as something illicit, a subject one wouldn't bring up in the company of lecturers or visiting parents, but which was seen as quite acceptable by everyone around me. Frankly, my rebellious Parisian student friends found the exotic Kurdish connection rather chic.

I obviously remained cautious in many ways. I stayed away from anything remotely linked to immigrants' rights or pressure groups. I had had quite enough of that.

And so I eased into a life that was rich in new experiences and discoveries, but at the same time lived in a somewhat more subdued, less confrontational manner. And if you find yourself frowning in disbelief at the contrast between my colourful past and somewhat dull present, then consider all the years that lie between the two. Years spent scrutinising potential allies, lying low, adjusting to new homes, striking up friendships, blending in and blending in again, until it was as though those sharp edges of my adolescent self had been polished away, smoothed into a bland surface that neatly slotted into any new environment and was, even in the most demanding setting, highly unlikely to cause offence.

Certain things would have been easier had I stayed put. Selim still needed to visit the immigration office, sort out the paperwork, make sure everything was on track for his permanent residency application. I was the silent partner, signing a stack of documents every time I went home for the holidays and otherwise remaining fairly remote.

245

'All the people at the immigration office, the social workers, everyone always asks me where's your wife, where's your wife,' he once complained to me.

'Yeah, well, what can I do.'

'I'm not blaming you, but you're never here,' he said.

'I come as often as I can,' I said. 'OK, I'll try to come more often. It's only for three years, I guess.'

'Yes,' he said. 'And then I will get my permanent residency.'

However, my moving away probably made the whole operation safer.

During those initial years, Selim occasionally mentioned his own plans and ambitions. He worked at the bike shop and embarked on various training schemes. He told me he was thinking of being a carer, both because there were lots of jobs in that sector and because he liked elderly people. They liked him back, with his calm, respectful manner. But to be a carer he needed better reading and writing skills, hence the project was on hold, like so much of his life.

I knew that he continued to maintain his political ties. I never asked him not to; it would have been impossible. The Kurdish diaspora and the Kurdish struggle for independence were Siamese twins, nourishing each other through one common bloodstream. I could no more have asked him to cut off any ties to the political movement than I could have asked him to cut off a foot or a hand. If someone had asked me, I would have said something along the lines of: *I guess he collects funds and helps organise demos, but I don't think he is directly active in the PKK or anything like that.* In any case, at the time, the PKK was still legal in Europe,

246

and even if he had been involved with them I wouldn't have been particularly concerned. Frankly, I didn't even give much thought to that side of things. Maybe I should have.

37

'My boyfriend can't make it.' Dynasty let herself fall onto the oil-stained sofa in the corner, sinking into the cushions. 'OK, OK. Actually, he didn't want to come.' She started crying.

Selim was not sure what to do. He moved towards her and lightly touched her shoulder.

'Sorry.'

'No, I'm so sorry. I know this is pathetic, making a right scene.'

'Oh, don't worry.' He thought of something comforting to say. 'I'm sure he likes you.'

'Yeah right.' She snorted angrily. 'He likes loads of girls. Sorry, that's unfair. Basically, the problem is, he doesn't like my little brother. That's really the only problem we have, basically. He's not a bad guy. Actually, you know him. He was in our class.'

'Yes, then I probably know him.'

'He's, it's . . .' She buried her head in her arms and started crying again, and through tears, snot and hair bleated: 'Hakan.'

'Oh. Yes. I remember him. He was loud.'

She looked up. He passed her a paper tissue. She blew her nose.

'Honestly, he was such a prat in school but he really isn't like that any more. He's got a job and he's like, you know, traditional, looks after me and takes me out and stuff. I mean, he's nice. You probably think he beats me up.'

Selim shook his head to show that no, he didn't think that at all.

'And actually, he says he wants to marry me.'

'Oh. Congratulations,' Selim said as he passed her another tissue.

'Yes but no, because, I mean, I've got to look after my little brother. It's all a bit complicated. Sorry. This is so embarrassing. Anyway, how about you? Are you going to stay in Germany now?'

'I hope so.'

'Everything sorted with your papers?'

'Yes,' Selim lied.

'But that's amazing! That's brilliant. And you've got a great job here.'

'Oh, but I'm not . . .'

A boy crashed into the shop through the stacked-up bikes. He wore his baseball cap with the peak pulled down so low it touched the tip of his nose, and was waving his oddly disjointed arms.

'Hoot hoot, anyone here?'

'Yes?' replied Selim.

'You!' With a swift flick of the hand, the boy turned around his cap, peak pointing backwards, to reveal his gaunt face.

'Yes,' Selim said.

'No I mean, hey, I know you.'

249

'Look at you,' Dynasty interrupted. 'School reunion, eh?' Then she turned to Selim. 'Come on, you remember. You must remember. It's Dwayn, right?'

'Yes,' Selim said, not remembering.

Dwayn hopped from one leg to the other, clapping his hands.

'So, right, ring ring ring, I'm looking for a pram.'

Selim shook his head.

'We sell bikes. And maybe, also, Dynasty was looking for—' He caught Dynasty's eye. She stared at him and discreetly put a finger across her lips. 'We sell bikes,' Selim repeated, unsure what Dynasty wanted but deciding it was best to say nothing.

'Shit, man, I need a pram.' Dwayn bit his lip and nervously rang the bell on one of the bikes once, twice, five times, twenty times.

'Go on, give us the news,' Dynasty said.

'Yeah, you know it anyway, right. Whole fucking town knows.' His thumb went on autopilot, working the little black lever on the bell so hard Selim feared it would fall off.

Dynasty, who was remarkably relaxed, smiled sweetly.

'Got a name?'

'My whole life's over, right. Over. We're going to call him Jet-Lee, sounds wicked, yeah? Jet-Lee Olshevsky.'

'Well . . . guess so. What does your girlfriend say?'

'Nah, not talking to me, pissed off about . . . fuck, you can't organise a pram, right? Know anyone who can?'

Selim, who had lost track of the conversation, stuck to what he considered to be the approved line.

'We only sell bikes.'

250

'Dwayn, you need to calm down a bit, chill,' Dynasty said in a soothing tone, but Dwayn was flitting erratically around the workshop, darting this way and that, slapping Selim on the back, giving Dynasty a friendly squeeze, trying out all the different bike bells, fingering the helmets. Everything he did only seemed to make him more restless and twitchy, and so, like a wasp that bumps against the window a few times, he darted back and forth and eventually buzzed out through the open door.

'That was,' Dynasty lifted an eyebrow, 'intense.'

'I remember him now,' Selim said, looking after the boy. 'He's going to be a father?'

'He seems to think so, huh?' Dynasty said. 'But you know what, my cousin knows his girlfriend and actually . . . well, she isn't really pregnant. Anyway. Anyway. Shouldn't gossip. And cheers for, you know, not telling him about the tricycle. For my brother. Just wanted it to be a bit, like, private.'

'OK,' Selim said, thoroughly confused now but vaguely pleased that this great big mess around him, this strange web of human relationships, truths and lies, for once, was not about him.

38

'People here break so easily,' Selim once said. 'Something small, like the girlfriend leaves, the job is bad, and already they are so *kaputt* they have to go and see a psycho. In Kurdistan, every day, people suffer so much. They don't have a psycho.'

Selim looked like an underpaid lecturer surviving on tea and biscuits pilfered from the weekly Marxist society meeting. You would think he spent his days sitting in a tiny study crammed with books, composing a political treatise or an epic Kurdish love poem.

'So what do they do?'

He lifted his hands and turned up his palms.

'Religion.'

'Hmm . . . but does that mean . . .'

I instinctively held off. And as so often when the subject matter became complicated, we left it at that.

One afternoon, Selim showed me a photo of his best friend, scrawny and lopsidedly bespectacled like Selim, standing on a dusty, yellow-green mountainside, dressed in camouflage and shaking the hand of a grey-haired man with a huge moustache.

'Abdullah Öcalan,' Selim said, pointing at the grey-haired

man in the picture, his soft voice reverberating with reverence. 'Apo. He leads the PKK.'

Selim gave me sidelong glance, as if considering something, then opened a box and took out another photo.

The backdrop was almost identical: dusty mountains with yellow-green stubble, jutting rocks, terrifying gorges, a misty sky. But, instead of a line of earnest young men, the picture showed two women. The older of the two was down on one knee, like a pleading suitor, her eyebrows furrowed over scrunched-up eyes, her black hair tousled by the mountain-top breeze. She had her hand on her knee, steadying herself as she leaned forward, scrutinising or maybe instructing the younger woman, who was lying on her stomach, her heart-shaped face, thick eyebrows and neat middle parting facing the camera, a long black braid dangling over one shoulder. There was a childlike look of concentration on her face. Her hands were feeding an ammunition belt into a menacing propped-up machine gun.

Selim pointed at the second woman, a girl really.

'My little sister Aynur,' he said.

I raised my eyebrows.

'She always wanted to marry my best friend.' He tapped the photo of his friend shaking Öcalan's hand. 'But she had to marry one of my cousins, you know, Şivan. Our parents said she should marry Şivan. Now she can't marry Şivan and she can't marry my best friend, because men and women in the mountains cannot be together.' He aligned his two index fingers and rubbed them against each other. 'But she's very strong.'

'She must be, if she's gone off into the mountains,' I said.

253

'You know, often I think, our women are a lot tougher. They milk the sheep, make cheese, clean the house, everything. I was sometimes a bit scared of my sister.' He giggled. 'My friend who gave me the photo told me she shot down a helicopter with a machine gun.'

I decided not to ask exactly how he obtained the photo, or the inside news from the mountain guerrillas. Before I married Selim, I could not hear enough about all that: illegal militias, smugglers, PKK activities in Europe, clandestine networks. Then there came a point when I felt I had heard quite enough about Selim's life. He would start a sentence by saying: 'You know that uncle I told you about, the one who was once arrested . . .' And I would try not to listen, I would cross my fingers and think, *Please, please, don't let the uncle be up to something illegal again, because his dodgy uncle is now kind of . . . my dodgy uncle.*

And then, later, I wished I had been more inquisitive.

I didn't see the older sister after our baklava-munching encounter. Selim mentioned her occasionally – there were the births of more nephews and nieces, and his continued attempts to join her, hampered by his residency status. Of course, as a teenager, he had been tied to my hometown. Now his asylum claim was no longer relevant, but he was still tied to the town. Moving elsewhere without me would have raised official suspicions about our marriage. It would also have meant transferring his entire case to a new immigration official, not a risk worth taking, however nice it would have been to be with his family.

Aynur was the more mysterious sister, intriguing in her remoteness. In Selim's childhood tales, she came across as

254

a tomboy, out-running and out-climbing the boys in the village, sheepishly lowering her head when scolded by her mother for the umpteenth time, sneaking out of the kitchen at the next opportunity to get up to more mischief. And despite all that, despite defying her family's idea of how a daughter should talk and behave, she was more beloved than anyone else in the village. Young mothers called her over to pass her sweets; grandfathers chuckled toothlessly at her latest pranks. Her older brother adored her.

In a family where girls were expected to shy away from suitors in timid modesty, she stood in the centre of the kitchen one morning, hands on hips, and announced to her mother and siblings that one day she was going to marry Selim's best friend. He was polite and well-spoken, she said, not a snot-nosed rogue like the other village boys, and she was going to marry him.

'Guess that's why I saw him running off to the mountains this morning,' said Selim, a snot-nosed rogue himself at the time. 'Never saw such a terrified groom.'

She blushed and stormed out of the kitchen, only to return a few minutes later, laughing.

Wherever Selim went, Aynur went too. It had always been that way, though like any older brother he spent much of his time trying to shake her off. The real problem began when he first ventured out on small political errands. As usual, Aynur tried to tag along. But this time he was firm. He conquered her little-sister stickiness with the help of his father and uncles: a wall of men surrounding the girl and telling her if they ever caught her following Selim she would get the thrashing of a lifetime.

255

She gave in, for a week or two. And then there was the day when Selim joined the big funeral procession, waving a photo on a banner made from a branch and a piece of cardboard, and turned around to see Aynur standing right behind him. There was a loud bang; the Turkish units started shooting.

'There was a lot of blood,' was all Selim ever said about the incident. 'There was a lot of blood.'

Was that the reason? Had that sown a resentment which would one day take Aynur high up into the mountains, a Kalashnikov slung over her shoulder? It was too easy a connection to make, and Selim looked uncomfortable when he mentioned it to me.

'One day you'll see her again,' I assured him, taking refuge in lame banalities the way people often do when faced with grief. 'And then you can ask her. But in my experience, people never take that kind of big decision because of one single thing.'

'Maybe,' Selim said politely.

The fact is, he did not want to stop speculating about her motivations and his own role in influencing her. Reflecting and speculating and theorising about Aynur was a way of keeping her alive, of vicariously sharing her guerrilla existence. He pieced together a vastly incomplete picture of her, based on childhood anecdotes, second-hand reports from the mountains, Kurdish television footage, a girlish statement of intent uttered years ago in a ramshackle kitchen. The rest he filled in with speculation.

Even what he thought of as fact was probably inaccurate or exaggerated. For a start, the real Aynur was probably never as wild, as brave, as cheeky or as lovable a little girl as the Aynur in Selim's memories. As for more recent developments, I never found out exactly how he obtained news of her. But whatever reports there were had been compiled weeks, maybe months before reaching his ears.

To him, this did not seem to matter. When he spoke about Aynur, he became quite a different person from the eternally wavering, softly spoken friend. He would grow agitated, not exactly aggressive but certainly determined. Amid all the uncertainties in his life, his commitment to Aynur and to their shared political dream was a constant: solid, unshakeable.

And so, when I think of Kurdistan, I don't think of shepherds, religious zealots, warriors or drug lords. I don't think of rebellious girls or baggy-trousered rappers. I don't even think of Turkish villages or Iraqi oilfields. I think of drinking tea in a damp little flat in a crooked house in a tiny medieval alleyway, looking at photos of brides and mountains, listening to a halting, word-mangling voice talk about home.

Selim would never have tattooed *KURD* onto his hand and he would never have composed a Kurdish rap song with the chorus *Fuck all Turks*, and it had been years since he last shouted 'BIJI KURDISTAN'. He wasn't a shouter, Selim.

But he was, in his passive way, a fighter. You think it's impossible to be a passive fighter? Well, sometimes fighting just means surviving. Surviving, staying put, and quietly biding your time.

257

39

Passive fighting: not as spectacular as firing a machine gun at a helicopter or posing for the cameras with a rakishly angled beret on your head, but not every true warrior looked like Che. In fact, even Che did not always look like Che.

The boy who crossed my path when I emerged from the Métro, however, did look like Che, at least from behind. He wore a black beret and a black shirt over low-slung, baggy jeans and had pushed his hands into his pockets so that his hunched shoulders made his back look even broader. His eyes were on the street and his head bobbed as if he was listening to music; and just as I passed him he looked up and I saw that it was Azad, the young bully who had come to see me at the town hall about his cousin's wedding.

I stopped and smiled at him, but he did not smile back. I could hear the muffled beats from his earphones.

'Azad?' I tapped his shoulder.

The beats stopped.

'Hmm?' the boy grunted, and with a cringe I realised it wasn't Azad at all.

'I'm so sorry, I thought you were someone I knew.'

He smirked, evidently reckoning I was trying to chat him

up. A swarm of schoolchildren came up the stairs and streamed past us, shrieking and giggling.

'You look like a guy I know, he's called Azad. Never mind. Sorry,' I mumbled.

Mothers with pushchairs bumped into us and pulled away. We stood there and then he gave another nod, the muffled beats started again, and he turned away, towards the town hall.

I briefly considered making a detour, or waiting by the Métro entrance, anything rather than trail him; but I was already running a little late for my appointment, and so I had no choice but to follow him like an enamoured skunk. After a few steps, he slowed and looked over his shoulder, smirking again.

'I work at the town hall,' I said helplessly.

The beats stopped.

'Huh?'

'I work at the town hall,' I repeated, pointing at the building ahead.

'Oh, right. I have an appointment there.' This time, he removed the earphones and took off the beret, shaking it out before stuffing it into his bag.

'Well, I'm happy to show you the way,' I said, seizing the opportunity to overtake him a little, so that he was the one following me now.

He laughed.

'I know the way. It's right there, the big building with the flag. In fact, the enormous flag with the building.'

'Exactly.'

'But thanks for offering, I mean, it's really hard to guess.'

259

He was about to stick his earphones back in his ears, but then stuffed them into his pocket. His black hair was glistening with gel, his sideburns shaved into neat rectangles. The black shirt was freshly ironed but his jeans were crumpled, as if he wanted to appear sort of respectable but not too bothered.

'So what do you do at the town hall?' he asked, catching up so we were walking side by side, Parisian town houses with wrought-iron doors to our left, the hilly park to the right.

'Paperwork, basically. Deaths, births and weddings. Well, the Deputy Mayor conducts the wedding ceremonies, but I organise them.' I glanced at our reflection in a wrought-iron-and-glass door with an oddly Christmassy holly-leaf pattern. How nice it would be to live in a spacious flat right next to the park.

'Then my appointment is with you.' He stopped and stretched out his hand.

My mind was still on wrought-iron balconies overlooking the trees, and I replied distractedly: 'Not necessarily, there are lots of . . .'

He shook his head.

'No, it's with you. You fit the description.'

Oh, of course. So this was the groom. I decided not to ask how Azad had described me, and instead shook his hand. His handshake was warm, friendly. He had Azad's large brown eyes, but without the hostile glare.

'I'm really glad you came,' I said, trying to sound genuinely pleased. 'I'm not sure what Azad told you—'

'He's kind of pissed off because, well, we wouldn't have

260

this appointment if my surname was Dupont.' He grinned. 'Hey, don't worry, that's just Azad. He takes things personally.'

'Hmm. I wish he could see that this isn't about, er . . .' I panicked, trying to think of the right phrase. 'This is not about cultural differences, you know. I mean, I'm less French than you, I grew up in Germany,' I said, too obviously trying to ingratiate myself with him.

'Germany.' He weighed the word a little, as if unsure whether this was a good or a bad thing. 'I've got a cousin in Munich. He's been working for Siemens for twenty years.'

He was kicking an empty beer can, alternating legs like a professional footballer, punctuating his replies with the clatter.

'Yes, all the Kurds I meet seem to have family there.'

He kicked the can again, less playfully this time.

'Kurds and Turks have such a shit reputation in Germany. It's a bit better here because, well, at least Paris gets all the Turkish poets, right? But still. My cousin is studying in the US and he says Americans have a great image of the Turks.'

'The Turks?'

'The Turks, the Kurds, whatever. He calls himself a Turk over there because Americans don't know what Kurds are. And they love him. In fact, when he does explain that he's a Kurd and from an ethnic minority and all that, they love him even more.'

He misjudged his last kick, sending the can right across the street. He paused for an instant, probably wondering whether it was worth pursuing, then shook his head with a slight expression of regret and turned to me.

261

'I really want to study in the States. Did you know that Muslims are richer than the average person over there?'

I didn't.

'Whereas in Europe they are poorer! Just think about that.'

I thought about it for about two minutes, while he was trying to balance a pine cone on the tip of his trainer. We were kicking random statements back and forth now, and I suspected that neither of us really wanted to talk about the wedding, that we were both looking for ways to make our appointment pass as quickly and painlessly as possible.

'Well then, shall we get it over and done with?' I said eventually. 'Let's go inside and have a proper chat. Part of the procedure, you know.'

He crushed the pine cone with his foot.

When we entered the *mairie*, I could not help feeling that this was a replay of my encounter with Azad. This visitor was quite different of course, much friendlier for a start, but I still felt a bit of institutional support would be helpful, and so I led him up the soaring, swerving main staircase, up the red carpet rippling over white marble, past a marble slab gold-engraved with the names of previous mayors, past a row of somewhat anticlimactic potted ferns, and into the empty wedding hall.

'No weddings this afternoon, and this is nicer than my office,' I said by way of explanation.

He strode over to the window, measuring out the oval room, then whipped around and looked up at the ceiling.

'Wow.' He drew his chin back, respectfully studying the knife-wielding man and the bull in the fresco. 'Is that a butcher?'

That wasn't quite the effect I had intended. I wished he had noticed the elegant, wall-length wedding portrait first, or even the inoffensive gouache in the corner, showing a ruffled pigeon.

'It's Zeus with the bull,' I lied.

'It can't be Zeus. Zeus turned himself into a bull, right, so why would he go around slaughtering bulls?'

'Maybe he was trying to get rid the competition.'

Mercifully, he ignored that.

I left him standing there, legs apart, arms crossed, scrutinising the ceiling, and went to my office to fetch a photocopied list of questions from *The Registrar's Manual*. I feared that bringing the whole booklet, with its barbed-wire wedding ring on the cover, would only invite more controversy.

When I returned, he had wandered over to the painting of cows and cattle traders.

'Reminds me of matchmaking,' he said with his back to me.

'Exactly.' I sat down on one of the red-velvet-covered chairs. 'I guess it's a French thing, you know, the farm theme. They just really love cows.'

'They do,' he said. 'You're right. They really do.'

He proceeded to the sun-dappled wedding portrait, and I started to feel like some bored sibling on museum Sunday, sitting there with my open folder on my lap.

'Do you know her well?' I asked a bit too loudly.

'Who?'

'The bride.'

He turned around and shot me the same look he had when I told him the butcher was Zeus.

263

'Of course I know her. We're about to marry.'

'Of course. I've just been wondering . . . I'm supposed to meet you two separately, and she's been ignoring my calls.'

'She's probably busy shopping.' He laughed. 'I'm not joking. You know, Turks and Kurds, we love buying new shit for weddings.'

'Well, she really needs to come. I know this must be annoying, on top of all the preparations. Though you've already had the big bash in Turkey?'

He leaned over the wooden table, feeling the carved laurel wreath as if he hadn't heard me.

'After the religious ceremony, I mean. Sorry, I thought Azad said that's all been done already.'

'Oh, that.' He stood up and paced around the room again, his feet searching for something to play with. 'The ceremony was kind of rushed. We'll have another party over here. You can never have too many parties, right?' He laughed nervously. 'Listen, it's just a wedding. What else can I say. If it seems so weird to you, why don't you come to the party afterwards and check it out. We'll all be locking our little fingers and dancing in a circle. Bride, groom, shitloads of people, and the next day the video goes up on the Internet and everyone writes a comment saying Kurdish weddings are the best.'

'Thanks. I'd love to.' I smiled. 'Listen, why don't you sit down and we'll go through the questions, get the formalities out of the way, and then I'll let you go.'

To my surprise, he complied.

I looked at the photocopy in front of me. The first question seemed easy enough.

264

'So,' I said, 'the way it works is, I go through the questions with you, and I'll ask the bride the same questions.'

That was probably not at all what I should have said; now they would be able to give the same answers. Or maybe I wanted them to? I tried to remind myself that this was a very different situation from Selim's, that this was not about wrecking a pact sealed out of solidarity, but about protecting a young girl.

I read out the first question.

'Why do you want to marry her?'

He shrugged.

'Because it's the right thing to do.'

That sounded like a reasonable answer. Or did it? What was the right answer, anyway? Should he have said, *Because I love her and want to spend the rest of my life with her*? Is that what anyone would say in this situation, in this wedding hall, facing an anonymous official below a painting of an abattoir?

'Sure,' I said. 'Fine. The next one is about how you met. If you could just—'

'If I get all of them right, do I get a prize?' He was resting his elbows on his knees, leaning forward and studying me with a mocking smile. His eyelashes were very long, almost feminine, lending him a sweet expression even as his jaw hardened in slight annoyance.

'The prize is a lovely wedding here in the town hall.' I gestured to the paintings, the carved laurel wreath, but he didn't laugh. 'OK, let's get back to this . . . how did you meet, and how did you propose?'

Another mistake. You weren't supposed to ask double questions. I felt so weary, so tense.

He, on the other hand, grew more relaxed.

'The traditional way,' he said, then paused as if to assess the impact of his reply. 'The traditional way. My parents talked to her parents.'

'I see.' This was not the answer I had expected. 'But you and the bride, you both agreed?'

'Parents want the best for their children, right?' He ran his fingers through his gelled hair. 'If my mother chooses a girl, then, well, it's going to be someone good. And my parents will have checked out her family, because with us you marry the whole family, so you want to be sure they're OK.'

I pondered this. It seemed quite sensible, really. At least it seemed no less sensible than printing *MARRY ME* on an aerial streamer, or paying a rock band to end their performance with the wedding march, or drunkenly, unsteadily going down on one knee in Las Vegas.

I flicked to the next page.

'So you work in a restaurant . . . but you want to go to university, you said? Would your wife accompany you to the States?'

'You're sounding like my mother.'

'Sorry. There's a section here on employment, but I can't see what that's got to do with anything. Let's skip this one.' I was on the brink of handing him the whole folder, just to prove that it wasn't me who had come up with this list of silly questions, that I was only doing my job.

'So you're happy with this arrangement?' I asked, though that question was not on the list.

'Don't I look like a happy man?' He flashed me a broad, gleaming-white grin. 'Don't I look happy to you? What more do you want, shall I stand up and sing? Get on that table and dance?' He jumped up and for a second I thought he was really going to do it.

'Fine, fine,' I said with a wave, keen to wrap this up. Now I would just need to meet the bride, ask her the same questions, then let them get on with their wedding preparations.

'There's no right or wrong answer here, please don't think there is. Let's just work our way down the list. Could you tell me a little bit about the bride – where she was born, and so on?' I turned the page and added, somewhat absent-mindedly: 'She really is quite young, isn't she?'

Still standing, he crossed his arms, looking down at me, no longer smiling.

'Are you saying all this fuss is because my fiancée is eighteen? Has it ever occurred to you that . . .'

Then he sighed and sat down without completing his sentence.

267

40

They filmed the girl from behind, her long, curly hair bunched into a ponytail, a Kalashnikov resting in the crook of her arm. She was gazing out at the foggy mountaintops. An avuncular German correspondent recounted her brief life so far, speaking with the exaggerated enunciation of the TV world: childhood in a mountain village. Teenage recruitment into the PKK. Guerrilla drills in the wilderness.

'. . . As they work. To rebuild. Their homeland. As well as the destroyed relations. Between men and women. Here,' the correspondent said to the camera, sweeping his arm over the breathtaking mountainscape, before adding with a dramatic flourish: 'in Kurdistan. After centuries of oppression.'

He waddled over to the camp with a chubby man's joviality, and I wondered how on earth he had made it all the way up to the mountaintop.

They showed images of the settlement where the girl and the others lived. A windswept open-air canteen, a vegetable patch and an improvised football pitch, a row of tilting tents. From there they would venture out on bone-breaking missions, into the scraggy mountains, into the treacherous valleys, into combat.

The women's guerrilla section had been founded in the mid-1990s, and little was known about their military campaign. The film crew was not allowed to record the planning meetings or daily self-criticism sessions but they showed the girl, her face blurred, recounting them in her own words. Selim frowned, straining with concentration as he tried to listen behind the stilted German translation that muffled her voice.

'Please forgive me, today I was very selfish. I failed to be passionate about today's history class. I wasn't paying attention. Yes, you're right, comrade, thank you for pointing it out. Not only was I not paying attention, I disturbed the class. I'm selfish and immature. Please help me improve my behaviour.'

Selim turned to me.

'It is very difficult to hear through the German. But, you know, it sounds so like Aynur. It is Aynur. I'm sure it is Aynur.' He rubbed his face in agitation. 'I know it must be my sister.'

The camera followed her on a photogenic exercise, probably set up for the TV crew. Perfect propaganda material. All the faces were either turned away or had been blurred, not, perhaps, at the request of the commander, but because the producer wanted to make the filming seem more clandestine. After all, what did it matter to the girls? They were outlaws anyway, they lived as such and had nothing to hide from the camera.

'It's better that they're blurred,' Selim countered when I shared my thoughts. 'Not for them now, but for the families. For those who stay behind in the village and tell the Turks my daughter is in Germany, my daughter got married and

269

moved to the city and she looks after her seven children there.'

The next images were of the girl on the mountaintop again, following another *tchemil* session.

'Please forgive me for another act of selfishness. While the others were washing dishes, I sat on the hillside and smoked. Then they made bread for the next day, and still I smoked. When they called me to order, I responded in a surly and childish manner. Yes, you are correct, even as I responded, still I was smoking. I ask for your forgiveness and promise I will improve my behaviour.'

'It's my sister,' Selim repeated.

'Hmm . . .' I tried to phrase my thoughts carefully. 'What do you make of the weird self-criticism? Do you think that, hmm, you know, she's in trouble?'

He waved aside my concerns.

'That's what self-criticism is for, you have to show you feel bad. Then they pass the results up to the commanders and to their commanders and so on. But the things she mentions are small, I don't think they will matter so much. And she seems well, no? I think she is doing well, and she seems well.'

The crew followed the women through their daily routine. Push-ups before dawn, lectures, drills and patrols. Like their nomadic ancestors, they packed up the entire settlement with strong-armed stoicism, advanced along hairpin paths and narrow ledges to a different position that was deemed more secure or more strategically useful, then spread out their movable home again.

Like their ancestors, they lived by the seasons. In snowy winter, they hid in caves. Come spring, the Turks started

270

bombing the mountains again, and the women swarmed out to plot guerrilla attacks on Army outposts and oil pipelines and, though Selim was reluctant to mention this, Turkish civilians.

'Yes,' I said. 'I guess from what you told me she does sound a bit like your sister. And surely if she's the subject of this documentary, she must be doing well. I'm sure she's fine. She'll be fine. They appear to call her Nihal but she probably goes by a fake name?'

Selim grunted in confirmation.

Just then, the German reporter tugged his moustache, frowned and said: 'For these women. Following tradition. And following their hearts. Is not a contradiction. Take Nihal.' The camera switched to Nihal at target practice. 'Nihal left. For the mountains. Without telling her family. Without telling anyone. After her father was tortured to death. By the Turks.'

I glanced at Selim out of the corner of my eye. He sat shock-still. Then he pressed rewind. Then he pressed play. The reporter repeated his statement.

'She may have made it up. She may have made it up,' he mumbled. 'They probably gave her a story to tell.'

'Your father . . .' I ventured. Selim often talked about his mother; hardly ever about his father.

'He's fine. He's at home, I spoke to him the other day. He's OK.'

'I'm sorry. I just remembered how you said he used to be in prison.'

Selim nodded. He pressed pause and stared at the screen.

Then he said in a matter-of-fact voice: 'My father was in prison in Diyarbakir. To punish him, they made him eat his own shit.'

271

He turned to me, suddenly talking very fast, urgently, as if trying to get all the facts across in very limited time.

'I told you, when I was little, maybe eight or so, someone accused my father of being politically active. It was not true. They tortured him and he said yes, I've messed up, but it wasn't true. He had eight children, he did not want to be political, he did not want to spend his life in prison.'

Selim had never told me that. I had never asked.

'Then my father went into hiding,' Selim continued, leaning towards me, almost blocking me in with his thin body as if he was afraid I would try to leave. 'The special units came to our house at night. They asked where he was. They took away our clothes and kicked me in the head, the skin came off and you can still see the scars, here.' He patted his head. 'They came every other night. Once, after the last beating, I became very ill. My father heard. He was very worried about me, he thought if he stayed in hiding I might really be in danger. So he came out of hiding, I got better, I recovered and was well again. And they arrested him and they put him in prison in Diyarbakir for five years.'

His voice was clipped and insistent, that of a witness wanting to make sure not a single detail of his testimony was lost or forgotten; but there was no jury listening to his account, there was only me.

'Aynur and I,' he went on. 'We went to someone's funeral, a man who had been shot by the Turks. All my friends were there. We heard a bang, someone started shooting. It was bang, bang, bang, and then there was a tank and it drove into the crowd. It drove into the crowd and it drove over the children.'

272

He sank back into his seat, held the remote control in his shaking hand and continued to rewind and play, rewind and play the scenes with the girl.

'What about your sister?'

'There was a lot of blood. And screaming. After that and the beatings, my mother was so afraid for me, she sent me away with the *Schlepper*.'

When I left Selim's flat, I knew that he would spend the evening and the following days that way, obsessively trying to spot a telltale detail, a birthmark, a gesture, the flimsiest bit of evidence that this young warrior was his beloved sister. He was leaning forward as if he wanted to stretch all the way into the television and over to the mountains, squinting through his round glasses, for once concentrating so hard he wasn't even smoking, he wasn't even picking at his lips.

I think that may have been the moment when Selim first thought about going back to Kurdistan.

Not in a general sense: returning to Kurdistan was on his mind at all waking hours and probably in his dreams, too. But I think that was the moment when he began hatching a concrete and realistic, if simultaneously mad and suicidal plan.

'By the way, did you get anywhere with that video?' I asked him a few weeks later over the phone.

'What video?'

'The one of your sister . . . of the women in the mountains,' I corrected myself.

'Oh, that,' he said in an unconvincingly casual way. 'Who knows. I'll have to watch it again.'

41

Those were the days when we were still talking to each other. When we were still talking about things other than signatures, documents and bureaucratic threats. That was when Selim still taught me things: about Kurdish bread, about Kurdish songs, about the struggle for independence, about the traditions and contradictions and violent struggle of his people. About guerrilla warfare. About warrior women. About religion, and culture, and homesick longing. About bespectacled militants.

That was when we were still asking each other interesting questions and giving each other interesting answers. When we still, I guess, liked each other. When we still found each other intriguing. And then, as time went by and our problems grew, we talked less about each other and politics and more about paperwork. Finally, we hardly talked at all. I came to dread his voice on the phone, which would always signal some new request: *I need a special certificate showing that all four of your grandparents are German. My uncle has been arrested – no, not that one – I will tell you when I see you. I need you to come to Neustadt to sign something, yes, your exams, yes, I am sorry but you really need to come, yes, thank you.*

Then there would be the calls from Julian, who had bought an accordion and was busy practising Jazz Manouche and Klezmer songs: *Selim told me you were a bit short with him on the phone. Well, he really needs you to come. Carl was supposed to accompany him, or Meredith or someone, but they can't make it. Hey, you're the one who married him. He's your responsibility.*

'Ich bin Selim,' he would always say when I picked up. *I am Selim.*

It was his version of the usual, casual way to introduce yourself on the phone, which was: *Ich bin's, Selim. It's me, Selim.*

I never corrected his version, sensing that it suited him and corresponded to his constant need to assert himself in the world.

'Ich bin Selim,' he would say. And I would think, Oh dear, what's up now.

When our marriage began knocking against the three-year limit, I began to get impatient. The three years had passed with a few bumps and potholes. Our sham appeared to be holding up: no impromptu police raids on our supposedly shared flat, no summons to interviews with suspicious investigators. All in all, I had become used to the situation, as far as you can get used to continually looking over your shoulder, but I was also relieved that our time would soon be up. After three years, Selim would obtain his unconditional, permanent residency permit, and divorce would swiftly follow.

I hoped we would stay in touch, somehow. I bore him no ill-will. But I was also keen to see our chaotic project come to a conclusion. It was the minor problems, the tedium and sheer drawn-outness of it all that ground us down. In this,

275

too, we were not that different from ordinary married couples. The initial enthusiasm and exhilaration had faded, and doubts had set in, mistrust. I never doubted his desperate need for asylum; I never doubted that he faced great danger if he was deported to Turkey. But I did, at times, doubt whether his intentions were the same as mine. I began to wonder whether he was really putting all his energy into applying for permanent residency, or whether, knowing that he would never be deported while he was married to me, he was quite happy with the status quo. I wondered who Selim was really hanging out with, what he was up to, how much of what he told me was true.

And just like ordinary married couples, we found ourselves unexpectedly, fiercely, loyally reunited once a real catastrophe blew up our little world.

But first, there was a little bit of paperwork to sort out.

PART THREE

The Difficulty of Lighting a Fuse in the Rain

42

'I'm just calling to see if everything's OK with the permit. I'm in a bit of a rush really.'

I was in a phone booth at the foot of Montmartre and it was pouring with spring rain. The three years were over, more than three years even, three and a half. I had granted Selim a little more time, knowing he was not the most efficient person when it came to pushing his case.

A felt-hatted woman with a pug walked past, stopped, turned around and knocked on the side of the booth.

'Selim? Hello? Can you hear me? Sorry, the line is bad, it's a public phone.'

'It's OK, shall I call you at home tonight?' he shouted back.

It was then that I grew a little suspicious.

As far as I knew, the residency procedure was pretty much automatic. Three solidly married years, and you got the permit, and then you could keep it even if your wife dumped you.

'Is there a problem?'

'What?'

'I said, is there a problem?'

'I'm sorry, I can't hear you, the line's very bad. I will call you tonight, please?'

279

'Sure.'

But later that night, despite a much better line, the message remained murky. All I learned was that, contrary to our information, contrary to Dr Habicht's information, the process was not automatic at all.

Certainly, three years was the usual period.

It was highly unusual for it to take longer.

Highly unusual, but not unknown.

In our case, because of the wife's frequent absences from the couple's shared flat, the German immigration officials had decided to take a deep breath. Fold their arms. Lean back and say well, let's take a good look at these two, shall we? For all we know, they might well be a decent, ordinary couple, but there's something about them . . . let's just tighten the line a little bit and watch our bait wriggle, why not?

'Oh shit.'

'Yes. It is very difficult. I did not expect this either, please believe me. I swear.'

'And Dr Habicht didn't know this?'

'It has changed a lot. Everything has changed, Germany is becoming different. It is getting more difficult.'

'Well, I guess it's not a good idea to talk on the phone then. Let's discuss it when I'm back home.'

We met in a cottage tucked away behind a red gate in the medieval part of town. The usual wobbly circle: Selim, Meredith, Dr Habicht and some others from the legal aid group. A tanned, sinewy woman in a low-cut tank top, apparently the owner of the place, brought us mugs of calendula tea.

'Nature's miracle drug,' she whispered as she set down my mug. 'It helps cure ear infections.'

'Aha,' I said. 'Thank you.'

'*De nada*,' she whispered, and I wondered why she was whispering, and why she was speaking Spanish, and whether I should whisper too. She placed her hand on her cleavage: 'Pushpa.'

Then she sat down next to Dr Habicht. From the way she snaked around the room, at one point rubbing Selim's shoulders in a strangely possessive way, I assumed she was his girlfriend. Meredith, however, with one decisive move, pulled Pushpa away from Selim and onto a huge reddish multilayered sofa cum bed.

'I can totally see that it would totally make it easier for you if you got the divorce sorted but it's such a super-difficult time,' squeaked Meredith from the depths of the sofa. She had somehow graduated into a leadership position.

Dr Habicht didn't offer any surprises. Having once vowed that I would never face him again, I found that relying on Selim as a messenger was even more stressful, and so we had re-established contact.

He gratefully sipped Pushpa's tea, and when she repeated loudly that it was good for ear infections, he downed it with a greedy gulp and asked for another. Pushpa collected his mug and peered into it, pursing her lips in vague alarm.

'Ooh.' She jiggled the mug a little. 'You aren't actually meant to eat the flowers. Just let them settle gently at the bottom of your mug.'

Dr Habicht stared at her in terror, his hand at his throat.

'Are they poisonous?'

Yes, yes, yes, I thought darkly, but Pushpa smiled and shook her head, then shook it some more to show off her glossy curls.

Why did we continue to surround ourselves with this crew of somewhat limited competence? Well, I guess we needed a lawyer, and it had to be someone willing to risk his reputation and liberty by acting as our accomplice. It had to be someone who could be trusted to keep our secret, and, in all his ineptitude, Dr Habicht had proven himself again and again able to keep his mouth shut as required.

'Let me put it this way,' Dr Habicht drawled, more sinus-blocked than ever despite Pushpa's tea. 'We are very close to being granted permanent residence, and so I would suggest that we just, you know, push ahead, hrrm, now.'

As far as I know, we already have the right to permanent residence, in fact we have German passports, you legal fruitcake, I thought. *As far as I know it's Selim, in the singular, who is close to being granted permanent residence and needs to push ahead, in the singular, and it's me, in the singular, who's bound to him.*

'No worries, darling, from what I heard about the situation it's actually swimming along really well,' Pushpa suddenly volunteered, imitating a swimming movement. I stared at her, aghast that yet another unofficial adviser was pitching in, but she continued unperturbed: 'If I interpret what you say correctly, your need is to follow a path, a road map that will lead to divorce, and you feel you want to have that reassurance, that sense of support and security.'

'I'm not sure there's much room for interpretation in, *I want to get divorced*,' I said.

'But you don't want to get divorced now,' she said with a

282

maternal smile. 'You only want that reassurance, that road map.'

'No.' I shook my head. 'I want to get divorced.'

'You see,' Meredith said in the kind, slow way of explaining something important to someone who was a bit dim, 'if you get divorced now, Selim will be deported. But the good news is, as long as you stay married, nothing can happen to him, and he's safe.'

She smiled at me and at Selim, who was wearing his most neutral and sleepy expression.

'Yes, that's great, but what if . . .' I could see that they were impatiently shifting around on their cushions, expecting me to accept the situation, but I needed to make my point. 'What if Selim *never* gets his permit?'

'As long as you stay married, that won't be a problem,' Pushpa declared with conviction. 'They can't do anything to him.'

'But if we remain married for as long as Selim wants to stay in Germany, and he wants to stay in Germany for ever, then we'll remain married . . .' I let the sentence hang in the air, almost choking back the final part: *'For ever.'*

When I think back to that peculiar scene now, it always gets mixed up with memories of my friend Anna's wedding to Philippe, even though the two events lie years and miles apart. It was a church wedding; Anna had converted to pacify Philippe's Catholic family. The priest was young and French and the sermon smooth and elegant, until the point where the priest, clearly quite excited by his first bilingual wedding, stopped, glanced at the assembled guests in their pews, took a deep breath and switched from French to

283

English, not letting his lack of fluency stop him from joining in the multicultural fun.

'God take these two, man and woman,' the priest declared, holding his two fists over his head, while Anna's eyes widened in dismay. 'And put them together.' He brought his fists together and interlocked his fingers. 'Until death come.' He unlocked his hands and spread them out. 'And take them apart.'

The congregation watched in stunned silence. He took another deep breath and switched back to French for the rest of the sermon.

'*That was completely off script,*' Anna, clasping her bouquet so tightly she crushed the stems, hissed in my ear before she and Philippe got into the flower-topped black limousine. 'We gave him clear instructions – no freestyle preaching, and certainly no English!'

Whenever I think back to that afternoon in Pushpa's cottage, that moment when I first thought Selim might *never* get his permit, might never agree to a divorce, the image of the priest comes up on my mental screen, like a signal disturbance, and I can see the priest interlock his fingers: 'Until death come. And take them apart.'

Dr Habicht, Pushpa and Meredith all rushed to disperse my doubts: *No, no, no, definitely not for ever, let's not exaggerate, it'll be another year max, OK, maybe two, anyway, it's a totally finite thing.*

I turned to Selim, who was studying the carpet.

But in the end, as always, I gave in.

In hindsight, it's obvious that I was one of those people who always protest and shout but ultimately give in. The complete opposite, in fact, of Selim, who silently stuck to the sidelines and yet, never truly yielded.

I think I have changed since then. I think that over time, I may have become a little more like Selim. I have learned to sit quite still, and look quite sleepy, and yet be very alert. I rarely shout these days. And I don't give in that easily any more.

After leaving Pushpa's flat, Selim and I patted each other's backs as veterans might, wishing each other luck and assuring each other that everything would be fine.

That was summer 2001.

43

The place where I worked as a waitress during uni was still there, on a busy street corner not far from where I lived now. Sometimes I walked past it, the students drinking beer outside, the oleander tree perched precariously on the first-floor balcony.

The meeting with Selim was some time in late June. By July, I was back in Paris. The couple I lived with were on the verge of breaking up, my deal with another flat-share had fallen through, I would soon be homeless, but at least there was a generous supply of booze at the bar. The owner, Lucien, a thirty-something musician, had recently divorced and we took to locking up shop together, then wrapping up the night with a civilised drink.

One evening, he pulled down the metal shutters, tossed the keys on the counter and rummaged around in the fridge with much clanging and clinking, before pulling out a bottle of champagne:

'Celebration! I bought a new guitar.'

We toasted the guitar. Then we toasted each individual string. Then we decided that the other guitars might feel excluded, so we toasted them, too, from his first acoustic to the Yamaha Silent.

'But you haven't even seen it!' he exclaimed as we mournfully examined the empty bottle. 'I must introduce you. No really, I must.'

We clambered up the worn wooden stairs. He poured me a glass of wine, then plugged in the new electric guitar and dug his hand into the strings, producing a deafening roar.

'Wouldn't the Silent be a better idea?' I suggested timidly. 'The neighbours . . .'

He beamed at me.

'Listen to this, it's like this, it goes . . .'

I thought I could hear the wine glasses tremble in the kitchen.

Then, unmistakably, there was another sound angrily trying to be heard: a fist hammering against the wall from the other side.

'Lucien, I love it and it's great and I love it, but the neighbours . . . hey, you're going to lose your licence.' I scrambled to my knees, put down my glass and stood up with difficulty. 'It's quite loud.'

He stopped, suspending his hand mid-air.

'I don't care. I'll go on playing for ever.' He strummed a few more chords as if to back up his threat, then paused again. 'I'll only stop if you kiss me.'

That was the first week of August. A month later, I packed my books and clothes into seven cardboard boxes and moved in with Lucien.

At night, we left the doors to the tiny balcony wide open but that only made the flat even hotter. The heat seeped in through the deep cracks in the walls and thickened under the low ceiling. Lucien had bricked up some of the windows and

287

bolted shelves and hooks to the walls to house his guitars and stacks of shoe boxes that contained, allegedly, lyrics. We would spend all morning in bed, I dozing off my hangover, he leaning against the headboard, tinkling the guitar while zapping from soap operas on TF1 to the LCI news channel to the live transmission of some motor race. He loved motor racing.

I was waiting for classes to start again, for my uni friends to come back from their holidays or work experience. My books and clothes were boxed up in Lucien's *cave*, gathering mould under dripping stone arches along with some gifts from his ex-wife.

Around lunchtime, Lucien would put his guitar aside, scratch his belly and pad into the kitchen to make coffee and roll the first joint of the day. Later, his friends dropped by or he went off to band practice and I sought out the few friends of mine who had stayed in Paris over the sweltering summer. And then, at night, the bar again, and more drinking and music-making and love-making.

Until, one afternoon, we were eating cheese in the park around the corner when my phone beeped.

Julian had sent me a message: *Pentagon burning, WH evacuated, switch on CNN.*

Lucien read the message and yawned.

'What does he mean?'

'Some kind of joke, I guess, or World War Three.'

'I don't have CNN.' He scratched his belly. 'Can't we stay in the park? Then if the world blows up at least we've got a nice view.'

We went back to his flat to flick through the French channels, watching them replay footage of the collapsing towers. It was

288

weird to see the newscaster as confused and anxious as her viewers; it upset the world order in which newscasters were always impassive no matter what tragedies rolled off the teleprompter.

Over the next few weeks, things changed, at first subtly, then not so subtly.

There was a Salafi shop and mosque down the road, and men in jellabas and women in niqabs had drifted in and out all day. Now the street was empty. Once I saw a bearded man hurry over from a nearby doorway and dive into the shop as if running from one air-raid shelter to another.

A wild-eyed boy stopped me in the street and demanded in an angry tone: 'American? You American?' No, I said, German, and he snorted and went away.

I received an e-mail from a Colombian friend living in Paris, a slightly unhinged performance artist who told me he felt sorry for all the people who had died, but nevertheless the day had put a big smile on his face: *The entire Third World is on its knees before the great Imperialist, except for the sons of the crescent moon who rise up and spit in its face.*

Classes started again and several friends offered me a room but I stayed with Lucien.

One of my lecturers, a Sikh from Singapore, warned us of manipulative elites who would try to use this event to their advantage. There were people who would try to incite riots, he said, and the masses would probably be all too happy to comply.

'It will start with something extremely simple. One single incident,' he said slowly. 'One man throws a pig into the window of a halal butcher. The next thing you know: riot.'

289

September usually saw the bar fill up with post-holiday crowds, but this year, people in the neighbourhood avoided public spaces and we were lucky to see a dozen punters per night. I guess the proximity to the mosque didn't help either. Lucien sold his bed to buy a new guitar. A friend donated an old mattress.

We were lying on that mattress, listening to the BBC World Service, which I had imposed on Lucien, who preferred French radio. He was tapping out the rhythm to some new song on my thigh. On the radio, various experts were announcing in roundabout ways that they had no clue what was going on or what would happen next, but that it was all very worrying.

And suddenly Lucien held still and said with uncharacteristic seriousness: 'I can tell you one thing, all those movements, Chechnya, Basque Country, all the separatists, they're finished.' He made a slicing movement across his throat with his hand, the one that had seconds ago so playfully patted my skin. 'America and Europe will say you're on your own now, and anything your government wants to do to you, we keep away. That's all over.'

It was only then that I thought about what all this would mean for Selim.

I rested my head in the soft hollow between Lucien's shoulder and his neck. He smelt of weed and smoke, but in a pleasant way. He pulled me closer.

'Lucien?'

'Don't worry, they're not going to bomb this neighbourhood, the terrorists, I mean. Too many Salafis here.'

290

'I'm not sure it works like that . . . but anyway, that's not what I was going to say.'

'We could always move the mattress down to the *cave* and sleep there, if you're scared. I'll take care of you.' He looked at me, intensely earnest now. 'I'll always take care of you.'

Taken aback by his solemn tone, I smiled uncertainly.

He cleared his throat.

'You know, when the divorce finally came through, the first thing I thought was, Never again. But bizarrely, I actually like marriage. I don't like my ex-wife, but I like marriage. And I think you and I, we'd be crazily happy, don't you think?'

I laughed, and he looked terribly hurt and I immediately regretted it.

'I'm so sorry, of course we'd be happy, of course, it would be perfect, it's just, this is so unexpected, and also—' I sat up. 'I'm married.'

His expression changed to disbelief and then annoyance, and he opened his mouth and shut it again without saying anything.

'Not *married-married*,' I said quickly. 'Let me explain . . .'

'Yes,' he said in a tone that I had never heard him use before, very dry and sarcastic and not at all like the bouncy Lucien I knew. 'That would be nice.'

'It's not what you think. I married a friend of mine, a Kurdish friend, so he could stay in Germany. *Un mariage blanc.*'

'*Un mariage blanc*! Hmm. Guess that's a fair reason for marrying,' he replied with forced good humour. 'In fact, I can't think of a better reason. Practical, and you don't have to worry about dividing up the *cave* when things go wrong.'

'Guess so. But you know what, sometimes he annoys me just like a husband would annoy me. And at other times I worry about him just as I would worry about a husband. Like right now, for example. I wonder how he's going to react to all this. Or if he's in danger, for some reason. I don't know . . . I just have this weird feeling in my stomach.'

'Maybe you like him more than you think,' he said. He reached for his guitar and started tinkling it absent-mindedly.

'No, no, that's not what I meant to say at all . . . I'm not sure what I meant to say. I think I'm a bit scared.'

I wanted him to look at me, to tell me again that everything would be fine, but he was looking down at the strings now, tinkling, plucking, strumming with nervous distraction. 'So, let me get this straight, I've just proposed to a woman who is married to a potential terrorist. This is getting better and better.'

'But for us, for you and me, this doesn't change anything, right? It's just a piece of paper. I'll obviously have to stay married to him for a bit, especially now . . .'

'Who cares about marriage anyway,' he said with a wave of the hand, putting down the guitar. His light-heartedness was as exaggerated as his previous seriousness, but I didn't know how to turn the conversation around.

We lay there in silence for a while, and I wondered whether he was mentally reshuffling all the plans he had laid out before me just a few minutes ago, the ones I had never even suspected existed, plans that involved us getting married, buying a flat maybe, having children. Who knows.

292

'Lucien, I really do want to stay with you. I'd love to marry you one day,' I attempted.

There was no reply. Even as the words left my mouth, I knew they sounded unconvincing and empty. I was being dishonest; in truth, I could not imagine ever marrying Lucien. It wasn't that I never wanted to get married again. It was more that my marriage to Selim had such a concrete purpose: to ward off all manner of threats and horrors. A bond based on some whirlwind romance seemed self-indulgent, immature by comparison. And yet, deep down, after all those years of sneering at bourgeois respectability, I had to admit to myself that the idea of a proper, life-long marriage, a promise made and a life built together, was lovely.

I dozed off, and was woken up by Lucien gently shaking my shoulder.

'Baby?'

'Mmm?'

'Listen.' He pointed to the radio.

'What?'

'They've started bombing Afghanistan.'

I propped myself up on one arm and listened to the correspondent telling us from far away what was going on.

293

44

I say I realised what it meant, but of course I didn't. Not really. Some of the fallout I could have predicted. The PKK was added to a global list of terrorist organisations; its leader, Abdullah Öcalan, was arrested. And I found out that, even after more than four years of marriage, a divorce would lead to Selim's deportation.

It was Julian who told me. He called me in Paris to inform me about the latest tightening of Germany's immigration policy. We were only sporadically in touch now. Starting with the time he and Selim told me about the child-benefit snag, there had been a number of rows. I resented Julian for his patronising interventions, for the way he lectured me on my fake marriage even though he knew as little or as much as I did.

'If it's all so easy, then why don't *you* go and marry a Kurdish girl,' I snapped at him.

Officially, we had made up and were friends again. I had applauded enthusiastically at a few of his chaotic accordion concerts in an abandoned pickle factory in Berlin, and he had promised to visit me in Paris and talk Jazz Manouche with Lucien.

He called me soon after his 'Pentagon-burning' text.

'But it's been what, more than four years! I thought it would be three. You said it would be three. And then the others said it would be four, *max*, and now it's been more than four, and now you're saying . . .' Even as I spoke, I knew how stupid and useless my protests were; what Julian had said didn't matter. He knew nothing, I knew nothing, our allies knew nothing. And Selim, well, Selim was his own mystery. I hadn't called him since 9/11, like a child who thinks she can't be seen if she closes her eyes.

'It's changed,' Julian said. 'If you pull out now, Selim will be sent back. And you know what that means. It's almost worse now, they are arresting Muslims left, right and centre, and if the Turks want to make some Kurds disappear they can simply claim they were part of a terror cell.'

I sighed.

'Whatever. OK. Let's just find a way of ending it this year before I graduate. Before I start applying for jobs.'

'You going to pop over for a visit at some point?'

'Guess so.'

'Right. I think Selim needs you to sign a few papers.'

'OK. I need to renew my passport anyway.'

'Listen . . .'

'Mmm?'

'I'm sorry it all turned out this way.'

'Whatever. Go and write a song about it.'

45

Renewing my passport: a routine visit, I thought.

Which was why it was so easy for them to trip me up.

Grey linoleum floors, grey walls, jolly little stickers of cats and tulips on some of the nameplates on the doors. I tried to find the capital letters that corresponded with my initials, but there was no discernible system. One door was labelled *E, B, H.* The one next to it: *Q, N, R.* Yet another, all the way down at the other end of the corridor: *A, Z, M.*

I walked into the room, sat down and told the woman I was there to collect my new passport. She smiled at me from underneath her spiky, sporty blonde haircut, one of those easy to maintain ones. I could almost hear her telling her friend: *I just wash it, blow-dry it while the kids eat their cereal, then I'm off to work and I don't have to worry about it.*

She knew it was all about customer service these days, and so she maintained her smile as she checked my details. Frumpy old bureaucrat? Not her. She read out a street name, a flat number, a house number, a postcode. I had never heard of the street.

'Sorry, could you repeat that?'

She repeated it.

'There must be a mistake,' I said, annoyed. Someone must have mixed up the records, I thought, hoping the glitch wouldn't mean I'd have to make another appointment. 'Looks like you've got the wrong street. My address is—'

She checked her screen, frowned.

'Oh, but it says here—'

'No, that's not my street,' I said, tapping my fingers on the desk. Impatient.

She lifted her face from the screen. Our eyes locked.

'Well, it says you live at this address with Selim . . .?'

'Oh yes,' I said. 'Of course.'

It had been ages since we'd last spoken; he must have moved to a new place without telling me. What an idiot; what a complete idiot. He'd moved, and he hadn't even told me. I wondered what other surprises he had in store.

She had recovered her smile and was entering something into her computer, tippety-tap. 'So your address . . .'

She was tanned. At weekends, she probably went to the lake with her family. They'd take their own deckchairs and barbecue. Her husband liked steak. The children liked sausages and ate them with too much ketchup. She'd buy chicken breast for herself, because it was lighter, but then she'd end up stealing some of her husband's steak. I could see her whole family before me, grinning and tanned, an ideal German family: after fifteen years of marriage, she and her husband still had a vigorous sex life.

'So could you just confirm your address?' she insisted.

I repeated the address she had read out to me, silently praising my memory.

'Sorry, got a bit confused. I've been travelling a lot.'

297

She pretended to be keying something in, but I was not fooled. She was a hard nut, this one. I knew her type, the Superdiscount Centre was full of them. Hard women. And yet, a perfect wife and mother and, judging from the red-blooming cactus on her windowsill, a skilled gardener. She had had maybe the odd affair with a colleague, a neighbour. Nothing serious. She still occasionally met up with a former lover for an evening of card games, joined by his unsuspecting partner. Sometimes the former lover drank too much, slammed down the cards with an almost sexual aggression, and she'd worry there would be unpleasant remarks. When the former lover won and the husband lost, she'd briefly hate both of them. When her husband won, she'd feel proud. Being a mother and partner came first for her, but she was not without ambitions in her job. She had participated in workshops and training seminars. She had learned to handle more complex cases, to deal with the challenges of the age. She had been taught to spot the signs. Since the September 11 attacks, she had been told to be especially vigilant.

'So, can I quickly get you to confirm a few details for the system here?' she said. 'Just for the system.'

I felt sick. And then the questions came in a quick succession of blows. She didn't even give me time to put up my guard. She was relentless. Her husband would never dare cheat on her. He would secretly ogle the sunbathing wife of a neighbour, but he would never dare cheat on his Gestapo officer of a wife.

'Wedding day?'

Shit. Wedding day. Wedding day.

298

I need to get out of here, I thought. Right now. Somebody get me out of here.

Wedding day. A week after my birthday. I added seven days, I gave her the date.

She nodded.

'Husband's place of birth?'

'Cizre, Turkey.'

'Husband's date of birth?'

Tricky. I subtracted four months and three days from my own birthday and told the date.

She nodded.

'Husband's parents' names?'

'I've never met them and my husband hasn't seen them in ten years. I think his mother is called Fatima.'

She glanced up from her screen, scanned my face. She nodded.

'Husband's address?'

I'm not stupid, woman. I repeated the address she'd read out ten minutes earlier.

'And the flat is number . . .'

I repeated the number.

'I get quite confused these days. I've been travelling a lot, which is why I came here to renew my passport . . . yes, I've been living abroad but he had to stay here, that's just the way it worked for us.'

'Previous address?'

'As I said, I've been living abroad . . .'

'What does your husband do now?'

Nothing.

I babbled something about Selim's odd jobs.

299

'What do you do now?'

'I'm a student.'

'Can you sign here, please. Your signature means that you acknowledge all of the above and confirm it is true. All of it, you understand. I have to inform you that signing a statement that you know to be untrue is a criminal offence and can be punished with up to *three years in jail.*'

I signed. I nodded, and I signed. And I wondered why Selim hadn't told me he'd moved to a new address.

46

They were standing on the parapet of the ruined castle, where the courtyard gave way to a sheer drop all the way down to Blood House. There was a metal safety rail and Selim reflexively tested it, pushing it gently with his palms before leaning his body against the barrier and gazing down into the chasm.

Below them were hundreds of wonky little timbered houses and stone churches, arranged in a neat pile between the modern high-rise settlements to the right and the villages to the left and the forest beyond. Somewhere out there, beyond the forest, must have been the former military barracks where Selim found refuge, but try as he might, he could not find the familiar shape on the horizon.

'Not bad, is it,' Dynasty said finally. 'I always think of our town as the armpit of Germany, but it's actually quite pretty, isn't it?'

Selim nodded.

'We're kind of lucky to live here, if you think about it. It could be worse, we could be living with the farmers.' She pointed at the fields and forest in the distance. 'Did you know Dwayn once went to visit his cousin in the village and his cousin asked him if he wanted to shag a cow? Like, as a kind of welcome.'

'I haven't been to any of the villages. Sometimes I've driven past with my uncle, on the way to Frankfurt.'

'Me too, when we go clubbing and stuff. But that's not the same, is it?'

'No.'

'So you go clubbing in Frankfurt as well?'

'No, I sometimes go there for official things. You know, immigration and that.'

'Oh right. But that's all sorted now?'

'Yes, no problem, I have a permit,' Selim said, staring into the chasm to avoid her eyes.

'Anyway, can't wait to leave this place. Like, it looks nice enough from above, but there's nothing here, is there?' She bent over the rail, plucked a light-green leaf from a shrub and dropped it, watching it sail all the way down to the twee houses.

'I can't leave. I'm always here,' Selim said regretfully.

'Of course you can leave, you've got a permit now.'

'It's difficult. It's not like a passport. It's more like, someone takes you into his house and says you can stay here because it's dangerous outside, but actually you can only stay if you stand behind the oven.'

She laughed.

'But it's good! It's better than being kicked out,' he hastily added, not wanting to whinge. It was complicated, explaining that part of his life. He knew that Germans expected a kind of gratitude for having allowed him to stay. And he did feel grateful, deeply grateful. But it was simply not possible

302

to live your life in a permanent state of gratitude, of meekness and humility, cringing in a corner like a dog let in from the rain. At some point, one had to grow up, be able to criticise and argue and be a partner, not just a long-suffering presence. It was difficult to explain, and whenever he thought about it, he sensed that he was probably in the wrong.

They left the parapet and squeezed through a gap in the protective fence around the rubble and boulders and climbed up the ruins, ignoring the signs forbidding it.

Dynasty started humming a tune, something from the charts.

'So where do you go out?'

'Here.' He straightened up on one of the boulders and pointed at the town below them.

'How do you do that? There aren't even any clubs here.'

'I don't really go to clubs. I go to concerts, sometimes. Or parties.'

'You're not into clubbing?'

'Always so much trouble in the clubs, and sometimes it's difficult to get in, when they don't let in Turks.'

God, she must think he was such a whinger.

'Ha! That reminds me of this video I saw the other day. I'll show you if you come to my place. Anyway, I bet you're one of those guys who stand at the back of the room, right, leaning against the wall, tapping one foot and smoking, and watching people dance.'

He laughed but his mind was feverishly at work. *If you come to my place.* That basically meant she wanted him to go to her place. Or maybe not. It depended on whether she meant, *Please come to my place so I can show you,* or, *If you ever were to come to my place, which of course is highly unlikely, then you could*—

'Am I right?'

'Mmm?'

'That you're one of those guys who stand at the back of the room and never dance.'

'I don't like to dance. Yes, I just like to listen.'

'Anyway, we should go there some time.' She pointed to the countryside in the distance. 'Not just the fake lake. Everyone goes to the fake lake, but really, just, like, nature.'

'OK. We can borrow bikes from the bike shop.'

She laughed.

'Bikes?'

'Yes.'

'Bikes are for hippies.'

'So how do you want to get there?'

'We'll take my car, obviously.'

He laughed.

'Why, what's wrong?'

'You can't drive your car into the forest.'

'If anyone from my neighbourhood sees me on a bike . . . they'll think I'm one of those mangy students.'

'I can teach you. It's not difficult. And I can teach you in the forest, so none of your friends will see.'

'What makes you think I can't ride a bike? I just don't like the idea, that's all.'

Selim smiled.

'Listen, do you have a video recorder?' she asked quickly.

He nodded.

'Let's watch it at yours then. It's always so noisy at my place. Hey, let's go somewhere warm, it's getting cold. Freezing.'

At this, Selim brightened up. He took the cue and offered her his jacket.

'Like, black people have this thing, look at all the musicians, that's our people, look at all the wicked athletes, that's our people,' the bull-like boy in the video said, jutting his massive head towards the camera. 'But if you're a Kurd it's just like, hey, you're a Turk. No, ey old man, I'm a Kurd. Whassat, you're a Turk, right. Yeah, wa'ever.'

They cut to a hip-hop video, the bull-like boy skulking moodily in the foreground in his low-slung trousers and black hooded top, shouting out his anger while a gang of half-naked lovelies writhed in the background.

Dynasty turned to Selim.

'I thought you might like that, so I taped it.'

The song finished and they cut back to the interview, the boy slouching on a sagging sofa, slapping his chest every now and then for emphasis.

They showed footage from a concert. Dynasty tapped her fingers to the rhythm.

'So what do you think? Deniz, you've heard of him, right?'

'Yes,' Selim said. 'He's my cousin.'

'You're joking!'

'I'm not.'

'You're joking!'

'I'm not! He's my Aunt Leyla's son.'

'So, what, he invites you to his concerts and his parties and stuff?'

305

Selim laughed.

'He lives on the other side of Germany. I've only seen him once or twice, at weddings, when he was small. I have so many cousins, but I remember him well.' He smiled. 'He's very loud.'

'He's wicked. I thought you might like him, you know, like, he always sings about going to the mountains and fighting the Turks and stuff.'

'Yes,' Selim said. 'He lives near Hamburg with my aunt. It's very far from the mountains.' He paused, considering something. 'My aunt has been living here a long time. I don't think Deniz has ever been to Kurdistan. If he's ever seen the mountains, it was when Aunt Leyla was still changing his nappies. But you're right, it's good that he sings.'

He coughed, gathering his thoughts.

'If you like that music, I can get tickets for a concert. Not Deniz, but similar.'

Dynasty nodded and smiled.

Everyone around Selim was wearing a hoodie. Out of hundreds of boys he was the only one wearing an ironed shirt and he felt like an idiot. Maybe he should have known, should have turned up in baggy jeans and a hoodie. But this was a date, an official date with a girl, and surely it was right to make an effort, to wear a decent pair of jeans and a shirt and some of Flo's aftershave.

He discreetly unbuttoned the top of his shirt. Great, that was even worse, he could see it just by glancing down at himself. The wide-open neck below the *keffiya* revealed his chest hair and made the simple green shirt look sleazy.

306

As so often in his life, Selim wondered why everyone around him was so very different. The Germans were different because they were German. The Turks were different because they were Turks. But even the Kurds were different! Even his own people! Even they were different from him!

Around him were beefy young men, their biceps straining the seams of tight black T-shirts with three buttons at the chest. They had shaved the sides of their heads, that seemed to be the fashion now, and they were so physical, leaning into each other, slinging arms around each other, resting elbows on each other's shoulders, slapping the spot above their hearts to pay respect to one another. And among these big, bulging gym rats was Selim, drowning in his ironed green shirt, a *keffiya* around his neck (that was the only thing he had in common with them), and he felt very thin and very floppy-haired and very bespectacled, like a dormouse.

The singer was a Deniz rip-off, but not bad. He shouted his lines in German and Kurdish and every now and then broke into song. Some of the boys unfurled banners and cried, '*Biji Kurdistan.*' The music was loud, thank God, which meant he did not have to say anything, and Dynasty seemed happy enough with it all.

Gradually, he relaxed. It was not a bad concert. Every now and then, a familiar face popped up in the crowd, a friend or a relative, and Selim would nod to them and they would come over and slap his hand.

Still, he made sure they were the first out the door as soon as it was over; he did not want to get stuck in endless banter, greetings and slapping.

He walked her home.

307

'You're so quiet,' she said. 'Didn't you like it?'

'They're very young,' he replied. 'They're all like my little cousins.'

'Like, they make you feel old?'

'Just different. You think I'm old?'

'*Ya, habibi*, you're the same age as me. If you're old I'm old.'

He put an arm around her shoulder as they walked on, and she didn't shake it off. *Habibi*, she had called him! He would tell her the story of Mem and Zîn soon. Soon.

47

A year or so after our conversation about marriage fake and true, Lucien moved back in with his ex-wife.

I wish I could say I didn't blame him, that I understood why my tangled personal life was too much for someone with so many problems of his own.

'It's got nothing to do with that,' Lucien claimed when I asked him if it was because of my marriage.

We were sitting by the canal, sipping beer out of scratched cans.

'But I thought we were, you know, reasonably happy,' I mumbled. And then I started crying.

He stiffly put his arm around me. I cried into his shoulder, mortified; it was like crying into the shoulder of some fellow passenger on the bus. He was moving his head, maybe looking around in case one of his ex-wife's friends was passing by.

'Of course we were really happy, but it just didn't work out, did it?' he murmured soothingly. 'I mean, when I married my ex, it was like finding a silver coin, and when I met you, it was like finding a gold coin.' He cautiously squeezed my hand.

'And then you found out the gold coin was a bit dented.'

He laughed.

'Sorry, stupid image, I was only trying to explain. It's all, well, a bit complicated, isn't it? Like that time you told me about when you went to renew your passport. If something like that had happened to me . . . hey, just thinking about it gives me the creeps.'

I hated him a little then.

A few weeks later, I applied for French citizenship. Recklessly, I stated that I was single. My gamble was that the French would be more interested in the documents that were provided – clean criminal record, birth certificate and such – than in any documents that were *not* provided. They were unlikely to go hunting around in my hometown to check if there was a hidden husband. I was sick of constantly looking over my shoulder. I reasoned that in the worst case I could always say that I was long separated, and therefore considered myself to be single.

I didn't even consult Selim before my decision. We had an unspoken agreement that each was free to do as they pleased, as long as it didn't harm the other. When I say unspoken agreement, I mean that this was how I saw it. I later learned that he interpreted it quite differently.

It was then that I decided to work in the public sector. Not a prestigious post; just a decent little position that would allow me to serve the public in a quiet, uneventful way. My experience with Selim, and in particular with the various well-meaning activists around us, had made me wary of charities and political movements. I wanted a job that would contribute to the common good, but with a clearly defined purpose.

310

Julian thought it was a bizarre choice. He had set up a small illegal business in Berlin, driving around eastern Germany, buying up cheap Soviet-era lamps and chairs and then selling them as highly prized design objects to young professionals. The business was illegal in the sense that he did not pay any tax. Officially, he was still a starving accordion player and songwriter hoping to create a fusion between Klezmer and Jazz Manouche, despite the fact that he could barely carry a tune. The fickle Berlin public had long tired of his cheerful tone-deafness, though sometimes he still managed to fill a bar with newcomers from the provinces.

'You'd think they could simply drive out and pick up all that junk themselves,' I said, wandering around his basement shop. He, too, had removed his piercings and adopted a more subtle look: chin-length hair, a carefully faded corduroy jacket, canvas shoes.

'There're not any old lamps.' He fondly patted a fluorescent-orange one. 'You've got to have an eye for stuff that will sex up a fancy living room, you know, fireplaces and parquet. Neon lights from factories, public toilets, that kind of thing. And to get into the old factories you need connections.'

'Hmm.'

'Yeah, I know, you've probably got some ideological objection to that.'

'What? Why would I?'

'Because you always have.'

'That's such a lie! I've got nothing against lamps.'

'Oh, you know exactly what I mean. Sometimes it's so hard talking to you. Like everything is some kind of political test.' The sudden bite in his tone took me by surprise. I

311

fingered the orange light, wondering what to say, but he was unstoppable now.

'It's like always having to report to some kind of chief ideologist,' he snapped.

'Julian, I don't even know what you're on about. We were talking about lamps.'

'You know exactly what I mean,' he repeated, but I didn't.

'Chief ideologist? What's that all about?'

'And then this whole civil-servant business. I just don't get it. The brazenness. Teenage rebel, chief moral lecturer, even though your brother is an Army engineer, and on top of all that, you get a state pension. Plus, somehow, you still manage to sneer at people who sell lamps.'

'That's ridiculous! I never said anything about your business, I think it's great, and my brother is, well, he's my brother. And if you're talking about Selim, that wasn't even political, well, it was political, but not in the sense of – oh, I'm not even going to get into this.'

Julian shot me a disbelieving look and we left it at that.

But it was true. My marriage to Selim was a political act, but not for international solidarity or Kurdish independence or any such lofty goals. It was a political act for a person. Which is why I saw no contradiction between my youthful ideological fervour and my current job, whatever Julian said.

You see, I would never have risked going to jail in the name of a state. I thought that notion was bizarre. In fact, when I was a teenager, the state as such did not exist for me. It was just a structure that we as a society created and then chose to believe in. All in all, I respected that choice. The laws here in Europe were broadly decent and I was mostly happy

312

to live by them. I was even happy to help apply them – through joining the campaign against forced marriages, for example. I would never have wittingly assisted a forced marriage, and I was doing my best to prevent them. Though as it turned out they were rather tricky to detect.

However, some of the laws were not decent. And in that case, when you have a conflict between the law and human decency, I would choose human decency.

Let me put it this way. Imagine observing our lives from far, far away, from distant time-space. All you see is a world of people trying to survive, to enjoy themselves even. Each of them has, say, six to nine decades to do so. From that far away, social conventions don't matter much, do they? They have been vanished into oblivion by the vastness of time. As have borders. What will a border mean in three hundred years' time? Look at Europe and how randomly it's been chopped up.

Consider, however, human suffering. Think of it from the human sacrifices of the Incas, the slaves in ancient Greece, the witches burnt at the stake in medieval Europe. I tell you, suffering is one of the few things in this world that does not age and that is not relative. It's always terrible. It will always be terrible. You hear a heart-wrenching story about child slaves in the Roman Empire and it touches you still, and saddens you still. And if you could do one thing to alleviate the suffering they caused, one act that might even have been despised by the society you lived in – a society that hardly existed in the greater scheme of things – well, then of course you had to do it.

313

48

The regional court near my hometown did not see things that way.

'After the testimony of the appealing parties, the court remains unconvinced that they left Turkey in 1992 in a situation that left them no choice,' the ruling read.

'The court does not recognise that the appealing parties were subject to or threatened by country-wide repression in Turkey that would have given them a valid claim to asylum. On the contrary, on the basis of the evidence concerning the situation of the ethnic Kurds in Turkey, the court is convinced that it would have been possible for them to live in other parts of the country, in particular the western cities, without reasonable fear of political persecution.'

The judge took his hands off the keyboard to blow his nose. Nasal channels unblocked, he returned to typing up his carefully considered decision.

'From the appealing parties' political activities in their homeland, it cannot be assumed that they would have been known beyond the circle of the local security forces in a way that would have supported a claim to asylum.'

Selim's temperamental uncle, his Aunt Hanife, his cousin

Şivan and several others were deported shortly after the ruling. Selim himself had received a similar ruling a few years before, which I had never read. In any case, he was married to me and could therefore stay.

I never asked what happened to the others. Selim never told me. However, we found out ourselves soon enough that the court's assessment was wrong.

49

Selim was carrying mended bike frames and greasy chains from one corner of the bike shop to the other. They were redecorating the shop, and after a morning of heavy lifting his hands were blackened and his torn jeans and T-shirt were stained with grease.

He wiped the sweat off his brow with his clean upper arm and stepped outside for a bit of cool air. He leaned against the doorframe, hooked his thumbs into the pockets of his jeans, and looked down the cobbled street just as Dynasty turned the corner and walked towards him. He shrank back into the shop, panicking, dashed into the back room to see if there was a clean shirt; no clean shirt, no time even for a quick wash at the basin, and so he wiped his hands on his jeans and his cheeks on his sleeves in one hasty, disjointed movement.

She came in, smiling, sending the wind chimes ringing. He smiled at her without saying anything, as usual, and then, for the first time in his life, Selim thought, Fuck it, fuck the ironed shirt and the timid smile and the ingratiating laugh, I'm so sick of myself, I'm sick of being me, and he lurched forward and flung his arms around Dynasty in an embrace

316

that would have been awkward had it not been carried out with so much conviction, and incredibly, improbably, he felt her embrace him back. They stood like that for a few heart-beats, their arms around each other, and then he pulled away a little, just enough to kiss her; felt her arms around his neck and her lips on his, and he kissed her neck and ears and inhaled her surprisingly sweet, almost biscuit-like smell, and felt her hands moving down his naked back under his shirt, and then they crashed backwards into the bikes but it didn't really matter, they just crashed on through into the back room behind the shop.

Those weeks were a gift, Selim felt. He tried to figure out what kind of gift. A gift like the spare room in Flo's house, which then transformed into the gift of lasting friendship? Or a gift more like the pocket knife Flo's father had given him for his fifteenth birthday, which someone at school stole a week later?

Better not think about it. Better enjoy it, and think about it all later.

Dynasty lived with her parents and little brother in one of the high-rises. Her flat was not all that far from Flo's family's, where Selim had spent his teenage years, and yet she never invited him up. He usually left her at the corner of her estate. Once or twice, he accompanied her to a staircase, but something about the way she slowly walked up, as if copying someone walking up the steps rather than instinctively heading home, made him doubt it was the staircase that led to her flat.

Not that it surprised or upset him. She probably didn't

317

want her parents to know she had a Kurdish boyfriend. He would have been the same with his family; in fact, he never introduced her to any of his relatives.

She worked at a recycling centre on the edge of town and had a fairly long commute. In the evenings and even at weekends, she would often have to babysit her brother. Selim would have liked to meet him, but she never brought him along.

And so they took to meeting between the grass and bark and undergrowth of the forest or the plastic and pine of Selim's bedroom.

One night, he switched on the light and rummaged around in his bedside drawer until he found the book. He hesitated, then turned and passed it to her.

She held it away from her like a slightly obscene object.

'What's that?'

'A book.'

'I know it's a book! I read books, you know.'

'Ehmedê Xanî, he's a poet. This is a famous epic in Kurdistan. *Mem û Zîn*. Can you read to me?' He gave her a sideways glance and said with a grin: 'I like it when women read to me.' He held his breath.

'Ha! Women?'

'When *you* read to me.'

'OK then.' She opened the book, leafed through to the first stanza and put her finger on the paper, reading loudly and clearly, like she had always done in class.

> 'So that wise men cannot say: The Kurds
> Did not choose love as their aim.

318

They neither desire nor are desired,
They neither love nor are loved.'

She looked up from the page.

'They neither love nor are loved! Pretty harsh. Why did he write that?'

'I don't know,' Selim said without opening his eyes. 'Because he is a writer.'

She threw a pillow at him.

'That's so not an answer.'

'Hey!' He sat up and chucked the pillow back at her. 'He doesn't say we are not loved. He says that men *cannot* say we are not . . . wait, now I messed it up.'

Dynasty frowned.

'The next line makes even less sense: *They are empty of love, real or symbolic.'*

'It's because he's a Sufi,' Selim said. 'They are like that. He wrote in Kurdish so the Kurds would have their own book. So that no one could say look, the Kurds don't have books, they don't have knowledge. For the Sufis, books and know-ledge and love are all the same.'

'Look at you! Sufi knowledge,' Dynasty mocked him. 'Where did you get that from?'

'Şivan told me.'

'Şivan?'

'Yes. He met a very nice Kurdish girl, very clever, so he asked one of our uncles to find some nice Kurdish poems for him. And the uncle gave him *Mem û Zîn* and explained it. Then Şivan went to the Kurdish girl and talked about Ehmedê Xanî. Don't tell him I told you that.'

319

'Well I can't, can I. He's gone. Poor Şivan.' She paused. 'And what about the girl, did it work?'

'No. She liked another boy, someone very loud, who is in prison now because he stole cars.'

'And I bet that boy had never heard of Xanî. It's always like that, isn't it?'

'Yes.'

'Well,' Dynasty said, snapping the book shut and rolling over to him, 'you're definitely loved.'

Later, she retrieved Xanî's epic from underneath the tangled sheets and duvet. She knelt on the mattress, naked, holding it before her like an open hymn book.

Selim propped himself up on one elbow. He rubbed his eyes and yawned, looking rather pleased with himself. His gaze wandered over her pale, plump thighs, her round hips, her strangely geometrical triangle of pubic hair (professional waxing, she had told him, had recently become all the rage in Neustadt).

He grinned.

'Could you lower the book a little?'

'Why?'

'So I can see your breasts.'

She laughed and threw the book at him, and he shielded himself with his arms, then stole another glimpse.

'That's better. Thank you.' He reached out and pulled her towards him, and they let their heads sink into the pillows.

She nuzzled his neck.

'I was just trying to find the right page. It's your turn now.'

'Mmm, not now . . .' he said lazily, kissing her hair.

She reached behind her, grabbed the book, opened it and propped it up on his chest.

'*So that wise men cannot say: The Kurds/Did not choose . . .*' he began.

'You're totally cheating! You're repeating what I read to you just now. This is a completely different page.'

'OK. No problem. Give me the book then so I can see.' He flicked through the pages. '*Oh bird! Oh lover! Oh river!*' he read. '*Oh candle! Oh Kurds! Oh Arabs!*'

'You're making that up! Stop it. Let's find the one where he seduces her.'

'You're so strict,' he complained. 'Like a teacher.'

She gave him a quick kiss, and then another one.

'Right. How about this one. Mem and Zîn alone in the garden at night.'

They turned over on their stomachs, and she indicated the line with a purple-varnished fingertip.

'*Their eyes,*' he read slowly. '*Their eyes, their lips, their chests, their necks, their shoulders . . .*

> '*Their faces, their cheeks and their ears*
> *Were devoured at times by kisses,*
> *At times by bites . . .*'

And yet, all through those weeks, he thought, This is a gift.

'I wonder what we'll do when winter comes around,' she said, brushing her hair out of her face as they walked away from a clearing in the forest.

He pulled her close to him and kissed her hair. Winter was in five months' time; and to think that he would be happy

321

not only today, but tomorrow too, and next month too . . . that was asking for trouble. That was upsetting the natural order of things, in which Selim was always the loser.

Surely, it could not last.

50

It didn't.

He was standing behind the counter at the bike shop one morning. The door was flung open. Dynasty stormed in. He saw her face, and he knew. And instead of resisting, he just let his arms hang by his side, like a man in front of a firing squad.

She pushed through the waiting customers. She didn't give a damn what they were thinking.

She leaned across the counter, grabbed his shirt and hissed: 'You're married?'

Selim looked at her, at the customers, who were pretending to be studying the bikes around him, looked back at her face, and she let him go.

'You have a wife?'

'Dynasty . . .'

'Tell me right now, yes or no.'

And Selim looked at her, her reddened eyes and determined mouth, and gave the only possible reply.

51

'Has Selim spoken to you?'

'We only fixed a date. Can you turn down the music? I can hardly hear you.'

'That's my washing machine. So he hasn't . . . OK, no worries, fine.'

'What?'

'No, there's just, hang on, let me try and switch the bloody thing off. I found it in a basement on the border with Poland, it's one of those top-loading ones and looks fucking cool but . . . oh shit. Hang on, can I call you back?'

'Julian, what is it? Just tell me. It's something to do with Selim, isn't it?' I felt worn out and yet oddly resilient. I had made up my mind: Selim and I would get divorced this summer. Selim didn't know this yet, but I did, and nothing could make me change my plans now.

'It might not be such a good time to get divorced.'

'But it never is! And I'm going to start a job soon, I need a proper story and—'

'Yeah, you've told me about a dozen times. But you know what I think, maybe you could just pull your boss aside and kind of explain the situation, right, we're all human after all.'

'My boss? You don't get it, Julian, that kind of unofficial smoothing over, it doesn't work that way over here. They're French.'

'See how you feel once you've heard what Selim's just been through.'

'Why? What happened?'

'I guess it all started when the bike shop folded, and then . . .'

'Oh, I'm sorry.'

'Well, he only worked there once or twice a week, but it's still sad.' His voice was drifting off and I heard a crash and a bang.

'Julian?'

'Yeah, no worries, you're on loudspeaker.'

'I had no idea. I thought he was working there full-time.'

'No.' He sounded puzzled, suddenly focusing on our conversation. 'I mean, he never really worked there anyway, right? He was *there* all the time of course, as in hanging out there and fixing bikes and helping out behind the counter, but he never really got paid.'

'What? I thought that was his job.'

'Er, no. I can't believe you didn't know that. You do know that Flo's father owns the shop, right? Well, he owned the shop before it went bust.'

'Yeah, I know that.'

'So, Flo and Selim used to help out, and then Flo trained as a plumber, and Selim . . . well, he just stayed at the shop. Because he didn't have anything else. But Flo's father couldn't pay him, because the shop never really made any money. Selim said that was fine with him. I guess it gave

325

him something to do. And Flo's father did of course pay him occasionally, when he could.'

'Gosh. Well, I'm sorry to hear it folded.'

'Yeah. Of course, that's only one of the reasons why . . . anyway, he'd better tell you himself. Sorry, I shouldn't have said anything, me and my big mouth . . . water fucking everywhere! Right, hang on, I'll climb on the table, hang on just one second.' I heard him cover the receiver and yell to someone: 'Paula? Paula darling, do you mind mopping up this . . . yes, I'm on the phone.'

I told him to ignore his washing machine for a moment and tell me what was going on.

'It's, hmm, sort of, a bit delicate, he'd better explain it himself.'

'Another one of Dr Habicht's brain waves?'

'That reminds me, what I also meant to say, when you see Selim, don't mention Dr Habicht.'

Our lawyer was not easily avoided. As it turned out, Selim had moved into his former home.

I climbed the stairs to the flat, tried to switch on the light. It did not work. Oh well.

I had a plan. This time, there would be no sighing and head-shaking. There would be no forlorn gazing at tightly typed documents. There would be no helpless shrugs. I had a simple objective: to get divorced. Specifically, to get Selim to agree to a divorce. This time, I told myself, I will not waver, I will not cave in, I will not be persuaded and cajoled and prodded into extending this hellish union for another year. I cannot take it any more; I have used a different marital

326

status for every visa, every contract, I can't even remember where I'm single and where I'm married. I'm starting a job. I'm going to work for the French state. I need an identity and I need a clear story.

With every step on the concave stairs, I felt a greater sense of relief and lightness.

I had entered into this deal as a teenager with little to lose; the only big worry at the time was the issue with my mum. Then I was a student, and for a while, the situation became easier. My friends weren't German; the university did not care much about my marital status as long as I didn't use it to gain favours.

But as the years passed, the weight grew. There was the fear of being discovered through a wrong word here, a wrong name or signature there. There were the paranoid fantasies about the immigration officials finally getting their act together. There was the simple fact that my freedom, my not being arrested, entirely depended on a group of insiders keeping their word and being discreet. In particular, it depended on the competence and organisation of someone I knew to be neither competent nor organised: Selim.

Most importantly of all, I was certain that, with a final push, a final concerted effort, we could sort out Selim's permanent residency. It was all looking good. Selim himself had said so. We just needed to make a final effort, make sure all the papers were in order.

Really, we were only still married because our initial urgency had given way to a kind of laziness, a kind of awareness that, like a leaky shower or ancient wiring, the status quo was somewhat awkward but not completely

327

unbearable, and changing it would possibly involve much greater discomfort.

Never mind: now we would end it.

And so, as I climbed the stairs, I felt a sensation of joy at the thought of my newly simple, conformist, respectable life. It would be over, all of it, the paperwork, the visits to the immigration office, the fear that my family would find out, the fear my employer would find out, the fear the police would find out.

Selim opened the door wearing a thick jumper and a scarf, even though it was not cold outside. The living room had not changed all that much. Dr Habicht had left behind the red-batik divider. Selim had removed the bits of cloth from the window frame, as well as the PKK poster. Only people with nothing at stake could afford to keep a PKK poster.

The main difference was that Dr Habicht's former home now smelt of smoke. The smell even slightly overpowered the damp. Clearly, Selim had lit a fag the minute he put down the first removal box, had smoked it right down to the filter, had used the dying sparks to light the next one, and had not broken the chain since. Except maybe to sleep.

He had grown a goatee, which only accentuated the gauntness of his cheeks.

We sat down and after the usual small talk I decided to ignore Julian's warning.

'How's old Habicht, still alive?'

'I haven't seen him.' His voice sounded strangely clipped. He tapped some ash from his cigarette into a glass ashtray. 'He moved to the mountains. Better air. For his lungs.'

'Well, good for you. That old charlatan, eh? The less you see of him the better, I guess.'

'Yep.'

'So.'

He bit his lip. I wondered what was up.

'So,' I repeated. 'I'm so sorry about the bike shop.'

'Yes. It was a nice shop. Now I work for the town.'

I decided not to ask what exactly he had been doing at the bike shop all those years, how he had supported himself. That was in the past now anyway.

'Sounds great,' I said, trying to sound cheerful. 'Public sector, huh?'

'It's OK. I pick up rubbish with a big pair of tongs. In the square and the park, and sometimes around schools. It's a small job. I will find something else.' He took a deep drag. 'Maybe.'

'Hey, if you need help with applications . . .'

He waved away my lame offer.

'I will find something. I've got my permit now, I can move anywhere. I am flexible.'

'You've got your *permit*?'

'Yes.' His eyes followed the smoke. 'I told you, no? Or Julian told you, maybe?'

'No one's told me anything. No one ever tells me anything. Hang on, you mean you've got your permanent residency?' I told myself not to get worked up, but before I knew it, I had jumped to my feet, rising on a wave of rage. 'You got your permit and you never told me? When did that happen? We've been waiting for years, for years, for YEARS! And—'

He held my gaze and I stood there, my mouth hanging open, and then I sat down.

329

'I went away,' he said slowly. 'To Turkey.'

'Oh really? I had no idea.'

This time, it was not an accusation; I had always believed in some degree of personal freedom. I had not consulted Selim on my application for a French passport, and I did not expect him to ask me for permission to travel to Turkey. We were so bound to each other on paper, so constrained already, that we needed the option to make certain decisions independently. That was how I saw it, anyway.

He got up to fetch two glasses of tea, put them down between us and slowly, carefully, arranged his limbs, as if at the same time slowly, carefully arranging his words. I plopped a sugar cube into the brown liquid and stirred it, then watched the cube shrink and disappear.

'Anything wrong?' I asked in the hope that he would shake his head. He didn't. I picked up the glass by the rim but had to put it down again. Too hot.

'I hadn't seen my mother in such a long time, you see,' he began. 'I last saw her when I was thirteen. Have I told you, I have a little brother, but he was born after I left. I spoke to Dr Habicht, and he said just go. You are a resident here now, you have a valid permit, you are married to a German, you left Turkey ten years ago, you've been in Germany such a long time. No problem, just go.'

'And?'

'The Turkish police arrested me at the airport.' He laughed. 'I stepped off the plane, went into the airport building and showed my passport. They arrested me right away and they told me I was a terrorist.'

52

It was an old newspaper clipping that led to Selim's arrest. A grainy black-and-white photo and accompanying article carefully cut from the respectable pages of the *Frankfurter Allgemeine Zeitung* on a grey February morning in 1994.

Most readers probably gave the brief report about a Kurdish demonstration in the centre of Frankfurt the quickest of glances before moving on to the sports page and their second cup of filtered coffee. *Some four hundred Kurds gathered in the city centre on Saturday to protest against* . . . et cetera. No self-immolations, no broken shop windows, nothing new in the cause or the rebels themselves. It was barely worth reporting, but the editor had, I assume, decided that it was good to keep the Kurdish story ticking over. Let it have a certain presence in the paper so that journalists and readers would not be caught unawares should something really big happen in that news story.

One reader, however, took more than a passing interest in the article.

The photo, in particular, caught his (or maybe her) eye.

A pair of scissors was taken from a deep wooden drawer. One hand smoothed the paper, the other neatly cut around

331

the edges of the photo and the story. Put down the scissors, wrote the source and date under the article in tidy black letters, and then . . .

Well, who knows exactly what happened next.

All Selim knew was that, almost a decade later, in an interrogation cell in Istanbul, he was shown that very newspaper article and photo, which happened to be of his fifteen-year-old self, holding a PKK banner.

'A photo from 1994? How on earth did they get their hands on that?' The story did not make sense to me.

'That's the Turkish secret services for you,' Selim offered.

He was taken to a bleak building. He heard agonised screams. The cries of men being tortured, the officers said. Better confess now. But what was there to confess?

They shouted at him, *You work for the PKK in Europe, we know about you, we've been looking for you.*

He replied, *I have nothing to do with the PKK.*

They struck him on the mouth with a baton.

You've only lived in Germany for a very short time, one of them said.

It's not true, Selim sobbed through bloody lips. *I have lived there for a long time.*

Liar!

The baton struck again: something cracked. His mouth filled with a metallic taste and his tongue could feel solid bits moving around in the cavity, like grit.

When did you move to Germany?

He couldn't remember.

I'm asking you, when did you move to Germany?

I don't know.

You only moved there recently.

I can't remember, he whimpered, his cheek against the cold stone floor. *I don't know.*

This is wrong, he thought, this is a mistake. Please make them stop. He pleaded over and over again in his mind, Please make them stop, but he did not know who he was pleading with.

If I can show that I am me, then they must let me go, he thought.

Maybe, he groaned, *yes, I moved there recently*. He thought, But it's not true, I have lived there for a long time. Then he thought, I can't really remember. Did I? Did I just say I have lived there for a long time? Or only a short—

And when the next kick came, all he could think of was, What do they want to hear? Whatever they want to hear, I'll say it.

He had to concentrate. He had to say the right words. If he said the right words, he would be released. If he said the wrong words—

He thought of his father.

Long after midnight, he stumbled out of the building and into the dark street. A car was waiting on the corner. He staggered inside, half falling, half being pulled into the seat. The door slammed shut and the car drove off.

'When I left, they told me the screams I heard were only on tape,' he said. 'Who knows. They sounded so real.'

His finger hooked the corner of his mouth and pulled it back like a curtain to reveal a gap where teeth had been. He turned his head and let me see a jagged bald patch on the back, and another on the side, just above his ear. And I imagined the older dents and scars hidden beneath his black hair, between the bald patches: such a young head and body, and yet so battered that it seemed miraculous to see him here, talking and drinking tea.

I wanted to comfort him, to hug him, but we had never hugged before and I was afraid of making him feel awkward. I cautiously stretched out a hand and let it rest on his arm. We sat there like that for a while.

'How did you get out?' I eventually asked.

'I gave 1,000 euros to one of the guards. He whispered to another guard, then they let me go. My uncle picked me up. He said they had mistaken me for someone else. Another uncle. They got it wrong.'

Another uncle who was in fact a PKK member? I decided not to dig.

'Well, it's good you had that much money on you.'

His arm trembled under my hand. He mumbled something I couldn't hear.

'I was going to stay there,' he repeated.

'Where?'

'In Turkey. In Cizre. Dr Habicht said it would probably be safe. My family told me everything was much better than before. I gave away all my furniture and gave up my flat and my German friends cried their hearts out, and I was going back.'

That certainly was not part of our unspoken agreement on personal freedom. And it dawned on me that it only existed in my own mind; I really knew nothing of Selim's mind. Throughout our difficulties, I had always been certain of one thing: neither of us would do anything stupid, or exceedingly

334

risky. It was obvious that we would both stay out of trouble, avoid any problems with the police. I had always assumed that we both saw our deal that way, and that it wasn't something that needed to be discussed.

For if Selim wasn't the chaotic but ultimately dependable ally I thought he was, then who was he?

This simple question gave way to such a rush of uncertainty, of anger and stomach-churning fear, that all I could do was bury my head in my hands.

'I felt so alone, I really wasn't well in Germany,' Selim pleaded. 'I thought I was going to go home. For good. I was going to go back home.' The last bit he only whispered, out of embarrassment maybe or because his voice failed him. 'It was good timing. I would be in the village just after Ramadan. For the *Zuckerfest*.'

I just wanted to howl.

Yes, I felt outrage, but this time it wasn't directed against Selim. What Selim had done was so momentously nuts that it burst through any framework of reason. Messing up some paperwork, hiring a bad lawyer, failing to sort out the child-benefit stuff, even failing to tell me about his permanent residency, those were problems I could get upset over. Concrete, annoying blunders.

For Selim to decide, however, after more than a decade in Germany – a country that was perhaps unlovable but at least safe – that he wanted to go back to the place where he had suffered so much; that his ordeal, his painful journey to Europe, his tenacious efforts to settle there could be disregarded; to decide, in essence, that nothing he had done so far mattered, and that he might as well live in a war zone; no, really, this screamingly bonkers logic was not something I could get angry about. It was so terribly sad, so insane, that it simply made me want to weep.

What Selim was really telling me was that he would discard everything he and I and his friends and family had worked for, and would willingly risk humiliation, beatings, torture, jail and even death, if it meant having the tiniest chance of being at the fucking *Zuckerfest*.

I wanted to rip open those warped windows and yell out my anger, not at Selim, not at myself, but at everything, everything!

Instead, I took a deep breath and said: 'Dr Habicht, eh?'

'Dr Habicht,' Selim echoed.

And then we looked at each other, and we shook our heads and rather than yelling I dissolved into desperate laughter. And he joined me, and we laughed and laughed.

'Dr Habicht!' I cried, releasing the disappointment, the frustration, the pain of more than six years, pouring all my disbelief and anger and, yes, amusement at this bloody joke that was life, pouring it all into that dreaded name.

'Habicht!' Selim shook his head.

'Habicht!' I flung my arms up in the air. 'What an idiot.'

'Yes. He wasn't right at all.'

'He was completely wrong.'

'He was wrong about everything!'

'And we were just amazingly stupid, weren't we, believing him every time.'

'But every time, he sounded so convincing! So I thought, OK, one more chance, he is more careful now, so now he will be right, *inşallah*.'

'But he's never right. Have you seen him since you got back from Turkey?'

'No. I don't want to. I don't even want to hear him say sorry.' Selim put his hands on his ears and shook his head.

'Of course you don't want to. What a fucker.'

And we sat there, and sighed, and laughed in a sad and stupid way, and sat there.

'But there's something else I need to tell you,' Selim said after we had calmed down, uneasily shifting about on his cushion.

'It's OK, Selim.' I waved off his concern. 'Don't worry about the divorce. I want this to end, OK, you know that. I really need to get out of this at some point, because of my work and stuff. But we don't need to do it right now. I'm just glad you survived.'

'It's not that.'

'What is it?'

'I told you, I paid the money so they'd let me go.'

'Yes . . .' Selim had never before asked me for money. I felt uneasy.

'And then, when my uncle picked me up in his car I thought, At least I will go to my village and see my mother.'

'You went on to Kurdistan? But that's mad!'

'Well, I had come so far. So my uncle took me to the village.'

'Oh wow. Wow. That's insane. Your village, the one in the photos, you mean, really? Right up in the mountains?'

'Yes.'

'And your family?'

'I saw my mother, father, and also the little brother I had

337

never seen. One sister is with the guerrillas, the other sister is here in Germany, as you know, with her husband. And many people, I did not even recognise them, so many visitors all day, I was ashamed, I had to ask who is this, who is that. Friends I had when I was little, and they had moustaches and big beards, and came in with their children.'

He went to his desk, pulled out a cardboard box, opened it and took out one photo after another, placing them between the glasses. There were boys and grandfathers in the photos, and Selim. A couple of white-bearded men wore crocheted skullcaps, waistcoats and drop-crotch trousers held up by sashes.

'God, your mother must have been ecstatic,' I said, studying the pictures.

'Yes. My mother.' He smiled at the memory. 'You know, when my father was in prison, my mother gave us everything, with nothing for herself. She gave us bread, and always courage. And I would say *Yade*, when I grow up, I will carry you day and night.' He raised his hands in emphasis. 'Day and night.'

'Well,' I smiled. 'And . . . what about your little sister?'

His grin vanished.

'I didn't see her,' was all he said on that matter.

'What . . . did you hear anything about her? Do you think she'll come down from the mountains one day? Like, what happens when they're too old to fight, do they retire?'

'They don't retire. In the mountains, you don't grow old.' We contemplated this for a bit. Then Selim added: 'There is almost no one fighting in the PKK who is over fifty.'

He winced, screwed up his eyes, then collected himself.

338

'It's very dangerous to be a PKK fighter, you know, thousands have died already. Some, if they are handicapped, they can go and live in northern Iraq, or the PKK smuggles them to Europe. A friend told me that Abdullah Öcalan's brother has a bakery in northern Iraq.'

He picked up my glass and saucer.

'More tea?'

I nodded. He poured me another glass, I stirred in another sugar cube and watched it dissolve. I felt a slight sugar high already and didn't really want any more, but the tea was unpalatable without it, far too bitter. How on earth did people manage to consume so much sugar? At least six, seven cubes a day, judging by Selim's tea habit. Maybe that was the secret to a sweeter character: more sugar.

'It was nice to be home, but it was strange as well,' Selim continued. 'The first night, after we had eaten, I went into the kitchen to help my mother do the washing-up. My mother chased me out with a kitchen towel! And she yelled at me, "What kind of man are you?"'

'Ha. All that practice in those hippie flat shares, huh. The New-Age man.'

'Yes. Not in Kurdistan.'

Things had changed in his absence.

The men criticised Selim for the way he spoke. His speech was plain and lacked any religious references, as if religion were non-existent, God were non-existent. The way he spoke was insouciant, failed to acknowledge and revere this divine presence who should be acknowledged and revered with every phrase, flourish and exclamation.

339

Maaşallah, inşallah, alhamdulillah. Did that not mean anything to him? Was he so contaminated by the foreign land that the very essence of speech and spirit, the delicious opportunity to praise God, appeal to God with every flick of the tongue, meant nothing to him?

The women, on the other hand, giggled about his womanly ways. A man in the kitchen! Too funny.

Maybe he had changed. Maybe years of mingling with anarchists and communists had driven Allah out of him, weakened the salt of his faith. It was Selim, after all, who had once so stubbornly rolled out his prayer mat in the snow. But it was also Selim who had stowed it away, abandoned it, forgotten it until it somehow absented itself.

That he had grown away from the people he loved so fiercely was perhaps not surprising. Washing the dishes, for example, was just something he had grown used to in Germany. Surely it was polite to offer to help out, to share the chores, whether in Frankfurt or Cizre. How could he sit on an embroidered cushion and digest his meal while his mother, his most beloved mother, was working her hands away at the sink?

He reminded himself that the kitchen had always been the realm of women and children. There was nothing new about this. Yet his own codes had softened and blurred while those of the village remained hard and steadfast.

And yet, he was sure the village had also changed.

There were the outward changes: TV sets, power lines. Outward signs of modernisation; but what surprised him was the simultaneous, internal shift in the opposite direction. And the opposite direction wasn't even tradition. The tension

340

that he felt so strongly in the village was not between CD players and coarsely played folk tunes. It was not between plastic-packaged cheese and curdled milk ripening in cloth sacks. No, the tension wasn't between old and new, it was between new and new. New gadgets, music, posters of heavily made-up pop singers chafing against a new kind of religious attitude, sharp and cold and unyielding.

Maybe nostalgia had softened his memories, but he had never thought of his family as particularly religious. They just did things in a certain way, because generations before them had done them that way. Allah this and Allah that – old men used to speak that way, pious widows, sheikhs. Now it was young men who used Allah's name in a display of aggressive defiance.

Then there was the question of his little brother, an alert boy. Selim loved him as soon as he saw him. His little brother. The awkwardness between them, that was normal. Selim was the older brother, the authority figure, even more so as his father was frail and there was an unspoken assumption in the air that he, the firstborn, had returned to take responsibility. To prepare for the succession of power. He had to make sure his mother would be fine, as well as this strange and serious boy. How difficult it was, though, to assume authority over someone you had never met. Selim hoped the awkwardness would at some point give way to brotherly ease. His family. This was his family.

It was a shock, then, when one afternoon his little brother told him he sounded like Satan.

He had thought about this, the little brother said calmly, had analysed it, and had found an explanation. All things

341

considered, it was not surprising that Selim sounded like Satan, having spent years in the toxic land of the infidels.

'Did you know,' the boy said over a glass of tea, earnest and factual as if relating another new wonder he had learnt in class. 'Did you know, when you kill an American, it's like a ticket to heaven.'

The little brother was studious. He went to school every day and when he came home he pored over chemistry textbooks and conducted mysterious experiments involving liquids, test tubes, little bottles procured from God knows where. Selim did not ask.

'Little Al-Qaeda, huh?' I said, looking at the earnest boy in the photo.

'Yes,' Selim said. 'Little Al-Qaeda, yes.'

'So what was he up to with those experiments?'

'I don't know. But I need to tell you something else.'

I vaguely thought he might come back to the bribe, to some question of money; there was a sense of awkwardness around him that I could only interpret as the embarrassment of someone about to beg.

'Go on.'

'There is a big problem. Please, please, please don't be angry with me.'

'Oh, I won't be.'

He went into the kitchen and came back with bread and bowls of Kurdish cheese and olives and pickled vegetables, as if hoping to pacify me.

'Of course, if you're angry with me, I understand, it's OK,' he continued, arranging food between us.

Then he sat down and looked at me, ready to talk business.

342

'So. When I arrived in the village, my mother ran up to me, she was so happy, she shouted, "I am so glad you've come! You've finally come!" And then later she said, "Look! I have found you a wife!"'

53

I laughed. It was a reflex. I laughed, and Selim laughed, too.

And then I stopped and asked: 'But what did you do?'

'My mother always had this wish for me to marry. She said before she died she wanted me to marry. Because you see, for men, marrying is safety. It means you won't be so politically active, you'll be calmer because you have to look after your family, not get into trouble, so your life will be safer.'

'But your mother knows we're married!'

'Yes, but it's different. In my village, only Muslim marriage counts. Without it you can't have any contact. The girl, my mother worked hard to find her, she was very pleased. The daughter of a sheikh,' he added, as if that explained everything.

'And so what happened?'

'I said to my mother OK.' He raised his palms. 'And then I married the girl.'

That shut me up. There was a long silence. I think neither of us could quite believe what he had said. The sentence made sense grammatically, it was in fact in perfect grammatical order, and yet it did not make any sense at all. Neither to me, nor to him.

344

'But you can't have married her,' I finally said. 'You're still married to me.'

'Yes.' He laughed again in a dry, hopeless way. 'I know. It's, what do you call it, it is a curse. Look, I never wanted to marry anyone. And now look at me.'

'Selim, you're a bigamist!'

'Yes.'

'So . . . you're a bigamist. And you know, that's illegal in Germany.'

'Yes.'

'And I'm married to a bigamist.'

'Yes. Well, no. When I married her, we only went to the imam.'

'Selim, I don't know, sometimes I think we're going to end up in jail.'

'I hope not.'

Another long pause.

'You had the wedding ceremony and the party and everything?'

'Yes.' He pulled out a photo. 'This is her.'

The girl in the picture was covered in a white doily of a wedding dress, her thick black hair teased into big curls that hung over her forehead, her mouth painted blood red. She was staring at the camera, wide-eyed, her mouth set in concentration.

'She looks very nice,' was my lame reaction.

'She is the daughter of a sheikh,' he repeated.

'You're both so serious. Don't people usually smile in wedding pictures?'

'It's our tradition, maybe.'

345

Then he placed the photo among the others. Uncles, cousins, donkeys, dry crumbly earth, stones, concrete houses and hills. Bride.

We both looked at the picture. Selim cleared his throat.

'I did not sleep with her, not like that. We slept in the same bed, of course, after our wedding, for a whole week until I had to leave. But for the seven nights, I only slept next to her and I didn't touch her at all. Because I thought, I cannot live with her, and if I don't sleep with her, if she is a virgin, maybe she can still find someone else.'

I nodded.

'She's a nice girl, I thought, but I don't know her at all. She's from the village, she has never been away, how can we live together? She cannot read or write, and she speaks Kurdish, Turkish, a little Arabic, but no German. And you know my life here, my friends, it's not the same. It's very different. I explained it all to her, we talked.'

I nodded again, half agreeing, half simply attempting to take it all in.

And I thought of Selim's bride.

In her twenties, a sheikh's daughter with fair skin and long glossy hair: a bit old, but still, premium goods in the marriage market. In her village, there were hardly any boys of her age. As soon as they could, they entered the political struggle, went off into the mountains, were thrown into Turkish prisons, fled to Europe. Her girlhood was spent polishing the silent hardness that characterised the women there, supporting the fighters, giving food and money to the PKK, being told that one day she too would bear sons for the struggle: what an honour.

346

With each year the village shrank. Other villages higher up in the mountains had been burnt to the ground, completely emptied. Their village, closer to the town, shrank gradually. It was not a gushing wound, rather it trickled blood. Worn out and frightened, more and more families packed up and resettled in the shanty towns around Diyarbakir, where children ran around freely just like they did in the village, but there were no friendly neighbours to look out for them, and there were busy roads and cars and trucks and strangers and hundreds of other neglected children roaming the city in pick-pocketing packs.

The bride and her family stayed. They watched their old friends and neighbours leave.

And then one day the news. So-and-so's son is coming over from Germany. He's enormously, unimaginably rich and successful. We have chosen a good husband for you, daughter. Did I mention that he is very rich and successful? He will take you back with him to Germany, you will have an excellent life! Daughter, I'm happy for you though it breaks my heart to think you'll be so far away; but maybe one day we can come and join you. You'll have a big house and, *inşallah*, a big family, and such a rich and important husband.

The sheikh's daughter begins to dream of that husband, so far away in a cold land. He was not much older than her, she heard, and was glad. She had seen too many eighteen-year-old girls married off to greying old goats. There were wedding songs only the women knew, sung by women for women and making fun of those besotted old tremblers and their liking for young flesh. Her husband was different,

347

young and successful. When he left Kurdistan he was still a child but already a respected fighter, they told her. He sounded like a young prince. She cried a little, she was a little scared of this stranger, who seemed so important and intimidating. What if he found her backward, stupid?

When the news arrived that he had been arrested at the airport, she was ashamed to feel a pang of relief. Oh, of course she was sad, it was terrible to hear that her betrothed was in prison. But she couldn't help thinking of an execution that had been stayed. She had been granted a reprieve. No, she shouldn't think of it like that, but at night she sometimes thought of this stranger, who grew ever bigger and scarier in her dreams, and the thought filled her with dread. She had heard terrible tales about the wedding night, whispers from sisters and cousins. At weddings, everyone shouted and cried with joy, but the tales she had heard from newly married friends were very different. Not so joyful.

And then, oh, he's been released and he's on his way! Daughter, let's turn you into something beautiful! Suddenly she was pampered, spoilt. Her mother slapped her when she caught her crying (*Don't cry, it will make you ugly*) but she was also indulged and coddled; bathed, exfoliated, moisturised, her hair smoothed and braided, she was sung to, and fed delicious food like a sheep being fattened up for slaughter. The wedding was going to be exciting and she had to admit that this stranger sounded like a good match, but Germany was so far away. She had heard that the country was very cold and so were the people.

We have many, many relatives in Germany, daughter, don't be scared, her mother told her. You will live in a big

348

house and your husband will take care of you. You are so lucky! Think how fortunate you are!

One morning, finally, her prince arrived.

The rattling *dolmuş* pulled up in the village centre, spat him out and bounced away over the potholed track towards the next stop. The bride-to-be kept to the back of the crowd and craned her head to catch a glimpse of him. Crammed between padded jackets, scratchy jumpers, beards and moustaches and the snotty noses of the children, she watched the groom's mother wrap herself around him in tearful ecstasy, watched the villagers wail and clap their hands over their heads.

But what strange prince was this?

So short and skinny; she almost laughed into her hand. To think that she was scared of him! That she was weepy, terrified, sleepless with fear of the violent love awaiting her. Now she saw him, battered and bruised, a stranger who stumbled into the village like a beggar. Yet when she looked around she found the villagers enchanted and bedazzled. Where she saw a scrawny stranger in rags, they appeared to see a sheikh in a cloak woven from the stars, the sun and the moon. A sheikh like her own father, generously visiting the village. Of course, it didn't surprise her that his family were making a huge song and dance, his mother beside herself with happiness. But the entire village was playing along as if possessed by a jinn, in thrall to this hero's homecoming, claiming their share of this rich and powerful guest from Germany.

The bride remained untouched by the spell. In the space where her radiant, big-shouldered, strong-armed prince should be, there was only a boy with glasses and a long nose.

349

Her husband, soon.

He never praised Allah. He tried to wash the dishes like a woman. He spoke a strange and stunted Kurdish, his trousers hung loosely where his buttocks should have been, he lay beside her for seven nights without touching her and then he left.

Daughter, it is sad to watch a husband leave, but don't you worry. Don't you be afraid. Already he is arranging for your documents and soon you will join him in Germany, where he is so rich and successful, and don't worry about your old mother, either; you will send money home and one day we too will join you, *inşallah*.

The young bride could not bring herself to crack open her secret, her shame, and confess to her mother that the scrawny boy in her bed told her he could not be with her, that he rejected her (for her own good, he said), did not touch her for seven nights because, as he carefully reasoned, that way, when he went back to Germany (where, she suspected, a rich and important and beautiful wife was waiting for him), when he flew away and left her behind, she could still find herself another husband.

350

54

'And then?'

'And then I came back here, and I thought about it,' Selim said. 'I thought about it all for a long time.'

I had eaten all the olives and half the cheese. He had not touched a thing. His deep-set eyes had sunk even further into their sockets and he appeared to be teetering on the brink of a long, deep sleep. During our conversation I noticed a new nervous tic: his smoking hand would put down its cigarette every so often and compulsively feel for the bald patch on the back of his head. The other hand fingered the dishes before him, the ashtray, his goatee, the rug, a piece of bread; and all that grasping and searching made me want to take his hands and hold them still. But his speech was clear, considered and deliberate.

'I realised she wouldn't be able to find anyone else now. She was married to me, I was married to her. It didn't matter that I hadn't touched her. No one in the village would want her.' He paused, puzzled by his own reasoning and yet unable to reach any conclusion other than the one he was about to put forward:

'And so I have to bring her over.'

'Bring her over? From your village?'

'Yes.'

'Over to Germany?'

'Yes. Difficult.'

'How are you going to feed the both of you?'

'I don't know. My sister lives in Bonn with her family. Now I have my residence permit, we can go there. She can help.'

'And your . . . your wife wants to come over?'

'I will need to travel to Turkey again and marry her in the government way first. We only had a religious marriage. I cannot bring her here with that.'

'Hmm . . . what I meant was, does she actually want to come here?' I tried to think of a way of phrasing my question that would not sound too rude. 'She . . . she wants to live with you as your wife?'

'She is my wife.' He shrugged. 'I'm her husband.'

'Yes, but does she actually . . . did you talk to her about . . . did you ask . . .' I gave up. Had I known then that another Kurdish bride would cross my path, I would have dug for more details, tried to understand. But that was before I had set foot in the town hall, and so I let it go and simply said: 'So you're going to bring her over.'

We sat there in silence. Selim looked at me, and his face, usually so placid despite its nervousness, broke into utter despair.

'I don't understand it, you know, all I wanted was to make a life,' he cried, exasperated. 'I had so many plans, to learn, to make something of myself. I wanted to make something of myself. But things are always changing. There are always

352

so many problems. Every time I solve one problem, another is already looking at me.'

There was nothing I could say, and so we both turned our gaze to the rug between us, silently, as if examining a little pile of discarded plans.

'I'm really sorry to hear that,' I finally said. 'But I think you're making the right decision.'

Selim winkled a cigarette out of a fresh packet, lit it, and stroked his goatee.

'I'm sorry too,' he said. 'So now you and I will need to get divorced.'

55

It never occurred to me to ask Selim for any evidence, any proof of the persecution he faced in Turkey. The first time we met, all those years ago, I sat with him for a couple of hours, drank orange juice with him, and listened to his story. Naive? Maybe. But remember, we were only seventeen, an age when instinct and personal ties are more important than written evidence. Someone tells you his story: do you believe him? That's all that matters. His German was broken, he chain-smoked, he was very thin and nervous and yet he could also be funny, he had a sort of gallows humour. He sounded as if he had just stepped off the plane from Cizre. All his consonants were at war with each other. They used his tongue as an ill-shaped launching pad from which they flew into conversation like erratic missiles.

'I need to turn my mouth inside out to speak German,' he told me then, pointing at his teeth and tongue with dismay. 'My teeth, my lips, they don't want to speak like this. I have to make them. I have to force them.'

He arranged his words in roughly the right order in his brain, but by the time they tumbled into his mouth and bounced off his tongue they were all mixed up. Like a box full of printing type that someone had given a shake.

As for the vowels: they were just padding to prevent the consonants from rattling.

'If we stay married for three years, my lawyer says it's enough. I have a good *Guntag*,' he said to me. It was the first time I had heard him use the word *Guntag*, a word I would hear so, so often over the following years. At first I thought he meant *Guten Tag*, then I reckoned he could mean *Kontakt*. Eventually I realised that he considered the two to be roughly the same. *Guten Tag*, *Kontakt*: he merged them in a word that meant an encounter, an interaction, and was both greeting and description.

Now, there is more evidence, printed and digital. The other day, I saw a story in the newspaper about a young Kurdish woman called Leyla who lived in a village near Cizre in the '90s. Her husband was shot dead by Turkish militias, she said, his brain leaking from his skull and his entrails hanging out of his stomach. She said she pushed his guts back inside and buried him as well as she could.

Stories like that are surfacing everywhere. Sad stories, but also hopeful stories, about Turkey and the Kurds making peace. That's good news, isn't it? People making peace. Germany seems quite supportive of the whole thing, too. I only wish they had thought about all this a bit earlier. I wish the Turkish and German officials had treated Selim and me a bit better. I wish I didn't have to worry, still, whether it might all come out one day, one day before the statute of limitations on forging documents and people trafficking and marital fraud kicks in.

355

None of it was known when Selim first presented his case to me in 1997 in that garden shed. There he was, in front of me, telling me his story. When he talked about Turkish politics, he laughed, a bitter laugh, but still he laughed. He did not talk about tribes or religion or clanship. He talked about Kurdish independence and recipes for making cheese. He told me how they used to make cheese back in Kurdistan by suspending the curdled milk in a cloth, surrounded by flies. I laughed. I knew his friends, I knew the family he had lived with, they were all good people. Good people had supported this boy for years, and that meant more than any court ruling. I believed him.

Overall, I'm glad I did. Selim was a good person, a better person than I was in many ways: kinder, braver, more patient. All the oddities that stirred my doubt – the political secrets, the changing addresses, the fake jobs – well, now that we lived such separate lives, they had come to matter less and less. The only remaining niggle was the issue of Selim's bride. I did sometimes wonder whether I should have said something about his marriage, about the fact that he so willingly played along with his family's scheme. I told myself that it was none of my business, that the bride was probably quite pleased with it all, that the situation was chaotic enough already without my probing questions. What did I know about how things were done in Cizre? What did I know about the best way to lasting love and happiness? Maybe an awkward wedding night and a few weeks, months or even years of getting used to one's spouse were an adequate price to pay for the security of a lifelong union.

356

There was, of course, the strange hypocrisy of it all: a family that would rush to condemn love affairs thought that sex between complete strangers, as long as they had an imam's blessing, was perfectly acceptable.

56

When the divorce came through it filled me with a sense of renewed freedom. Selim kept his right to stay in Germany and was free to bring over his new wife. As for his experience in Turkey: I think he simply decided to let it lie.

A judge decided, quite reasonably I suppose, to look into our assets and pension payments. I was working for a French think-tank at the time, where no one had an inkling that I was divorced. One morning, I received a letter from HR saying they had been contacted by the court and had replied with a copy of my pension plan. I quit the job. The following days and nights were spent hatching one panicked plan after another: move to the countryside, take on a new name, emigrate somewhere far, far away (Thailand? Argentina?).

The town hall position came up not long after. I thought about it for a bit, then took a deep breath and applied.

The judge never contacted the town hall, but I felt the unpleasant sensation of being slowly encircled by a high fence. Whoever was building the fence was making connections, linking up the separate elements of my life, pursuing enquiries. The divorce ended seven years of marriage, but it did not delete those seven years. I was no longer married, but I would always, indelibly, be someone who was once married under false pretences.

My last meeting with Selim took place in a car park. I was sick of living rooms. We sat in his deported uncle's car and then, all of a sudden, with uncharacteristic passion, he slapped the wheel and cried out: 'Sometimes I think, what have I done to this human being?'

'It's OK, Selim.' I cautiously placed a hand on his shoulder. 'No worries. I was shocked when I got the letter, I never thought German courts would bother tracking me down in France. Never mind. I hope they won't contact me at the next place I work. Guess I can always quit again.'

'It's all very difficult,' he said, his slender hands resting on the wheel.

'Yes,' I said, seeking refuge in my usual platitudes, so well known and worn-in by now. 'It's difficult. But we'll be fine.'

And I wondered whether it would go on like this for ever. I had a vision of Selim and me aged ninety, rocking back and forth in our chairs, croaking to each other, *It'll be fine, don't worry, it's all very difficult, yes, spoken to the police lately?*

I was about to share this with Selim, to cheer him up a bit, when he said slowly: 'When bad things happen to people, they shout and cry. But when the worst thing happens, they are suddenly very quiet.'

And then he told me about the couple he met on the ship to Puglia, and about their little daughter, Evin.

'What?' I said, not understanding. 'She drowned and . . . they buried her on the beach? You buried her there in the sand?'

'Yes. There was very little time.'

'Do you know where it was?'

359

'No.'

'I guess someone must have found her.'

'I guess so, yes. Maybe.'

'And what happened to the parents?'

'They were deported some years ago. Maybe four, five years ago.'

'Did you see them when you went back?'

'No. I heard that they live in Diyarbakir now. It's a big city, the Kurdish capital. Life there is very hard, you know. So many poor people from the villages moved to Diyarbakir during the violence. Maybe they will be able to move back to their village one day.'

'Oh Selim.'

We gazed through the windscreen of the parked car. Black-and-white timbered houses, a billboard with a manically grinning Santa Claus in swimming trunks, and in the distance the Superdiscount Centre. I considered asking Selim to drive me over and drop me off for a visit to Frau Brock, but then I thought, She probably doesn't even work there any more. After a while, I turned towards him. His face, that drowsy, placid face, had turned all tight and hard and snarled.

'The best thing about my permit is, I can finally, finally leave this town,' he said through clenched teeth. 'I hate this town. I hate it so much. I have spent my life here, and I hate it.'

I stared at him, astonished. In all those years of our unconventional married life, that one thought had never occurred to me: that Selim could hate this town as much as I did. Could have the same yearning to fly away, to escape, to see and taste and hear and touch and smell something new. And yet, in the years when I put as much land as possible

360

between myself and the medieval spires of this stifling little place, his enclosure had shrunk and shrunk, until it only stretched from the bike shop to Dr Habicht's flat and the immigration office.

'There was a girl I met a while ago,' he said, still looking straight ahead. 'You know, she was nice, she always wore nice clothes, I liked her.'

I nodded in encouragement, wondering where this was going.

'We got together, it was nice, we got on very well. Then one day she came running into the bike shop, in front of everyone, and she screamed at me in front of everyone you have a wife, you have a wife!'

I groaned with dismay.

'It was the worst day of my life. Really, I felt like the very worst man in the world. I felt so bad.'

'Selim, if you want to tell her it was a fake marriage, that's totally fine with me. I would do the same, if someone was important to me. Honestly, it's OK with me.'

He shook his head.

'You can do it because you live in a different country. But here, everyone talks. And of course, now, we are divorced but I married the Kurdish girl from my village. I am only waiting for some arrangements, she will come soon, I will have to look after her.'

After a while, I asked him how he had left things with the other girl.

'I said yes. She was standing there like this, you see, in front of everyone and she said is it true that you are married. And I said yes, I have a wife.'

361

57

Anna picked me up from work. She wanted to check out a new cheese shop in my street. The space used to house a sweatshop-fed clothing chain, which I knew well because I had made several ill-fated purchases there. Once, a blouse unravelled on its hanger as I was carrying it from the shop front to the changing rooms. Anna had heard that, in its latest incarnation, the shop was the only place in Paris where you could buy Sardinian lamb's cheese.

'What, like pecorino?' I asked her as we perused the yellow-white rounds and slabs under the glass counter.

'Hmm,' she mumbled. 'Not quite.'

She exchanged some words in Italian with the shop owner, who scurried into a back room and returned with a mysterious parcel and a little plate. He gave the parcel to Anna and pushed the plate under my nose. On it were slices of bread smeared with a rancid-smelling paste. I tried one; a pungent top-note of fermented guts hit my taste buds and the paste stuck to my palate, refusing to be dislodged by my tongue.

'It's really hard to find,' Anna told me, proudly clutching her parcel. 'Basically, they let the lamb suckle for a bit, and when its belly is filled with milk they slaughter it, take out the full stomach, sew it shut and let the thing ferment into cheese. With the milk inside.'

'You're joking.'

'I was going to invite you over right now to share it.'

'Oh, I'm fine, thanks.'

'Listen, are you OK? You're always so tense these days. Has David called you?'

'Not since he left my flat this morning, no. He did send me a really sweet text around lunchtime though.'

Anna almost dropped her cheese.

'Girl, you are full of surprises,' she eventually said. 'Good for you though. Go, tiger. Or should I say, go, cougar.'

'He's the same age as me,' I protested. 'He just looks younger because he dresses like a backpacker.'

'So how did this happen?'

'Well, he brought over some books that he thought might be useful. You know, that business with the bride. He had some books on that sort of topic. He called me up and offered to bring them over, and we ended up having dinner at my place.' Something occurred to me. 'Actually, come to think of it, I flicked through the books and most of them were on mosque construction in the Middle Ages, so it might have been a ruse.'

'Who cares. The important thing is that it worked.'

Yes, I thought, it worked.

And the other important thing was that around two a.m., in the warmth of the night, I told David about Selim; and guess what, he found my story neither shocking nor amusing, but simply interesting, and he asked me lots of questions,

363

good questions actually, like why I decided to marry Selim, and why I stuck with him, and how this affected my life and Selim's life, and how it might help me figure out today, now, whether a Kurdish family in this neighbourhood was trying to make me an accomplice in forcing their daughter to marry.

I would have liked to have told Anna about some of that, but didn't even know where to start. I had never told her about Selim, perhaps because I had never found the right moment, perhaps because I had wanted to protect her. I think she would have been worried about me. Come to think of it, that's probably the same reason I never told my mother or Martin: it was easier to deal with all the problems and the paranoia on my own than to feel the guilt of dragging other people into it.

And when I looked at Anna standing there with her suede handbag in one hand and a plastic bag with lamb's cheese in the other, I thought, It's OK this way.

Oh, I knew, there was this whole modern obsession with openness, with honesty, whatever that meant. Keeping secrets was supposed to be bad for you, like letting some kind of mould fester in your bathroom or leaving an ingrown toenail untreated.

But in my case, as I listened to Anna chit-chat in front of the cheese shop, I decided that secrets might not be such bad things after all. Certain parts of my life would never mix. Anna and Selim, for example, would never mix.

Anna hurried home with her cheese, and I walked on to my flat. I noted, as I did every night, that the staircase needed repainting and one of the light bulbs wasn't working and the lock on my door was getting moodier by the day.

And then I sat down on the sofa and looked at the phone and thought to myself, You've been meaning to do this for ages, why not do it now.

She picked up the phone too quickly; I hoped she wasn't sitting at home by herself, bored and lonely, with Stefan away building a bridge somewhere. But she sounded as chirpy as ever. She talked about the neighbours, and my brother, and work, and Stefan's bridge, and again the neighbours, as if she knew I was going to tell her something she wouldn't like.

'Mum, I have to tell you something. Remember that Kurdish friend I had, years ago?'

'Hmm, not really.'

'Well, there was a Kurdish friend . . . not exactly friend . . . a political refugee, remember? A guy I knew. He came to Germany when he was thirteen, and when I met him he was nearly eighteen and about to get deported.'

'Gosh, that's terrible. I'm so sorry.'

'You remember him, right?'

'No.'

'Well, there was only one way of keeping him in Germany, and that was to marry him, and I asked you about it, I definitely asked you, but you said no, and, well, I married him anyway.'

Silence.

'When was that?'

'Just after I turned eighteen.'

Silence.

'You married him?'

'Yes. I'm sorry. I wish I'd told you earlier.'

'So you have a Turkish husband? Have I met him?' I heard

365

a sharp intake of breath. 'Wait, was he that flatmate you lived with in your first year?'

'That flatmate was French-Moroccan. And my friend is Kurdish, not . . . anyway, we divorced a while ago, so no, you never met him.'

There was another long silence.

'Mum?'

'Well, what can I say? That's certainly . . . well, what do you want me to say?'

'I don't know. Tell me I did the right thing.'

'Do you think you did the right thing?' She didn't sound angry, just a bit surprised, and somehow sad, maybe because she was wondering how she could have missed such a big part of her daughter's life.

'He's doing fine now, I think, in his way. So, yes, over-all . . . well, I'm glad I did it.' I slowly rolled up the edge of the bamboo mat under the phone. 'Yeah, I think it was the right thing to do. And it sort of worked out, I guess.'

I too felt both relief and a certain sadness. I wondered whether she was going to tell Stefan about it, and what he would say. She would probably call back the following day, once she had thought it over; she would be full of questions, and I would have to answer them. And then she would tell my brother Martin, who was serving the German nation as an Army-trained engineer in Bavaria, and he too would call with all sorts of questions, and then . . . Oh well, I thought. That's family.

After that final meeting in the car park, and a couple of phone calls to sort out the legal mess, I never spoke to Selim again. As for the pension payments and the division of assets and the court's letters and fees and enquiries, all that was resolved eventually, the way we had resolved so many problems big and small: amicably, and with a deepening sense of exhaustion.

The other day, I pruned my hotmail inbox: e-mails going all the way back to my school days.

It was among the flirty missives from former lovers and chatty, gossip-sharing messages from friends that I found Selim's last message to me. I don't think I paid it much attention at the time. I was probably impatient and annoyed, as usual. But when I reread it, I could not help but feel moved, and I wished, wished so strongly I had been kinder, more generous, more easy-going, and that we had somehow managed to turn our strange alliance into friendship.

DEAR FRIEND, HEY HOW ARE YOU I HOPE YUR WELL. I AM VERY GRATFL FOR YUR HELP I WILL NEVA FOGET YUR HELP. JULYAN TOLD ME YOU HAVE PROBLEM WITH CORT BUT I DONT NO WAT IS ESACLY. CAN YOU MAKE COPY OF LETTER PLESE. I AM THERE FOR YOU ALWAYS PLAESE BECAUSE OF SMALL THINK DONT MAKE YOURSELF KAPUTT NO MATER WAT WE WILL SORT IT OUT YOU ARE STRONG WOMAN. YOU CAN CALL ANY TIME. I WISH YOU ALL GOOD THINGS. AND ALL BEST. SELIM

58

He saw Dynasty as soon as he entered the yard of his old school. She was talking to a former teacher and appeared not to have spotted him. Not many people had turned up for the reunion. Selim himself would have stayed away had it not been for the fact that this would be his last visit to, oh, so many old haunts before moving away. Of course he had hoped she would be there. Of course.

She looked nice. Other girls in his class had become rather dowdy somewhere between the first and third child, sapped by the long nights of screaming children and stinking nappies and drunken boyfriends. Twenty-four, twenty-five, and haggard already. But Dynasty looked lovely. Her hair was mousy brown now and the hoop earrings had been replaced with little silver stars, but she still wore those tight jeans, a pink hooded jumper and an easy smile.

And he thought, She'll always look very nice.

She's simply a really nice woman.

Whoever grows old with her will be a very happy man.

He had stopped in his tracks, unable to chat to his teachers and classmates now. She turned away from the teacher she had been talking to, saw Selim and came towards him.

'Hi.'

'Hi.'

'I've been here for five minutes and I'm already fed up. Do you want to go for a coffee?'

No, Selim thought, because if we go for a coffee we will have to talk to each other, and I won't know what to say, and it will be strange and embarrassing. How much nicer it would have been to stay unobserved, to look at Dynasty for a while and then walk away.

'OK,' he said.

They walked past the botanical gardens and up the hill into the medieval town centre. In a café with metal chairs and posters of saxophone players, she ordered a coffee with froth on top and he had the same, even though he disliked the milky froth.

He knew what she was going to say before she said it. She put down her spoon and looked at him with the kind of friendly, understanding look that always made him feel queasy.

'Listen, I heard. I mean, I'm sorry. When I slapped you back then.'

'It's OK.'

'No, I'm really sorry. I shouldn't have slapped you and I heard she wasn't really your wife. I mean, I know you married her so you could stay here.'

'Hmm. Who told you?'

'Oh, I heard it the way . . . like, everyone knows everything here, right?'

'Yes. Everyone knows everything.'

'Don't worry, Selim, I won't tell anyone that it was fake or anything. I just wanted to say I'm sorry.'

369

Selim would have liked for once to have the right words, but language, as ever, failed him. He smiled weakly.

'So, I thought, now that I know your secret, I want to be honest with you too, right. Like, I reckoned, now the cheese is eaten, isn't it, so to speak, and I wanted to tell you something I hadn't told you before, about my little brother.'

'Dynasty, it's OK.'

'Well. It's not a big deal really, lots of people are fine with it but I know you're quite traditional and . . . right, you're going to think God knows what but basically he's not actually my little brother. We just said that at the time because I didn't want people to talk.'

'Yes,' Selim said. 'I know.'

They sat there in silence for a while.

'So . . . if you want, I thought maybe we could be friends again. At some point. In the future. Like, we used to get on so well together, that summer and everything. Even now I sometimes think of that summer, and, well, it was just great. It was the best summer ever.'

'Yes.'

'And I thought it's such a shame we lost that.'

'Yes.'

'So, maybe we could meet up some time and do something together. Go to the cinema or something.'

Selim shook his head.

'I'm going to move away soon. To another town.'

'Oh.'

And I'm married again, to another woman, and I've resolved to treat her like my wife and be good to her and start a family with her, and so, no, I can't go to the cinema with you.

370

He tried to think of a way to put that thought into words, words that could actually be spoken. He couldn't.

'Well, if you're going to move away, then I probably won't see you around much, huh?'

'No.'

They sat in silence. He stirred his coffee and drank.

'That's . . . I'm sorry. That's shit, that's really sad. I mean, I wish . . .'

He nodded.

The cup was empty and he was wondering whether he should order another one just to avoid speaking.

'Selim?'

'Hmm?'

'You're going away anyway, and so much has gone wrong, but what I meant to say, well, I just wanted to say, I really like you. You're great.'

'Yes.' Selim nodded. He felt a sudden urge to laugh. He wanted to explain everything to Dynasty, about the comical monstrosity that was his life, but he didn't even know where to start.

Dynasty, you're great, too. I feel very happy when I'm with you. It's very nice when we're together. I have not felt this way about any other girl. I would like to play Kurdish music to you and listen to you sing and, yes, go to the cinema with you. I would like to tell you the legend of Mem û Zîn; I would like to tell you the entire story, about the festival and the disguise and the traitor, and I think you'd like it. I would tell it really well, and I'd make you laugh. We get on very well, we do.

But, you see, none of this matters. Because, no, I cannot go to the cinema with you. Not in this life. Never. Because, you see, I saw

371

a tank drive through a crowd of schoolchildren, and then I swam through a carpet of shit to a country that did not want me, and then I married a woman to save myself, and then I married another woman to save her, and sometimes I feel I am still out there bobbing between the waves, splashing like a dog, eternally facing a floating carpet of shit.

So, no, I cannot go to the cinema with you.

And it occurred to Selim how much he would have just loved to do precisely that: go out with Dynasty and watch a nice film, and go home with her, and take her to bed, and make love to her, and wake up the next morning with her, and repeat that sequence for as long as they both wanted to. Night after night after night, day after day after day. It seemed a very simple and happy thought. And yet, it would not happen, not in this life and probably not in any other life, because whichever deity was steering Selim's course was riotously drunk at the wheel.

After this unspoken declaration of his sincere and yet so cowardly love, Selim felt so exhausted from having not said in such detail everything he had meant to say, from having not declared his feelings with such passion and honesty, that when he finally opened his mouth to speak the words tumbled out almost as incoherently as when he had first arrived at Dynasty's school, and the only phrase that reached her ears was: 'Dynasty, really. Honest. I hope life will be good for you, I swear. I hope it will all go very well for you and your son.'

372

59

The few who knew, rarely asked me why I married Selim. I found that heartening. It was fashionable to say that everyone was greedy, materialistic, unable to comprehend any motive other than self-interest. But the truth was, most people wanted to do the right thing. Which was surprisingly hard.

I, for example, was trying to do the right thing by reaching out to the Kurdish bride. Having followed me this far you may not be surprised to hear it all ended in a bit of a hash. But I hope you will at least have some sympathy for my good intentions.

'The opposite of good is good intentions,' I hear my brother Martin say.

'The good thing is, you'll be doing this job for the rest of your life, so you've got plenty more opportunities to try and get it right,' said Julian, the eternal optimist.

He was coming to visit at the weekend, by the way. He was the only one who could really, fully understand what this forced-marriage business at the town hall meant to me. Of course, he thought the whole situation was rather typical. He said I was a magnet for that kind of stuff. I said at least I wasn't a magnet for mobsters (his lamp business went bust after a run-in with some Polish electricians).

Well, he was coming to visit. I wondered if he and David would get on. We'd see what happened. David still wanted me to go along on one of his research trips to Cizre, but I didn't think that was such a good idea. Maybe we'd go to Armenia and look at Mount Ararat from there.

As for the persistently evasive bride, three appointments went by without anyone knocking at the door of my little office. Mohammed did not go to the mountain, so the mountain decided to go to Mohammed. In violation of a stack of rules, old and new, I dug out the private addresses of both bride and groom. The bride's family lived in a nineteenth-century building not far from the town hall, but there was no one at home; or whoever was at home had spied me from the window and preferred not to answer the door.

The groom lived further afield. I took the Métro to the depressingly named Stalingrad, walked through a haze of urine scent and, gripping my rucksack, boarded another train to Aubervilliers, one of the run-down north-eastern suburbs.

I got off the train and rose up the escalator towards the gritty street level. A little boy with a big shoulder bag swung himself onto the moving handrail. I looked up and all I saw through the square frame of the Métro exit was the white sky and, diagonally across it, the moving handrail carrying the little boy, who looked away from me and up at the sky; and the beautiful image took me by surprise and made me stand still and watch, simply watch.

Outside everything was noise: Arabic, Swahili, patois,

Senegalese French, Maghreb French, Russian French. Cars, howling motorbikes. Shoppers haggled over prices and grocers swept squashed fruit and cabbage leaves from the pavement with big brooms. The square outside the Métro was strewn with smashed bike locks.

The building had no door code; as it turned out, none was necessary. The lock was broken and the door opened easily with a single push. Inside, the doors on the ground and first floor were unmarked. I worried that I wouldn't find my target, but on the second floor I struck lucky. Three small children spilled out of the flat on the left, cackling and sprinting down the stairs, and when they tumbled towards me I quickly threw the groom's name at them. The eldest of the three stopped and pointed at the flat on the right before racing away.

I pressed the doorbell and stepped to the side, out of range of the spyhole. After a while, I heard footsteps inside. Then nothing. Then again footsteps. Finally, someone opened the door and I slid into the gap. Before me stood the groom's cousin, the boy who pestered me at the town hall, the middleman or helpful relative or whatever you wanted to call him. Azad.

We were both taken aback, but he collected himself first and greeted me with his usual charm and eloquence.

'Yeah?'

'I've got an appointment with—'

'You do home visits now? This a raid?'

'I'm looking for—'

'He isn't here.'

With one hand on the frame and the other on the door,

375

Azad blocked the way; not that I would have tried to wriggle past him anyway.

'Can I come in?'

'Why?'

'I've got an appointment with your cousin,' I lied.

From inside, the smell of fried tomatoes and onions and herbs wafted out into the corridor. A woman called out from somewhere, gradually drifting into song.

'Looks like he stood you up.'

'I'll wait for him.'

Azad sniggered.

'Have fun waiting. You haven't heard?'

I shook my head, wondering why I had ever embarked on this ill-fated mission. Azad looked strangely pleased, as if he was about to pour his bubbling tomato sauce over my head.

'PKK got him.'

I laughed out loud in disbelief.

Azad frowned.

'It's true! Guys from the PKK, they came in a car, picked him up, drove off.' He put on a mock-concerned expression. 'Shouldn't even be telling you this, but I guess you've heard about them. Forced recruitment. You might have heard, given that you know so much, right?'

'Azad, that's bullshit.'

He jerked back his head in denial.

I sighed.

'Listen, you're trying to tell me that two PKK members drive into this neighbourhood in broad daylight, out of nowhere, and just kidnap a bloke and drive off? Where are they taking him, Kurdistan? Are you trying to tell me they're, like, sitting in some battered BMW now, driving east along the Autoroute?'

'I don't know what brand the car was.'

'Listen, that's absurd. That's an absurd story. Like, what, a PKK raid in the middle of Paris? I met your cousin, he wants to study in the States. Joining the PKK is just about the last thing he would do.'

He sneered.

'We're not in the middle of Paris and the PKK is already here. You don't know them, but they're already here.'

It was absurd. Without any pretence at politeness, I turned around and walked down the stairs. A woman in a white dress and a white headscarf stood on the first floor, singing. I thought of asking her about the man I was looking for. But when I walked past, she spat at me.

60

'You heard?'

'Naturally,' said Derya, serious and spiky-haired as ever, bundling together a dog-eared stack of documents as if nothing had happened. Her office had spawned additional towers of books and folders since my last visit. On the chair where I once sat and asked about forced marriages there was a pile of leaflets. I leaned against a bookcase, but it began to give way so I quickly straightened up.

'It's absurd. The PKK invading some suburb . . . though he says they're already there.'

Now it was Derya who laughed out loud.

'You don't believe that story, do you?'

'I don't know what to believe. It's such a mess. The one thing I can say is, I wish Azad had never turned up at the *mairie*.'

I would have liked to sit down, not for comfort but to give an air of permanence, to signal I was not going to leave until I found out what was going on.

'Well, I can tell you one thing, it's all a bit of a mess but it's got nothing to do with the PKK,' Derya said. 'He's right on one count, there are a lot of PKK men here, naturally, and

378

some shopkeepers pay them fees or tax or whatever you want to call it. But no one kidnapped the groom. They just cooked that up.'

'Who's they?'

'The family, who else?'

'Right.'

I was starting to think that Derya, too, was probably lying. Somehow, that thought made everything easier. They were probably all lying. The groom, my elderly predecessor, Derya, Azad; it was liberating to think that I did not have to believe any of them, that I could simply listen to all their stories and then conclude that none of them was true.

Derya looked at me defiantly.

'I don't know the whole story. And to be honest, there's only so much I can tell, because we don't want to put him at risk.'

'Well, Azad seemed pretty chilled to me.'

'Not Azad, the groom. He's with us now. Not here-here, obviously, but in a safe place. It's rare for us to get approached by boys, but sometimes it happens, and naturally we help them just as we'd help any girl. So that's the whole story, simple. The groom didn't want to get married, he was scared the bride's family would be after him, he came to us for help, we helped him. No PKK.'

I thought of the groom, of his joke about the painting of the cattle traders, of his playing football with an empty, dented can.

'You know, I actually met up with the groom once. We had quite an interesting chat in the wedding hall. He was nice. Really nice, in that slightly sarcastic way ... anyway, he seemed completely OK with his parents' choice. He mentioned something about his mother – trusting his mother to pick out a nice girl for him. He seemed fine.'

'He would tell you that, wouldn't he?'

I bit my lip.

She stood up and smiled as if to say now, now, surely you're not offended by that? But I was. And at the same time I knew it was utterly ridiculous to feel, well, hurt. What had I expected: that the groom would see me as some kind of transcultural confidante, just because of a bit of banter about cows and France? Just because his cousin had spent twenty years working for Siemens in Germany? Well, yes, basically.

'So is he OK?' I asked quietly.

'Not exactly,' Derya said. 'But he's as well as he can be under the circumstances.'

'He'll be fine, you think?'

'Yes. I think he'll be fine.'

And I thought she would say that, wouldn't she? There was no way of establishing what was really going on here.

Derya seemed ready to escort me out. I moved into the space between the filing cabinet and a poster with a razor blade on it.

'Derya, I think there's great scope for cooperation between the *mairie* and your organisation, say, in terms of funding. But it has to come from both sides.'

She shrugged.

'There's not much else I can add. What else do you want to know? It's simple really, he didn't want to marry the girl, but his family wasn't giving in, and rejecting her wouldn't have gone down well with her family, either. You won't be

380

surprised to hear her brothers are pretty pissed off now, so we helped the groom disappear. That's all.'

'But what's the PKK got to do with it?'

'Nothing, except it's a clever lie to get French police to help track down the groom.'

'I . . . yes. I don't know what to believe now.'

'That's OK. You can believe whatever you like.'

'Well, I can tell you right now I'll have to inform the police, you understand . . . I'm an official.'

She shrugged as if to say that's up to you.

'Yes,' I said. 'I'll think about it. And, hmm, the bride?'

'No idea. With her family, I assume.'

'Right. Right.' I scratched my head. 'Right.'

I picked up my bag. A thought occurred to me.

'You know what my problem is?' I asked but didn't wait for the answer. 'I sag a lot. It's something to do with my posture. I will sit straight for a bit, until I get distracted by something, and then I sag and hunch my back. Someone pointed this out to me once, but I don't seem to be able to do anything about it.'

And I thought if ever there was a person who could teach me to go through life with a straighter spine, it would be Derya.

She knitted her brows, critically assessing my problem.

'Well,' she eventually said. 'You could try Pilates.'

I hadn't quite meant it that way, but I thanked her anyway and left the office.

Three o'clock, I thought, time to grind some coffee. I swivelled around on my chair and pressed the button on the matt black machine. Nothing happened. I checked the plug, the wire, the clear plastic funnel with the coffee beans. It all seemed fine. I unplugged the machine and opened the back to see if the blades were jammed, using my pen to dislodge some half-ground beans. Brown powder spilled out of the machine and onto my lap, the floor, my folders.

There was a knock on the door.

'*Entrez*!' I called out, hoping Sandra might help me find a dustpan and brush.

Instead, an elderly man with bottletop glasses stiffly entered the room, carefully closing the door behind him.

It was Monsieur Dubois, my predecessor.

'Surprise!' he said with a smile, opening his arms wide as if for an embrace, a black walking cane in one hand like an elderly entertainer.

'Monsieur Dubois! That's ... how nice to see you.' Brushing coffee powder off my trousers, I stood up to shake his hand.

He did not move towards me but remained by the door, and it took me a second to realise he was waiting for me to guide him.

He sniffed.

'It smells of coffee.' He sniffed again.

'It does,' I said, helping him into one of the more comfortable chairs. 'I've just broken the coffee machine.'

He chuckled, shaking his head in amusement as he arranged the walking cane across his lap.

'Can I get you a glass of water?' I offered.

'A cup of coffee would be lovely,' he said, letting out another chuckle. 'He-he! Only joking.'

382

He leaned forward and lowered his voice.

'I was having lunch with *mon ami le maire* just now and thought I'd come over. Don't worry, I didn't say a word about the little conversation we had, you and me.' He mimed zipping up his mouth. 'I had a feeling you'd want to keep that private.'

'Oh, thanks,' I said cautiously. 'It's no big secret. Well, I never told the Mayor I'd spoken to you, but it's not a big deal if he finds out.'

He shook his head again, thoroughly enjoying himself now.

'My dear friend, if the Mayor found out you'd been driving around the countryside talking about confidential cases at the town hall . . . let's just say it's an unusual way to behave. But don't worry, your secret is safe with me.' He pointed his cane at my desk. 'Now where is my little manual? I do hope you keep it on your desk. Right next to the photo of your boyfriend, may I suggest.' He giggled, and noticing the reddish glow on his cheeks and nose, I suspected the Mayor had ordered *une bonne bouteille* with their meal.

The manual was indeed right there on my desk, its cover with the barbed-wire wedding ring on full display for potential visitors. I placed it in Monsieur Dubois's thickly veined hands and he patted it with satisfaction.

'Very good. I asked the Mayor about how things were going with the manual, you know, discreetly. I was careful not to mention our secret conversation, of course, I only asked him if there'd been any unusual cases at the town hall, any cases of weddings being stopped, say, by a registrar.' His

383

smile, a mixture of cunning and complicity, made me feel uneasy.

'I haven't stopped any weddings,' I said quickly.

'So I heard. Am I right then in assuming that you changed your mind after our little chat?'

'I'm not sure what you mean.' I glanced at the door, wondering whether Sandra was at the other side of it. 'I was very grateful for your advice, of course.'

'No need to be embarrassed, my dear. We all learn, we all make mistakes, and there is no shame in admitting that after listening to your older friend you realised there was no point meddling with the wedding plans for that poor girl. And I am here, my dear, to tell you there is nothing wrong with that. You did the right thing.' His hand felt across the desk until he found my arm and gave it a reassuring squeeze. 'As I told the Mayor . . . well, I was really very careful not to bring up your name, but I did suggest that some of the younger registrars might be taking the manual a little too seriously. And he quite agreed. The Mayor is very pleased to have my clever booklet, of course. It looks wonderful and it's something he can give to journalists and show that we are moving with the times. But it's really not meant to be used.'

'Thanks.' I nodded. 'I'll keep that in mind.'

'Don't worry, he understands that younger staff can be a bit rash at times. Hot-headed, maybe. He knows you mean well. We only referred to you in passing, of course. He was a little concerned about . . . well, you may want to be more prudent in the future.'

'Sure.'

He twirled his cane, as if to signal that the serious part of the conversation was over and we could switch back to easy chuckles.

'If only my eyesight was better, I would ask you to unlock the wedding hall for me. You know, that Gervex portrait of the bride, so prim and proper . . . I do sometimes wonder if he used the same model for his naked Marion.' He sighed. 'That little bride!'

At the town hall, no one had been particularly surprised when the Kurdish wedding was called off. We celebrated twenty weddings a week, after all. And every year, dozens more were scrapped at the last minute. God knows why. Maybe the lovers suddenly realised they didn't want to spend the rest of their lives together, or the woman fell for someone else, or the man escaped and went into hiding. We didn't ask. Well, my colleagues didn't ask.

I accompanied Monsieur Dubois to his car. The young woman I had seen at his house sat behind the wheel, waiting.

'Don't worry too much about these weddings,' he said before he slipped into the car, raising his hand as if to prepare me for a particularly good joke. 'From what I hear on the radio, this whole debate about forced marriages is going out of fashion anyway. Now it's all about headscarves and polygamy. Ladies turning up at the town hall in long black veils! Didn't happen in my time.'

And with that, he closed the door, waving at me through the window as they drove off.

Sometimes we can radically change the script that someone else has written for us. At other times, our own script gets ripped up and rewritten.

I did get a few strange looks at the town hall when a short piece appeared in *Le Parisien* recounting the bizarre twist in the alleged PKK kidnapping. Police soon aborted their investigation of the PKK link and shone their searchlight on the bride's family. But nothing came of that, either. No one had seen anything, no one had heard anything. Sandra told me about a rumour going around that I had advised the bride against the marriage.

I never tried to explain to my colleagues, or indeed the Mayor, what really happened. I hoped the groom was well, wherever he was now, with his hyperactive feet and his dreams of a US degree; keeping quiet about his escape seemed the best way of ensuring his safety. It was also the best way of keeping good relations with Derya and her colleagues. After all, I might need their help again at some point in the future.

In fact, though this may sound soppy, I left my contact details with Derya and asked her to pass them on to the groom. Did I expect him to get in touch? Not really. Certainly not any time soon. But, say, if he did end up moving to the States, or somewhere else far away – well, you never know, maybe one day he'd drop me a note, and if it was safe we might even meet up and I'd hear his side of the story.

But I'll have to put my pen aside now: here she comes. Not Kurdish, this one, judging from the name. Not that anyone is Kurdish in this neighbourhood, or Moroccan, or German. We are all French here.

She isn't crying, and she isn't wearing white. It's only the town hall after all. The groom looks tense, but I think he'll

386

relax once they sit down. They'll write their names on a piece of paper. The witnesses will add theirs. I'll make sure everything is in order, and then I'll send them off, away, into a future that, for better or worse, will be theirs together.

61

He bought a new shirt for the occasion. It was slightly ridiculous, he knew that; after all, she had never seen any of his old shirts and would not have noticed the difference. His brother-in-law, however, noticed. So did his sister. They teased him about it mercilessly. They accompanied him to the airport, along with three of their eight children, squished into a battered Mercedes: a proper reception to welcome the young bride into the fold.

Selim felt a queasy mix of disappointment and relief. Relief because the loud and boisterous group could be relied on to fill in any awkward silences (in fact, with his family around, the mere idea of an awkward silence would die before it was conceived; it never stood a chance).

And yet, that hint of disappointment. He was once again being driven here and there, being pulled this way and that by aunts, uncles, siblings, cousins, with half the family coming along to the airport, the other half staying behind to prepare the big feast (the women) and talk politics (the men). It would have been nice to show his young wife that this was fundamentally his own decision, that he alone was picking her up from the airport, welcoming her into his life, looking after her and taking responsibility for their new life together, and, yes, suffering through awkward silences with patience and dignity.

The first time they met, he had felt like an impostor. His mother had probably advertised him shamelessly, marketed him as a wealthy entrepreneur fit to marry a sheikh's daughter. That first night, he was certain he detected disappointment in the young bride's eyes. There was his stunted Kurdish, his ignorance of local seduction techniques, his chicken-chested boniness where she had maybe dreamed of a broad manly chest. And then, of course, his lying beside her for a week without once trying to caress her face, her shoulders, let alone her breasts or thighs. Despite his explanations, she must have thought it strange, offensive even.

Now, he could hardly remember what she looked like. But at least he had more to offer her than before. It still wasn't much, but it was more than before. He was training as a carer, lifting old and infirm people every day. He liked to imagine his chest and arms had grown a little stronger. He would find a proper job, maybe. There was a greater need for carers than for bike mechanics. He had a residency permit now. He was here. He was legal.

To his left, his eldest nephew was climbing onto the steel rail. To his right, his sister was leaning over the partition, scrutinising every female face among the arrivals, comparing it with the photo in her chubby hand; evidently not trusting her brother to pick out the right girl.

A young, pale woman stepped out of the sliding doors, pushing a trolley laden with bags and suitcases like an overburdened donkey, glancing about nervously, looking lost, and he decided that must be her.

389

He smiled and walked around the partition, but before he knew what was happening, the clan had already overtaken him, rushing to greet her, sweeping her up in their cacophonous warmth and bustling her to the car, and that was it for the rest of the day, a loud and crowded day full of questions, gossip, food, tea, womanly chatter, much hugging and kissing and clapping of hands.

His brother-in-law had organised a little one-bedroom apartment for them, just a few floors above his own. From the window, Selim could see the boxy grey housing estate and beyond that, fog. It was almost midnight by the time the rest of the family withdrew, leaving them in their new home, alone with each other.

They sat on the sunken sofa, a gift from his sister, and studied the rug on the floor.

'Would you like some tea?' Selim finally asked into the silence, which was exhausted more than awkward.

She looked up at him with surprise. Of course, at home, making tea would have been her job. Even in his sister's home below, it would have been the woman's job. Well, this would be different.

'Would you like me to make you some tea?' she asked, still looking slightly confused.

'I'll do it, you don't know where everything is,' he said, regretting the words as soon as he uttered them; they must have sounded harsh. 'Well, come and we'll do it together, and I'll show you the kitchen. Our kitchen.'

'Wait.'

She went into the bedroom, opened one of the big, sagging nylon suitcases and lifted out a carefully wrapped

390

bundle of cloth, which she untied to reveal the shiny chrome components of a brand-new Kurdish teapot.

Making tea was not an activity designed for two people. They kept bumping into each other in the small Formica kitchen, splashing each other with water, spilling dried tea leaves over the worktop, and at one point Selim burned the side of his hand on the hot metal, but swallowed the cry of pain he was about to let out.

When she finally poured the tea into two glasses and opened the cardboard box with the sugar cubes, he remembered something he had been taught a long time ago.

'Look at this – this is how the Palestinians drink their tea, did you know? A Palestinian boy once showed me, ages ago.'

He placed a sugar cube between his teeth and sip by sip sucked the bitter tea through it.

She giggled, then took a sugar cube out of the box and copied him.

They looked ridiculous, standing there with the disintegrating cubes between their teeth, and Selim suddenly thought, I bet no one actually drinks their tea this way. It's completely impractical. No one in the entire world could possibly think this was a good way to drink tea. The Palestinian boy must have made it up. He was just having a bit of fun with me. He was simply pulling my leg.

And yet, for years Selim had earnestly told his German friends that this was exactly how the Palestinians drank their tea!

He laughed out loud at his own gullibility, at that of his German friends, at the thought that, all over Germany, well-meaning tea-drinkers were perpetuating the myth: 'Look, this is how the Palestinians do it . . .'

Selim's new bride, infected by his tea-spraying outburst of mirth, began to giggle, trying to swallow the sugar cube to prevent it from falling out of her mouth; it got stuck half-way down her throat, and she coughed, and Selim slapped her back to dislodge the lump (sudden panic – what if she choked?) which made her laugh even harder, and by the time they had jointly managed to clear her throat, the awkwardness between them had, at least for the moment, disappeared.

They wiped their sticky mouths with paper napkins. Selim explained in great detail why he had laughed, explaining about the Palestinian boy, the refugee shelter (you never knew; she might think he had laughed at her. Better dispel any hint of misunderstanding right away). She refilled their glasses and he admired her elegant, efficient gestures, the way she handled the hot teapot, the delicate glasses. Then she opened the suitcase again and took out a brown paper bag.

'My aunt lives in Van,' she said quietly. 'They drink their tea that way, you know, *kıtlama*. With the sugar between their teeth. But it doesn't work the way you did it, with the cubes, because they dissolve, right? You should try it with these.'

With a special knife, she cut a small chunk from a big rocky lump, stuck it between her teeth and took a sip of tea. He copied her.

'It's quite difficult, isn't it?' he said from the corner of his mouth.

It would be different, he decided. He would make sure

she learned German, learned to read and write. Their children would go to a proper school. They would build a life together, he and she. They would not lead the kind of married life he knew from his cousins and cousins' friends.

Yes, he was like thousands of young men who had agreed to marry a stranger, but he was also different. He would not take out his disappointment and frustration on the young wife, turning her into a domestic slave, letting her be bullied by older female relatives while her husband was out gambling or chasing other women. This was his life, too, after all. They would make it theirs.

Selim and his wife sat down on the sofa, each balancing a glass of tea on a saucer: two people who had not much to say to each other for now. He was a bit worried that she might cry. His sister had warned him, had said that the bride would probably be homesick, would cry for days or even weeks, that it was a good sign, it showed the bride cared about her home and family. The thought almost brought tears to his own eyes.

He carefully put one arm around her, holding the saucer with his other hand, and glanced at her face. No tears. She is beautiful, he thought, astonished that he had not noticed it before. Her laugh had surprised him: it had been deep and womanly and sexy. Not at all the kind of laugh you would expect from a girl.

And as they sat there, very close but still quite distant, he felt a tepid glow that was not unlike happiness.

393

A NOTE FROM THE AUTHOR

The Kurdish areas of Turkey, Syria, Iran and Iraq have attracted travellers for centuries. Their accounts helped me to shape the adventures of Prof. Tournesol and fill his notebooks. Overleaf is a bibliography listing the resources I used at the Kurdish Institute of Paris. Given that the spelling of Kurdish names is in itself a subject of controversy, I have replicated the spelling that appears on the cover of the relevant book. This means, for example, that there are several versions of Ehmedê Xanî's name in the bibliography.

On the subject of forced marriages, the Paris town hall and women's rights associations such as Elele and Voix de Femmes have provided useful reports, pamphlets and other material. In 2009, the Paris town hall issued a manual to help officials prevent forced marriages – needless to say, it is completely different from the fictional manual in this novel.

Rummaging through the older books and pamphlets at the Kurdish institute, I found that the debate over forced marriages is nothing new. As early as 1936, Prince Sureya Bedr-Khan, eager to gather support for an independent Kurdistan, told a European audience in Brussels that 'the Kurdish woman has never had to fight for any rights' and

395

'no Kurd would even consider a marriage between his daughter and someone she hasn't met and spent time with before.'

Several books were particularly useful in shaping the story of Aynur and her family. Olivier Touron's *Amazone: Farachine, Rebelle Kurde*, a portrait of a French-Kurdish teenager who leaves Paris to join the PKK, offers a fascinating glimpse of guerrilla life in the mountains. A collection of letters from Leyla Zana, who was the first Kurdish woman to be elected to the Turkish Parliament and was subsequently sentenced to fifteen years in prison for her political views, helped me understand the role of women in the Kurdish struggle. *Women of a Non-State Nation: The Kurds*, edited by Shahrzad Mojab, is crammed with essays covering every aspect of the situation of Kurdish women, from politics to religion. Gina Lennox's *Fire, Snow & Honey: Voices From Kurdistan*, a vast collection of testimonies and folk tales; *Mémoire du Kurdistan*, a selection of songs, poems and fables edited by Joyce Blau; and Ferit Edgü's novel, *Une saison à Hakkâri*, provided an excellent introduction to the Kurds' creative heritage. Bekir Yildiz's travel memoir about southeastern Turkey was particularly moving.

Finally, the hundreds of Turkish-German and Kurdish-German amateur videos and discussion threads on www.youtube.com are a rich source of modern slang and colourful sayings that I have done my best to convey in English.

BIBLIOGRAPHY

Bedr-Khan, Prince Sureya, *La femme Kurde et son rôle social* (Paris/Brussels, 1936).

Blau, Joyce, ed., *Mémoire du Kurdistan* (Paris, 1984).

Bois, Thomas, *Connaissance des Kurdes* (Beirut, 1965).

Chaland, Gérard, *Anthologies de la Poésie Populaire Kurde* (Paris, 1997).

Dagtekin, Seyhmus, *Couleurs Dèmêlèes du Ciel* (Bordeaux, 2003).

de Bellaigue, Christopher, *Rebel Land: Among Turkey's Forgotten People* (London, 2009).

de Cholet, Armand Pierre, *Voyage en Turquie d'Asie: Arménie, Kurdistan et Mésopotamie* (Paris, 1892, republished as a facsimile by Elibron Classics www.elibron.com, 2006).

Düzen, Husên, ed., *Zehn kurdische Erzaehler* (Winterthur, 1996).

Edgü, Ferit, *Une saison à Hakkâri* (First published in Turkish in 1977. Translated by Gertrude Durusoy, Paris, 1989).

Khanî, Ahmedê, *Mem et Zîn* (First published in Kurdish in the 17th century. Translated by Sandrine Alexie and Akif Hasan, Paris, 2001).

Khani, Ahmed, *Mem and Zin* (Translated by Salah Saadalla, 2008).

Kreyenbroek, Philip and Allison, Christine, eds., *Kurdish Culture and Identity* (London, 1996).

Lennox, Gina, ed., *Fire, Snow & Honey: Voices from Kurdistan* (New South Wales, 2001).

Massignon, Louis, Preface to: *Les Kurdes*, Basile Nikitine (Paris, 1943).

Meiselas, Susan, *Kurdistan: In the Shadow of History* (New York, 1997).

Mojab, Shahrzad, ed., *Women of a Non-State Nation: The Kurds* (Costa Mesa, California, 2001).

Nikitine, Basile, *Les Kurdes* (Paris, 1943).

Pamuk, Orhan, *Neige* (First published in Turkish in 2002. Translated by Jean-François Pérouse, Paris, 2005).

Randal, Jonathan, *After Such Knowledge, What Forgiveness? My Encounters with Kurdistan* (New York, 1997).

Shwartz-Be'eri, Ora, *The Jews of Kurdistan* (Jerusalem, 2000).

Touron, Olivier, *Amazone: Farachine, Rebelle Kurde* (Neuilly-sur-Seine, 2009).

Uzun, Mehmed, *Im Schatten der verlorenen Liebe* (Translated by Hüseyin Dozen and Andreas Grenda, Zurich, 1998).

Yeşilöz, Yusuf, *Steppenrutenpflanze: Eine kurdische Kindheit* (Zurich, 2000).

Yildiz, Bekîr, *Südostverlies: Drei literarische Reportagen über Anatolien* (Translated by Gisela Kraft, Berlin, 1987).

Zana, Leyla, *Writings from Prison* (Cambridge, MA, 1999).

ACKNOWLEDGEMENTS

It takes many people to write a novel, especially one set in different countries and communities. Old and new friends in Paris, Diyarbakir, Istanbul, Tokyo, London, Philadelphia and Edinburgh helped me with my research and encouraged me in my writing, making this book a truly global effort. Any improvements are thanks to them; any errors or controversial statements are all my own.

I have been extremely lucky in finding an editor and an agent who were passionate about Selim's story right from the start. I would like to thank my agent, Mark Stanton, for taking the time to read my submission while dealing with the demands of newborn Alfie; and my editor, Jessica Leeke, for believing in this book ever since I pitched it to her by the rubbish bins in front of her house. I am deeply grateful to them, to my copy editor, Mary Tomlinson, and to the staff at Simon & Schuster, for their enthusiasm in turning my manuscript into a book.

The Kurdish Institute in Paris provided unlimited access to its treasure trove of novels, folk tales, political tracts and travellers' accounts. Joyce Blau, head of the institute, patiently answered my questions about all things Kurdish.

Sandrine Alexie, the institute's generous and knowledgeable librarian, shared her French translation of Ehmedê Xanî's epic, *Mem û Zîn*, and helped me work an English version into the novel.

I would like to thank Türküler Isiksel for her invaluable advice on all those wonderful details that cannot be found in reference books; from tea-drinking habits in Van, to suitable names for fifteen-year-old boys. Speaking of the little details that make a novel come to life, I am grateful to Arif Shah for taking the time to discuss the purity of sand and snow.

Wendell Steavenson helped me prepare my research trip to south-eastern Turkey and shared her experiences in Iraqi Kurdistan. Alexandra Hudson also kindly helped with the trip, not least by looking after us in Istanbul. Jack Balaban, Yilmaz Akinci and Bülent Ipek introduced me to Kurdish food, music and everyday life in Diyarbakir. Bülent expertly translated a list of phrases into Kurmanji. Rozan Kahraman at EPIDEM, a women's rights organisation in Diyarbakir, told me about the social and economic problems faced by women in the region. A special thank you goes to Sophie Lee Taylor, whose adventurous spirit and patience in the face of yet another interview about sugar lumps made the trip a lot of fun.

Reading groups in Tokyo and Paris gave me early feedback and advice, and formed the friendly and supportive audience that every writer dreams of. Rafael Herrero, in particular, hosted the Damrémont Writers' Group with warmth and kindness. Staff and students at INSEAD business school in Fontainebleau generously let me use their library when I

400

needed a quiet space to write. In London, Olivia Satite provided support, enthusiasm and a comfortable bed.

My fellow writer Melinda Joe cheered me on during difficult moments. I am grateful to her and all my friends and family for their optimism and kind words.

Above all, I would like to thank Dan Lerner, my most inspiring reader, for sharing the ups and downs of a writer's existence and for filling my life with sunshine.

Sophie Hardach
Paris, September 2010